WAR OF THE ARCHONS

HANGMAN'S GATE

BOOK TWO OF WAR OF THE ARCHONS

HANGMAN'S GATE

R·S·FORD

TITAN BOOKS

Hangman's Gate
Paperback edition ISBN: 9781785653094
Electronic edition ISBN: 9781785653100

Published by Titan Books
A division of Titan Publishing Group Ltd
144 Southwark St, London SE1 0UP

First edition: June 2019
2 4 6 8 10 9 7 5 3 1

A CIP catalogue record for this title is available from the British Library.

Printed and bound by CPI Group (UK) Ltd, Croydon CR0 4YY

What did you think of this book?
We love to hear from our readers. Please email us at:
readerfeedback@titanemail.com, or write to us at the above address.

To receive advance information, news, competitions, and exclusive
offers online, please sign up for the Titan newsletter on our website:

www.titanbooks.com

WAR OF THE ARCHONS

HANGMAN'S GATE

1

*T*HE *grass was wet underfoot, blades slick between her toes. She held onto that feeling, thrilling at the sensation. It was strange that such a trivial thing was so important to her. Strange because she could not remember her own name, yet neither did she care. All that mattered was the feel of that grass between her toes.*

Looking across the bright, green field she tried to remember how she had come to this place, but there were no answers. No answers in the distant mountains or the endless dark blue sky that pressed down on her from above. No answers in the river running murky and brown to her left. No answers in the wooded grove and its lush tree line to the right.

No answers.

And none of this bothered her. Perhaps that was the strangest thing of all.

Despite her verdant surroundings nothing flew in the air, nothing sang in the trees, and the only sound was the breeze rushing through the grass, the gentle swaying of the boughs, the incessant trickle of the river.

It gave the place an eerie sense of wrongness she couldn't shake. Like a dream that wasn't a dream. This land had a lucidity that no dream could harbour. This was reality, not the invention of her fuddled head. And yet it could not be real. How else would she have no recollection of… anything?

The ground squirmed beneath her feet. She wiggled her toes, the grass becoming slimy underfoot. Looking down she saw her hands, skin pulled paper-thin over finger bones, nails cracked and yellowing.

Rot.

She turned them over, looking at the cracked and calloused palms. Likewise the flesh of her wrists and forearms was weathered, like the cover of an ancient, battered tome. Within this fertile environment it seemed that she was the one out of place. A carcass among the ripe landscape.

When she turned her hands back over there was a spider sitting on her knuckle. Its back was blue, yellow dapples on the carapace. Black legs splayed, clinging to her desiccated skin.

She viewed it without emotion as it moved, clambering along her hand. Even when the sharp sting of teeth penetrated her old flesh she did not react, but watched curiously as it fed, as her white flesh turned yellow around the wound, veins darkening as venom coursed through them.

A tickle on her toes. Movement across her foot. Ignoring the troublesome spider she looked down at her bare legs. The grass at her feet roiled, churning with life. Insects squirmed, the ground alive in a writhing mass. It moved up her shins towards her knees, and she began to feel a stirring of emotion. At once she appreciated that this was real. The beasts had come for their carrion, and it meant danger.

She moved. First, a stuttering step. Then a stumble. Then a loping run as she bent to sweep the swarm from her legs. Her hand stung from the spider venom – the sensation flowering along with the dawning of emotions.

The sky rumbled overhead as her stumble turned into full flight. Beneath her feet the wet grass gave way to a bed of carapaces, myriad insects stretching as far as the eye could see, her footfalls crushing their fragile shells. Around her the environment was in a frenzy, chittering creatures harrying her flight, tangled in her brittle locks, creeping across her limbs.

Panic set in like an iron choker at her throat. Where before she had felt empty, now she was filled with fear. The need to escape. It was all that mattered.

She ran on through the muck of skittering creatures, feeling them claw at her, desperate to pull her down and feast. Her panic heightened to the point of hysteria, every fibre of her being now focused on the instinct to escape.

As though answering her unspoken plea, she saw a pulsating light ahead. Where a moment before there had been nothing but an open field, now stood a portal. Ancient blue stone framed a doorway, surface shimmering like a pool of quicksilver.

She ran for it. Vision focused, trying to shut out the landscape of cloying, fluttering insects that surrounded her. When she was a few feet from the portal she leapt. The doorway drew her in, clutching her from the air and dragging her through…

Silence.

She was submerged in a cloud of grey. The deafening noise of insects now hushed. All feeling gone from her limbs. She was floating for the longest time in limbo – or was it no time at all? – before she was dumped unceremoniously at the other side.

Silence was replaced by the din of battle.

The sound of metal rang next to her ear, the hum of steel momentarily drowning out all other noise. It buzzed in her head as her rheumy eyes focused on the slaughter. An axe battered against a shield, its sigil long since hacked to splinters rendering it unrecognisable. She foundered, turning away from the violence only to be faced by two men in armour writhing in a muddy pit. One forced the other's head down into the wet, his desperate breath coming in bubbling gasps. A horse raced past, headless rider bobbing along, arms limp by his sides.

Slowly she stood, watching a body collapse a few feet away, innards hanging loose from bent and torn armour. She knew she should have run, escaped once more, but she was locked in a daze, the violence overwhelming her, paralysing her with…

Was it fear? No. She knew she was not scared, despite the peril that churned all around her in a brutal dance.

A lance pierced the breastplate of a charging swordsman, lifting him in the air. His scream was shrill as he was raised high, impaled on the impetus of his own charge, but still she did not feel compelled to flee.

None of the berserk warriors seemed to pay her any heed as she began to walk among them. When one charged at her, bellowing from within his helm, she stopped and faced him. At the last moment he veered, a black iron blade catching him, stifling his cry. A mounted knight came galloping, barding and armour drenched in blood, but before his steed could trample her beneath slick hooves it leapt aside.

She seemed impervious to the combat: untouchable as she trod ankle deep in the mud and gore. A white-haired hag passing unseen among the slaughter like some goddess of death.

In the sky above her head, something screeched.

Leathern wings beat as dark creatures swooped to attack, claws reaching eagerly for their prey. It was as though a host of gargoyles had torn themselves from the side of some temple and were now on the hunt. A fury of fangs and talons rent armour wide, exposing flesh and bone and blood. The beasts flew amok, wings still beating as they tore their quarry apart.

Just as it seemed the winged demons might slaughter all in their path, there came a boom like thunder. The battlefield fell silent and the two armies paused in their slaughter.

To one side of the battle the massed ranks parted, allowing a giant to step forth. Its tread shook the ground, throwing up muck and gore as it loomed out of the fray. Its head was bald, with knobbled skin reaching down to a heavy black brow. Its face was a mass of gnarled flesh and broken teeth atop a thickly muscled body. In one hand it grasped a club that resembled the trunk of a massive oak.

With a laboured swipe, the giant beat aside half a dozen of the winged beasts. Another beast cast aside the armoured knight on which it was feasting and leapt at the giant, claws rending, jaws biting. The giant grasped the creature in one meaty hand. The crack of its bones was audible over the din as the giant bit down and tore off its head.

In a flurry of leather the rest of the creatures took to the sky, fleeing in fear of their indomitable adversary.

The two armies stood apart now, facing one another over a mass of bodies. The giant waited on one side, silence overtaking the field as though heralding something new. Something even more deadly.

Unease crept up within her. A new feeling she had not yet experienced as an unseen menace struck fear into the two warring factions.

Just as the silence became impenetrable, a gap appeared among the ranks facing the giant. A dark figure strode from their midst. He stood at least nine feet tall, obsidian armour writhing, as though flames danced beneath the reflective surface of every plate. In one hand he held a sword, its blade a shaft of blackened lava constantly flowing, steam billowing from it in dark gouts. Atop broad, armoured shoulders sat a tall helm, spikes rising to form a crown, their tips glowing with white heat.

The armoured behemoth stood before the giant, which glared down at its foe, brows furrowing with momentary doubt. Then the giant roared, raising his club high to smite the burning king.

It was a blow that would have crushed an entire phalanx, but the king simply raised his molten blade to meet the descending club. A percussive boom swept from the combatants, consuming the battlefield. When it subsided the giant was left holding nothing but the smouldering stump of its own arm.

The hag watched in awe as the giant took a step back, its foot shaking the earth. It raised its head to cry out in anguish, but the burning king was already leaping, his sword of lava raised, smoke billowing in its wake. With a mighty slash of the sword, the burning king split the giant from shoulder to waist.

As the two halves of the giant collapsed to the earth, splashing in the mud, the king looked on at his enemies. One by one, their will crumbled, each falling to their knees in the dirt, offering up their weapons in supplication.

The burning king was motionless as his defeated enemies threw themselves on his mercy. He surveyed them with little pity, smouldering yellow eyes scanning the field for any sign of defiance.

Until those eyes came to rest on her.

She was the only one left standing amidst an army of kneeling supplicants. Though she had thought herself invisible it was clear the burning king could see past the glamour that had kept her impervious to the battle. Under his gaze, she realised that those burning eyes did not glow from within a black obsidian helmet... they were part of it. The burning king wore no crown, it was his own dark skull that reached, clawlike, towards the dark skies.

Fear gripped her heart in its ice-cold fist, and she took a step backwards. Slowly the burning king raised his arm, pointing an accusing finger at her. As one, every fighter in both armies turned their head to look at her.

Whatever bravery had kept her here fled in an instant. She took a stumbling step back, turning and taking flight. Mercifully, no one raised a hand to stop her as she raced from the battlefield, through the mud and blood until it transformed to soft grass once more. Until the pall of mist through which she raced lifted, and she was once more under blue skies.

She carried on running but her breath never shortened, her legs did not tire, and no matter how far she fled those icy fingers still gripped her chest like a vice.

Though she had no clue who she was or from where she had come, she knew one thing...

She knew fear.

2

The Ramadi Wastes, 105 years after the Fall

ALL he wanted was to leave the stink of this desert behind. Just keep going, don't look back, one foot in front of the other. Even that was getting more difficult. He needed water and fast, but that wasn't all.

Josten had wanted redemption. He'd worked out a long time ago that redemption was the reason he'd come all the way to this hell. It hadn't worked out that way though. He'd managed to fuck that up as well, but then his whole life was one long list of fuck-ups. After everything he'd done, now would be a bad time to start with the regrets, but regrets were all he had left.

Letting Randal live, that was pretty high on the list. He should have cut that bastard into pieces when he had the chance. Hadn't though, had he? Randal was alive, walking the desert somewhere, and Mullen was dead. That was no justice, but letting Randal live had seemed like the right thing to do at the time.

Worst of all was knowing he'd failed Livia. That innocent girl he had followed halfway across the world. Now she was gone too.

Josten had made a vow to her. His word had never been

worth much, but this time he had meant to keep it. Now it was worth nothing more than piss in the desert.

Whatever that woman was back there, that wicked thing that had set him free, it wasn't Livia Harrow.

As he walked, he kept the coast on his right-hand side all the while. As long as he followed the sea he knew he was heading south. He'd looked out over the barren expanse of water more than once, thought about walking down to where the waves lapped up against the beach. It would have been so easy to let the sea take him, to swim out as far as he could until his strength gave out.

The long walk south turned from stride to step to stumble, until eventually he was barely on his feet. It seemed like he'd walked miles but there was no way of knowing the truth of it, he could have travelled less than one for all he knew.

When eventually he saw some kind of shanty port up ahead of him he tried to laugh, but his throat was so dry it just came out like a strangled cough.

The closer he got the worse the place looked, and the more it seemed exactly the kind of place he deserved. He could see rickety roofs, a few mangy animals and a few mangier people lurking in the streets. At the makeshift jetty there was a ship moored. That was something at least. For the first time since he started this journey he thought that maybe he was going to make it out of this alive after all.

As he walked into town, Josten started to realise what a state he looked. Everyone was giving him the side-eye and in response he tried to look as confident as possible. Avoiding trouble was as much about looking the part as being the part.

No one would fuck with him if they thought he was trouble, but there was a nagging voice in the back of his head telling him he looked like an escaped slave. The western coast was rife with pirates preying on easy meat. If he wasn't careful he'd end up in chains all over again.

As he reached the makeshift harbour there was the usual bustle. Men were loading the ship with supplies, possibly ore from the mines of the Ramadi. It was how those death cults made their wealth when they weren't dealing in war. Slaves were traded for iron, copper and nickel, and the last thing Josten needed was to be trafficked for a few hunks of raw metal.

Three mariners were talking to a merchant, most likely finalising their deal. Josten focused on them, trying to read what kind of men they were, but what did he need to know? They were pirates and slavers. They would kill a man soon as look at him, and sell their own mothers if it made a few coppers.

When the deal was done the trader left the men to their conversation, and Josten picked his moment to approach. Despite his fatigue he tried to make a decent show of looking confident.

'I need passage down the coast,' he said as he reached them, trying to sound gruff enough to fit in with a bunch of cutthroats. 'I have no money for a berth, but I guarantee once we reach Canbria you'll be handsomely rewarded.'

The three men looked him up and down, appraising the ragged figure before them. Then they burst out laughing.

'Handsomely rewarded?' said one of them, the tattoo of an eagle's claw marking one side of his scarred face. 'And we're supposed to believe you're some rich Suderfeld lord I suppose?'

'Something like that,' Josten replied, realising he'd probably made a mistake and any moment he was going to end up in irons.

'Little bit lost aren't you?'

Lost wasn't the word. This had definitely been a mistake, but what choice did he have? 'I'm a mercenary,' he replied. 'Just trying to get back to my company. They'll pay to have me back… in one piece.'

'You're worth that much?' The pirate looked him up and down. 'Because right now you don't look worth a shit.'

They'd stopped laughing now. Josten wondered whether it would be best to just turn and run, but he didn't have the energy to take more than a few steps, and pride wouldn't let him be chased down and made a fool of by a gang of lowly pirates.

Then one of them clapped him on the shoulder. 'You're in luck, mate,' he said, smiling widely, his teeth filed down to points. 'We're heading to Canbria on the next tide. And since we lost three crew in the last week we need all the hands we can get.'

Josten stared. Was this a joke? There was no way his luck could turn just like that. And should he even trust a man who looked like he was half shark?

His question was answered when the men turned and made their way back to the ship. He watched them, all the trust squeezed out of him, then the shark-toothed one turned.

'Well? Are you coming or not?'

Josten didn't wait to be asked twice and followed them onto the ship.

They led him to the quarterdeck. Shark Teeth said, 'Best if you meet the captain before we set sail.'

With that he knocked on the door set in the aftcastle. 'What's his name?' Josten asked before they entered.

'We call him Mad Vek,' answered the mariner. 'But it's best to leave out the "Mad" part when you're addressing him.'

With that, a voice shouted for them to enter. The sailor opened the door and beckoned Josten inside. He walked into the dimly lit room, and was hit by the stench of stale sweat and spirits.

'New hand, Captain,' said Shark Teeth, before closing the door and leaving Josten alone.

Vek sat behind a desk covered in nautical charts. Three candles burned, wax dripping over the table edge. A bottle of some spirit sat half empty in the middle of the charts as a paperweight.

'By the Kraken's eye, you look like shite,' said Vek, as Josten stood there.

'So they tell me.'

'Well, don't just stand there making the place look untidy. Sit down.'

Josten gladly accepted the invitation and slumped in the weathered chair opposite the captain.

'So what do they call you?' asked Vek.

Josten told him the truth. He doubted these pirates would have heard of him before.

'You look like you've been in the wars,' Vek said as he poured a glass of spirits from the bottle and placed it in front of Josten.

'You don't know how right you are,' he replied, staring at that glass. All he wanted was water. A jug of it. But it seemed the only thing on offer was some rank-looking rum. Josten had a bastard of a thirst and he considered necking the drink, but after swilling it around in the glass, the pungent aroma hitting his nose, he thought better of it.

'Worked a ship before?' Vek asked.

Josten had only ever set foot on a ship once and it had made him sick as a leper. 'I'm a quick learner.'

Vek seemed to find that funny. 'Lucky for you we're shorthanded. But even so, if you don't pull your weight you'll be food for the fishes.'

'Sounds like a fair deal,' said Josten, despite it sounding like a pretty shit deal if he was honest.

'Good. That's settled then. Kento is below decks. He'll do the tattooing.'

Josten thought he might have misheard. 'The what?'

'You're part of my crew now, Josten Cade. We all have the mark of the Kraken on us. Otherwise it's bad luck.'

Vek stood, pulling his shirt over his head. In the candlelight, Josten could see a tattoo etched on Vek's back; a huge sea beast rising up from the base of his spine, tentacles winding up and over his shoulders, then down each of the pirate's arms.

'That's… impressive,' was all Josten could think to say.

'And it burned like fire when I was having it done,' Vek replied. 'But I suppose you'll find that out soon enough.'

'I only need passage to Canbria. When I get there I can pay you.'

Vek closed one eye and stared at Josten through the other. 'We'll see,' he said. 'But I think it more likely you'll want to stay with us. I think you'll find this life suits you.'

Josten wanted to say like fuck he would. 'We'll see.'

'Ha!' Vek picked up his glass. 'Then here's to the sea, and everything in it.'

Josten stood, raising his own glass. Vek downed his drink, then looked on expectantly. Josten had never been one to shirk a challenge, and he gulped down his own. The rum stung his dry throat, and he had to grit his teeth to stop himself throwing it back up all over the parchment-strewn desk.

Vek sat back down with a satisfied grin, and Josten left the cabin. Once outside the air hit him, fuddling his senses, and he almost stumbled across the deck. The rest of the crew were waiting, looking amused at Josten's condition.

'Captain's taken a shine to you then,' said one of them.

'How can you tell?' asked Josten.

'Cos you're still alive.' The rest of the crew broke into laughter.

'I need to see a man named Kento,' Josten said, when the laughing had died down.

'Sure you don't want some food first?' asked one of the younger mariners. 'You look fit to drop.'

'No. I think it's best to just get this out of the way.'

That seemed to spark a grudging admiration from the men. It was clear they respected that kind of tough stubbornness. For a moment Josten thought Vek might be right – maybe this life would suit him.

They led him down to the galley. Kento was waiting,

puffing on a long pipe. Every inch of him from the top of his bald head to his yellow toes was covered in ink.

'This one's for the Kraken's mark,' said the young mariner.

Kento nodded, beckoning Josten to a table. 'Assume the position, new-fish,' he said in a thick accent Josten didn't recognise.

There was no turning back from this now, and he removed his shirt, lying on the table and staring at the filthy floor.

Kento rummaged for something in a bag, pulling out a rolled leather scroll. When he spread it out before him, Josten could see there were wooden needles, ink and a little hammer. He'd seen men with tattoos before but never had the inclination to have one of his own. They generally marked a man out as member of a guild, but Josten had never felt loyal enough to join one. He guessed he was joining one now.

'This is going to hurt,' said Kento. 'Want something to bite down on?'

'Let's just get it over with,' Josten replied.

They were words he began to instantly regret as Kento went at him with needle and hammer. Vek had been right – the pain was like fire. Mercifully, just as it started to feel like Kento was tearing off his skin with white-hot pincers, Josten passed out…

3

THE tattoo burned like a bastard. It stung him from neck to arse crack, red-hot pain like someone was cutting through his flesh, but there was nothing to take your mind off a new tattoo like being sick ten times a day.

It hadn't taken Josten long to realise why he'd never wanted to be a man of the sea. The boat churned up and down on the waves, and not even big waves. The rest of the mariners had laughed at him at first, taking some sadistic pleasure in the way he'd been throwing his guts up over the side of the ship. After two days even they weren't seeing the funny side anymore.

Days of walking through the desert had already left him feeling weak, and he needed to eat, get some water in him, but every time he tried to keep something down the buffeting of the ship would see it come right back up again. All he wanted to do was find a dark quiet corner and lie down, but that hadn't been an option. Josten knew he had to pull his weight. Had to earn his stripes aboard the ship or he'd most likely be thrown overboard after his own puke like so much flotsam.

Just keep going, and all this will pass. At least that's what he'd told himself. And eventually, after three days of hell, he was right. The sting in his back relented and he managed to keep some food down. On the fourth day he was like a new man. And a new man was exactly what it was going to take for him to survive this.

Whatever he'd expected the pirate life to be like, it wasn't this. The tales he'd been told about savages of the seas turned out to be so much horseshit. The crew were disciplined and focused, every man had a job and knew it well. Despite the look of them, they kept the ship in fine condition, and Josten's first job was scrubbing the deck. He kept a shirt on while he went about it, the flesh of his back already tender enough without letting the sun burn it to a crisp, and for those first few days all he knew was the sound of the wire brush scrubbing the wood in between the occasional cry of a seabird and the laughter of the men. It was hard work, honest work Josten had spent years trying to avoid, but it beat dying in the desert or drowning in the sea, so he took to it with all the vigour he could muster.

Not long after there was a promotion of sorts, and Josten was trusted to learn how to adjust rigging and hoist sail. There were new words to learn like halyard and braces and vangs, and new pain to endure as his hands blistered with every new pull of a rope. Still he didn't complain, determined to prove his worth, determined to survive long enough to reach home.

It wasn't long before Josten was climbing the rigging like he was born to it. Within a month he would often find himself looking out and seeing nothing but open water on every horizon, feeling the salt breeze on his face and regretting he hadn't sought out a ship's company as a younger man.

Their carrack was called the *Storm Cow*. Josten thought it odd that nobody else found that funny, and at first he thought maybe it was misspelled. The *Storm Crow* seemed a much more fitting name for a ship full of reavers. Still, it wasn't really his place to question it. Not since he was one of them now.

The pain from his tattoo had long since relented. Josten couldn't see exactly what it depicted but he hoped it was something akin to the other crewmen. Every one of them bore a tattoo depicting a huge sea beast, tentacles winding across shoulders and down arms. He could see the tentacles on his own tattoo all right, winding down his arm to the wrist. Hopefully Kento had done a decent job on his back – he hadn't suffered so much pain for it to look shit.

That wasn't all that had changed. His hair was growing out, the cropped look he favoured now swapped for an unkempt mop that he tied back with a leather band. His usually clean-shaven jaw was covered in stubble and he was enjoying the prospect of a beard for the first time ever. Before, he had cursed the brightness of the desert sun, but now the salt sea air soothed his sunburned skin and he welcomed its touch.

Josten had also got to know the crew. To his surprise they weren't the fearsome bunch he had expected. In the mercenary companies Josten had mixed with more cutthroats and murderers than he could care to remember. By comparison this band of mariners were almost civilised. The one with the shark's teeth who he had first been intimidated by was quite an amiable chap. Predictably they called him

'Shark Teeth', but his real name was Dolan. After their first conversation, Josten learned his new shipmate had an encyclopaedic knowledge of history, and took great pleasure in relating tales from the Age of Penitence.

The young lad who had suggested he take food before having his tattoo was known as Lonik the Fidget, since the lad couldn't keep still for a second. In fact most of the crew had names that described their looks and habits. The most apt was a man they called 'The Crapper'. Josten still shivered when he remembered the day he'd found out why they called him that.

Every man on board worshipped a god they called the Kraken, which explained the tattoos. Paying homage to the Kraken was not to be shirked or questioned, that much had been made clear to Josten from day one. He made a show of it, there was no point being stubborn, but Josten had seen real gods. He knew this Kraken wasn't real and was nothing to be feared. The real gods were more terrifying than any deified sea creature.

For days the crew went about their business like ordinary mariners and Josten learned his new trade; climbing rigging, hoisting sail, scrubbing deck. He began to wonder when any actual pirating would occur, but he needn't have worried.

It was on one clear night that land finally came into view. A city shone on the horizon, and even in the twilight, Josten could see it was beautiful.

'Tallis,' said Lonik, tapping his thumb against the gunwale as he stared out at the sight. 'Always gets me right here.' He jabbed a finger to his chest.

25

'I can see what you mean,' Josten replied. And he could.

He'd heard of Tallis – the jewel of the Cordral. It was said for all the cities that had lost their splendour after the Fall, only Tallis had managed to increase it. If Kantor was the Cordral's beating heart, then Tallis was its bejewelled head.

'What business do we have here?' Josten asked.

Lonik just shrugged. 'Ask Vek if you dare. None of us have any clue what that mad bastard's up to, but he hasn't led us wrong yet, so we ain't about to argue.'

Josten wasn't about to argue either. Vek had saved his life. If he owed him anything it was to keep his mouth shut and follow. At least until they got back to Canbria, then he'd go his own way no matter what he owed.

The *Storm Cow* slid into the harbour of Tallis like a robber, the crew going about their business in silence. They flew some colours Josten didn't recognise, but he guessed it was to mark them as traders rather than pirates. As they began to moor up, Vek appeared, looking almost respectable. He'd put on clothes of some finery, his beard neat and oiled.

'Right, Lonik, Dolan, with me. Rest of you, stay out of trouble.' Then, before he moved to the gangplank, 'And you.' He pointed at Josten. 'Let's see if you're worth more than scrubbing decks.'

Josten wasn't about to protest and he followed Vek ashore.

His legs felt like jelly as he stepped onto the hard stone of the harbour. Another new sensation to add to the rest. Vek and the others didn't seem bothered as they made their way towards the city. Josten did his best to walk in a straight line, none too ready to look like an idiot but all too aware he was walking like a man who'd been riding hard for a week.

Vek led them up to the city, nodding at the harbourmaster who returned the gesture as he walked by. When they reached the midst of the port, Josten was hit by all the sensations he'd missed while at sea.

The smell of hot spicy food wafted down the narrow street. People chattered in funny northern accents. Two dogs barked at one another in the distance, as though relaying messages above the hum of the city.

There wasn't much time to appreciate the beauty of Tallis; its rising minarets were little more than silhouettes against the night sky. The men and women they passed were dressed in loose-fitting robes, hair worn long as was the fashion. Josten had known a few men from the Cordral in his time, men who'd fought for coin in the mercenary companies. For the most part they'd been good talkers, but they couldn't fight worth a shit.

Vek led them through the labyrinthine streets until they reached a busy alleyway. Stalls jutted from every dwelling, covered with multi-coloured awnings. Vendors touted exotic textiles and trinkets in between glowing braziers cooking a multitude of spiced meat and fish. Vek ignored them as he made his way to an open doorway. A thick-set bouncer pulled aside a heavy curtain, allowing Vek to enter. It seemed the pirate knew Tallis well, and it knew him right back.

Josten followed as they walked down a set of well-worn stairs and into a vibrant chamber. A band were playing a collection of strange-looking instruments in one corner, making a right racket to boot, but the patrons seemed to love it. Men and women danced, though to Josten's eye they were more writhing around one another like coiled snakes. Drink flowed and pipe smoke filled the small space, but these pirates were all about the business, ignoring the many temptations on offer.

Vek spied his contact in the corner, leading the three of them to a secluded booth. A man sat puffing on some contraption that filtered weed through a jug to a pipe stem. It bubbled as he drew in the smoke.

'Erral,' Vek said, spreading his arms as though inviting the man for a hug.

'Vek, my old friend.'

Erral slapped the rump of a girl sitting on his knee, and she slid out of the booth, smiling at the pirates as she did so. Lonik smiled back, unable to take his eyes off her. Josten could understand the allure, but there'd be time for that later. For now, they were here on other matters.

They crowded into the booth as Erral set the bubbling pipe aside. 'I'm glad you could make it,' the man said. Josten recognised his accent was from the Suderfeld, though he couldn't place exactly where.

'I wouldn't be anywhere else,' Vek replied.

'Then I take it you're in the market for work?'

'Aren't I always?' Vek smiled, but Josten detected a hint of impatience about him.

'Very well,' said Erral. 'Then to business. A cargo ship is coming out of Canbria laden with grain. As usual the job will be simple: ransack the ship, take the cargo, and return it to Canbria intact. There, its original owner will take it back and sell the cargo on again.'

It was a treacherous move. Josten admired the simplicity of it. 'And you'd be the original owner, I take it,' Josten said without thinking.

All eyes turned to him, and he realised he'd spoken out of turn.

'New crewman?' Erral asked.

Vek was looking at Josten as though he'd let off a deathly stink.

'Still breaking this one in,' he replied, clapping a hand on Josten's shoulder and squeezing it a little too tight.

'Well,' said Erral with a smile, 'let's hope he's as quick with a blade as he is with his tongue.'

Josten wanted to tell this fucker that he was quicker than most, but he thought maybe he'd said enough.

'He'll get his chance to prove it soon enough,' said Vek.

Oh I'll prove it all right, Josten thought. *Just you give me the chance.*

4

Not a week later, Josten found himself standing alongside the crew, every man armed to the teeth, ready to slaughter a ship full of traders at the behest of a man everyone said was mad. Strange how life had a way of turning around on you.

The sky was dappled with cloud. A 'mackerel sky', they called it. It was a beautiful day but Josten doubted it would stay beautiful for long.

He and the rest of the men could see the ship across half a mile of waves, the telltale yellow flag marking it as a trader out of Canbria. This was their target all right. It looked so far away, but Josten had been assured the *Storm Cow* could catch anything that floated on the water.

Around him, the other crewmen were getting nervous. Sure they knew the sea, yes they knew how to raid, but Josten reckoned he'd seen more battles than any of them.

In his hands were a cutlass and a knife. He was used to a good sword and a stout shield in a battle, but like he'd said to Vek, he was a quick learner.

Lonik was standing next to him, trying to look tough, trying to look like he was relishing this, but Josten knew the truth. He'd seen it a hundred times before – he'd even been that lad, standing next to the tested veterans, hoping some of their know-how would rub off. It wouldn't. As a rule, the veterans were just as scared as the new blood. Sometimes more. If you were seasoned in battle you knew what was coming. All the blood and screaming. There was no getting used to it. You just had to learn how to handle it.

'Been here before, lad?' Josten asked.

Lonik paused before saying, 'Yeah.'

Josten was pretty sure that meant 'no'.

'Just keep your eyes open. Don't get too carried away with yourself. If you take a man down don't stand there congratulating yourself. When your blood's up there'll be a voice inside telling you you're invincible. Don't listen, it's likely to get you killed.'

'I know I'm not invincible,' Lonik replied.

'None of us are,' said Josten. 'But I reckon we're more than a match for a trading ship. You'll be fine.'

The crew on the trade ship had seen them now. They were desperately trying to change course, hoisting sail to get more speed. It was already too late. Or so Josten hoped. As much as he had been assured the *Storm Cow* was the fastest vessel on the sea, it seemed to take an age to catch up with the cargo ship. Josten had been in more battles than he could count, and the waiting was always the worst part, but this was ridiculous. It was about now he'd be flicking the cross-guard of his sword, but instead he slapped the blade of his cutlass against his leg. The feel of the metal on his thigh calmed his nerves a little, keeping him focused, quelling the panic.

31

When they were within fifty yards of their quarry, Josten could see they weren't just chasing helpless traders. Armed men waited on the ship and they looked determined to defend it.

Vek took his place at the prow. The rest of the crew were stripped down, tattoos showing, bare heads gleaming in the sun, but Vek stood stark bollock naked. His beard smouldered, smoking like fresh kindling, and the look in his eyes told Josten where his name had come from.

'There's our payday, lads,' he said, rattling his cutlass at the trade ship. 'The Kraken demands his due. Let's give it him in blood.'

An arrow flew overhead, thudding into the mizzenmast. It was quickly followed by a volley, most missing the mark, some hitting the deck. One hissed past Josten's head and struck one of the crew, who went down with a wail. Vek didn't seem to care, but then neither did the rest of the lads as they homed in on their prey.

If Josten was going to make an impression, if he was going to fit in with this mob, he'd have to show them he was just as insane as the rest of them. For all he'd told Lonik not to get carried away with himself, Josten was about to do that very thing. But then he'd never been much for taking his own advice.

He tore off his shirt, eyes focused on the ship, on its crew, slapping that cutlass against his leg like his life depended on it. Vek was still talking, rambling on about death and blood and pain and the Kraken. All Josten could hear were the waves lapping at the side of the bow, mixed in with the panicked cries of men on the trade ship and the whistle of arrows. The prospect of battle was in the air now. He had no shield but there was a knife in his hand. He had no armour but there was a tattoo all across his back. He'd soon find out if the Kraken would protect him as well as a shirt of chainmail.

Vek had worked the crew up into a frenzy now: this was it, they were almost upon the ship. Josten wasn't about to wait for any orders. He pushed past Shark Teeth and Lonik, ran across the deck, past Vek still jabbering on, planted his foot against the bulwark and leapt.

An arrow flew past his face as he jumped, nicking the flesh of his cheek. All he could see were panicked faces glaring at him from the trade ship as this madman came screaming at them through the air. He landed on the deck of the other ship, bowling into an archer, sending him flying. Somehow he managed to stay on his feet and he struck out at the nearest sailor. The cutlass hacked a divot of flesh, blood spattering his arm. He raised his knife in time to parry an incoming blade. Another hack of the cutlass and two men were down.

All he could see around him were desperate faces. Some fearful, some furious. Josten didn't distinguish, he was in a frenzy of his own now, fighting for his life. There was screaming, but there was always screaming when you were in the thick of it. Another swipe of the cutlass, another dead man.

The surprise of his attack had worn off. He could see the crew of the cargo ship steeling themselves, coming to their senses. Josten was just one man, a madman maybe, but they had the strength in numbers. For the brief moment he took to think, he guessed that death at sea was the same as death on land. It would just be easier for them to bury him.

With a roar, Mad Vek appeared, axe hacking the head from a hapless sailor. He looked elated, face locked in a gleeful grin, smoke billowing from his beard. The sight of this naked bastard put the fear in the sailors. It put the fear in Josten too, but instead of standing there and staring he joined Vek in the joyous kill. They celebrated together, weapons hacking at the crew as the rest of the pirates joined them.

In a blur of violence they bloodied the deck. It was warm between his toes, slick beneath the soles of his feet. He didn't need a sword and shield, these were his weapons now and they were as good as any.

Another hack of the cutlass and he sheared a red line down a man's face. Stabbing with the knife he put a hole in his neck for good measure. The man went down silently. Across the deck and through the flurry of hacking pirates Josten spied Lonik. The lad was backed up against the gunwale, strugging with a sailor. For all he was holding his own, the sailor looked strong and desperate.

Josten ran through the fray, lifting the cutlass and swinging it in a deadly arc. The sailor's head fell from his shoulders, spraying Lonik red. Josten stared at him as the lad stared back, before he barked a laugh.

'What I told you earlier,' he shouted. 'Fucking forget that. You're invincible, lad. Now show me!'

Lonik kept staring, breathing in hard before his eyes went mad, infected by the slaughter around him. Lips pulled back from his teeth and he let out a snarl before barrelling into the melee with the rest of the crew.

Someone shouted for the crew to surrender. Josten heard it over the din, but his fellow crewmen seemed in no mood to accept. The slaughter went on. No one wanted to face him, the sailors cowering from the merciless blades of the pirates, and Josten stood in the centre of the fray, watching as men were cut down and butchered.

When the crew of the trade ship had lost all spirit for the fight and the pirates their spirit for the kill, the survivors were driven to their knees. In the silence that followed, Vek called for the captain, and to his credit one of the surrendered crew bravely rose to his feet. He didn't look much, but then Josten reckoned to captain a trade ship you didn't have to be the fiercest man on the seas.

Vek stood before him, axe in hand. It was like there was an unspoken agreement between them. The captain just closed his eyes before Vek took his head off with one swipe of that axe.

Then there was a frenzy of activity. Josten could barely focus on any of it. Half the pirate crew rushed below decks, dragging out crates, throwing them onto the *Storm Cow*. The other half went about executing the crew. It was clear no witnesses would be left. Josten was all about the battle, all about the slaughter, but murdering beaten men was something even he wouldn't sink to. It sickened him enough that he turned away, looking out over the bow of that ship at the mackerel sky.

'This is a good day,' Vek said.

Josten turned to see the captain's beard had stopped smouldering now, it was just a black twisted mess on his chin.

All the madness had gone from his eyes, and he looked more like a friendly uncle, but for being naked, cock dangling between his thighs.

'Never seen a man so eager to jump into the fray,' Vek continued. 'You got some kind of death wish?'

'Just trying to do my bit,' Josten replied.

'You did that all right. And they say I'm mad. If I'm not careful you'll be taking that reputation from me.'

'Trust me, there's no danger of that.'

Vek's brow furrowed as he thought on that. Then he laughed a deep belly laugh.

'We'll see, Josten Cade. We'll just see.'

5

FERRABY was perched at the northern end of the Canbrian coast, the perfect place for them to drop off the cargo. It wasn't a port Josten was familiar with, but he supposed it could still be classed as home to him. The signs were there anyway – the temperature had dropped and the sky was overcast. If there was ever any doubt he was back in the Suderfeld, the change in the weather set that aright. All he needed now was to smell the shit-stink of horses and it would be like he'd never left.

How long had it been since he was here? Weeks? Months? Was it a year? Time hadn't seemed to matter while he'd been at sea. On board, the days didn't seem to pass like they did on land. Josten liked that feeling. It was like being young again.

'You'll be coming with us,' Vek had said. 'It will do us well to have a native on shore when we finalise the deal.'

Of course Josten had agreed, despite his fears. He wasn't sure exactly what he was fearful of, but something about being back in Canbria made him want to stay on the boat. Josten wasn't scared of any man alive, but this place was giving him the fear. Was he scared of meeting someone from a mercenary company he'd wronged? No, he'd come too far to care about that. Maybe it was the knowledge that once he was back in Canbria that was it; he'd failed. That pact he'd made with Livia all that time ago was done and dusted, and there was never going to be a way to make it right.

By the time they walked down the gangplank to the dockside, Josten had an empty feeling. This place wasn't home. He had no ties here anymore. No friends, no family, nothing. All he had now was the ship and these men.

They followed Vek through the drizzle to a tavern, but then these kind of illicit dealings always seemed to happen in taverns. When they walked in, it looked like the usual kind of place – salty patrons, salty serving wench, salty tavern keeper. There was even a mangy dog under a table.

Vek didn't pause to order drinks, he was straight down to business, and Josten liked that about him. The pirate captain saw his contact, Erral, sitting in the dimness of the inn and made his way straight to a corner table. Vek, Josten, Lonik and a one-eyed mariner named Keelhaul all sat around the man. If Erral was intimidated by four pirates, he didn't show it. Josten thought he looked more out of place than he had in Tallis, with his fine jacket and hat, peacock feather dancing on one side. For a backstreet fence he was pretty conspicuous.

'Three days I've been waiting in this… establishment,' said Erral. 'Please tell me it wasn't for nothing.'

'It'll be worth your while,' Vek replied. 'We're ready to unload when you are.'

'Well, that's just the good news I was hoping for. The carts will take the goods off your hands at midnight under cover of dark.'

'And our end?'

'You get your payment when I have the goods back. You know me better than that, Vek.'

Keelhaul was growing restless, hand straying down to the knife at his side.

'Sounds reasonable,' Vek said. 'Don't be late.'

'Am I ever?' Erral smiled, gold tooth glinting at the back of his mouth.

Vek stood. Josten and Lonik took that as their cue but Keelhaul stared for a moment longer before he too rose to his feet. Josten had learned that Keelhaul, of all the pirate crew, was not to be crossed, so it was with relief that they all left the tavern. Outside in the drizzle Keelhaul was still bristling.

'You should let me gut that slimy bastard someday,' said Keelhaul.

Vek patted the man on the shoulder. 'Someday I will,' he said. 'But while he's useful you'll have to leave his guts where they are.'

They continued their way through the shitty streets, and Josten didn't feel safe until they were back on the ship. Then they just had to wait.

This was the worst time. All Josten wanted was for them to cast off, to set sail and get back on the open water. To get away from this place and all it signified.

He watched from the deck as day turned to night. As the bustle of the dock subsided, and the noise of the town turned to silence. When he eventually heard the sound of cartwheels rumbling along the cobbles, his stomach began to churn with excitement. Two carts rolled into view, sitting themselves at the end of the jetty. Everyone was on deck now, the cargo they had stolen sitting in neat piles waiting to be unloaded.

A man walked towards their ship in the silence, holding a lantern at arm's length.

'I'm here to collect the payload,' he said in a thick north-Canbrian accent.

Josten squinted through the dark. This wasn't the fence they had met earlier.

'Where's Erral?' Vek called from the deck.

The man with the lantern shrugged. 'You don't expect that pompous ass to do any of his own dirty work, do you?'

That seemed a good enough explanation for Vek, and he ordered the men to start unloading. As uncomfortable as Josten was with the situation, he mucked in with the rest.

He and Shark Teeth grabbed one of the bundles of cargo and hoisted it off the ship. The drizzle had turned to driving rain as the night drew in, and the sailors were soaked through in no time. Josten and Shark Teeth squinted at each other, water pouring down their faces.

'Sooner we get out of this shitty weather, the better,' said Shark Teeth.

Josten was about to agree with him when a crossbow bolt flew out of the dark and embedded itself in Shark Teeth's neck. The barrel they were holding hit the jetty as the pirate fell. Josten ducked as more crossbow bolts flew from the night. Someone shouted to get back on the ship. It was too late for that. Armoured men were already jumping from the back of the carts, swords drawn, and by the look of them they'd be more than a match for a bunch of rain-soaked pirates.

Despite the look of these knights, a couple of the crew decided they could take on their ambushers and rushed to the fore, taking the fight to the enemy. Josten admired that, even though he knew it was stupid.

Crapper and Keelhaul both ran in screaming. They both died screaming too.

Squinting through the rain, Josten recognised the livery of Duke Lensmar. It seemed the fence, Erral, was either a turncoat or had been captured by the Duke's men. Not that it mattered now. All that mattered was escape.

Through the confusion and the sound of clashing weapons, Josten spotted his escape route along the dock, but before he could sprint to safety he spied Lonik lying on the ground. His hands were covering his head, protecting himself from the hail of crossbow bolts, not that it would do him much good if one of them hit its target. Josten thought for a moment – just for a moment – about leaving the lad. He might have changed recently, become a pirate, a fearless man of the sea, but he still couldn't leave the lad behind.

Grabbing the boy by the scruff, Josten dragged him to his feet, pulling him along behind as he fled. There was no skill to running away. You just had to keep your head down and go. Hope nobody saw you. Hope nobody came after you. Hope everyone else was so preoccupied with battle you could just slip away. It was a risk, but not as much of a risk as charging headlong at armoured men with nothing but foul language to back you up.

They ran down the street until the cobbles ended and they were squelching through the mud and the wet. Josten dragged Lonik to one side of the road, pausing for a moment in an alleyway. He checked himself, relieved to find he wasn't wounded.

The two of them stood there, trying to get their breath back. Everything had suddenly turned to shit. All Josten had left were the clothes on his back and the knife at his side. Not even a pair of boots for his muddy feet.

'What now?' asked Lonik.

Josten answered by clapping his hand over the boy's mouth. Someone was coming down the street. Could have been one of Duke Lensmar's men. Could have been town militia. Either way, with nothing but a knife he hoped the element of surprise might keep them both alive.

The sound of running feet got louder and when they were almost at the alley Josten burst out from his hiding place, knife in hand.

Vek almost ran straight into him.

Both men stared at one another. Then Vek burst out laughing. 'You got the same idea as me?' he said. 'Live to fight another day, eh?'

'I guess you're not as mad as they say you are,' Josten replied.

Vek didn't answer that, just waved Josten and Lonik behind him as he ran on through the port. They made their way through the muddy streets, the sound of the rain lashing down masking their footfalls as they went. Soon they were almost at the edge of town, but the place had burst into life after the attack at the harbour. There were voices raised, bells jangling, dogs barking.

Down the street, their exit was blocked – the gate leading out of town was manned by armed men. The three of them paused in the shadow of the town walls, watching.

'What do we do now?' asked Lonik.

'We need a diversion,' said Vek.

'Like what?'

Vek looked at Josten then at Lonik. 'Like someone makes a lot of noise and draws those guards away.'

'But who—'

Before he could finish his sentence, Vek had drawn a knife across the back of Lonik's leg. The boy screamed, and Josten grabbed Vek by the throat, other hand on his wrist holding the knife away.

'What the fuck are you doing?' Josten growled, ready to throttle the bastard where he stood.

Vek's eyes bore that tinge of madness again. 'We need to go, now,' he said.

Josten glanced towards the gate. Lonik's cries were drawing the guards right to them. He looked down at the boy, who was grasping his leg, screaming in pain. There was no escape for him now, and if they hung around there would be no escape for any of them. Just the noose.

As the guards made their way closer to Lonik's screams, Josten and Vek slipped away into the shadows, moving around the edge of the wall towards the gates. By the time they got there the way was clear, and as Josten listened to Lonik's mournful cries behind them, he and Vek crept off into the night.

They ran until they left the noise of Ferraby far behind them, but still Josten could hear Lonik's cries echoing in his head. That boy's screaming brought back the long journey north. Brought back his failure to save Livia. He'd abandoned her too – what was left of her. Left that girl to the desert, just like he'd left Lonik to the guards of Ferraby.

Josten and Vek eventually reached the edge of a wood, where they paused for air. Vek was breathing hard but he still had a smile on his face.

'Close one,' he said. 'They almost had us.'

Josten didn't reply, still thinking on what had just happened. Mad Vek they called him, but it was clear he wasn't mad at all. Just another bastard willing to abandon his own men to get what he wanted.

Vek looked back towards Ferraby. 'They'll be coming after us. This is your country, Cade. Which way do you think we should go?'

'I don't think it'll make any difference,' Josten replied. He'd already slipped his knife from his belt.

'Why not?' asked Vek.

Josten plunged the knife straight into Vek's gut, twisting it, slicing it, shoving it in as far as it would go. He grabbed Vek beneath the jaw, moving his head until they were staring into each other's mad eyes.

'Because everyone gets what they deserve,' he growled.

Vek stared until his accusatory look glazed and he slid to the ground.

Josten left the body next to the wood, striking out on his bare feet. He'd have to see how far he got. A part of him hoped it wasn't far.

6

Running. *Always running. She didn't want to stop but she knew she had to. The landscape flashed by in a haze of forest and hills, blurring into one until eventually she found herself in a field. All about her was green. All above her was blue and the fresh crispness of the air filled her nostrils. It was a welcome change from the stink of battle and death.*

She laid a hand to her breast, feeling the fluttering of her heart against the thin cavity of her chest. Her flesh felt paper thin, her heart threatening to beat its way through her fragile ribcage.

The hag took a moment to compose herself. Closing her eyes, she listened to the steady thrumming within, the blood pumping in her ears, coursing through her veins. The fear had subsided somewhat, but still she felt the echo of it within her. She remembered those baleful eyes, the burning king staring into her soul.

Reality was beginning to coalesce. Where before this had all seemed like some dream, now the reality of it had hit her. As though waking from a nightmare she tried to breathe deep and even, tried to take solace in the solidity of the real world. But this was no real world. This was something other; something wicked and twisted.

She heard a distant noise… a cawing in the air. She opened her eyes to see a bird, distant, wheeling and spinning in the clear sky.

It pitched and swooped, dancing in the air until it was joined by a second bird, then a third. Three eagles, pivoting around one another, calling out, singing their screeching song.

Their aeriform dance caused the harsh memory of the battle she had fled to fade. She watched them for as long as she could before the brightness of the sun began to sting her eyes. When she closed them against the glare, something struck her, sharp and stark. She was being propelled, as though falling into a bottomless well, her stomach lurching all the while.

Until she came to a sudden stop.

She was a young woman. Flush with the bloom of youth, she ran in fields; the open grasslands that surrounded her home, a farm on the edge of the town, on the edge of the county, on the edge of the kingdom.

Her run came to an end as she reached the top of a hill overlooking endless green land. Birds twittered their song. She belonged here. She was safe here. There was nothing to fear.

You will never return to this place.

The voice struck like a knife through her ribs. It was an alien voice, malevolent in its nature. It shook her from the memory but she couldn't open her eyes, she couldn't escape it.

All this is gone now. You are gone now. And I am here.

Her memory darkened, the blue sky consumed by black cloud, the green that surrounded her turning to ash grey.

'Who are you?' she asked. 'What do you want?'

Another baleful laugh. Want? I have everything I need from you. All you are is but a distant memory, a shade. Soon there will be nothing of you but dust on the breeze.

She looked down to see she was a young girl no longer. The flesh of her arms had withered, her legs little more than skin and bone.

'What is happening to me? Why are you doing this to me?'

My need is greater, *said the voice.* You are nothing but a vessel. That's all you ever were. Your whole life was without meaning other than to fulfil this purpose.

'But why?' *She was pleading now. Desperate to know the reason she was made to suffer like this.*

Because it pleases me, I will show you.

Her memory shifted again. The ashen land that surrounded her turned to desert. Copses of trees shifting and rising into ancient temple walls that might once have been resplendent but now looked to be all but ruins.

She stood in the midst of a vast courtyard. Surrounding her were an array of warriors, some savage, some noble, some heavily armoured, some in resplendent robes. Every one of them had their head bowed in supplication. In front of her, the hag could see a raised platform, ancient stones elevated above the crowd, a makeshift altar at which they worshipped. Upon it stood a woman dressed in red, white hair flowing down past her shoulders. She stood over these warriors like a queen, like a goddess, but there was nothing benevolent about her. Everything in her demeanour spoke malice. Yet still the warriors worshipped her, and in turn she consumed that worship like a leech sucking the blood through their flesh, letting it nourish her.

This vision spurred something in the old hag. She remembered this place, remembered her fear, and even as she closed her eyes against it, the memory would not fade. The goddess stared at her from the platform, lips parting in a dreadful smile. Then she opened her mouth and screeched.

The old woman opened her eyes. She was back on an open field and for a fleeting moment she hoped she was back in her memory of childhood. But no, the eagles flew above her, their screeching growing louder, more frantic. When she looked up she saw that they no longer wheeled in a dance, but instead fought in a frenzy. Beaks tore, talons ripped. Blood and feathers flew in a storm. It was hideous to behold, but as with so many sickening sights she had witnessed, she could not turn her gaze away from it.

Nausea slowly overwhelmed her, dragging her down into the pit. She closed her eyes once more, feeling the ground begin to consume her, this whole place swallowing her. Before she was buried alive in the grass, someone grabbed her hand.

She opened her eyes. There was a farmhouse she recognised in the distance. Her body once more felt full of vigour and she was a girl again. Holding her hand was an old man, his kind face marred by age. She didn't recognise him but something inside told her not to be afraid, that she could trust this man.

'Hello,' he said.

'Hello back,' she answered.

His smile grew wider, showing his lack of teeth.

'Who are you?' she asked.

The old man paused for a moment, raising his eyes to the sky as though the answer might be written there. 'Now that's a question,' he said finally. 'But perhaps the real question you should be asking, is who are you?'

She shook her head. 'I have no idea.'

'Yes, it's a tough one,' said the old man. 'But then again, who are any of us anyway?'

That annoyed her. She had enough questions as it was without this old goat getting philosophical.

'Do you know who I am?' she said, not even trying to hide her annoyance.

'If you don't know, I can't tell you,' he replied. 'What I do know is that you don't belong here.'

That much was obvious. 'So where do I belong? And how do I get back there?'

The old man thought on that for a moment. Then looked straight at her and shook his head.

'This is pointless,' she said, feeling her frustration build.

She felt trapped in a cage, surrounded by torturers and fools. There was no way to tell what was real and what was a lie. Or even if this whole place was one big trick. Was she dead? Or merely dreaming?

The girl turned from the old man and sat down on a log. The weight of it all was getting too much. Perhaps she should just sit here and wait for it all to pass. Wait to be awoken from this nightmare. The old man came to sit down beside her, and they both looked out at the countryside surrounding them.

'I wish I could help you more,' he said. 'But I have problems of my own. There's always work to do around the farm, and with no help I'm scuppered. If I just had a pig or two—'

'You're all alone?' she said.

'Yep. Have been for a while now. Ever since...' His brow furrowed as though he were trying to retrieve a distant memory.

'Why don't I help you?' she said. 'I could stay here and work with you on the farm.'

As she said the words, the feeling that she knew the old man grew within her. He was special to her. She knew him, that much was obvious, but the memory of him was beyond her reach. Nevertheless, she felt that staying here and working on the farm with this old man was the most natural thing in the world. That was her purpose. Not to be a 'vessel' for some witch-queen.

'That would be nice,' the old man said. 'But you can't stay here. You have to go.'

'No. Why? I don't want to go, I like it here. I belong here. And where would I go? How do I know where I have to go if I don't even know where I am?'

'You have to go,' he said once more.

'But go where?'

'Go!' he screamed right at her, his face contorting, stretching into a beastly visage.

The old woman opened her eyes in time to see a wide-open beak. One of the eagles was swooping in low, right at her, its screech deafening.

She dived to the ground as the eagle swept over her with a whoosh of feathered wings, talons clacking shut, tearing the cotton of her dress.

The other eagles were wheeling above her, their animosity forgotten now they had a common target.

She scrambled to her feet, running again. Always running, the memory of that old man already fading. The beat of wings rushed through the air behind as her withered legs propelled her. Nearby was the edge of a forest, her only escape.

This time as the eagle plunged in there was no screech of warning. She sensed the attack nonetheless and dived to the ground, hearing the snap of talons that found nothing but air. Again she was on her feet, legs pumping for all they were worth. The tree line was just ahead, the tantalising safety of the wood. With a last burst of effort she rushed into the sanctity of the forest, hearing the frustrated screeches of the eagles above her.

Gasping for air, she clung to the trunk of a tree, gripping it as though it were her rescuer. She was enveloped in the dark cloying safety of the wood, hearing nothing now but the quiet rush of leaves in the wind. She should have felt safe but it was obvious there were yet more dangers ahead.

The hag closed her eyes, desperate to get back to the old man, willing herself to return to that farm, to the land where she knew she was safe, where she was young again. But that place was gone, already drifting away like the memory of a dream fading in the morning light.

With no other choice, she pressed further on into the wood.

7

The Cordral Extent, 106 years after the Fall

CTENKA Sunatra had been a model recruit. When he first enlisted in the Great Eastern Militia he would leap from his bunk every morning, his enthusiasm boundless. His eagerness to prove himself meant he attacked every task with all the vigour of youth. Drilling and weapons training, cleaning his uniform, polishing his armour and weapons until he could shave his wispy facial hair in the reflection.

Six months into his posting at Dunrun and all that had changed.

The sun lanced into the barrack room through slats in the wooden blinds, and Ctenka Sunatra stared at them with one bleary eye. He could barely raise his head from the pillow, groggy with wine, his mouth dry as a dead dog.

Another day.

One more endless bloody day.

He sat up, dragging one leg after the other over the side of the bed. The rest of the tiny barrack room was empty, its ten bunks in varying states of disarray. At least he wasn't alone in his apathy.

The Great Eastern Militia had once been a powerful military force. Indeed, its training grounds in Kantor were still a testament to that. But on the fringes of the Cordral, where old outposts lay in disrepair to rot in the sun, it was an entirely different story. Since the Fall most of those great monuments had crumbled. No longer did thaumaturges and sorcerers stand upon the battlements defending the city-state and its people from invaders. Now its soldiers were left to suffer the vagaries of the wilderness, waiting for an enemy that would never come.

Ctenka's father had once told him of what nobility there was in service. The old soldier had a hundred stories of bravery in the face of insurmountable odds. Last stands fought on the fringes, as the soldiers of the Cordral rallied to defend their great nation. Ctenka had discovered something very different. All he had learned was how apathetic an army can become when there are no more wars to fight.

He pulled on his trews, once again ignoring the hole in the knee. His unpolished boots sat in a heap along with his tunic, the eagle symbol sewn on the front long since frayed.

A year ago he had appeared immaculate in this gear. When first he came to Dunrun he had looked out of place – a pearl amidst pig shit. Now he fitted right in. Another turd in the pile.

Picking up his sword, Ctenka headed for the door. The weapon rattled in his grip, blade far too loose in the scabbard, pommel and cross-guard rusted, leather binding worn paper-thin. Good weapon maintenance had been drilled into them in the training grounds but out here no one seemed to care, and Ctenka had soon fallen into the same bad habits as his peers. It was a regret, but not one so keen that he would want

53

to change his ways now. What would be the point?

Outside the sun had already risen over the Crooked Jaw, beaming down onto the courtyard, stamping everything beneath its oppressive foot. Ctenka squinted, the light only making his fuddled head throb that much more.

Saying a silent prayer to Sol that he made it through the day without throwing up, he walked towards the Hangman's Gate. It was the innermost of the five gates that defended the Cordral Extent from the Shengen Empire. Where the Skull Road spilled out from the Crooked Jaw stood the vast and ancient fortress of Dunrun. It was once manned by almost a thousand soldiers of the Eastern Militia, vigilantly guarding the important trade route against any sign of attack from imperial invaders. Now there were less than fifty men rattling around within the ancient ramparts.

Some were green recruits like Ctenka, sent for whatever reason to the arse end of the Cordral to waste away in the sun. Most were veterans, too old to hold a place among the Kantor Militia and too broken from a life of military service to be of any use elsewhere. Among those veterans there were some who seemed to still give a damn, executing their duties with dedication and putting their younger counterparts to shame.

One such man waited for Ctenka beneath the oppressive shadow of the Hangman's Gate.

He stood a little over six feet, and though well into his fifties he was still broad at the shoulder and thick in the arm, his wide chest running to a slim waist, giving him the silhouette of a much younger man. His face though showed the truth of his years. His close-cropped hair and beard were

54

silver, bright blue eyes peering from within brows wrinkled by decades of care.

'Morning, Ermund,' Ctenka said as he approached the militiaman.

'Late again, Ctenka?' said Ermund without any humour.

'I am nothing if not a creature of habit, my friend,' Ctenka replied with a smile. It was not returned.

They continued on their way, walking beneath the shadow of the Hangman's Gate. It was the largest of the great gates of Dunrun, a huge barbican twenty feet thick spanning the entryway to the pass. In years gone by, the warriors of the militia had hanged bandits and invaders from its walls, hence the gruesome name. Now all that hung from it was the same stench of despair and ruin that lingered over the rest of Dunrun.

'Good to see you've taken the usual pride in your appearance today,' said Ermund.

Sarcasm was something Ctenka had come to appreciate from the big southerner.

'We don't all have the skills of a seamstress,' he replied. 'Some of us have talents that lie elsewhere.'

Ermund's uniform was always meticulously spruce. There was certainly nothing frayed about him, despite the years of wear. Though Ermund's past was something of a mystery, and a great source of debate among the militia of Dunrun, it was commonly accepted he must have been a military man through and through.

'Yes,' Ermund said, his eyes locked on the Skull Road ahead as it led through the remaining four gates of Dunrun.

'Perhaps one day you'll demonstrate exactly what those talents are.'

Ctenka laughed. Ermund retained his stern demeanour. One day he was sure he would see the big southerner crack a smile, but clearly it was not this day.

They crossed the wide courtyard and reached the Chapel Gate. Upon it was built an annexe that had in years past been devoted to prayer. There were still idols symbolising every god of the Cordral pantheon within it, but Ctenka did not know a single militiaman who used it to worship. Now the only gods venerated in Dunrun were those of wine, the only spirits invoked those found in the bottles that were delivered from the capital on rare occasion.

'It's very well you complaining. But what chance will I have to prove myself out here in the armpit of nowhere?' Ctenka said, splaying his arms wide to take in the confines of the fort. They had walked beneath the Chapel Gate now and come out into the wide courtyard of the Tinker's Gate. It had once been a burgeoning market, where the traders of Shengen and the Cordral would meet to ply their wares. Spices, livestock, precious gems, even ancient codices, would be bartered for within the shadow of the Crooked Jaw. Since the Fall, the Cordral had degenerated into a wilderness, its former agriculture diminishing to little more than the odd farm, scrabbling for existence in the desert. Now Dunrun was derelict – the sand having long since consumed every stall.

'Prove yourself?' said Ermund. 'You could start by showing some attention to your appearance.' His accent was so thick that Ctenka couldn't tell whether he detected a hint of disdain or if it was merely his way of speaking. But then big old Ermund always had a way of seeming superior – even when he was conversing with senior officers.

'Any man can wash a uniform,' said Ctenka. 'I want to prove myself in battle. There is war brewing to the west and here we are, guarding a stone ruin.'

'Have a care what you wish for, Ctenka,' Ermund replied.

Ctenka waved the big man away. 'Are you about to tell me of the horrors of war, Ermund? Save your breath. I've heard it all before from my father.'

They walked beneath the Tinker's Gate. Here the pass narrowed to a width of twenty feet and ahead was the Sandstone Gate. Once it may well have been a thing of beauty, but now it was crumbled, the heavy iron portcullis it housed broken and skewed. Nothing now but a useless archway.

'I would not presume to tell you anything, Ctenka.' Ermund kept his eyes fixed on the narrow pass ahead. 'I have seen young men like you before. Seen them lust for glory. Seen them die in misery.'

'Of course you have.' They passed beneath the Sandstone Gate and Ctenka quickened his step slightly as he always did – wondering if this might be the day the ancient portcullis came crashing down upon him. 'And one day you may want to tell me some stories from those joyous times. But until you do, I will fill my dull and empty days with dreams of victories to come.'

They walked across the last courtyard of Dunrun towards the final barbican. The Eagle Gate stood tall, built spanning the twenty-foot width of the pass. From it, the Skull Road wound all the way through the Crooked Jaw to the border of the Shengen Empire. A fifty-mile span of cobbled pathway that was now an abandoned trade route since Emperor Demetrii had been slain. It was said that back in the Age of Apostasy the tyrant Garul Hedtcheka had paved the road with the skulls of his enemies. It was either a tall tale or those skulls had long since been prised from the ground to be replaced by ordinary cobbles. Whatever the truth of it, the name had stuck.

Betul and Munir stood atop the fifty-foot high battlement. Ctenka gave a wave as he approached and Munir waved back enthusiastically. He was even greener than Ctenka, his eagerness for his duties not yet worn down to the nub by their pointlessness. Betul, however, was every inch the jaded recruit. He walked down the twisting stairway from the gate's summit, his impatience to see his night's watch end and return to bed obvious from his haste.

'Day's greetings, Betul,' Ctenka said with a wink as they met at the bottom of the stair. 'You look like I feel.'

'I'm sure,' Betul grunted.

His stomach had been fragile for the last two days after eating some spiced lamb none of the other men would touch. It was clear he was suffering for it now.

Ctenka was about to make a poor joke about the prospective state of Betul's morning shit, when Ermund gripped him by the shoulder.

'Look,' said the southerner, pointing through the open gate.

Through it, Ctenka could see down the Skull Road for a half-mile.

Someone was coming.

No one had travelled along the pass for some weeks. The last they had seen were refugees from Shengen, fleeing the harsh rule of their new overlord. Now came what looked like a crowd in the distance.

'Munir, seal the gate,' Ermund ordered. The young recruit rushed to obey without a word of complaint; when Ermund barked an order it was generally obeyed, even by those of superior rank. 'Betul, find Marshal Ziyadin. Ctenka, with me.'

With that Ermund rushed up the stairs of the Eagle Gate with the vigour of a much younger man. Ctenka was at pains to keep pace with him, and when finally they reached the summit it was he, not Ermund, who was out of breath.

From the top of the barbican they could see down through the pass. There was a group of soldiers coming, heavily armoured but moving at speed. A scout party for a larger force perhaps? They were certainly too few in number to be mounting any kind of invasion.

'How many, do you think?' Ctenka asked.

'Forty-two,' Ermund answered, his keen eyes surmising their number at a glance.

'Well... what do they want?'

Ermund slowly turned his head to gaze at Ctenka with a raised eyebrow. 'Why don't you go down there and ask?'

'I think I'll let you do the talking,' Ctenka replied.

'I see. Not that keen to earn yourself honour and glory after all.'

'There's a time and a place, my friend,' said Ctenka,

watching as the soldiers neared the gate, their armour and weapons looking in much better condition than those of the Dunrun militia.

Well, Ctenka had been hoping for some action.

All he could think was that in future, he should be careful what he wished for.

8

THEY were standing there in ranks – two rows, tower shields locked, spears at rest, pointing upwards to the midday sun. Only forty-two of them, Ermund had said, but there may as well have been an entire legion blocking the narrow pass.

Ctenka could barely take his eyes off them. He had never seen soldiers like this, not even back in the training grounds of Kantor. They were silent and disciplined, well armed and armoured. And all that stood between them and the Cordral was a poorly maintained fort. Should the Emperor of Shengen launch an invasion with his entire army, what could the militia of the Cordral do to stand against them? For the first time Ctenka realised why the fortress of Dunrun was such an important outpost and why it was still manned in this time of relative peace.

A noise below alerted Ctenka to someone ascending the worn stairs of the Eagle Gate. He looked down to see Marshal Ziyadin heading a retinue of militia. The marshal's jowly face shone with sweat as he reached the summit, puffing for all he was worth. Dark, greasy hair and moustache were slick to his head and face and he used his sheathed sword as a walking stick to help navigate the final few stairs.

Without a word, Ziyadin peered over the parapet, breathing heavily as he took in the scene.

'What do they want?' he said finally.

Ctenka looked at Ermund, who looked back at Ziyadin. 'They have made no demands, Marshal,' he replied.

Ziyadin glared down at the shield wall as his retinue spread out along the battlement of the Eagle Gate, the archers among them half-heartedly nocking arrows.

'So what do we do?' asked the marshal.

It was only now, after so many months of wallowing in this undisciplined shithole, that Ctenka wished they had a more inspiring commander.

'Perhaps someone should speak to them?' suggested Ermund.

Ziyadin nodded, still staring down at the ordered ranks below.

'Good idea,' he said. 'Ermund, go and find out what they want.'

'Marshal,' Ermund replied, 'would it not show more respect if they were greeted by an offi—'

'Just get on with it, Ermund,' Ziyadin barked. 'And take Ctenka if you're too afraid to do it alone.'

Ctenka felt something prickle on the back of his neck. He almost raised a hand to clean away whatever it was, but he realised that no amount of wiping would rid him of this sudden arse-clenching terror.

Ermund signalled for Ctenka to follow as he headed down the stairs. All Ctenka could focus on was the back of

Ermund's grey-haired head as they made their way below. The words *you're going to die today* rattled around his brain again and again as he picked his way carefully down each of the crumbling stairs. Halfway he considered feigning a trip so he could pretend he was injured, but that would have done little good. Ermund would have seen through the ruse and dragged him along anyway.

When they reached the bottom, Ermund ordered the gate open. To his left and right, militiamen rushed to lift the vast bars that secured the Eagle Gate. Despite the crumbling battlements at least the gate was secure. And what was Ctenka doing? Oh yes, walking right through it to face a grim-looking wall of would-be invaders.

'What are we going to say?' he whispered to Ermund as he followed the southerner through the gap in the gate.

'*We're* not saying anything,' Ermund replied in a low voice. 'You're going to keep your mouth shut and I'm going to politely ask them what they want.'

'And what if they *want* to kill us?' Ctenka's voice went up involuntarily at the end.

'Then I imagine it'll be a short conversation.'

Now he makes jokes, Ctenka thought. *After all these months he picks now to make bloody jokes.*

Both men walked out onto the Skull Road. Ctenka let Ermund lead the way, more than happy to keep his mouth shut as the southerner had suggested. When they approached the shield wall a gap suddenly appeared in its midst, well-drilled soldiers moving aside to create a corridor through which a single warrior strode.

He wore the same burnished steel as the rest, his dark hair tied in a topknot. Deep green eyes were set within the saturnine features of his handsome face and he walked with all the confidence of a man surrounded by forty-odd of the hardest killers you could find.

The warrior stopped a dozen feet in front of the shield wall, one hand resting casually on the pommel of his curved blade, the other cradling his plumed helmet in the crook of one arm. He was calm as Ctenka and Ermund approached. Ctenka couldn't help but be reminded of a cat watching a rat the instant before it pounced for the kill.

Ermund came to stand just before the warrior, Ctenka waiting further back. In his head he made a plan of attack should things go awry. Deep down he knew the best response would be to flee, but the Eagle Gate had been closed behind them. There was little else he would do but die if this all went tits up.

Neither the Shengen warrior nor Ermund spoke at first, each happy to stand there sizing the other up. Neither man seemed willing to break the tension until the big southerner said, 'I am Ermund of the Cordral Extent's Great Eastern Militia.'

The warrior replied in a thick eastern accent. 'Laigon Valdyr. Centurion, Fourth Standing of the Shengen Imperial Army.'

Ctenka couldn't help stifle a sigh once the introductions were out of the way.

'You are far from home, Centurion,' said Ermund.

Laigon nodded. 'It is our home no longer.'

'Unfortunate. And you would seek safe passage into the Cordral?'

Laigon looked up at the high battlements of the Eagle Gate and at the men looking down pensively.

'I would speak with your commanding officer, Militiaman Ermund. Though it seems he is loath to grant me audience.'

'You must understand our caution. We have received no envoy from the Shengen Empire in a year. Your arrival is something of a surprise.'

Ermund sounded as though he had welcomed foreign envoys before. His voice did not quaver, his body language confident and rigid, despite the air of tension that hung over the exchange.

'Our arrival was not planned. And we bring grave news from the east. If I were to speak with your commander I could explain.'

Ermund nodded. 'Then speak you will, Centurion. But your men and your weapon must wait outside the gates.'

Laigon nodded, spinning on his heel and walking back to the shield wall. He unbuckled his sword belt and handed it to one of his men. Ctenka could see words briefly exchanged, the soldier expressing his concerns to his senior officer, but Laigon remained adamant. Ctenka noted that, up close, the warriors arrayed before him were not quite as splendid as they had appeared from the battlements. There was weariness in their eyes, their armour and shields dented and scratched from battle.

When Laigon returned unarmed, Ermund led him

back towards the gate. Ctenka stood beside the centurion as though guarding a prisoner, but the man carried an aura of power about him that was undeniable. Even though Ctenka was armed he doubted he'd ever be a match for this warrior.

The gate opened wide enough for the three men to walk through, and once they were inside it was hastily barred. Marshal Ziyadin had climbed down from the summit of the Eagle Gate and stood waiting, his expression one of ingrained suspicion.

Ermund stopped before the marshal. 'May I present Laigon Valdyr. Centurion, Fourth Standing of the Shengen Imperial Army.' Ctenka was amazed at how the southerner had remembered the full title. In all the excitement Ctenka had barely remembered the Shengen's name. Ermund continued, 'This is Ziyadin. Marshal of the Cordral Extent's Great Eastern Militia.'

Laigon raised a fist to his chest and bowed. 'Marshal. My thanks for opening your gates.'

Ziyadin looked unsure of how to proceed. In the meantime, Ermund had taken a waterskin from one of the surrounding militiamen and offered it to the centurion, who took it with a grateful nod and drank deeply.

'So... what can we do for you, Centurion Valdyr?' Ziyadin asked, the sweat trickling down his brow.

Laigon glanced from Ziyadin back to Ermund, as though he recognised the marshal for the useless ape he was. It was clear Ermund was the most capable veteran here. Ctenka could see Laigon was not a man to suffer fools.

'The centurion brings grave news from the Shengen Empire, Marshal,' Ermund said.

'So grave that a contingent of legionaries comes to give us the news?' asked Marshal Ziyadin.

'Legionaries no more,' said Laigon. 'We are exiles from the empire. Men still loyal to Emperor Demetrii. The past year has seen the empire fall foul of usurpers and we were lucky to survive.'

'We learned that the emperor was dead,' said Ziyadin.

'Indeed. Slain by a warlord known as the Iron Tusk. Every Standing in the Imperial Army has bowed to his will. The Iron Tusk has conquered Shengen and the territories of the Mercenary Barons. Now he turns his eye west. Before long he will march the armies of the empire along the Skull Road and this place will be overrun.'

'So you have come seeking safe passage?' asked Ziyadin. It was clear he was unhappy with the idea.

'No, Marshal. We have come to defend this place, and your lands, from the onslaught. But we will need reinforcements. If word is not sent to Kantor, if Dunrun does not stand against him, then the Iron Tusk will destroy every kingdom in the western lands.'

Ziyadin was silent as he pondered the gravity of Laigon's words.

'How do we know this is not a ruse?' said Ermund, breaking the silence. 'How do we know you have not been sent to take Dunrun in advance of this warlord's arrival to weaken our defences?'

'You have only my word,' said Laigon. 'If it is not good enough then take us prisoner, but I beseech you to send word to Kantor at the least. You need an army to stand against this warlord. Your walls will not be enough, trust me on that.'

'I... I need time to think on this,' said Ziyadin.

'You cannot delay,' Laigon replied. 'Even now, five Standings muster at the eastern edge of the Crooked Jaw. The Iron Tusk will lead his armies here in weeks. You must send word.'

'On the testament of a self-confessed exile?' said Ziyadin, shaking his head. 'You expect me to trust what you say?'

'Clap me in irons, if you don't trust me. Take my head if you must. But if you do nothing this place will be ashes before the month is out, and you will be responsible.'

Ziyadin looked at his men, even at Ctenka, before his eyes came to rest on Ermund.

'What should we do?' he said.

Ermund didn't take long to mull it over. 'Take their weapons. Allow them inside the walls under guard. Time will tell if what the centurion says is true. Whatever happens, we must send word to Kantor.'

Laigon seemed relieved. Ziyadin even more so that someone had made the decision for him.

'Very well,' said the marshal. 'Ermund, you will take word. If the aldermen of Kantor wish to send us a cohort then so be it.'

'A wise decision,' said Laigon. Whether that was directed at Ermund or Ziyadin it was impossible to tell. 'But believe me when I say, a cohort will not be enough to defend the pass against the force that is coming.'

'I will do my best to persuade Kantor to send its best,' replied Ermund, before turning to Ziyadin. 'Now, I suggest we allow these men inside the walls of Dunrun. Under guard, of course.'

Ziyadin considered Ermund's suggestion for a moment before conceding with a nod.

Laigon saluted his appreciation and turned on his heel before marching back through the gate. The centurion spoke to his men. They dutifully abandoned their arms in strict military order, shields lined up in uniform rows, spears and swords propped behind.

Marshal Ziyadin summoned the entire retinue of militia to guide the Shengen warriors inside the walls of Dunrun under armed supervision. Up close, Ctenka could see some were wounded, all dishevelled as though they had fled a great conflict and barely survived.

'What if he's telling the truth?' Ctenka asked Ermund, as they closed the gates behind the soldiers. 'What if a mighty army is on its way here?'

'One thing at a time,' Ermund replied. 'First we have some travelling to do.'

It took Ctenka a moment to process Ermund's words. 'We?'

Ermund looked down. 'Of course. You don't think I'd set off on such a dangerous mission without you. Now come. We must learn everything we can about this Iron Tusk and his army before we make the journey to Kantor.'

Ctenka followed, open-mouthed. As much as he relished the prospect of leaving this place now it was under threat, he hadn't anticipated embarking on such an important mission. Either way, it appeared he had no choice in the matter.

Later they sat in the mess room beside the rearmost courtyard of Dunrun. Ermund, Ziyadin and Ctenka were across from Laigon. He and his men had been fed and watered, consuming everything as though they had not eaten for days.

'We ride tomorrow,' Ermund said, when Laigon had finished. 'Before we take word to Kantor, can you tell us what has happened in the empire?'

The centurion sat back and took a deep breath. A sadness crossed his eyes, and Ctenka found himself pitying this great warrior.

Eventually he looked up and said, 'I'll tell you everything I know...'

LAIGON

I

A SPEAR punctured the earth at his feet. He paused from shouting orders at his men long enough to wrench it from the ground and send it soaring back towards their attackers. Laigon's voice was hoarse from yelling and now all he wanted to do was kill.

'Tulius, lock your damn shield,' he barked.

Before Tulius could obey an arrow struck him below the cheek guard of his helm. He fell forward silently, leaving a gap in the shield wall that was quickly filled by another legionary.

Half a dozen brigands came screaming down the mountain path, axes and swords high. It was suicide, but Laigon could see the zeal in their eyes. They threw themselves against the armoured might of the Fourth Standing, breaking on the shields, run through by a dozen spears, still screaming in fury even as they fell.

More arrows followed from the ridge above, most tamping harmlessly off legionary armour. Laigon felt one hit his chest and heard the telltale *thunk*. Looking down he could see it protruding from his breastplate but the steel held.

His anger simmered as he pulled the arrow from his armour and flung it aside.

'We have to get out of here,' shouted Primaris Vallion. Laigon's second-in-command was not easily flustered but it was obvious they were fighting a losing battle. Despite how poorly armed their enemy was, they more than made up for it in overwhelming numbers and fervour. It seemed the tales of this bandit king were true – he had turned disparate tribes of brigands into a fanatical horde.

'Fall back by ranks,' Laigon shouted over the din. More bandits were racing down the pass. This time there were more than Laigon could count at a glance.

With their shields still locked, the survivors of the Fourth retreated steadily, their footfalls resounding in well-drilled unison. Laigon felt the regret cut him deep. Further up the pass were the corpses of the rest of their cohort, his brothers lost to the enemy. He could only imagine how these foul savages would desecrate the bodies, but for now he had to focus on the living.

The enemy was almost on them. Laigon's troops were still retreating and would be off balance once the wave hit. Despite their need to retreat, they would also need to weather this attack or all was lost.

'Brace!' Laigon screamed, a moment before the first of the bandits threw themselves at the legionaries. The resounding clang of weapons hitting tower shields rang throughout the pass. Arrows continued to rain down and Laigon fought the instinct to take cover. He carried no shield and held only his sword in hand, but he had to stand tall and resolute in the face of the enemy. He was an example to his men. A centurion could show no fear, even in the face of defeat.

The second rank of the shield wall stabbed forward with their spears, impaling their attackers as the shield bearers held back the horde. Laigon glanced back, seeing the pass clear behind them. It was their only way of escape.

'Disengage!' he shouted above the noise, arrows whipping past his head.

'Retreat!' Vallion confirmed and the legionaries backed away as one.

Laigon stood firm; he would guard the rear as his men escaped. If necessary he would stand and die – better that than face the shame of his failure back in Nephyr.

The troops retreated past their centurion, as Laigon planted his feet, sword raised. The first of the brigands came at him, face a mask of scars and ill intent. Laigon took his head off with a deft swipe of the sword, then stepped forward, foot churning the soft earth of the mountain pass. Another hack of the sword and he had broken the haft of an axe, blade slicing through an arm. Another step and he severed the leg of a screaming bandit.

Laigon was surrounded now. He felt his lips move back, baring his teeth, his breath deep and even as he fought the temptation to unleash his anger – staying in control. If he succumbed to the lust of battle he would leave himself vulnerable. He had to focus. That was the only way he could—

Behind him the pass exploded in blinding light and shuddering heat.

Laigon foundered. He was on the ground now, his helmet

lost. Around him lay a score of bandits, burned and moaning. He checked himself, seeing his armour had taken the brunt of the explosion, but it was now tarnished and blackened.

As the ringing in his ears subsided there was screaming. Laigon rose to unsteady feet, turning to see some of his men flailing, still on fire. From the cliffs that overlooked the pass the bandits had dropped flaming, pitch-covered bundles. Their escape route was now blocked by an inferno.

A screaming bandit came at Laigon through the smoke, his back consumed with flames. With no sword, Laigon had to make do with grasping the burning man by the throat. It stifled his scream, turning it into a pitiful choking sound as Laigon throttled him to death.

Vallion appeared from the smoke, followed by a dozen surviving legionaries.

'Form a line,' Laigon growled as he squeezed the last of the life from the flaming brigand.

'Shields,' Vallion ordered.

Laigon could only admire the discipline of his men as they formed a rudimentary shield wall, despite some of them being badly wounded.

The fire crackled and sparked behind them. Through the smoke they watched and waited for more charging bandits to come racing at them, but no one appeared. As the smoke gradually cleared, Laigon could see the enemy standing in a mob, waiting. Glancing up at the cliffs overlooking the path there were more of them looking down, bows nocked, a score of arrows levelled and ready.

'Do we attack, Centurion?' Vallion asked.

'Hold your ground,' Laigon replied. 'Let them come at us.'

They waited. But the brigands did not move. Laigon watched the enemy standing there. Every eye harboured madness, every fist held a weapon, but still they stood waiting – though for what, Laigon couldn't tell.

'Warriors of the Shengen,' came a shout from the crowd of bandits. 'You cannot win. You cannot flee. Throw down your arms and live.'

Laigon shook his head. Even if the shame of surrender were not too much to bear, could he trust these savages to spare them? If they fought they would die, but perhaps Laigon could take a gamble for the lives of his men.

He stepped forward through the smoke, getting a clearer look at what he faced. These brigands were true savages; faces painted and scarred – some of those wounds were shaped in strange patterns as though they had been self-inflicted.

'There is no need for more needless slaughter,' Laigon announced. 'I will fight the best among you. If I win my men go free. I lose and my men will surrender to you.'

'Centurion—' Vallion protested, but Laigon silenced him with a gesture.

At first there were subdued mutterings within the crowd. Then a voice said, 'You will have your wish, Shengen. Let us find our champion.'

That raised some mirth from among the brigands, their laughter seeming at odds with the fanatical zeal they still bore in their eyes.

Laigon turned back to his men. One of them, Retuchius, had found his sword in the dirt and handed it to him reverently.

With a nod of gratitude, Laigon took it and kneeled. Quietly he said a prayer to Portius the Trickster that he would find victory, but only so his men would live.

From behind he suddenly heard disquiet among the horde of bandits. Some began to chant over and over – *Tusk, Tusk, Tusk* – as though they were summoning some vile demon from the pit.

Laigon turned to see the crowd part, allowing something monstrous to pass through their midst.

A huge bear walked among them, its tread slow and measured. The face of the creature was concealed behind a mask of metal, chains and rings pierced through its flesh, coat mange-ridden and scabbed. It was truly a grotesque sight, but no more grotesque than the creature that rode upon its back.

With fear rising within him, Laigon realised that it was no bandit champion he was about to fight, but their warlord himself.

The Iron Tusk was huge, his bare chest a mass of swollen muscle. One meaty hand rested on his thigh, the other held the reins attached to the bear's helm. Atop the warlord's shoulders was the most fearsome visage Laigon had ever seen in all his days of fighting the emperor's foes.

At first he thought the warlord wore an ordinary helm, but as the Iron Tusk rode closer it was clear the metal that encased his head had been hammered and riveted to his face and skull. Half the pale flesh beneath was still visible and he stared with one baleful green eye. A horn protruded from one side of his head, the flesh around it raw and livid, and Laigon almost gagged at the sight.

As the warlord guided his bear through the crowd, Laigon fought the urge to turn tail and run headlong into the wall of flames. This was a battle he could not win, but fight it he must.

Without a word the Iron Tusk dismounted as the great bear bellowed a roar that echoed throughout the mountain pass. He walked forward, single eye intent on Laigon, who stood his ground despite every fibre in his body screaming for him to flee.

The warlord stopped in front of him, no weapon in his hand, no armour bedecking his tree trunk of a body.

'The Iron Tusk accepts your challenge, Shengen,' shouted a voice from the band of brigands. 'Feel free to fight him.'

Someone laughed. A cool gust of air blew along the mountain pass, whipping the smoke into swirls. Laigon swallowed as best he could. All the while that single eye looked down at him, more animal than human.

With a grunt, Laigon swung his sword, a blow that would have split timber. The Iron Tusk caught the blade in one huge fist and gripped it tightly. Laigon tried to wrest the weapon from his foe but it was as though it were wedged in a wooden post.

The Iron Tusk held tight, no sign of any blood dripping from his clenched fist. Laigon realised he had already lost. That there was nothing he could do against this monster. Slowly he loosed his grip on the sword, all the fight draining from him under the scrutiny of that one green eye.

They stared at one another then, for the longest time, until the Iron Tusk raised a huge hand and placed it on

Laigon's shoulder. It was a hand that could have crushed rock, but it was gentle as it compelled Laigon to kneel.

All the while he stared into that eye, feeling his resistance wane and die. Behind him, his men likewise let go of shields and spears and dropped to their knees.

'Abandon your false gods.'

The command was clear in Laigon's head, though the Iron Tusk spoke no words.

'Abandon your mortal emperor.'

The command was anathema to him, Laigon was nothing if not loyal and pious, but still he knelt. Still he listened.

'I will be your god and your emperor. I will embody all you worship. All you serve.'

Laigon stared into that one eye. He knew he should resist, should fight, should stand and spit in that eye, but there was nothing he could do against such will. Against such power.

'Pledge yourself to me, Laigon Valdyr, and you shall have everything you have ever coveted. You shall have glory. You shall win honour on the field in my name.'

As the words were spoken, Laigon felt the last bastion of his will crumble to dust. There was no being in the world he would rather serve than the Iron Tusk.

'Pray before me, and you will be rewarded beyond anything you could imagine.'

The fire crackled and the wind blew through the pass, and Laigon Valdyr prayed to his new master.

II

THE shining streets of Nephyr had never seemed as alien to Laigon as they did today. He had walked the White City's marble-paved Road of Immortals a thousand times, but now he felt like a stranger in the city of his birth.

Where before a victory parade would see the streets lined with the cheering masses, now there was silence. Streaming garlands and a petal-strewn path were replaced by crowds of sullen citizens staring blankly at their passing. Nothing but the sounds of marching feet echoed through the city. They even seemed to have frightened the birds from the rooftops.

At their head rode the Iron Tusk, surrounded by his retinue of faithful brigands. Over the months of conflict, Laigon had watched as the noble legionaries of every Standing had fallen to their knees in supplication. Every army Emperor Demetrii had set against the Iron Tusk had proclaimed the warlord their new god-king or died at his hand.

And all the while, Laigon had watched and done nothing.

Not a day went by when he did not regret his decision, but pledging himself to the Iron Tusk had seemed the only thing to do – as though he had no choice in it. Every man had a choice, every man walked his own path, but in this Laigon had felt compelled. It was a decision he was helpless to change. He was servant to a new master now. Or was he a slave?

What had made him succumb so easily? What had made so many others follow in his wake? What magic was at work here?

No, it could not be magic. The ancient sorcerers were dead and gone. Magic had been struck from the world, never to return. This was the inexorable power of one man... no matter how inhuman that man seemed to be.

Laigon could see him up ahead now, that horned head and powerful torso elevated above the crowd. The vast beast on which he rode making its way through the streets of Nephyr as though they had always belonged to him.

The warlord mounted the white stone stairway up to the imperial palace. With every step the Praetorian Guard that lined the way dropped to their knees, bowing their heads to a new sovereign.

So easily the Iron Tusk was able to bend men to his will. So naturally they abandoned their former loyalties and pledged themselves to this eidolon. And yet still Laigon tried to convince himself this was not magic. It could not be. His former loyalties could not have been abandoned because of some enchantment. Surely he was simply doing what was right? What he was meant to do?

The centurion shook his head, loosening a bead of sweat which ran from beneath the rim of his helm and down his forehead. This was no time for doubt.

He followed the procession up the great stairway and beneath the arched entrance to the palace. The huge domed ceiling soared fifty feet above them, but loomed over Laigon as though he had entered the darkest cave, the sense of foreboding ominous.

At the far end of the grand temple stood the emperor's throne. Demetrii sat in all his regalia – golden armour making him seem more than a man, decorative helm bestrewn with a plume of red and blue feathers. He watched impassively as the Iron Tusk rode that bear towards him. Laigon could only admire the emperor's courage.

Demetrii stood from his throne as the Iron Tusk approached. Even elevated as he was on the throne's dais, the warlord stood at the same eye level. Laigon was close enough to see the emperor's face, his expression rigid. So many times Laigon had knelt before that throne and now he watched as an interloper desecrated its sanctity. And yet he did nothing.

There was a fleeting moment where Demetrii seemed to consider his actions, as though he doubted whether or not to offer fealty to this monster. He glanced across the gathered ranks, the warriors of the Standings, and his gaze hovered over Laigon. Shame filled the centurion, and he could not hold his emperor's glance, looking away rather than be cut further by the betrayal on Demetrii's face.

Taking every step with reverent care, Demetrii descended the dais to stand before the Iron Tusk. He opened his mouth to speak. Laigon remembered that voice; one that spoke with such authority. But before he could utter a word the warlord said, 'Kneel.'

One word, but it held such power that it silenced an emperor.

Demetrii dropped to his knees before the Iron Tusk and bowed his head.

'See,' said the warlord, turning to face the gathered rows of warriors. 'See how your emperor kneels. See how he is made to yield. Know that none can resist. Not one among you can defy me.'

He walked forward and laid a hand on the huge head of that armoured bear. There was a sound, a whisper of something in a language Laigon could not catch.

In an instant the bear leapt forward. Its growl cut through the palace hall, drowning out Demetrii's scream as those fetid jaws took hold of his head. There was a grinding of teeth on metal as the creature's maw crushed the helm encasing Demetrii's head. For a moment his scream grew shrill before it was silenced.

'Know there can be no defiance,' said the Iron Tusk when all fell silent. 'There shall be no one you shall worship above me. But those who follow willingly will be rewarded in abundance.'

The Iron Tusk strode forward along the path between the men of his army. Representatives from the First to Fifth Standings watched, every eye on this conqueror.

'I will not be stopped,' said the warlord. Their new emperor. 'Once I have crushed the Mercenary Barons to the south I will look west. The Suderland, the Cordral and the Ramadi will all fall before me. I will sweep across those lands like a plague. Those who do not join me shall be destroyed.' His single eye swept across the ranks of armoured men, until it fell on Laigon himself. As though he were the only man present, powerless beneath that inscrutable gaze. 'Will you follow me?'

As one, a thousand men dropped to their knees in obedience as their dead emperor bled on a white marble floor.

Laigon's villa was a humble affair on the eastern outskirts of Nephyr. Other centurions lived in almost palatial splendour, paid for by the spoils of war, but ostentation was not for Laigon. He had always been a defender of the people. It was only fitting that he dwelt in a place as modest as those of the citizenry he protected.

Every time he returned to this haven, no matter how bloody the campaign, no matter the slaughter he had witnessed, Laigon always felt his troubles lift. Now, as he walked through the neat gardens and along the mosaic path to his door, he felt more troubled than ever before.

Petrachus burst through the door as Laigon approached. His son was growing fast, almost twelve summers. It would not be long before the boy was initiated as a young cadet. Laigon should have been proud of the fact, but there was no joy in him now. He felt numb as Petrachus rushed into his arms, hugging him tightly. The happiness that should have filled him evaded him, and he knew why. Laigon had helped condemn the empire to rule beneath the heel of a despot. He had abetted the Iron Tusk in bending Shengen to his will. Only now did Laigon feel the true weight of what he had done.

Nevertheless, he picked up his son, forcing a smile as Petrachus took his helm and placed it over his head.

'One day soon it will fit,' Laigon said as he approached the open doorway.

'One day soon?' the boy replied. 'Then will I be a centurion too?'

'Perhaps,' he said. Though now it was the last thing he would have wished on his son.

Laigon crossed the threshold and entered his house. Verrana stood waiting inside, busying herself with a pot of flowers as though she hadn't already known her husband was about to arrive. It was a charade she went through every time he came home.

'I didn't expect you back so soon,' she said. He had not seen his wife for the best part of three seasons.

Without a word Laigon gently put Petrachus down and embraced his wife, breathing her in deeply. Laigon opened his eyes to see she was looking at him curiously.

'What is it?' she asked, reading the troubled expression he was wearing like a caul.

Surely she must know by now. The emperor was dead. A usurper sat upon the throne and it was the empire's own armies who had put him there.

'What have I done?' was all Laigon could think to say.

Verrana laid her hands on his armoured shoulders. 'You did what you had to, Centurion. So that you could return to us. You are Laigon Valdyr. You are a warrior. A survivor. Never apologise for that.'

Laigon nodded, feeling some of the weight upon his shoulders lift.

His burden lightened further when he stripped off his

amour and laid his sword aside. Verrana had prepared a sumptuous meal for him that reminded Laigon it was not just her beauty that had urged him to take her as his bride. As he ate, Petrachus sat opposite, watching with an expression of adoration, without doubt or question. Though Laigon's men would have followed him anywhere, he knew the devotion Petrachus held for him was without equal. When Verrana walked by and kissed him gently on his temple, Laigon began to realise how deeply he had missed his family.

And how much everything had changed.

After dinner he watched Verrana put their son to bed, then kissed her goodnight. When he was sure she slept, he took a single rushlight and walked from the villa, out into the garden, silent but for the sound of chirruping crickets. The path that led to the side of the villa was cool underfoot, and he had to shield the rushlight from the gentle night breeze.

Laigon entered the tiny chapel that sat beside the villa, lighting the candles within and illuminating the meagre altar to the gods. He knew he was committing heresy. The people of Shengen now had no god but the Iron Tusk, but still Laigon could not resist the old habit and the old gods. Or at least one god in particular.

Portius had always been his. He knew it was strange for a warrior to follow the trickster god, but something about the portly deity had always appealed to Laigon. As he knelt before the statue, three foot of poorly moulded clay, he bowed his head and prayed.

He had no idea what to expect. Whether he would feel nothing or be overcome by some epiphany. What he hadn't expected was such an overwhelming feeling of grief. Whatever false loyalty he held for this new warlord seemed to slough off him in an instant, to be replaced by the weight of what had happened. Of what he had done. Laigon had been born to serve, had been raised on loyalty to the throne of Shengen. Now all that had been cut away and Laigon had helped wield the knife.

No matter how hard he prayed, no matter the forgiveness he begged for, he knew he would never shed the guilt of his inaction. He should have died in the mountains defending Shengen and his emperor. Should have given his life rather than become slave to some inhuman monster.

Laigon prayed for redemption, but there were no words of support from Portius. Every time he had prayed before there had at least been some notion of comfort. Now it was clear no one was listening.

When finally he opened his eyes the candles had long since burned out. Laigon stood and crossed the garden under the hazy predawn light. Back inside his villa his wife and son were still sleeping. He crept to his bed and lay beside Verrana. Despite the warmth of her beside him, Laigon had never felt so alone.

III

Laigon had never seen a fortress like it before. Not even the white walls of Nephyr looked so insurmountable. Lord Koad's stronghold sat like a solid block of granite atop an unassailable rise. It would cost Laigon hundreds of men to reach the foot of it in a full frontal assault, and even then there was no guarantee they could scale the walls. It seemed Laigon's campaign of dominance over the Mercenary Barons had all but come to a halt, but perhaps there was a solution other than sacrificing his entire Standing. Not that he could persuade Jodba of that.

Across the campfire, Jodba was even now planning the attack. How Laigon would have loved to walk over there and throttle the pig, but he was one of the Iron Tusk's most loyal. He had been the first of the bandit kings to follow their emperor when he began his conquest of the Crooked Jaw, and he held a position of trust. Laigon wasn't sure how they stood as far as hierarchy went – whether it was he or Jodba who was considered the most senior – but he knew that strangling one of the Iron Tusk's generals wouldn't put him in the emperor's good graces.

Jodba had decided to stage a full frontal assault: ladders, rams, grappling hooks, scores of men flinging themselves at a sheer approach. Scores of Laigon's men that is. The loss of life would be devastating, not that Jodba cared.

Laigon had heard enough. There was no way he was willing to make such a sacrifice when there were other options to be explored.

He strode towards Jodba, his annoyance getting the better of him. 'This is not the way,' Laigon said. 'Your plan has no chance of succeeding.'

The Iron Tusk's underlings ceased their conversation and turned to him. Each one had been a criminal, nothing more than a robber in the mountains. These were the scum of the earth and now Laigon had to suffer them as his equals. It could not stand.

'So what is the way then?' Jodba asked, peering up from within that dimwit face. 'Have you got a better way of cracking open the fortress?'

'If I have my way, we won't need to.'

'What you talking about?' Jodba looked even more confused, if that were possible.

'We have the fortress surrounded. Their supply chain is cut off. A protracted siege will take weeks, maybe months until their supplies run out. If I offer them terms of surrender we could end the siege here and now.'

Jodba laughed. He was joined by his lieutenants. They all seemed to find the idea hilarious, but Laigon wasn't laughing.

'You would offer them mercy?' Jodba said. 'Those that defy

the Iron Tusk must be destroyed. No matter what the cost.'

'If I can make Lord Koad bow before the Iron Tusk he could be a valuable ally. They say he is a wise man and he knows much about his fellow Mercenary Barons. He would be much more useful alive than dead.'

'I disagree,' said Jodba. 'And so will the Iron Tusk.'

'You will not lead my men on a suicide mission,' said Laigon.

'Are you refusing to obey my orders?'

'I don't take my orders from you.' Laigon squared up to Jodba, staring into his beady eyes. 'I serve the emperor.'

Jodba's lieutenants began to spread out, sensing the coming violence. Laigon was all too aware he faced half a dozen men on his own. All of a sudden he missed the presence of Vallion at his shoulder.

'I am the voice of the Iron Tusk,' said Jodba. 'Not you. I am the one to be obeyed.'

Laigon stared deeper at the bandit. 'And yet here you are talking.' Laigon reached a hand to the hilt of his sword. 'And still I don't give a—'

'Enough,' came a deep resonant voice.

Immediately Laigon stood to attention, standing as straight and still as he could as the Iron Tusk loomed from the dark. The campfires lit him in baleful light and his one eye shone like a cat's in the night. The air of tension grew that much thicker at the approach of their emperor.

'My lord,' said Jodba, 'I was trying to tell the Shengen that we must—'

Jodba fell silent as the Iron Tusk raised a thick meaty

finger. 'I heard. And yet the centurion chooses diplomacy over violence.' He stared at Laigon, who found it difficult to hold that gaze. Yet hold it he did.

'A siege could take weeks. Lord Koad is a wise man, and will most likely have stocked his supply sheds in preparation. His walls are practically unassailable and we will only be wasting lives in a frontal assault.'

'And your solution is to offer clemency?'

'Surrender,' Laigon replied. 'Conditional on Koad pledging his fealty to you, my emperor.'

The Iron Tusk turned his massive head to the fortress looming over them all. 'And you think Koad would accept such an offer?'

'If I were a betting man,' Laigon replied.

'Would you bet your life on it, Centurion?'

Laigon didn't have to think on that. 'Yes, my emperor.'

'Good,' the Iron Tusk replied. 'Then so you shall. At dawn you will make the proposal to Koad yourself. For your sake, I hope he agrees to your terms.'

With that, the Iron Tusk turned and stalked back into the night.

Laigon didn't sleep, but instead spent the night staring up at the fortress, wondering if he'd even reach the main gate to make his offer to Koad before he was riddled with a volley of artillery fire. As the sun rose over the overlooking ridge, he didn't wait to find out.

When he handed his blade and helm to Vallion, his Primaris said nothing. They both knew there was little Vallion could do now to stop Laigon. Not after the Iron Tusk had given his order. The men of the Fourth Standing stood and watched as their centurion walked towards the twisting path that led up to the fortress. Laigon kept his pace slow and steady, not wanting to spook any of the defenders who would inevitably be watching from behind the ramparts. The last thing he needed was an arrow in the face before he'd even had a chance to speak to Koad.

The further up he got, the more eyes he could see peering at him from within the fortress, but no one took a shot. It was clear he was no threat, and with the Iron Tusk's army standing ready to besiege the place they were clearly more than ready to hear what an emissary might have to say.

When Laigon reached the iron-bound gate there was already someone waiting for him outside. He was clearly no warrior and smiled the easy smile of a man in charge.

'Centurion Laigon Valdyr,' the man said. 'You honour us with your presence.'

Clearly his reputation preceded him. 'The honour is mine...'

'Jazhek Shaer, personal advisor to Lord Koad.'

'Good to meet you, Jazhek. I wish it were under better circumstances.'

'Indeed. But I hope your presence means that there might be a parlay.'

Laigon nodded. 'If I might speak with Lord Koad we may be able to find a peaceful solution to this siege.'

Jazhek shrugged. 'Alas, my lord will not be meeting with any of the Iron Tusk's representatives. These gates will remain locked until he has certain assurances.'

'I understand,' said Laigon. 'And assurances I can give. If Lord Koad presents himself to the Iron Tusk before the day is out and pledges his undying fealty, he will be allowed to live as a vassal to the great emperor himself. He will be granted his current lands and title and his servants allowed to live.'

Jazhek raised a pointed eyebrow. 'Merciful indeed.'

'The Iron Tusk rewards loyalty above all things,' Laigon said. And he mostly believed his own words, despite what he had so far seen. Though it was true, the Iron Tusk rewarded his followers most generously, he also punished their failures in the harshest manner.

'Very well,' said Jazhek. 'I will relay your terms to my lord. I hope that for all our sakes he accepts them.'

With a respectful nod, Laigon turned and made his way back down the twisting slope from the entrance to the fortress. Vallion was waiting at the bottom, still holding Laigon's sword and shield.

'How did it go?' asked the Primaris as he handed Laigon back his sword.

'We'll soon find out,' Laigon replied, buckling his sword belt.

'So what now?'

Laigon looked up the long, sheer hillside to the fortress above. 'Now we wait.'

The day wore on and Laigon and the Fourth Standing stood patiently at the foot of the mountain. Every long hour, Laigon became more nervous. If Koad did not take up his offer the implications would be dire indeed. He could see Jodba lingering, watching, waiting for all this to go wrong so he could be proven right. Or perhaps it was more so he could witness Laigon's punishment.

As the sun set, Laigon felt relief wash over him as the gates to the hilltop fortress opened and a column of torch-bearing warriors came forth, making its way down the ramp. Laigon watched the procession, seeing Jazhek Shaer at the front leading the way through the darkness with his own torch. He looked an odd figure, at the head of these men, and Laigon could only admire his bravery. He wore no armour and carried no weapon, yet he led the vanguard to face their enemy.

When the warriors reached the bottom of the ramp they formed into ranks, presenting themselves to the Iron Tusk's forces. Laigon stepped forward.

Jazhek smiled in greeting. 'May I present the inestimable Lord Koad of Rhema.'

From the ranks of soldiers walked a portly figure. He looked out of place among his soldiers, and though still bedecked in armour it fitted him poorly. If this Mercenary Baron had ever been a warrior it was clearly long in the past.

Laigon bowed in greeting, ready to accept whatever speech of surrender Koad was willing to give, when a roar cut the valley. From out of the dark strode the Iron Tusk atop his armoured bear. A pall of fear fell over the ranks of soldiers, though no one dared to move.

The emperor slipped down from his mount, all seven feet of him striding towards the Mercenary Baron.

'So this is Lord Koad, come to pledge his loyalty to me,' the Iron Tusk said, glaring down at the cowering figure.

If Koad had planned some grand speech it was all but

forgotten now. He merely stood and stared in awe.

'No matter,' the emperor said. 'It is too little. And all too late.'

He turned his back on Koad and, as though it were a silent signal, a hail of arrows fell from the dark shadows surrounding them. Laigon could only watch as volley after volley soared from the darkness. He could only imagine Jodba and his lieutenants lying in wait, commanding their men to fire until none of Lord Koad's men were moving.

It was then, seeing the last of those men flailing in the dirt, that Laigon began to realise how he had been used. How he was just another weapon in the Iron Tusk's armoury.

The arrows continued to fly long after the last of Koad's warriors had fallen still. In the aftermath, Laigon walked among the bodies until he found the motionless Jazhek, his robes peppered with arrows. In death he bore an accusing look, and Laigon knew it was reserved for him alone. He had betrayed these men, albeit unknowingly.

Whatever honour Laigon had left, whatever his word had been worth, it died in that valley with Jahzek Shaer. Now he was nothing more than another brigand, no better than Jodba. When he looked into the eyes of his men, he could see many of them knew it too. For many that might have been enough – to blindly serve the word of their emperor. But for others Laigon saw this was a test of loyalty too far.

How much longer he would stand to be tested, Laigon could only guess.

IV

LAIGON looked out from atop the ridge, at the sea of corpses that lay cooling in the shadow of the Crooked Jaw. After the murder of Lord Koad, the last Mercenary Barons had been swiftly defeated and all that remained of their armies was a handful of sorry-looking prisoners.

They hadn't stood a chance. The Mercenary Barons paid for the loyalty of their armies in gold. How could they ever have stood against an army devoted to its immortal warlord? A leader who commanded the undying devotion of a standing army. A fighting force of true faith and determination.

As he stood viewing the carnage, Laigon felt neither faithful nor determined. He was sick to his stomach. The clawing doubt that had festered in his mind since the death of Demetrii was beginning to consume him. Now all he felt was sorrow and regret, as though drifting on a sea of his own mistakes. The only solace was in knowing he wasn't alone.

Primaris Vallion stood beside him, and Laigon could see the conflict in the officer's eyes. There should have been pride there after such an overwhelming conquest, but he saw only lamentation.

'What have we become?' asked Vallion. He looked nervously towards Laigon, as though he had been caught in a lie. It was clearly a thought he would rather have kept to himself, and he bowed his head in shame. 'Apologies, Centurion. I am overcome.'

'No need to apologise, Vallion. I see it as well as you do.'

Already legionaries of the Fourth were beheading corpses and mounting them atop pikes – a custom the Iron Tusk had insisted on after every victory. *A message*, he had told them. As though their crushing victory were not message enough. But this was not just victory – it was annihilation. Not only had the Mercenary Barons been slaughtered without mercy, but so had the innocents that lived beneath their yoke. Laigon had seen the slaughter of women and children. Of slaves and livestock. It was as though the Iron Tusk were purging their memory from the face of the earth.

'If it were within my power to change this, I would,' said Laigon. 'But what would we do? Walk away from this place? From the empire and everything we know? We serve or we are outcasts. That is no choice for legionaries.'

'Surely there would be no shame in it,' said Vallion.

'No, my friend,' he replied. 'There would be no shame. But where would we run to? Nowhere would be far enough. We would be condemning ourselves to death.' He found himself trying to pick apart the suggestion, but the more he thought on it the more the notion appealed.

'Not if there were enough of us,' Vallion replied. 'There

are more within the Fourth who feel as we do. I know it.'

'And there are more still who remain bewitched by the tyrant who holds our fealty.'

'But surely we have a duty to do what is right, Centurion? We must flee to the west. We must warn the nations across the Jaw what awaits them.'

Laigon looked out at the butchery and could not deny that Vallion was right. They should warn the westerners of what was to come, but it seemed an impossible task. Besides, was it not better that his own nation survived? Laigon had been a servant of the Shengen Empire since first he was inducted into the Fourth. Surely he should stand with his own countrymen rather than counsel the western nations so they were forewarned and ready to fight against Laigon's own people? But then, this was not the Shengen he had devoted himself to. His countrymen were no longer the free subjects of an empire but the servants of a despot.

'We should not speak of this, Vallion,' Laigon said, turning back towards the command tent. 'It is treason. Best we look to our duties and forget we ever uttered such heresies.'

He took the long walk back towards camp, passing the massacre, the wounded and the dying. Kneeling at the edge of the encampment were scores of prisoners. Men in chains, all hope gone. Every face looked forlorn as they awaited their fate. Laigon knew only too well what that fate would be and the prospect sickened him yet further.

Back in his command tent, Laigon began to strip off his heavy armour. With every piece of plate he unbuckled, the more his burden seemed to lighten until he was standing in nothing but his tunic. The answer to his troubles seemed clearer as he stood in the sanctity of his tent. He would return to the White City, take Verrana and Petrachus, and whatever possessions they could carry, then head east. Away from this fallen empire. Away from the doomed nations in the west.

And he hadn't even needed to pray for the answer.

Laigon went to the small chest that contained his meagre belongings. Inside was a small pewter figurine of Portius; a portly figure in a pointed hat. He picked it up, feeling the weight of it in his hand. It was cold to the touch, the crudely carved face smiling up at him. Laigon ran a thumb over that head, and felt a sharp pain. The tapered end of the trickster god's hat had drawn blood. Laigon almost laughed at the tiny smiling face.

'Another great victory.'

Laigon turned to see a praetorian standing behind him, and silently cursed himself that he had so easily been snuck up on. Luckily it was a face he recognised, though one he would have preferred not to see. Manse's well-oiled hair and pristine armour was testament to how little he had contributed to their recent victory. He and Laigon went back a long way, though it had not always been on the best of terms. 'You are fast earning yourself a reputation, Centurion,' Manse continued. 'The Iron Tusk will be pleased.'

'I'm glad you think so, Praetorian,' Laigon replied, though in truth he could not have cared less how the Iron Tusk regarded him.

'All that remains is to perform our sacrifices and we may cast these Mercenary Barons into history.'

Laigon turned to regard the praetorian. He could see the same zeal in his eyes he had observed in so many of the Iron Tusk's servants.

'Sacrifices? What do you mean?'

Manse shrugged. 'There are prisoners, Centurion. The Iron Tusk would have his benefaction. Your duties are not done yet.'

'I am a soldier,' Laigon replied. 'Not a butcher. If you want a sacrifice performed, find a priest.'

'This is how we do things now, Laigon. You know—'

'It is not how I do things, Manse.'

The smug expression fell from the praetorian's face. 'Are you refusing to carry out the will of the Iron Tusk?'

'I am telling you we have slaughtered enough enemies for one day. Perhaps for all the days to come. The Mercenary Barons are defeated. Beaten and on their knees. What difference is a sacrifice? Do you not remember the teachings of the Eleusian? Mercy in victory is the only way to earn your enemy's respect.'

Clearly Manse had never been taught the tenets of the Eleusian scriptures. 'If you refuse this, there will be repercussions, Laigon. We are all servants to—'

'To what, Manse? A year ago we were servants to the empire. Now what are we? Slaves? Murderers?'

Manse shook his head. 'What has got into you?'

'No! What has got into you? All of you! This is not how the Standings go to war. This is not how we raised our empire. This is not how we built a nation.'

Manse looked flustered for an instant, but then it was gone.

He ran a hand over his pristinely coiffured head. 'You will carry out the sacrifice or you will suffer the consequences.'

'Consequences?' Laigon suddenly felt naked in front of the armoured praetorian. For a moment he wished he had not been so hasty to remove his burdensome armour. 'And where were the consequences when the Iron Tusk murdered our emperor? An emperor you were sworn to protect?'

'He was not worthy of—'

'Not worthy? Demetrii was like a father to all of us. And you stood by and watched while he was torn apart by a wild beast. You fell to your knees with the rest of us when that animal took his throne.'

'You speak heresy.' Laigon could see he had provoked the praetorian but he didn't care anymore. He didn't care about any of this.

'I speak the truth, Manse. We serve a tyrant. I'm not the only one who thinks it.'

'Who else thinks it? This sacrilege has clearly spread like an infection. It must be cut out.'

It was obvious now that Manse was never going to throw off the glamour as Laigon and others had. He was a fanatic, addicted to the Iron Tusk like some men were to the poppy.

'No, Manse. We are not the ones who are infected. You are.'

There were no more words. Manse drew the dagger at his side. Laigon managed to grab Manse's wrist before he could stab him. The dagger was aimed at his midriff, and the two men tested their strength for an instant before Laigon realised he was about to lose. Manse was the bigger, more powerful man, but Laigon had trained for a lifetime in how to overcome stronger opponents.

He felt the figurine still gripped in his right hand, cold against his palm. With a growl he balled a fist and punched Manse in the throat.

The praetorian reeled back, raising a hand to his neck as Laigon wrested the dagger from his grip. Manse recovered, surging forward to stop Laigon before he could deal a killing blow. Both men struggled, upturning a table as they fell. By some freak of luck Laigon was on top, forcing the dagger down. Before Manse could cry out for aid, Laigon punched down on his dagger hand, forcing the blade into the praetorian's neck.

He held it there, his breath coming heavy, as Manse's became shallow, mouth filling with blood, eyes glassing over as his life ebbed.

When there was no resistance left in Manse, Laigon rose to his feet.

There was silence as he stood and waited. It seemed no one was coming to see what had befallen the praetorian.

Reverently, Laigon donned his armour, feeling the weight of it encumber his body once more. But this time he did not feel weighed down by the guilt of his actions. He had murdered one of his own, but it was the most just killing he had performed in over a year. For the first time in so long, Laigon was cleansed of guilt and focused of purpose.

Returning to Nephyr would be suicide. Even if he could reach his wife and child he could never escort them out of the White City in safety. They would be caught and condemned alongside him. The only way they would not be held complicit was if he left them behind.

Laigon gritted his teeth, his heart sinking with the knowledge he would have to leave alone, strike out west and warn the armies of the Cordral what was coming.

One last glance down at Manse's corpse and he knew there was nothing left here for him. He opened his palm, gazing at the figurine of Portius one last time before he wrapped it in a linen cloth and slipped it in his belt. Laigon would have at least one good luck charm, even if all the other gods had abandoned him.

He left the command tent, still buckling on his sword, and scanned the area until he spotted Vallion by one of the fires burning on the battlefield.

'Gather the Fourth,' he said to the Primaris.

His second-in-command obeyed without question, and as Vallion called for the men of the Fourth Standing to attend, Laigon watched the prisoners sitting in their sorry droves. There was nothing he could do for them, but perhaps there was something he could do for the men of his Standing.

In short order, what remained of the Fourth Standing were gathered about him, bloodied and battle weary. They had fought a hard campaign for the best part of a year, their numbers heavily depleted in the costly war, and now he was to ask yet more of them. One last sacrifice.

'Men of the Fourth,' Laigon began. There were barely four hundred men left from his legion. Four hundred out of two thousand. 'You have fought bravely for the past year. You have served the Empire of Shengen proudly. But you were deceived.' Laigon could already feel the disquiet brewing among them. 'We have all been deceived. Used as slaves, not soldiers. The Iron Tusk is a false god. A false emperor.' Men began to shake their heads, unable to rid themselves of that insidious influence. 'And so I can lead you no longer. I will take the Skull Road west. If any of you wish to join me you are welcome at my side, my brothers. To those of you who refuse, I only ask that we are allowed to leave unmolested.'

He did not wait, but turned his back and walked towards the shadow of the Crooked Jaw. It would not have been wise to let his men think on his words for too long. Those whose loyalty to the Iron Tusk was strongest may have answered his mutiny with violence, but Laigon gambled on their devotion to him.

As he walked away he was relieved to discover he had gambled wisely, and though he expected a spear in the back at any moment, he was allowed to leave in peace.

The walk to the mountain took half a day. Laigon did not turn until he had almost reached the rugged pass that marked the start of the Skull Road. Only then did he look to see how many of the Fourth Standing had put their loyalty in a centurion above that for a despot.

Forty-one men had followed him.

Not enough to stand against an empire.

But it was a start.

9

The Cordral Extent, 106 years after the Fall

CTENKA listened to Laigon's story like it was a tale from before the Fall. Part of him still couldn't believe how easily the Shengen had fallen foul of a single warlord from the mountains, and in such a short space of time. Perhaps Laigon's suspicion that there was something more to this Iron Tusk was right. Or perhaps his tale had become more fanciful in the telling. Either way, if there was even the slightest chance his words were true – if the Shengen Empire had crushed its enemies in the east and was now turning its eye to the Cordral – they had to act.

'This Iron Tusk,' said Marshal Ziyadin. 'What is he? The way you describe him, he can be no mere man.' The way his voice wavered it was clear Ziyadin was fearful of the tale. He was on the frontier after all, and would be the first to face the Shengen army if it truly was on its way along the Skull Road.

'He is just a man,' Laigon replied. 'One who inspires loyalty like no one I have ever seen. He is as divine to his followers as any god.'

'Gods,' said Ermund. 'Fanciful tales of legend. This Iron Tusk is a man like any other. And can be killed like any other. But with the might of the Shengen Empire behind him it will take more than a poorly garrisoned fort to hold him back.'

'How far away are your countrymen?' Ziyadin asked, the fear in his voice now palpable.

Laigon shrugged. 'With the Mercenary Barons defeated it will not take long to muster the rest of the Standings. A few weeks at most.'

'Very well,' Ziyadin said. 'Ermund, when you reach Kantor you will need to explain the gravity of this situation. We need reinforcements. This place must be fully garrisoned before the Shengen arrive. Ctenka, you know the Cordral as well as anyone. It will be your responsibility to ensure he gets there in one piece.'

Ctenka doubted Ermund needed any help getting anywhere, but he knew he couldn't argue with the marshal. Besides, if Laigon was right, and the Shengen army were only going to take weeks, it might be better if he was far away when they arrived. Better he return to this place behind an army than be standing at the wall with a few old men and green recruits when the Iron Tusk turned up.

'Then we need to rest,' said Ermund, rising to his feet. 'It's a long road to Kantor. And thank you, Centurion. We appreciate your bravery and the sacrifice you have made in coming here.'

Laigon nodded his appreciation, but said nothing. As they left, Ctenka couldn't help but feel for Laigon. The centurion had fled his homeland in disgrace, with no idea what might become of his family, all so that foreigners might better defend themselves from an army he had recently been a part of. Ctenka could never imagine being so courageous.

That night he hardly slept. All he could do was stare at the ceiling of the barracks, half excited, half terrified at what was to come. His memories of Kantor had faded over the months and all he remembered was the hard training he had suffered. Perhaps this time he might get to appreciate the majestic spires and lush gardens, but how could he appreciate the prospect when such a threat hung over the Cordral Extent? The weight of his responsibility kept him awake for most of the night until, bleary eyed, he was forced to drag himself from his bed.

Ermund had already risen and was checking their horses as Ctenka left his room and headed to the stables.

'Good to see you are at least taking this task seriously,' said the southerner, without looking up.

'I know my responsibilities, Ermund,' Ctenka replied.

'Do you?' Ermund looked his usual grave and serious self. 'We cannot fail in this. We have to secure reinforcements, perhaps the entire Kantor Militia, if we are to hold back the Shengen.'

'I'm not an idiot.' Not everyone could be so dedicated to their position as Ermund, but Ctenka knew the importance of their mission, and the constant suggestion that he was some kind of slovenly ingrate was growing tiresome.

'No,' Ermund replied. 'You're not. So time to stop acting it.'

'I'm here, aren't I?'

'Yes.' Ermund turned to face him, looking the young recruit up and down. 'Uniform still in a state. And have you

106

even drawn that weapon since you brought it from Kantor?'

Ctenka looked down at the sheathed blade. He couldn't remember if he had.

Before he could make up some excuse, Ctenka saw Ziyadin crossing the courtyard, his eyes bloodshot from the previous night's wine. At his side was Laigon, still bearing that solemn nobility, despite the fact he had been stripped of his armour.

'It's good to see you are keen to be off,' said Ziyadin.

'Almost ready, Marshal,' Ermund replied.

'Good. I'm sure I don't have to explain the magnitude of your task.'

'No, Marshal,' Ctenka said quickly. Ermund had already more than covered it.

They mounted their horses. Ctenka hadn't even bothered to inspect the saddlebags at his mount's flanks, trusting Ermund had already taken care of it. Silently he made a note that in the future he would check his own supplies. Better that than give the southerner yet more reasons to admonish him.

As they rode out of the gate of Dunrun, with the sun rising ahead of them, Ctenka took a glance back. Ziyadin and Laigon were both watching in silence. Despite the marshal being his superior officer, it was the centurion that Ctenka suddenly felt responsible to. He didn't want to let the man down. A man who had already sacrificed so much for a people he barely knew. Even when he had harboured an idealistic view of his future in the militia, Ctenka had never felt such a sense of responsibility as he did now.

★ ★ ★

The road west was barren for the miles that they plodded along it. Where once might have stood field upon field of verdant crops was now nothing but dried scrub. The occasional derelict outbuilding or abandoned irrigation machine stood like broken statues in the sun. Testament to how far his country had sunk in the hundred years since the Fall. Beneath the oppressive Cordral sun, Ctenka felt exposed. Without the walls of Dunrun to protect him he felt vulnerable, despite this being the country of his birth. As much as he was supposed to be the guide on this journey, he suddenly felt glad he had Ermund to protect him.

Glancing over at the tall southerner, Ctenka realised there was no other man in the world he would have rather been on this journey with, despite the lack of conversation. There had always been something about Ermund that commanded respect. A confidence about him that was undeniable. It made Ctenka wonder about that mysterious past and what might make such a man leave his former life to pursue a lowly position in a foreign land.

'Have you spent long on the open road, Ermund?' he asked, fishing for anything from the implacable veteran.

'I've had more than my share of years in the saddle, if that's what you mean,' he replied, scratching his grey beard.

Ctenka could hold back no more. 'So a sellsword in the southern companies, then? No... a captain. You commanded your own band of mercenaries?'

Ermund shook his head. 'Why the sudden interest, Ctenka? You want to know the quality of the man you travel with? Or is there a bet among the militia recruits?'

'Pah. If I had to bet I'd say you were some kind of bandit chief. Cast out by a treacherous second-in-command.'

'That's something of a stretch, Ctenka. Perhaps you fancy yourself as a fireside storyteller?'

Ctenka laughed at that. As usual it didn't even raise a smile from Ermund.

'Well, it's clear there's more to you than meets the eye. All anyone knows is your first name. If that's even the one your mother gave you.'

'There's not much in a name,' Ermund replied. 'You should not put so much store by them.'

'Really? That strikes me as words from a man who once held a great name. A feared and respected name.' As he spoke, Ctenka realised his inquisitive line of thought may have run away with itself. For his part, Ermund said nothing, merely creasing his troubled brow yet further. Perhaps Ctenka had struck upon the truth after all. A truth Ermund would rather have stayed buried. Still, it did not stop him, and against his better judgement he pressed further.

'Were you always so bloody dour? At least tell me there was once some joy in the life of Ermund of the Suderfeld, before he lost everything.'

Ctenka was surprised when Ermund replied, 'A man who has felt no joy cannot call himself a man.'

'And now he speaks philosophy like a sage.' Ctenka laughed. It felt dry in his parched throat.

'Not philosophy. Just sense.' Ermund looked at him with those deep blue eyes, shining in the sunlight. 'But if you must know, yes. I have lost much over the years.'

Ctenka had so many more questions, but he satisfied himself with that for now. He had already learned more about Ermund in one brief conversation than in the past six months of living with the man. And it was a long road ahead. No need to rush.

As the evening wore on into night, Ctenka couldn't help but feel relieved to be out of the sun. It was clear his horse felt much the same as they plodded along the arid roadway, but his sudden good humour faded fast when Ermund spied a campfire up ahead.

'What do you think?' Ctenka asked.

'I think bandits wouldn't make such a large fire in the middle of the night,' Ermund replied.

'Maybe it's a trap?'

Ermund kicked his mount towards the fire. 'It's good that you have your wits about you, young Ctenka. So let's introduce ourselves. If they rob and murder us you can be satisfied that you were right.'

Ctenka hung back, surprised at Ermund's uncustomary disregard for caution. As they drew closer he relaxed a little as the sound of music and laughter greeted them. Closer still and Ctenka heard voices he recognised.

'Merchants,' Ctenka said. 'How could you know that?'

'Because they are due to arrive at Dunrun tomorrow,' Ermund said matter-of-factly. 'If you ever checked the fort's supply ledger you'd know that.'

Yet more veiled admonishment. Ctenka wondered how much more he could take on one journey.

Both men dismounted, walking their steeds into the

camp. Immediately Ctenka recognised Mohanan, the bearded tinker whose smile was almost as big as the belly that protruded over his thick sash.

'My boys,' Mohanan said over the sound of lilting tamburs and the singing of his fellow merchants. If any of them were surprised at the arrival of two militiamen in the night they didn't show it.

Ermund and Ctenka were greeted like old friends, and it was a relief to know they didn't have to build a fire or even prepare their own food on the first night of travel.

Ctenka was buoyed by the subsequent music and conversation, until Ermund asked the merchant about the current mood in Kantor. A sudden shadow fell over Mohanan's usually jovial countenance.

'Kantor prepares for war,' he said, pulling at that long beard. 'The queen is eager for the Cordral to retain its neutrality. After the death of the king she is desperate to raise the prince to be a strong ruler, but the White Widow in the north presses for an alliance. She has already united most of the Ramadi cults and turns her eye to the Cordral. I see a darkness descending.'

'And to the south?' asked Ermund.

'Not much better, my friend. The War of Crowns is all but over. The three kings of Suderfeld are now united.'

'By what?' Ermund sounded surprised by the fact. Ctenka found it curious that Ermund appeared troubled by news that the war in his homeland was now over.

'No one knows. But now war in their own lands has passed, it appears the three kingdoms have come together, and they too look north towards conquest.'

111

'And Kantor is stuck in the middle,' said Ctenka. It seemed the importance of their mission had now grown.

The two men remained silent then, as the merchants played on into the night.

With the threats from north and south, Ctenka could only hope the queen would take seriously the grave news they were bringing from the east. As he lay down beside the fire, the sound of music still ringing in his ears, Ctenka wished he had not been so eager to be the bearer of such dark tidings. For the second night in a row sleep evaded him.

10

CTENKA wanted to complain about how hungry he was, but there was no way he was going to whinge to Ermund. His southern friend had moderated his rations and still had an abundant supply of dried fruit in his pack. Ctenka on the other hand had nothing, but then moderation had never been his thing. How he wished he'd packed some wine in one of their waterskins, at least then he'd have something to take his mind off the hunger.

As it was, all he had was the desolate scenery – the wide-open sands, interspersed with the odd tree. In the distance they'd now and again spy a farm as someone tried to scratch out a meagre living from the harsh land. The further west they went, the more of these tiny homesteads they saw. It made Ctenka suddenly grateful he'd left his own settlement behind to join the militia. Rather that than be just another tragic farmer, wasting his life in the desert.

Ctenka hadn't remembered the land being so bleak when he'd first travelled east to Dunrun. But back then he was filled with a sense of naïve duty and optimism for what was to come. He hadn't been battered by the endless days with nothing to do but drink his wine ration and gamble. Now he saw this place for what it really was… doomed.

It was getting late and still no sign of Kantor. Four days should have been enough, but still they plodded on with not a sign of another traveller along the road. Ctenka was almost at his wits' end. What he would have given for a hearty meal and some grog.

'Do you think they'll give us beds in the capital?' he asked, bored of looking at the back of Ermund's head.

'What do you think?' Ermund replied.

'I think we deserve something. Perhaps a dabble in the harem as a show of gratitude? That might be nice.'

'Of course they won't give us beds, you dolt,' Ermund snapped. 'And harem? The city's ruled by a queen. If she has a harem it'll be full of strapping young men with square jaws and broad shoulders. If you fancy a dabble with one of them you're more than welcome.'

Ctenka made a mental note to think things through more before he wished for something.

Just as the sun was going down they reached Ankrav Territory, passing a field sporting a surprisingly fertile crop. A lone farmer toiled in the midst of it, filling a little cart with sheaves of corn. Ermund was about to ride on but Ctenka slowed his mount.

'Do you think he's got a spare bed?' Ctenka said absently.

'A bed?' Ermund replied. 'He hasn't even got a mule to help him with the crops. I think a spare bed might be pushing it.'

'He must at least have a roof. Maybe he'll let us stay under it if he knows what an important mission we're on.'

'We haven't got time to make friends with farmers.'

'I'm not talking about making friends. I'm talking about getting us a roof to sleep under rather than a sky full of bloody stars, out in the wilderness, exposed for any animal or bandit to come along and murder us.'

Ermund sat and looked at him. Ctenka thought he was about to argue, until he shrugged. 'All right. By all means, get us a bed for the night.' He motioned towards the farmer.

Ctenka hadn't expected that response at all, but he wasted no time in jumping down from his horse and handing the reins to Ermund. As he made his way across the field towards the farmer he expected the man to stop what he was doing and hail him at any moment, but the man was so intent on his labours he didn't stop until Ctenka was almost upon him.

'Evening,' said Ctenka. 'I'm with—'

'Militia,' the man said. He looked well into his fifties, back stooped from years of working the fields, face a craggy sun-blasted landscape that told the tale of his years. 'Am I late with my tax?'

'No, nothing like that,' Ctenka replied, gleaning some strange satisfaction from the man's appreciation of his authority. 'My companion and I just wanted some shelter for the night. Would you be able to—'

'Of course,' said the farmer. 'Anything for Kantor's elite.'

Ctenka didn't have the heart to point out he was just a green recruit, and far from 'elite'. As the man began to push his cart across the field, Ctenka couldn't resist turning to Ermund in the distance and giving him a thumbs up sign.

'My name's Markhan,' said the man, struggling with his burden. 'My house isn't far.'

'I'm Ctenka. And let me help you with that.'

'Oh, thank you,' said Markhan, standing aside and letting Ctenka brace himself against the cart. He pushed with all his might, but it wouldn't move.

'Wheel must be stuck or something,' Ctenka said, after he almost burst a vein in his head.

'Yes,' said the farmer with a wry smile. 'There's a knack to it.'

Markhan took over, easily pushing the laden cart which rumbled over the dry ground. Ctenka followed him, wondering how anything could grow here, but clearly Markhan had chosen to farm a hardy crop.

They made their way over a ridge, Ermund following with the horses in the distance, until Ctenka could see the little white farmhouse. Farm*shed* would have been a better description, but from where he was it looked like it had a sturdy enough roof, and Ctenka was happy with that.

As Markhan wheeled his cart to the side of the house and began to stack his sheaves under a rickety-looking awning, the door to the house opened. A woman stood there, a big smile on her face as though she'd not seen another human for weeks. Her teeth were yellow with liberally spaced gaps, her bosom the largest Ctenka had ever seen, but still he feigned a smile in return. Ermund came to stand beside him now and both men looked at the woman, unsure of what to do.

'Markhan?' she called eventually. 'What trouble have you got us in now?'

Before anyone could answer she slapped both thighs

and guffawed at her own joke, throwing in a little snort for good measure.

'Just helping these fine fellows out, my dear,' said Markhan, now finished with his labours. 'Bed for the night and some vittles. Least we can do for the queen's men.'

'Oh. Well, why didn't you say so?' said the woman. 'Come in, don't be standing on ceremony round here.'

She ushered them inside, and Ctenka was immediately hit by the smell of something cooking on the stove. It was hardly the best thing he'd ever smelled, but his stomach wasn't too fussy about what he put in it after a few days of dry rations.

The woman introduced herself as Felaina, and bid both men sit. Ctenka and Ermund pulled two wobbly chairs up to an even wobblier table as she tended to the stove.

Markhan entered and began washing himself in a bowl of water, and Ctenka suddenly felt self-conscious. He was very aware of the dirt caked on his hands, but the couple didn't seem to mind as they joined them at the table.

Despite the questionable smell of whatever broth Felaina had made, Ctenka couldn't wait to dig in. He reached out a hand for some of the stale bread Felaina had served with it, when Ermund grasped his wrist. The couple bowed their heads to say grace to Sol the Life Giver before he could dig in. Ermund bowed his own head, and Ctenka quickly did the same so as not to insult their hosts.

When they were done with the simple prayer of gratitude to Sol, Ctenka took it as his signal to dive in. He needn't have bothered – it was the worst thing he'd ever tasted. The broth was weak and sour, more like goat's piss than the hearty meal he'd expected. For his part, Ermund shovelled it down as quick as he could. Ctenka thought he probably had the right idea. Get it over quickly.

When they were done, Ctenka turned to their hosts, hoping for some kind of meaningful conversation. Again, he needn't have bothered.

'You have a lot of land to farm, Markhan,' Ctenka began. 'Is it hard to work?'

'Yes,' the farmer replied. But then, that much was obvious.

'I imagine Felaina's a great help in the fields as well as the home?'

'Oh, I won't have my wife working in the fields,' he said. 'She's a precious one, and no mistake. I wouldn't have her all wrinkled and stooped from a life of tending crops. She's too beautiful for that.'

He tousled her chin as though she were some pretty maid and not an old boot with a face like a hog.

'Get off, you daft devil,' she replied, swatting his hand away playfully before she rose to clear up the plates.

The rest of the night carried on with their inane conversation. The couple were clearly unused to strangers, and took the opportunity to regale Ctenka with stories about farming the land in such harsh conditions. As much as he sympathised with them, Ctenka almost resorted to asking if they had a book in the house, but he quickly thought better of it. He doubted if either of them could even read.

Eventually, as the sun went down, Felaina brought the men two blankets and cleared a space in the main room for them to sleep. Then the couple bid them goodnight and went to their bedchamber. Before long, Ctenka could hear Markhan snoring gently from behind the closed door.

'I'm starting to think another night under the stars wasn't that bad a prospect after all,' Ctenka whispered into the dark.

'You really are an ungrateful little shit, aren't you,' Ermund whispered back.

'Ungrateful? That food wasn't fit for swill.'

'It's all they had, and they shared it with us. Count yourself lucky we found such a generous couple.'

'Come on, these people are halfwits. For a start, what kind of farmer tries to scratch a living in barren land like this? Secondly, what kind of farmer lets his wife swan around all day while he grafts? Especially when she has no children. And that's another thing – where are the young ones? Flown the coop I'll wager. Couldn't wait to leave this shit tip and those two halfwits behind them.'

He listened for a moment in the dark. All he could hear was Ermund's gentle breathing as the man slept soundly.

Fair enough, he thought, curling up in his blanket and trying to get as comfortable on the floor as he could.

Morning came with Markhan banging around in the bedchamber. At first Ctenka thought he may have been making amorous advances to his horror of a wife, but he appeared all too soon, smile on his face as though mornings were his favourite time of day. Yet another reason for Ctenka to be suspicious – he'd always had his doubts about morning people.

Of course, Ermund had already risen and gone outside to tend the horses. Ctenka stood up gingerly, stiff from sleeping on the floor, and went outside to take his inaugural piss of the day. He walked out into the morning sun and with no better alternative, went around the back of the farmhouse. Ctenka closed his eyes and breathed a sigh as he unleashed that first pitter-patter of piss on the ground. When he opened them, he noticed half a dozen mounds had been dug in the earth – little hills, most likely the product of desert vermin.

Once he'd finished he met Ermund around the front, already waiting with their mounts.

'You won't stay for breakfast?' asked Felaina, standing on the doorstep.

'Thank you, but no,' Ermund replied. For all his defending her generosity the night before, he was clearly in no mood to sample any more of her cooking.

Markhan also appeared to wave them off, and when he did Ctenka couldn't resist.

'Thanks for the hospitality anyway,' he said as he mounted up. 'Just to let you know, you might have a problem with prairie rats. Back of your house is riddled with mounds.'

Felaina's face turned sullen, her eyes lowering, bottom lip quivering. Without another word she turned and entered the house.

'Pay her no mind,' said Markhan.

'Thank you again for your hospitality,' said Ermund, kicking his horse and guiding it back towards the road.

'Yes,' said Ctenka, still confused at the woman's reaction. 'We'll be sure to recommend you. Top notch.'

With that he guided his horse after Ermund. It didn't

take long as they made their way west before the southerner turned in his saddle.

'You really are a fucking halfwit, you know that, don't you?'

'What have I done now?' asked Ctenka.

'Prairie rat mounds?' Ermund snapped.

'I was only trying to help. I didn't know she'd get so upset about it.'

'They were graves, you idiot.'

'Graves?' Ctenka wasn't quite with him. 'But they were tiny.'

'You don't need to dig a big hole for a stillbirth, Ctenka.' With that he kicked his horse on ahead.

Ctenka watched him go as the word *graves* went around and around in his head. There had been so many of them.

Damn his bloody mouth, why was he always so quick to judge? What a fucking idiot. Maybe he should go back and apologise, though by now it was too late for sorry.

But with Ctenka Sunatra wasn't it always?

11

I**T** was almost as Ctenka remembered it, though when he last came to Kantor he hadn't been stinking of horse and parched beyond measure. His village was only a few miles west of the capital, and the walk had been much easier than the horse trek from Dunrun.

He and Ermund rode through the vast city gates, the black iron portcullis half raised, red stone archway carved with myriad shapes depicting the Cordral gods. The Lover and Serpent intertwined, Vane the Hunter battling Karnak the Reaver, Lilith the Masked, the Scorpion, the All-Mother and the rest, all beneath the watchful eye of Sol, glaring down in judgement. It had made Ctenka shiver the first time he passed beneath that arch and he felt that same sense of awe now as he and Ermund entered the city.

'Is this your first time in Kantor?' he asked Ermund.

'It is,' the southerner replied. 'But in my experience one great city is much like another. Though this one seems to bear its own unique odour.'

Ctenka laughed. 'It smells of life, my friend. And this is a city unlike any other. I guarantee it.'

Ermund glanced around at the bustling streets, at the

merchants touting wares, at the urchins rushing in and out, at the beggars on the corners. 'Looks just like any other shithole to me. Everyone just wears different clothes and speaks in a slightly different accent.'

'This is the seat of life,' Ctenka said, eager to impress the implacable veteran. 'They say this was the first city. Where man first crawled from the desert to begin civilisation itself.'

'Civilisation?' Ermund said, as a screaming merchant chased a woman across the road in front of them, wooden stick raised high.

'Well, nowhere's perfect.'

They continued towards the palace where it sat looming at the centre of the city. The closer they got the more the city's military were visible. Ctenka would have expected to be greeted with friendly smiles from the other militia, but in the six months since he had been here it appeared the mood had changed. Now there was an oppressive air. The guards were vigilant, not one of them wanting to greet their fellow soldiers. When finally the pair reached the palace their way was blocked by a heavy military presence.

Ctenka stared up at the palace in awe. It was clad in the same red stone as the gate, with mortar of yellow and blue streaking the walls in concentric patterns, giving the impression of a storm raging across the stronghold's surface.

Both men pulled up their horses in front of the main gate. Guards holding shields and spears barred the way, greeting them with stern looks.

'We've ridden from Dunrun,' said Ermund. 'We must speak with the queen immediately. There is a grave threat from the east and she must be informed.'

One of the sentries took a step forward, his brow furrowing. 'You'll be lucky,' he said. 'No one is allowed entry. And from the state of you two I'd suggest a bath before you go anywhere.'

'Invasion is imminent,' said Ermund. Ctenka could detect the anger growing in him. 'The entire Shengen army is heading along the Skull Road. Dunrun must be properly garrisoned—'

'Why don't you take a look around, you southern shit,' replied the sentry, losing patience. 'Of course invasion is imminent. Why do you think—'

Before he could continue, Ermund had jumped down from his horse. The sentry backed away and the rest of the guards braced their spears. Ctenka considered dropping from his own saddle, but he froze. This was getting out of hand and he had no idea what to do.

'What's going on?' A marshal came through the gates, summoned by raised voices and the prospect of violence.

'This fucker thinks he can just walk into the palace,' said the sentry.

The marshal looked Ermund up and down, clearly unimpressed.

'We've been sent by Marshal Ziyadin,' Ctenka blurted, before Ermund said anything to make this worse.

The marshal looked up at him. 'Ziyadin? Is he still rotting out east in the arse end of nowhere?'

'Yes, Marshal,' Ctenka replied. 'And until recently we were rotting alongside him. But we have grave news that must be presented to the queen.'

'I see,' said the marshal. 'Then you'd best follow me.'

Ctenka let out the sigh he'd been holding and climbed down from his horse. As they walked through the gates, he and Ermund were relieved of their weapons and escorted towards the palace. A wide staircase led up to an archway. Sentries stood everywhere amidst red carved fountains. Ctenka noticed there was no water flowing from them anymore, but they might once have looked an impressive sight.

Once inside the palace they were led to an anteroom, three studded iron doors leading from it.

'Wait here,' said the marshal, and he disappeared, slamming the door and locking Ctenka and Ermund inside.

'What do you think?' Ctenka asked.

'I think we wait. What do you think?' Ermund answered.

Ctenka was about to say he thought Ermund had almost got them killed at the gate and maybe he should calm down, when one of the iron doors opened.

Both men stood to attention, Ctenka ready to bow in fealty, but it was not Queen Suraan who entered. Instead a little boy, his head shaved close to his scalp, red silk tunic looking threadbare, ran into the room and quickly hid behind a nearby plant pot.

Ctenka looked at Ermund with a *what's going on* look on his face. Ermund gave a reciprocal *I haven't got a clue* look back. Moments later, a girl rushed into the room after the little boy. Her head was equally close shaven, her face stern beyond her years. She was lean but well muscled for such a youth. The way she moved was like a dancer, and when she saw the two men she stood tall, surprised but not in the least bit threatened.

'Rahuul, come out this instant,' she said, still regarding

Ctenka and Ermund suspiciously, despite their uniforms clearly marking them as men of the militia. The little boy giggled from his hiding place, the leaves of the flowered plant shaking as he did so. 'Now, Rahuul. The game is over.'

As the boy crept from behind the pot, a grin on his face, Ctenka began to work that name around in his head. What was familiar about it?

Rahuul walked past the girl and out of the door, giving a quick look back before popping his tongue out playfully and running off into the room beyond. The girl bowed, then left the men alone.

'What was all that about?' asked Ctenka.

'That was Rahuul,' said Ermund.

'Yes, I got that. But—'

'The Prince of Kantor?'

Ctenka stared at the doorway. The boy who would be king had just played hide and seek in the room he was standing in. Ctenka was still staring when the door opened again. This time it was not a boy who entered.

The man was tall, well over six feet, but there was little meat to him. The dark blue of his robes was barely visible beneath innumerable scraps of parchment – rolled scrolls, sheets of vellum, scraps of yellowed papyrus – all pinned or tied with ribbon, and hanging from his thin frame like old rags. A wispy beard grew from his wizened face and deep-set eyes bore into Ctenka.

Following him were acolytes, three in all, each wearing a black habit, heads shaved, dark scrollwork tattoos marking them as the crown's bonecasters.

Ctenka realised the man in front of him must be Egil Sun, Keeper of the Word, Vizier to the Queen Regent and the second most powerful man in the Cordral.

'I am told you seek audience with the queen?' he said. Ctenka opened his mouth to answer, but Egil carried on regardless. 'That is not possible. Whatever missive you bring from Dunrun should be delivered to me.'

'Listen,' said Ermund. 'We need to speak to the queen, now. The entire Shengen army is about to fall upon Dunrun, and we need reinforcements.'

Ctenka stepped forward, placing a restraining arm on Ermund's shoulder. The southerner was clearly unaware of Egil Sun's reputation. This was not a man you made demands of.

'Oh great and wise Egil Sun,' Ctenka said. 'What my comrade means to say is… the Cordral is under threat. We beseech you to send troops east. A great warlord has risen beyond the Crooked Jaw—'

Egil raised a wizened hand. 'No. My bonecasters have had no visions. This has not been foreseen.' He gestured to the silent men in black robes. Their eyes were cast down at the ground, but still they filled Ctenka with disquiet. 'If there was a threat from the east I would know of it.'

Before Ctenka could think to protest, another figure entered the anteroom. This one he recognised.

'This is a military matter, Egil,' said the huge warrior. Musir Dragosh stood like a giant, the glint of his polished armour reflecting the thick, bronzed flesh of his arms and face. 'You need not concern yourself.'

Egil smiled from behind that threadbare beard. 'I was merely seeing to matters for the queen.'

'And I am grateful. But I can deal with this now.'

The two men stared at one another in a silent standoff. Ctenka could sense the animosity between them. In silence, Egil Sun and his bonecasters left the room.

Ctenka couldn't help but feel relieved, despite Musir Dragosh being an equally imposing sight. When Ctenka had been in the training grounds, the leader of the Desert Blades had overseen some of their trials to measure if any recruits were good enough to join his cohort of elite guard. None had been found worthy.

'Follow me,' said Dragosh.

Ctenka obeyed, relieved that Ermund also followed rather than try and get them in further trouble with that mouth of his.

Once outside in the bright palace courtyard, Ctenka could see what had once been a magnificent garden, now fallen fallow. It seemed the whole of Kantor was being left to ruin.

Musir Dragosh sounded grave as he spoke. 'I hear you would have an audience with the queen. Well that won't happen.'

'We need troops for the reinforcement of Dunrun,' said Ctenka. 'You must believe us, Musir. The Shengen are coming.'

'I do believe you.'

Ctenka almost jumped for joy. 'Thank you, Musir. Thank you.'

'But I cannot spare the troops you need.'

Ctenka felt like he'd been punched in the throat.

'But if Dunrun is not properly defended the whole of the Cordral is under threat.'

'The whole of the Cordral is already under threat. What is one more warlord?'

Ctenka was about to press further when he saw someone he recognised watching from a balcony above the garden. He had only seen her once before – part of a procession through the centre of Kantor. Ctenka had been a raw recruit then and he remembered Queen Suraan was more beautiful than any woman he had ever seen. Now she looked careworn, her hair tousled, shoulders slumped as though they bore the weight of the world.

Dragosh was the first to fall to his knee upon seeing her. Ctenka quickly followed, relieved when Ermund did the same. All three men bowed their heads, and Ctenka knelt there waiting, wondering when it would be customary to stand. After a moment, Musir Dragosh rose. Ctenka stood, looking up sheepishly, only to see the queen had vanished.

'Look,' Dragosh said, seeming to grow suddenly impatient. 'I can pledge some men. How many I don't know yet. But if you need more you'll need to look elsewhere.'

'But…' Ctenka was about to protest but he knew there was little point. He doubted the leader of the Desert Blades would change his mind at the behest of a militia recruit.

'Then we will look to the Suderfeld,' said Ermund.

Both Ctenka and Musir Dragosh stared at the southerner, who had remained silent all this time.

'Suderfeld?' Dragosh clearly did not see the sense.

'There may be someone who can help us. Once this

eastern warlord has taken the Cordral he will not stop there. It may benefit all the western nations if there is an alliance. I may be able to persuade—'

'Do what you must,' interrupted Dragosh. 'You will have men. That is all I can promise.'

Musir led them from the courtyard and through the palace. Before they left he bid them good luck and had them supplied with fresh horses and rations.

As they headed for Kantor's southern gate, Ctenka found he couldn't contain himself anymore.

'So, you have allies in the south? I knew it. I knew you were a man of breeding.' Ctenka couldn't wipe the self-satisfied smile from his face, but Ermund looked unimpressed as usual. 'I have never seen the Suderfeld Kingdoms before. These allies of yours, will they treat us like lords?'

'Aye, they might,' Ermund replied. 'If they don't kill us first.'

'Kill us?' Ctenka said.

Ermund didn't seem too keen to fill in the details.

But of course. Ctenka should have known it would never be so simple.

12

THEY headed south on the Penitent Path for two days. The fresh horses given to them in Kantor were a vast improvement on the nags they'd ridden from Dunrun, and by the end of the second day Ctenka was beginning to think himself a plains horseman reborn, even taking some joy in the journey. It didn't last long.

The air began to cool with every mile they travelled, the landscape growing more lush. As the sky turned dark and the first rainfall began to hit the ground, Ctenka realised why the Suderfeld Kingdoms were so renowned for their greenery and the miserable mood of their populace.

For hours they plodded until the rain finally relented. As they rode in their sodden clothes, Ctenka spied a waystone, the legend scratched into the worn granite long since faded. It reminded him that the Penitent Path had once been a grand thoroughfare. Much like the Skull Road it had drawn trade and culture to Kantor from a far-off nation. Since the War of Three Crowns that trade had subsided and the two militiamen seemed the only ones who had travelled its length in an age.

'That marks the border,' Ermund said as they passed the waystone.

'And how much further are we to travel?' Ctenka asked, glancing up at the grey sky with a feeling of foreboding.

'Perhaps another two days.'

Ctenka thought about Ermund's words as they left Kantor – how he had suggested they might well meet their end once they reached their destination.

'This is not the kind of country I would like to die in,' he said.

'With any luck you won't. Although I can't think of any country it would be a good place to die.'

'My own country,' Ctenka replied. 'With the sun above me, not this…' he gestured at the grey pall, '…this curtain of doom above, waiting to soak me through.'

'You'll get used to the rain.'

'I'm hoping we won't be here long enough for that.'

'Then you'd best put heels to flanks, boy,' said Ermund, encouraging his mount into a canter.

'Forgive me if I'm not so eager to face my death,' Ctenka replied, but if Ermund heard he didn't bother to reply.

It didn't take them long before a building rose up from the greenery in the distance. Ctenka felt his hopes rise at the prospect of sheltering from the inclement weather but they were dashed as soon as the place was in sight. Though the building was large and had clearly once been some kind of hostelry, now it was dilapidated, its roof long since caved in. Nevertheless, the closer they got the more they heard signs of life.

As they made their way through the trees, Ctenka could see a group of men camped under awnings, a fire lit within the open walls of the place. Something was cooking on a spit and his stomach growled in appreciation.

Ermund reined in his horse and dismounted. Ctenka did likewise and followed the southerner towards what used to be the doorway, but now stood as a gap in the crumbling wall of the inn. The place was sodden, but one side of the main room had been covered with a hastily nailed canvas. Beneath it stood a miserable-looking man, skull cap pulled tightly down over his fat head.

'Do you have shelter for the night?' Ermund asked. 'Maybe a hot meal?'

'Aye,' said the innkeeper, barely looking up. 'Three bits apiece.'

'Three bits?' Ermund asked, clearly perturbed by the expense, but then he shrugged and fished for the coins.

As Ermund paid, Ctenka couldn't resist leaning forward. 'Lovely place you have,' he said to the innkeeper. 'Nice and airy.'

The innkeeper gave him a sullen glance that spoke volumes about what he thought of Ctenka's levity.

Their shelter turned out to be a leaky stable, the hot meal a few pieces of stringy rabbit and some watery broth. As the evening went on they hunkered around a fire in the centre of the open building and Ctenka gave thanks that the heavens held onto their load.

Other than Ctenka and Ermund, there were five others who had paid for the innkeeper's 'hospitality'. Five women, their dull grey robes and the braided girds around their waists marking them as priestesses of some denomination Ctenka didn't recognise.

'You are pilgrims?' Ermund asked, making polite conversation as they sat about the fire.

The oldest of them nodded. 'We are,' she replied. 'Travelling south from the shores of Devil Sound, taking the Penitent Path to its source in the Suderfeld. I am Le'Shan.'

Under her hood, Ctenka could see a lean and scarred face, her hair cut short in tight dark curls.

'You are the leader of this group?' Ermund continued.

The woman shook her head. 'We have no leader among us. But I am the oldest, so it often falls upon me to speak for the rest.' She looked nervous, but that was hardly surprising. Women unaccompanied on the road, even priestesses, would be vulnerable to attack from all kinds of miscreants.

'You come from the Ramadi?' Ctenka asked, his curiosity piqued. He had heard hellish tales of the northern desert lands and was keen to hear more.

'We come from many places,' said Le'Shan, gesturing to her fellows.

In the firelight Ctenka could see all five of them looked very different. One bore the dark skin of a Scorchlander, another the olive tint of the western Cordral, the rest Ctenka had no idea. There was a wariness to them, as though they might be attacked at any moment.

'And... which gods do you serve?' Ctenka asked, fearsome stories of sacrifice playing at the back of his mind.

The woman glanced for a moment at her sister priestesses, who all averted their gaze to the ground. 'We respect all the gods,' she answered.

'That's a good policy,' Ctenka said. 'Hedge your bets. I've

134

never seen the point myself. All that praying takes up a lot of free time. Although I guess you haven't got much else to do.'

'You're right,' she replied. 'We don't.'

Ctenka began to get the impression the woman was merely humouring him. Served him right for trying to hold a conversation with a bunch of priestesses. He'd always found religious people to be the most tedious – why would this bunch of women be any different?

Ermund leaned forward. 'Perhaps we will accompany you on the road tomorrow,' he said. 'Increased numbers may serve us both.'

Le'Shan shook her head. 'That won't be necessary. The road holds no trepidation for us.'

'It should,' said Ermund. 'This is dangerous country.'

She fixed him with a steely gaze. 'It's all dangerous country.'

Ermund couldn't argue with that.

The pair got little conversation out of the priestess for the remainder of the evening, so they returned to the stable with their horses. Ctenka was thankful for the roof, and managed to sleep well enough considering the chill air. In the morning he awoke to the fresh smell of horseshit, and as usual Ermund had already risen and was saddling up.

Ctenka was quick to stamp some life into his chilled limbs before leading his horse to the road. He noticed those priestesses had already left, but the innkeeper was still there, watching as they began their journey.

'Your hospitality is much appreciated,' Ctenka commented to him. 'I'll be sure to recommend your establishment to all my acquaintances.'

135

Again, the innkeeper didn't appreciate the mirth.

A few miles down the road and Ctenka was starting to feel the boredom of the journey setting in once again. He was sure it would have been alleviated slightly by a wineskin or two, but it was clear Ermund was almost as pious as those priestesses. The chance of him enjoying a wineskin was about the same as him belly laughing at a joke.

When they eventually spotted the priestesses ahead of them on the road he knew the company was hardly likely to improve.

'Just keep riding past and they might not notice us,' Ctenka joked, remembering the stilted conversation he'd had the night before.

'Nonsense,' Ermund replied. 'We can't just let them travel unaccompanied. This is bandit country.'

Ctenka glanced around him at the thick woodland. 'It's what? You never told me that.'

Ermund ignored him, kicking his mount forward to catch up with the five women.

'My ladies,' he said, sounding all formal. 'It's a pleasure to see you again.' The priestesses nodded at him politely. 'I'm afraid I must insist you allow my companion and I to join you on the road. As you're strangers in this land I feel obliged to make sure you reach your destination safely.'

Le'Shan tried to argue, but Ermund had already climbed down from his horse and started walking beside her.

Reluctantly, Ctenka climbed down from his own nag, grasping the reins and pulling it along behind him. The priestesses carried on walking, heads bowed, hoods up. Clearly the chances of a decent conversation hadn't improved.

They walked for a couple more miles, the silence beginning to grate as much as the birdsong, until Ctenka noticed one of the priestesses surreptitiously glancing at him. She looked younger than the rest, and prettier. Ctenka immediately expelled any sinful thoughts from his mind – these were priestesses after all. Then again, they were priestesses from another country. Perhaps in the north they weren't so strict about the whole celibacy thing.

'I am Ctenka,' he eventually said to her.

She looked up and smiled. Her tousled blonde hair poked out from beneath her hood and Ctenka noted she had a nasty scar from her left eye that ran down her cheek.

'I am Sicabel,' she replied, nervously.

'You're a long way from home,' he replied. 'As am I. Though I think there's a rural charm to this place. Not so keen on the weather though.'

Sicabel nodded and smiled. 'I'm not so keen on the wet, either,' she said.

'How long have you been on the road?'

Sicabel looked up, as though the answer might be in the treetops. 'Sixty-seven days,' she replied.

'That's a long time to be away from home,' Ctenka said, hoping he wouldn't be away for half that.

'It is,' Sicabel replied. 'But Mandrithar willing, we'll be heading back soon.'

'That's enough,' said the priestess in front of her. The woman looked at Ctenka and forced a smile. 'My apologies, but Sicabel often forgets the vow of silence she made before we began our journey.'

The priestess gave Sicabel a withering glance and the girl fixed her eyes on the ground once more.

Served Ctenka right for trying to be friendly to priestesses. But the more he thought about what she had said, the more it bothered him. Mandrithar was a name he was familiar with but he couldn't quite place it. It bounced around in his head until eventually it came to him like an arrow from the dark. Wasn't Mandrithar the name of a Ramadi death cult?

He was about to walk forward and tell Ermund it might be best to take their leave, when a rustle from the nearby undergrowth made his right hand stray for his sword.

Before he could draw, he heard the sound of ringing metal. Ermund already had sword in hand, but it mattered little as a dozen men erupted from the surrounding scrub. Ctenka looked to his friend for a sign of what to do, and Ermund duly raised his hand, palm down, to signal Ctenka be still.

A grim-looking bandit stepped forward, his face a mass of scars. 'What do we have here?' he said as he eyed the militiamen and the five priestesses.

'They've got coin,' said another voice Ctenka recognised, as the innkeeper from a few miles back stepped out of the bush. 'And horses. And that one...' He pointed at Ctenka. 'He's got a fucking smart mouth.'

Ctenka glanced back at Ermund, who had already dropped his sword to the ground. 'Oh shit,' he said.

As usual, Ermund had little to add.

13

THE hag walked the forest until the sunlight that encroached through the canopy turned to dark. Only the moon and stars lit her way now, and they were little use as a beacon. As she followed the only light she could see, the thick roots threatened to turn her ankle, the twisting branches reaching out for her hair, face and arms, as though they sought to enmesh her and keep her in this forest forever.

A spider's web, thick and viscous, caught about her face and she heard the skittering of something near her ear. In a panic she ripped it from her cheeks and mouth, crying out as she stumbled forward in the dark.

When would this nightmare end? When would she be released from this purgatory?

She stopped, crouching beneath the boughs of a mighty oak, eyes wide as she searched in vain for comfort in the dark surrounding her. Still she could not remember her name or where she had come from. But then she had so far not given it much thought. This place had plagued her with images of war and death and pestilence since she'd arrived, and given no respite since her first moments. She had to gather herself. To remember.

Closing her eyes she tried to think back to the beginning. To *before she had found herself on the empty plain. It was difficult, like trying to break through a barrier she couldn't see, but there was no doubt the barrier was there. It stood tall and wide and stopped her from remembering. With eyes shut tight she willed it away, desperate to see what lay beyond. Her fists clenched, nails digging into her palms, the pain focusing her on tearing down the wall that blocked her memories. Teeth ground as every muscle tensed, but still she could not break it down.*

'Relax,' she whispered to herself as she let go. There was no point in forcing this.

Instead of battering the wall with her anger and frustration, she instead moved towards it with care. And in return it spoke, breathing whispers, teasing her with a past that was just beyond her reach.

Hot wind whipped about her, a desert dryness in the air. Men being slaughtered by the score. A seed in her gut growing out of control. Eating her from within. Consuming. The weight of its power overwhelming. Victory and helplessness tearing her apart. Ripping her from the world.

She opened her eyes.

It was still dark. Still silent but for the chirruping of some night creature. She listened to its lilting voice in the distance before she realised that it was the sound of no animal. There were words tangled within the tune. Somewhere in the forest a voice was singing.

She stood once more, stumbling on through the dark, trying to home in on the song. Despite the disorienting environment she worked her way closer, discerning words in a language she couldn't understand. Up ahead a weak light permeated the trees, and her breathing came faster the closer she got.

Slowly she crept up on a clearing in which a fire glowed and crackled. *Three creatures sat around it, their hairless heads reflecting the firelight. Each had pointed ears, eyes huge and dark, despite the fire's light. One of them continued to sing his strange verse as the other two looked on with gleeful smiles. All three seemed like cheerful little imps, dressed as they were in trews and waistcoats, their bare feet tapping in time to the dainty tune.*

She knew she had to reveal herself. These were the first friendly faces she had encountered, despite their outlandish nature.

As she walked into the clearing the singer stopped and looked at her. The other two turned fearfully.

'Hello,' she said. 'Can you help me?'

It was all she could think to say. It was clear she needed help, though what these three creatures could offer she had no idea.

The one who had been singing jumped to his feet. Unnaturally large smiles crossed all their faces.

'Yes, yes,' he said, his voice high-pitched and tuneful. 'Sit. Sit by the fire.'

He gestured eagerly and she walked forward, feeling it warm her. She crouched down, rubbing some feeling back into her limbs. She hadn't realised how cold she'd been wandering in the forest.

'I am Mahata,' said the singer. He gestured to his companions. 'These are my brothers, Rahata and Kahata.'

She nodded at them in turn, and after several moments of silence, Rahata said, 'And who are you?'

She looked at the three creatures in turn, hoping to put off having to explain that she had no idea who or where she was.

'I don't know,' she said finally. 'I have only been in this place for…' She couldn't even tell him that much. In truth she had no idea how long she had been here.

'Ah!' Rahata's smile grew even wider. 'Then you are a newcomer.'

'A newcomer?' she replied. 'What do you mean?'

Rahata looked at his brothers. 'A new arrival. Fledgling. Just ripe.'

Looking down at her wrinkled hands, and the white brittle hair that hung about her shoulders, she thought she was anything but 'ripe'. Nevertheless, one of the brothers, Mahata or Kahata or whatever he was called, sniffed at her like she was some fragrant flower. She leaned away from him, only to find the other brother had also moved in on the other side, his grin malevolent in the firelight.

'Yes, I suppose I'm new here,' she answered, discomfort growing as the two creatures stared at her longingly. 'But I don't know where I came from. Can you help me?'

The three looked at one another, then shook their heads frantically.

'No,' said Rahata. 'We can't help you.'

'So you have no idea where I'm from?' She could hear the yearning in her own voice and it embarrassed her to sound so pitiful.

'That's not what I said.' Rahata's brothers began to giggle. 'We know exactly where you're from. We're just not going to tell you.'

She stood, gripping her fists to her sides. The brothers stood too, their faces twisted in mock fear.

'What is wrong with you?' she asked. 'Why won't you help me?'

'Oh, we'll help you,' said Rahata. 'We must put you out of your misery.'

'Consume you,' said one of the brothers.

'Take your soul and suck it dry,' said the other.

142

Their eyes took on a darker hue and one of them blinked, a translucent film flashing across his eyes like some forest lizard.

She had made a mistake and yet again, fear gripped her in an icy embrace. These were not the benevolent imps she had thought.

As she tried to back away Rahata grasped her arms from behind.

'Wait,' she pleaded. 'Why are you doing this?'

The creatures ignored her, their faces becoming twisted and evermore bestial.

'Can you smell it?' said one of them.

'Can you taste it?' said another, his forked tongue flicking forward in anticipation.

'She is so ripe,' said Rahata, burying his head in her white hair and breathing deep. 'So, so ripe.'

'Let go of me,' she said, struggling in the creature's grip, but she was held tight. She issued an animal scream fuelled by panic and thrashed wildly. There was nothing she could do to loosen Rahata's hold.

'Don't worry,' said one of the brothers. 'It won't hurt... for long.'

As he moved towards her she felt as though something inside was squirming for release, as though her innards were being pulled every which way. She tried to hold onto it, but it seemed as though her very soul were being drawn out of her body.

The darkness of the forest grew more oppressive, looming in with tenebrous fingers. She was going to die in this unholy place, her soul consumed with no idea of who she was or even why this was to be her fate.

As the last of her strength ebbed, she could resist no longer.

Someone ran from the shadow of the trees and into the fire-lit clearing. Through fading vision, the hag could just make out a woman, eyes wide with fury, sword in hand. The creatures screeched, turning to face the intruder, faces contorting in rage as they hissed at this warrior woman.

Rahata loosed his vile grip and the hag slumped to the ground as the warrior attacked. She cried in rage as she swung the sword, taking the head of one creature from its shoulders. The other brother attacked, dark claws raking an armoured shoulder. The warrior span, sword flashing again, cutting a furrow across its chest. Rahata issued a final hiss of rage at the death of his kin before turning tail and fleeing into the dark forest.

The warrior stood panting for a moment, then glanced down.

'Are you all right?' she asked.

Was she all right? The hag could not tell. It was as though the creatures had been tearing at her essence, eating her from the inside out.

'Who…? Who are you?' was all she could ask.

'I am Hera,' said the warrior, offering a hand.

The hag took it, allowing the woman to pull her to her feet. The bodies of the two foul creatures lay still beside the fire. One was headless, the other had a gash across its chest, but neither of them was bleeding, as though they were old man-shaped sacks of meat.

'I am grateful to you, Hera,' she said. 'It was lucky you happened upon me when you did or those creatures would have…'

What would they have done? She still had little comprehension of exactly what they would have done to her.

'Happened upon you?' said Hera. 'It is not luck that caused our paths to cross. I have hunted you for days.'

'Hunted me?' For a moment her panic returned.

'I had to find you.' Hera sheathed her sword. 'Before you succumbed to the dangers of this land.'

'You know me?' the hag asked, her fear abating slightly. 'Then you know how I got here?'

Hera shook her head. 'No. I do not know who you are. All I can tell you is that we're drawn together. Whatever force brought us both to this place compels us towards one another.'

'But I cannot remember anything. Nothing from my past beyond arriving in this accursed place.'

'Memory will come, in time,' said Hera. 'And perhaps you will regret it when it does. As your link to the land of the living weakens, so your memory of it grows stronger.'

'The land of the living? What do you mean? What is this place? Where am I?'

'You haven't worked that much out yet?' said Hera, glancing around at the brooding environment. 'You are in Hell, girl. Of that there is no doubt.'

The hag let that sink in and it made a strange kind of sense. Even though she could not remember where she had come from, the concept of Hell was one she knew.

'Then we are damned,' she breathed. The prospect of facing damnation alone filled her with dread. But then she was not alone. 'Others? If this is Hell are there more of us? More lost souls?'

Hera nodded. 'Yes, there are others,' she said. 'It was one of them who sent me to find you. Come. I will take you to him.'

With that, Hera led the way through the forest. All the hag could do was follow.

145

14

The Suderfeld, 106 years after the Fall

CTENKA had seen someone hogtied once before, but he'd never appreciated what it did to a man until now. A bounty hunter had come through their village when he was a boy, prisoner in tow. His quarry had been tied hands to feet, lying there like he was waiting to be butchered then hung for ageing. Ctenka and the other village children had laughed and taunted the prisoner. How Ctenka regretted that now.

The rope burned his wrists and he could feel his legs cramping up as he lay on his stomach, breath coming hard and laboured. He could barely suppress the panic rising within. What were these bandits going to do to them? Worse still, what were they going to do to those priestesses?

The seven of them were in a clearing surrounded by their captors, around a dozen in all. They hadn't bothered to tie the women up, and at the moment they were jeering and poking sticks at them, trying to take a peek under their robes. Ctenka knew that wouldn't satisfy them for long. He and Ermund had been tied and dumped at the side of the clearing, so they were being ignored. For now.

He could hear Ermund struggling with his ropes. It was

futile, he knew that much, but he could only admire the man for his persistence.

'You'll only wear yourself out, my friend,' Ctenka whispered.

Ermund gave him a withering glance, before seeming to come to terms with the finesse with which he had been bound. The southerner finally gave in, exhausted from his efforts.

'So what now?' asked Ctenka.

Ermund glared at him. 'How the fuck do I know, Ctenka? What kind of stupid question is that?'

'I thought you must have had a plan when you surrendered so quickly.'

Ermund's brows furrowed. 'What were we supposed to do, fight a dozen bandits with nothing but a bunch of priestesses for back-up?'

'At least we'd have gone down fighting and not ended up trussed like livestock.'

'Really?' said Ermund, his face turning a darker shade of red. 'That's how you see yourself? A brave warrior dying in the midst of battle?'

'Well…' Ctenka realised how stupid he had sounded.

'The only thing you'll die fighting is liver failure, you drunken little shithead.'

Ctenka turned away embarrassed, as Ermund went back to struggling against his bonds.

As one, the bandits fell silent. A figure walked from the surrounding undergrowth and into their midst, head and face matted with red hair, eyes glaring down at his prisoners. From his position on the ground Ctenka thought the man looked like a giant, and his need to piss grew suddenly more urgent.

'A sorry bunch,' said the red-haired man. 'And you thought these were worthwhile marks, did you?'

The question was directed at his men, who now stood on the periphery of the clearing.

'We didn't touch any of the women, boss,' one of them said. 'Thought we'd wait for you before we started.'

The giant ignored the man, still intent on his prisoners.

'I am Tarlak Thurlow,' he said. 'I'm sure you've heard of me.' Ctenka hadn't, but he doubted he'd earn himself any friends by pointing that out. 'And you have the misfortune to have fallen foul of my band of... loyal followers.' He said the word *loyal* as though he could quite as easily have exchanged it with the word *dim-witted*. 'I wouldn't normally bother with you myself, I'm after richer pickings, but now you're all tied up I guess you'll have to be dealt with...'

He paused as his eyes fell on Ermund, who stared back defiantly. Tarlak's deep ginger brow creased in thought.

'You look familiar,' he said, glaring down at the southerner. 'Have we met?' He shrugged when Ermund failed to answer. 'No matter. Since you're a sorry fucking bunch and don't have anything between you worth taking, you'll have to compensate me and my men in some other way. I don't think I have to spell out what way that is. If it was up to me I'd make it quick, but my men... they're in need of some sport. So who's first?'

The priestesses gave no reaction. They were huddled together now, heads covered, awaiting their fate in silence. At any moment, Ctenka expected the bandits to fall on them like wolves, but the silence pressed on.

'That one,' said a voice from behind Tarlak. Ctenka craned his head to see the innkeeper, finger pointed accusingly. 'That fucker's got a smart mouth. Cut his tongue out before you fuck him.'

Ctenka opened his mouth to protest, but before he could say a word, one of the priestesses stood up.

Le'Shan pulled back her hood, revealing that head of tightly curled ringlets.

'I will be first,' she announced, not one hint of fear in her voice.

Thurlow seemed impressed. He walked forward, towering over the priestess. 'I like your spirit,' he said with a grin that made Ctenka want to vomit. 'Impress me, woman, and maybe I'll keep you around.'

She didn't answer, just slowly dropped into a crouch in front of the bandit leader. Tarlak Thurlow grinned the wider, reaching down to unbuckle his belt.

Before he could drop his leggings, Le'Shan produced a wickedly curved blade from within her robes. Two quick swipes and she'd opened up deep lacerations in Tarlak's thighs.

As the bandit leader fell with a strangled cry, the other priestesses bolted into action. Ctenka saw them abandon their robes, revealing tight-fitting leather tunics beneath. Each of them carried twin blades, the same wickedly curved weapons Le'Shan had used, and they went at their captors with swift efficiency.

The bandits shouted in panic as the women attacked. Three of them went down clutching their throats before the rest even realised what was happening, but it didn't take them long to rally.

'What the fuck is happening?' Ctenka said to Ermund, as the battle erupted around them.

Ermund said nothing, just watched, waiting for his opportunity. It didn't take long to come.

One of the bandits fell gasping his last, right next to where Ctenka was lying. They stared at each other for a moment as the bandit mouthed words that wouldn't come, his throat open to the world, blood spilling all over the grass.

'Blade,' Ermund snarled.

Ctenka dragged his attention away from the dying bandit to see a fallen knife on the ground. As the battle continued to rage, both men shuffled towards it. Ermund was there first, and he turned, fingers probing for the weapon in the wet. Eventually he managed to grasp it, and Ctenka turned, presenting his ropes. The blade was keen, cutting the ropes with ease, and Ctenka let out a long breath as he was finally freed. Quickly he took the knife from Ermund and cut him free.

Both men stood to survey the battle. The bandits still fought, Tarlak Thurlow barking his ire at them from the ground, legs pissing blood everywhere.

The priestesses attacked like animals. After their initial attack, the bandits had managed to steel themselves, but they weren't a match for these women. Ctenka watched in awe as they moved around the clearing like dancers, slashing with those knives, probing at the bandits who did their best to hack at the women clumsily.

There was no way he was going to let them take all the glory.

Ctenka looked for where their equipment was piled. His sword lay discarded next to their saddlebags and he grabbed it with shaky hands.

By the time he'd unsheathed the weapon the fight was almost over. Some of the bandits had fled, but the rest still fought on, too scared of Tarlak Thurlow to disobey his bellowed orders to 'kill these bitches'.

Then Ctenka spied the innkeeper, standing back from the fray, creeping up on Sicabel who stood at the edge of the clearing nursing a wound in her side. Ctenka saw his chance. Moving swiftly he raised his blade and brought it down on the side of the innkeeper's head.

Whatever Ctenka had expected to happen when he first killed a man, this wasn't it. The impact of the blow jolted up his weapon and into his hand. The innkeeper went down silently, with no last cry of pain. This wasn't what he'd expected from all the tales he'd heard. Where was the feeling of triumph? As Ctenka stared at the body all he felt was ill, his arms starting to shake.

One of the bandits turned, seeing the blade in Ctenka's hand and what he had just done to the innkeeper, and without a word raced off into the woods. Looking around in a daze, Ctenka saw the rest of the bandits were dead or fled now. The only one left alive was Thurlow, still foundering on the ground. Ctenka, his blood up, panic rising in his throat, stumbled over to the bandit leader.

'Yield, you fucking bastard,' he screamed. His voice

was shrill like a different Ctenka, a more terrified version of himself, had said it.

Tarlak Thurlow looked around, seeing he was the last one alive, that his men had bolted and left him to his fate. His laugh was deep and rumbling.

Ermund walked forward, breath coming fast, mouth and nose bleeding from the fight. Thurlow looked up at them both and smiled.

'I know you,' he said to Ermund. 'I knew I'd seen you before. You've changed. The years haven't been kind, have they? What happened to you?'

'What's he talking about, Ermund?' Ctenka asked, trying his best to stay calm, blood coursing through his veins.

Tarlak laughed at that. 'Ermund? Is that the name you go by now? This one doesn't know who you really are?' He looked at Ctenka. 'Your friend here isn't who he says he is, boy. This is—'

Ermund buried his sword in the bandit leader's head and split it with a crack. He remained stock still for a moment, before one of his eyes dripped a single tear of blood and he keeled over into the brush.

It was quiet in the clearing. The women – priestesses, if that was even what they were – stared at the two men.

In the aftermath of the battle, Ctenka couldn't help but admire the way these women had dispatched their enemies.

'Well fought,' he said, arms still shaking. 'We make a formidable team.'

The women looked at one another. Then, with an almost imperceptible nod from Le'Shan, they surrounded the two men.

'Drop your weapons,' said the dark-skinned Scorchlander.

Ctenka immediately dropped his sword.

Perhaps they didn't make a formidable team after all.

15

'LET'S just kill them and be on our way,' said the olive-skinned priestess.

'They just helped us,' said another with a spiral tattoo up her neck. 'These are clearly honourable men.'

'No men are honourable,' said the Scorchlander. 'Did you not see the way the young one looked at Sicabel? Let's just cut their throats and be done with it.'

Ctenka was regretting dropping his sword so readily. He could see Ermund was thinking the same.

'But what would She want us to do?' said the tattooed one. 'We are here at Her word. We came to this place to—'

'Enough,' said Le'Shan, standing up from where she had been bandaging Sicabel's wound. 'No more talk.' She looked at Ctenka and Ermund. 'I am sorry. But we cannot let you tell anyone you saw us.'

'We won't say a word,' Ctenka replied, looking at Ermund. 'Tell her. We won't say a word, will we?'

Ermund stared at Le'Shan, refusing to be cowed despite the imminent threat of murder. 'She's already made her mind up, lad. Begging won't help us now.'

'Wait!' Ctenka said, not ready to die just yet. He picked

out Sicabel from the group and saw the guilt written in her expression. 'We helped you. We saved you... I saved you.'

'It will be quick,' said Le'Shan, ignoring his pleas and drawing one of those curved blades.

Ctenka closed his eyes. *Let it be quick. Please gods let it be really really quick.*

'Wait!' Ctenka opened one eye at the sound of Sicabel's voice. 'This one saved me,' she said, pointing at Ctenka.

Le'Shan looked around at her with an expression of annoyance. 'You mean you owe him a life debt?'

Sicabel nodded, looking embarrassed at the notion.

'Stupid girl,' said the Scorchlander. 'You know what that means?'

'Does it mean you have to let us live?' Ctenka smiled in relief.

'No,' said the woman. 'We just kill one of you.'

Le'Shan shook her head. 'If we let one live then what difference both of them? We owe a debt and it must be paid, no matter the consequence. You may be on your way,' she said to the men. 'In return I would only ask you do not speak of our meeting to anyone.'

'It's the least we can do,' said Ctenka, feeling relief wash over him like the Suderfeld rain.

The women gathered what meagre belongings they had. He could see each one had an array of blades about them, which they covered up once more beneath their grey robes. As they disappeared into the woods, Sicabel turned and gave Ctenka a last grateful nod, before she too was gone into the trees.

Ctenka let out a sigh. 'Fuck, that was close.'

Ermund ignored him, already moving, searching the bodies of the bandits for anything useful.

The ground was littered with corpses. Ctenka suddenly felt sick to his stomach. Killing had seemed so much more heroic in the stories. His father had told him a hundred of them, but not a single one had ended with him shaking like a leaf and needing to shit.

The innkeeper was staring. Out of one eye at least, the other was a red mess, his arms and legs splayed awkwardly like he'd slipped down the stairs. He hadn't slipped down the stairs though. Ctenka had smashed him over the head with a sword and now he was dead. A man who'd wanted to see Ctenka raped. A man who'd seemed to take some kind of gleeful satisfaction in the prospect.

So why was Ctenka feeling shitty about it?

He should have been elated. He'd defeated his enemy in mortal combat. Well, he'd blindsided the fucker, but the result was much the same. This should have been a great moment, but all Ctenka felt was emptiness. All he could do was stare at that corpse, shaking like he was getting a fever.

'Are you all right?'

Ctenka turned as he felt a heavy hand on his shoulder. Ermund was looking at him with concern, Tarlak Thurlow's blood spattered all across his face.

With a retch, Ctenka turned, stumbling off to the side of the road where he heaved stinging bile on the ground. It welled up in his nose, causing him to gag and retch again. He spat out the foul taste from his mouth and stood, beginning to feel somewhat better.

When he turned he saw Ermund was still regarding him, but now more with disappointment than concern.

'What now?' asked Ctenka, trying to divert attention from his weak stomach.

'What do you think?' Ermund replied curtly. 'We carry on south.'

In the confusion their horses had taken flight; where they were now was anyone's guess.

'That's a long walk,' said Ctenka.

'Then we'd best get started.'

They walked the road south for three days. Despite the verdant countryside, there were clear signs that this place had been ravaged by war in recent years. Here and there were the remains of a burned-out hamlet, and for two nights in a row they found inns that were abandoned, furniture left intact as though the owners had upped and left in a hurry.

'What happened to this place?' Ctenka asked as they walked further south, passing the rotting skeleton of a horse by the side of the road.

'Arethusa endured the brunt of the war in Suderfeld,' Ermund replied. 'Mercenary companies fought more battles in this land than Canbria and Eldreth combined.'

'And now?'

Ermund looked around him at the open fields left unploughed and took in a deep breath. 'And now the war is over. The three kings have come to some kind of accord.'

'And we are on our way to?'

'Northold. Capital of Canbria. King Stellan still holds court there. He was a fair man once, though when last I saw him...' Ermund trailed off as though the memory were painful.

'Let me guess – it wasn't on friendly terms?' The way their journey had gone so far, Ctenka could only anticipate yet more adversity.

'I was betrayed,' said Ermund. 'The king was turned against me and would not listen to what I had to say. But this time he will.'

'How can you be so sure?'

Again Ermund thought on it. 'Because he has to. What we face threatens the peace in Suderfeld. He is a shrewd man. He will listen to reason.'

'And yet he didn't listen before...'

'Do you have to question everything? Just trust me.' Ermund turned to face him, and Ctenka felt a flash of fear at Ermund's annoyance. He held his hands up to placate the southerner, but Ermund had already stormed off down the road.

They walked for a short distance before Ctenka saw another waystone. This one marked the northern border of Canbria. They were almost at their destination.

Soon enough they'd find out if Ermund was right about whether this King Stellan could be reasoned with. He'd just have to trust in Ermund's judgement. As Ctenka watched Ermund forging ahead, he could only hope that his trust wasn't misplaced.

16

THE route they travelled became better maintained the closer they got to the city, turning from muddy path to worn stone road to cobbled thoroughfare when they were within a few miles of their destination.

It also became busier, and Ctenka took some relief in the fact that these were ordinary folk – farmers, traders, tinkers – who seemed to go about their business without fear of being assaulted on the road.

At one point a troop of soldiers passed them by, their livery showing a golden lion upon a red field. Ermund stood to the side of the road to let them pass, and Ctenka followed his lead.

'King Stellan's men,' Ermund told him, as the knights rode their powerful-looking steeds down the road.

They were an impressive sight. Ctenka had heard of the heavily armoured warriors of the Suderfeld, but only in stories. He had to admit they were more fearsome in the flesh and he took some solace in the fact they now travelled in protected lands.

When finally they reached the city of Northold it stood at the eastern side of a wide, fast-flowing river. A great feat of engineering had seen the river diverted via a tributary that enclosed the city's western half, creating a moat to protect the entire perimeter.

Surrounding the city for miles was a wide flat plain interspersed with the occasional copse of trees. This was beautiful country, that Ctenka could not deny, but it did nothing to allay his sense of foreboding as he approached the city. The further he made his way through the beautiful green fields the more he yearned for the arid landscape of his home.

'A veritable fortress city,' Ctenka said as they made their way over a wide stone bridge that led to Northold's eastern gate. 'Doesn't rival Kantor for its magnificence, but I'm sure it would be as difficult to besiege.' His eyes were drawn up the sheer stone walls surrounding the city on every side.

'It's the greatest city in Canbria,' Ermund replied. 'A hub for trade throughout Suderfeld. Before the War of Three Crowns merchants came from beyond the Ebon Sea exchanging silk and wine for steel and wool. Now the war is over I'm sure it will have returned to those days of prosperity.'

At the other side of the bridge stood the main gate. It rivalled any of the gates of Dunrun for its size and splendour, two great stone warriors flanking it on either side. The pair weren't challenged as they made their way in, and Ctenka found himself holding his breath at the opulence that might await them.

He needn't have bothered.

The first thing that hit Ctenka was the smell – pig shit mixed with rotting vegetables – which almost made him gag. The second was something flung by a street urchin. Ctenka ducked, then stared angrily at the little shit as he ran by, chasing a mangy cat that he was clearly never going to catch.

No sooner had they started along the street than Ctenka was ankle deep in mud, though from the smell there was likely a fair amount of dung mixed into it. To strike a contrast with the impenetrable walls that surrounded the city, the dwellings within looked dilapidated to the last, crumbling wood and brick holding up roofs of chipped slate and unkempt straw.

Ctenka looked at Ermund. 'Mmm, those days of prosperity really do look just around the corner.'

Ermund stared about him as though he barely recognised the place. 'Even in the darkest days of the war, Northold never looked this bad.' He moved aside as someone walked by, coughing their lungs up, face riddled with pox. 'I don't understand how Stellan has let the place fall to such ruin.'

'Well I don't know about you, but my legs are killing me from the walk and I'm parched. Any chance we can stop at an inn before you reacquaint yourself with this King Stellan, who may or may not be pleased to see us?'

Ctenka was surprised when Ermund nodded in agreement. He was even more surprised when Ermund began asking passers-by where they could find the most expensive hostelry in the city.

They made their way through the streets until they eventually found the place – the Gorgon's Rest. It wasn't the palace Ctenka had been expecting, but considering the state of the rest of Northold he was sure it would do.

When they walked inside Ermund asked for two rooms

and a bath for each of them, slapping enough coin in the innkeeper's hand to keep the pair of them fed and watered for the next week.

'Where were you hiding that?' Ctenka asked, before they were led to the bathhouse.

'Let's just say our stay is courtesy of Tarlak Thurlow.'

Ctenka stifled a laugh. Clearly Ermund had found more than weapons and supplies when he'd been ransacking the bandit corpses. Ctenka could only wonder what other secrets his friend was keeping.

The two met up again when they had bathed. Ermund suggested they would make a better impression if their uniforms were cleaned and the innkeeper had arranged for a washerwoman to launder their attire.

'Might be worth having a quick drink while our clothes dry,' suggested Ctenka, and once again he was taken aback when Ermund agreed. It was as though his usually taciturn friend had changed into a different man, and it was good to see he'd taken the flagpole out of his arse for once.

They drank well into the night, and Ermund was more comfortable than Ctenka had ever seen him. When a band of minstrels entered the inn and regaled them with a tune or five, Ermund even began tapping his foot and throwing coins at them like he was a prince of the realm.

Ctenka took to his bed feeling sated and happy, but the following morning saw him cursing the foul southern ale for the bastard it was. When he managed to materialise from his chamber, head fuddled and stomach churning, Ermund was already waiting, fully dressed. Some things didn't change.

The two of them made their way across the city to Stellan's palace. It leered over the rest of Northold like an oppressive bully, and the closer they came the more Ctenka's nerve began to falter. He looked to Ermund for reassurance, but his friend's previous good mood seemed to have withered overnight. Now the southerner's face was set with his usual grimness, stone-jawed and heavy-browed.

They reached the palace gates. Where the entrance to the city had been open, here it was heavily guarded by more men bearing the golden lion livery of Stellan's knights. Ermund walked forward, holding himself imperiously. Ctenka knew his friend usually had a noble bearing but here he somehow seemed to hold even more authority.

'We seek audience with the king,' he announced to the guard. 'We are envoys from the court of Kantor, beseeching aid.'

'The king sees no one,' said one of the guards when Ermund had barely finished his entreaty.

'What do you mean the king sees no one? Stellan invites audience from anyone who needs help. He always has.'

The guard shook his head. 'Not now he doesn't.'

'Is he taken ill?' Ermund seemed nonplussed at the rebuttal.

The guards fell silent, glancing at one another as though they didn't know quite what to say. Then one of them walked forward. He had the look of a commander about him though his dress was the same as the rest of the guard.

'King Stellan has given orders that no one is to be allowed into the palace. If you need to make any petitions I can take a name and arrange for you to speak with his counsellor.'

'His counsellor?' Ermund was growing annoyed, and Ctenka could sense the rising unease. 'Stellan needs no counsellor. Tell him...' Ermund paused, as though reluctant to give a name. 'I must speak with Stellan himself.'

'It's his counsellor or nothing.' The guard seemed to be growing impatient.

Ctenka took Ermund's arm. 'Maybe we should come back another time. When it's more convenient?' He half expected Ermund to shake him off and begin railing at the guard, but instead the veteran took a step back as though defeated. Silently he turned and walked away from the palace gate. All Ctenka could do was follow.

They made their way back to the inn in silence, Ctenka not daring to ask what they would do next. When Ermund ordered a flagon for them, Ctenka didn't complain. They sat at a table and Ctenka watched as Ermund downed his drink before quickly refilling it. Had his friend forgotten the urgency of their mission?

'We should try again tomorrow,' Ermund said finally.

'You heard what they said. We should leave our names and meet with the king's counsellor.'

'No. I have to see the *king*. It has to be Stellan. I have to tell him...'

Ctenka waited for Ermund to finish but instead his friend drank more ale, gulping it down like he was dying of thirst. Ctenka had never seen him so much as smell alcohol before, and this new side of him was becoming a concern. Not that Ctenka was averse to getting shitfaced, but they had a job to do, and Ermund was supposed to be the responsible one.

'What is it between the two of you?' Ctenka asked. 'Why don't you just tell me what the fuck is going on?'

Before Ermund could answer, the door burst inwards. A dozen knights in red rushed inside, swords already drawn, and Ermund stood slowly to greet them.

'There he is,' said the guard Ermund had spoken to earlier at the gate. 'I knew I recognised him.'

From behind the knights came a solitary, unarmed figure. She was slender, walking with the regal splendour of a queen. Her hair hung in black tresses, dark piercing pupils set in her jade eyes. Ctenka was hard pressed to remember when he had seen a more beautiful woman. She rivalled even Queen Suraan.

'Hello, Harlaw,' she said, a wry smile teasing the corner of her mouth. 'It's been a long time.'

Ermund did not respond.

'Who?' said Ctenka. 'Ermund, who is this? And who the fuck is Harlaw?'

'Throw down your weapons,' said the commander of the knights. 'No one has to get hurt.'

Ctenka could see Ermund tighten his grip on his sword, knuckles whitening.

'Are we fighting?' Ctenka asked, hoping against hope they weren't about to die here in this shitty inn.

'No,' Ermund said. 'Just…' He stared at the woman who had called him Harlaw. 'Just put it down.'

When Ermund dropped his own weapon, Ctenka did the same.

As the knights came forward to secure them both in chains, Ermund pleaded with the woman, 'Selene, let him go. He has no part in this.'

That smile never left her lips. 'He was a part of this as soon as you brought him here,' she replied.

As they were dragged from the inn, questions clamoured in Ctenka's head. If Ermund never told him anything else in his short life, Ctenka was damned sure he owed him an explanation for this.

HARLAW

I

I T was an old keep, some wreck from the Age of Penitence. Duke Harlaw didn't even know the name of it, but names didn't matter right now. All that mattered was it served its purpose. The building hunkered at the apex of the three kingdoms of the Suderfeld. Neutral territory. Or at least that's what he hoped.

They sat in the only room that was still held up by four walls. There were five of them, each sworn enemies, shut in around a table of rotten wood. Their knights and bannermen were outside and Harlaw could only hope that this business was concluded before someone tried to settle an old score, inside the keep as well as out.

Harlaw was at the head of the table, but that was only fitting since he was the one who had arranged the meeting. It had been hard for him to persuade King Stellan that it was time for talks, let alone the four envoys who had come to attend. This was a risk. But then the War of Three Crowns would never end unless someone took a risk. The chance for peace, to end the slaughter, was a slim one but worth it.

To his immediate left sat Clydus, consul of King Ozric and his father Leonfric before him. It was no secret the old goat was the real power in Eldreth. He was a wizened skeleton of a man, who reminded Harlaw of the stories he'd been told of the Crown Sorcerers of old. Harlaw could well believe the man held Ozric under some kind of enchantment, but everyone knew there was no magic in these lands anymore. Clydus' power was in his poisoned words, not in any sorcery he might spew from his wrinkled lips.

On Harlaw's right was Manssun Rike, champion to King Banedon of Arethusa. He was a hulking brute, arms wrapped in iron bands and tattoos, face a mass of scars. His red hair and braided beard were as fiery as his temper, and it had taken all Harlaw's powers of persuasion to make him leave his huge broadsword outside the room. Not that it would stop him killing everyone here if the mood took him.

Beyond those two was even more trouble – two individuals Harlaw hated more than anyone. They represented the real reason the War of Three Crowns had lasted so long.

Mercenaries.

Castor Drummon was a lithe snake, all sinew and leer. His right hand drummed on the chipped wood of the table, restless now it no longer held the knife he used to constantly pick at his teeth. He was leader of the most ruthless mercenary company in the Suderfeld and had spent the past year harrying counties in Canbria at the behest of King Ozric. Of everyone at the table he was the one Harlaw would have most liked to see hanged at the end of a rope, but this was not a time for settling scores. Harlaw had to remember that.

Beside Castor was an equally lean woman, head shaved at the sides showing faded tattoos in concentric patterns around her head. Maud Levar sat in silence but she was likely the most dangerous of them all. Her mercenary company had fought for all three kingdoms over the course of the war and she held no loyalty to anyone. Harlaw suspected she would rather have slaughtered every man here than see peace prevail in the Suderfeld, but her company was the largest of them all. If Harlaw had to persuade anyone that reconciliation was the answer then it was her.

'King Stellan wishes peace in the Suderfeld,' said Harlaw. There was no point dancing around it. 'There must be an end to this slaughter.'

'I'm sure he does,' Clydus replied, his croaky voice grating on Harlaw's nerves like a knife on a mirror. 'He is losing this war.'

'We are all losing this war,' Harlaw replied, desperate to keep his own temper in check. 'How much has King Ozric wasted in coin and corpses over the past year alone? There will be no winners at the end of this. Only a kingdom of dirt and bones.'

'So what does he suggest?' said Manssun Rike, rumbling voice resounding through the small chamber. 'A truce? We tried that once. You're old enough to remember the Treaty of Iron. And how did that end?'

'So we must try again,' said Harlaw. 'A new treaty. Stronger than iron. One we are all committed to.'

Manssun laughed. 'And built on what? The last time the kingdoms united it was to fight a common enemy. Once that enemy was defeated the three kings were at one another's throats again. We have no common enemy now. Only a common hatred.'

'Then we must set that hatred aside,' Harlaw insisted. 'Unite the realms by other means than war.'

'By what means, exactly?' asked Clydus. Harlaw had a feeling the old bastard already suspected what the solution would be.

'Stellan has sons. Ozric and Banedon have daughters. Join the three kingdoms by marriage and this hatred ends in a family united under a single banner.'

Manssun slammed his meaty hand on the table and Harlaw heard the wood crack under the blow. 'So Stellan's heir is the one who becomes king of the Suderfeld? And you expect King Banedon to accept such an arrangement?'

'There can be no unity in the Suderfeld as long as three different kings rule. It is time to end this destructive feud.'

'By handing Stellan's line the key to the three kingdoms,' said Clydus, his voice dripping with contempt.

Harlaw opened his mouth to argue that all three lines would inherit a single realm, when he was cut off by another voice.

'And where do we fit into all this?' Castor Drummon spoke quietly but it still silenced the room. 'I have a host of bastard heirs. Will you offer one of them a crown?'

Harlaw had already anticipated this, but had hoped to broker the offer from a position of unity with Clydus and Manssun. His position was now weak but he had to try anyway.

'You will all be compensated handsomely for a cessation

in hostilities. The mercenary captains will each be offered manses and a generous stipend for retiring their companies.'

'Paid for by whom?' Castor asked. 'I doubt Stellan's coffers will stretch to compensating every company in the Suderfeld.'

'The three kingdoms will contribute,' Harlaw replied. 'Each king will donate an equal share.'

There was a moment of silence before Clydus and Manssun began as one, berating Harlaw for his idea, accusing him of trying to rob their kings of both coin and crown.

'Enough!' This time it was Harlaw's turn to slam a fist on the table, only there was no crack of wood. 'Those are the terms I suggest. Return to your liege lords and give them the offer.'

Manssun rose to his feet, chair falling back with a clatter. 'King Banedon would rather gut Stellan's heir than see his only daughter wed to that cow-eyed cunt. As for paying mercenaries for peace, the armies of Arethusa will ride over their bones before they see a single piece of gold.'

Maud Levar was next to rise, and Harlaw saw the glint of a dagger in her hand. They had all been checked for weapons before they entered the room – someone would pay for their lack of diligence.

'You want to try and ride over my bones, you ugly fucker?' she said.

Clydus and Castor likewise rose to their feet. The old man already had the blade of a punch dagger protruding from between his knobbly digits. Could no one check for weapons these days?

Everyone was shouting at once as Harlaw gently pushed his own chair back. They were still in the throes of screaming at one another as he opened the door to the chamber and walked out, taking a deep breath of the fresh evening air. Of everyone gathered, he knew best the smell of defeat when he tasted it.

Warriors still milled around the courtyard, every one turning expectantly as he appeared, and Harlaw took some solace in the fact that none of them seemed ready to start a fight. Sir Arlis sat astride his horse, waiting patiently.

'Let's get out of here,' Harlaw said as he mounted his own white steed.

As they made their way from the courtyard, Harlaw could still hear the sound of argument pealing from within the old keep.

'Things not go to plan?' asked Sir Arlis, as they made their way down the long road to Northold.

'You could say that,' Harlaw replied, as they were joined by yet more of his knights. He took some comfort in seeing their familiar red eagle livery.

The ride back was mercifully swift, but as Harlaw saw the fortress-city of Northold in the distance he suddenly wished it had been longer. Now he had to report yet more ill news to King Stellan. It seemed of late that was the only news the beleaguered king ever received.

The throne room sat at the heart of the palace. It had once been a place of revelry and mirth during the days of King Harald but now it was little more than a sepulchre. The golden lion banners of the Canbrian kings hung all around, but even their majesty did little to lighten the air.

But then what could Harlaw expect? As well as being a nation riven by war it had also recently lost its queen, and her husband now had to rule alone. Harlaw would have sympathised had his own marriage been more than one of convenience.

King Stellan stood, tall and straight, his hands clasped behind his back. The armour of his office made him look like a giant.

'My liege,' said Harlaw as he entered.

Stellan turned from the window, a trace of a smile crossing his face as he saw his faithful duke, but it was gone as soon as it came. Clearly the king was expecting bad news. He would not be disappointed.

Harlaw dropped to one knee, bowing his head. 'My apologies. I made the offer as best I could. It was not well received.'

There was a pause. Harlaw wondered if this would be the news to finally spark Stellan's ire but the king merely said, 'Stand, my friend.'

Harlaw rose to his feet, looking at the king's impassive face. It seemed he was unmoved by the news. More than likely he had simply been anticipating the worst.

'So, it is war?' asked the King.

'Ozric and Banedon know we want peace. They will naturally assume we are weak and seeking amnesty because of it. We will prove them wrong. And quickly.'

'How?' Stellan asked.

'Our troops are battle-fatigued, but the right offensive in the right place will make Canbria at least appear a force still to be reckoned with. I have already made plans for our next attack.'

'Then make it so, Duke Harlaw.' Stellan clamped a hand on his shoulder.

'You would trust me with this after I have so recently failed you, my liege?'

This time Stellan's smile remained on his face. 'You took it upon yourself to perform an impossible task, my friend, and yet you still carried it out as best you could. Of course I trust you, Harlaw. You were my father's man, and now you are mine, are you not?'

Harlaw bowed his head. 'Now and forever, my liege.'

'Good,' said the king. 'Because we have a battle to plan.'

II

As Harlaw rode through Ravensbrooke, past the hedgerows and rolling hills, he could only feel a certain sense of guilt at how untouched it was by the vagaries of war. This place was an oasis among the carnage. But that was none of his doing. Harlaw didn't choose the battlefields of the War of Three Crowns. He could only fight on them.

And fight on them he had.

The past year had been the hardest of his life. He had seen many victories but suffered nearly as many losses. It had been a year of slaughter, and for what? Another stalemate. The three kings at an impasse once more. For all his guilt that his own lands had been spared from the war, Harlaw knew he had more than earned this brief respite from the long campaign.

He and his men rode into the grounds of Ravensbrooke manor and the old statues greeted them with their proud indifference. Harlaw jumped down from his steed, a smile crossing his face as Donal and the stable boy came rushing out to greet him.

'It is good to see you, my lord,' Donal said, taking the reins. The stable boy stood, eyes down, wringing his skullcap in his fists. Harlaw made a mental note to learn his name at some point.

'It's good to be back, Donal. Is the duchess inside?'

The old man nodded. 'She is, my lord,' he replied. Donal fidgeted, clearly uncomfortable that she had not come out to greet Harlaw on his return home, but it wasn't necessary. Selene had made her feelings clear long before now. Her disdain for him was Harlaw's fault and no one else's.

'Well, draw me a bath and make sure the men are taken care of. It's been a long ride.'

'The maids are already boiling the water, my lord.'

Harlaw squeezed Donal's shoulder in gratitude. Of course they were; the old man had seen to Harlaw's needs for thirty years. He knew what his duke needed even before it was asked.

Harlaw walked the empty corridors to his chamber, the familiarity of the place doing little to raise his spirits. A bath was already waiting, and Harlaw wasted no time in stripping off his road-battered attire and slipping into it. The warm water relieved the aching in his body but his mind was still alive with recent memories of what he and his knights had suffered. For every hard-won victory there had been a defeat lurking in wait. Every report of enemy casualties came with news of his own losses. Friends and allies he had made now gone. It reminded Harlaw that with every new battle he was more alone than the last.

When he was washed and dried Donal came, asking if he

should organise a welcome feast for him and his men. Harlaw thought on it for a moment. It would do his men good, but there were more pressing matters.

'I will dine alone with the duchess tonight,' he replied.

Donal nodded, dutifully heading off to arrange the dining hall and pass on the news to Selene. He could imagine her shrewish response, and he felt somewhat sorry for Donal taking the brunt of her ire, but she would not refuse. She never refused a request from her duke, though she would make her displeasure clear for all to know it.

Harlaw dressed in his finery. Blue doublet embroidered in red, black boots polished to a mirror sheen. He even trimmed the silver beard that had grown into a mass of tangles over the past weeks. The figure who stared back at him from the mirror looked every part the noble duke, though he felt like a battle-weary old man.

Then he waited. Dinner would be served at sundown but Harlaw stayed in his candlelit room for as long as he could before making his way to the dining hall. It was the same game every time – who would keep the other waiting the longest? He wasn't surprised to find he had lost again. Selene was nowhere in sight, but he took his seat at the head of the table regardless.

A fire roared in the hearth, the only life to fill the room. It should have been filled with Harlaw's heirs, should have been echoing with conversation and laughter, but this was the life he had whittled out for himself and now he was forced to live it – a hollow carving indeed.

Donal entered, leading servants who carried trays of

quail and trout, spiced eggs and roasted beets. It was fare fit for nobility, but the feast only added to Harlaw's guilt. These were lean times and here he was living like a king. He would be sure the servants dined well on leftovers tonight.

Harlaw sat and waited while the food went cold. He stared at the fire, the crackling of wood the only conversation, before the door to the chamber opened and she walked in.

Selene did not look at him as she sat, treating him as though he didn't even exist. Still she took his breath away as she had the first time he laid eyes on her. A marriage of convenience they had called it. A union of two duchies to rival any in Canbria. If only they had known the way he really felt. If only they had seen into Harlaw's heart at how much he loved this woman. But he had known from the beginning that his affection would never be reciprocated, and so he had chosen to hide it. Her eventual betrayal had been inevitable.

They both sat in the dark room, fire blazing, food left untouched. Harlaw had not seen his wife for months yet there was still no notion of a greeting. But what did he expect? It had been years since he had ordered the death of her lover. Few knew that Harlaw suffered as much pain as she did over that. Josten Cade had been his friend. A man he trusted with his life. A man he trusted to take care of his bride. Josten had taken that duty far too literally.

'You have been well?' Harlaw asked, finally sick of the silence.

Selene turned her gaze to the fire as though she had not heard him. Harlaw cursed himself for being the first to surrender to the discomfort, and her silence cut him to the core. Nevertheless, he persevered, for what other choice did he have now?

'It was a hard winter. I trust you were not troubled too much by the cold?'

She wasn't troubled by the cold. More likely the cold was troubled by *her*.

Selene continued to stare into the fire. It seemed to ignite the green of her eyes and Harlaw noticed how she wore no jewels. It was as though she were in mourning...

Josten Cade was not dead. He had murdered one of Harlaw's most trusted knights and fled into the dark. He had carved out a name for himself in the mercenary companies fighting in Arethusa. Very much alive by all accounts, but as far as Selene was concerned he was dead and buried.

'I haven't seen that dress before.' His tedious attempts at conversation were starting to sound pathetic, but Harlaw had always been a stubborn man. 'Where did you—'

'The king is visiting with us tomorrow,' Selene said before he could bore either of them further.

'Stellan? Here? But why?'

Selene averted her gaze back to the fire. If she knew the reason she was in no mood to tell, and Harlaw was in no mood to beg. He would learn soon enough.

Donal led his servants back into the dining hall to clear their untouched plates. Suddenly all Harlaw's appetite had fled him. Before he could at least offer his wife some wine, she stood. Harlaw stood too, and she paused, turning to him.

'Goodbye, Ermund,' she said, before leaving him alone by the fire.

He had always hated that name and she knew it. She used it like a barb to prick him with whenever she pleased.

Harlaw stared at the wine on the table, and it tried to entice him just as Selene used to. It had been a long time since he'd drunk anything more than boiled water, but with the prospect of a visit from his king it wouldn't do to indulge now. With nothing to keep him, he returned to his chamber and slept.

The sound of horses' hooves in the courtyard woke Harlaw from a deep sleep. He swung his legs from his bed, feeling every ache in his back and neck. As he stood, there was pain in his knees and ankles from months of battle manoeuvres. Another reminder that he was not getting any younger.

From the window of his chamber he saw men in red livery being greeted by Donal. Stellan was among them, his armour making him seem more regal than ever. He must have set off from Northold in the dead of night to arrive at Ravensbrooke so early.

Harlaw had no time to don his armour of office. It would not do to keep his king waiting. With difficulty he pulled on the clothes he had worn the night before and made his way down to greet the new arrivals.

Stellan was already waiting in the main hall, knights in red and gold surrounding him. Harlaw thought it curious that he should come so closely guarded.

'My liege,' said Harlaw, bowing as low as his stiff back would allow.

'Duke Harlaw. It is good to see you well.'

Harlaw stood, trying not to look puzzled. Stellan had seen him not more than a tenday earlier in Northold.

'What brings you to Ravensbrooke?' Harlaw asked.

'Walk with me,' the king said.

Harlaw obeyed, following his king's huge frame from the entrance hall of the manor and out into the gardens. Stellan's knights followed closely, and for an instant Harlaw wondered where his own men were. It was a fleeting thought, but one that lingered in the back of his head.

'You have served me well these past months,' said the king.

'As I served your father before you,' Harlaw replied. 'It is both a duty and an honour, my liege.'

Stellan nodded. 'I know. That is why this is so difficult.' He looked out to the fields surrounding the manor. 'I'm sorry, my friend, but I require your wife.'

Harlaw stopped walking, suddenly ever more conscious of the nearness of the king's bodyguard.

'I– I don't understand,' said Harlaw.

'Selene's family controls two duchies. With the loss of Queen Eurelia I need a new union to reinforce my hold on the crown.'

Harlaw could barely comprehend what the king was saying. His manner was as though he'd just announced he was buying a horse at market.

'My liege… she is my wife.' Harlaw could think of nothing better to say.

Stellan shook his head. 'The marriage has already been declared invalid. I have the letters of annulment. You have no heirs, there is no evidence of consummation. The legal writs were simple enough to obtain.'

'I have signed no such—'

'Yes, you have,' said the king. He was staring right at Harlaw now, his matter-of-fact manner gone, replaced with one of steely determination. 'You have also rescinded your rights to the Duchy of Ravensbrooke and bequeathed your holdings to me.'

Harlaw bristled, but in his periphery Stellan's guard had their hands on their weapons.

'This will not stand,' Harlaw said, his mind focused now as he tried to contain his temper. 'The knights of Ravensbrooke—'

'Are now mine,' said Stellan. 'Look around, Harlaw. Do you see them here? The knights of Ravensbrooke are now bannermen of the crown. Don't make this any more difficult than it needs to be. You have your life, I owe you that much. Take a horse, ride north, or wherever you wish. A resourceful man like you will make his mark somewhere.'

Harlaw looked out at the knights arrayed against him. He had no weapon. He had no men. No allies. His home loomed large against the morning sky but it was his no longer. Was Selene watching him from somewhere within? He could only hope she was satisfied with her vengeance.

'Why not just kill me?' he asked.

'Harlaw, my friend,' said the king, a wide smile crossing his face. 'You have been a loyal servant. And I am no monster. Consider this a gift. No more fighting. No longer having to share your bed with a woman who hates you. What better reward could I give a man who has served me so faithfully?'

The king was almost convincing. If Stellan truly considered Harlaw a friend, he could only wonder how he must treat his enemies.

With little choice, Harlaw made his way back to the manor to pack for the road. He was sure it would be a long one.

III

HARLAW ran his fingers through a tangle of white beard. His horse, Mestilus, needed rest and water, but there was nothing that passed for an inn for miles as far as he could see. He had ridden hard to clear the Canbrian border, but even though he was deep within the Arethusan countryside he still didn't feel safe.

What was it Stellan had said? He was no monster? There was no way Harlaw could rely on that being true. A king who would so easily betray one of his loyal followers could just as easily change his mind on a whim. Mercy could turn into murder quicker than Harlaw could pack his bags.

Harlaw could not dwell on the vagaries of kings. He had to work out what to do, and fast. As he skirted a thick wood the rain started to pour, hard and straight, soaking him through. He would have thought it yet another sign of his poor luck had he not immediately seen an inn up ahead.

It was a sorry building, but intact at least. He could only hope it would be dry enough inside. After tying Mestilus beneath an awning, he entered and was hit by the welcome smell of wood smoke and ale. Harlaw began to feel a little relief from his worries. At least he had enough coin for bed and board for the night, best worry on the gods being set against him later.

A few coppers and he found a warm place by the fire, a stable boy taking care of Mestilus, and a bed awaiting him when he was ready. Memories of the hard road fled as he ate a hearty broth, and he even accepted the offer of ale. What did it matter now if he drank? What else could the fates do to him if he was in his cups?

Someone took a chair at his table.

Harlaw realised he'd never have time to pull the blade at his side if whoever it was decided to stick a knife in his throat. As he looked up at the newcomer and her smiling face, he still had no idea if that was exactly what she'd do.

'You're either very brave or very stupid coming in here,' said Maud Levar. She raised a hand and scratched at the stubble covering one of her head tattoos.

'Where would you suggest I go?' Harlaw replied. 'Stellan has—'

'I heard,' said Maud. 'And after all you did for him too. That betrayal must have stung like a bastard.'

It did sting. More than Harlaw would ever admit. 'So you know I've got little choice about where I go and who I fight for.'

'Who you fight for? Are you thinking of pledging your blade to another king? Or joining one of the companies? Because I doubt either option would be a good one.'

'And why is that?'

Maud shook her head. 'You've really got no idea the trouble

you've caused, have you, Harlaw? Ozric wants you dead after you led Stellan's forces to so many victories against him.'

'I would have thought that's the perfect reason for him to accept my allegiance.'

'Know your enemy, Harlaw. Ozric is as treacherous as Stellan. And twice as vengeful. He'd rather see you hung from his city gates than leading his armies. Banedon is much the same, only more vicious. With all three kings after your blood that makes you poison for any mercenary company.'

Harlaw suddenly felt his troubles worsen. He glanced behind Maud and saw men waiting casually in the background. Clearly she wasn't here alone.

'And what about you?' he asked.

'Same goes for me. If Ozric even knew I was talking to you there's every chance he would end our contract and have me branded a traitor. I'd love to have a man like you in my company, Harlaw, but mercenaries only trust their own. You're no mercenary. You're a duke. And one with a big fucking target on his back.'

'I'm a duke no longer,' Harlaw said. 'And I hold no loyalty to anyone.'

'And there's your problem. You no longer have friends in the Suderfeld. It's widely known you wanted an end to this war. What was it you said? *There will be no unity while three kings rule.* And for that, everyone wants you gone.'

'Everyone?' Harlaw said. 'Does that go for you too, Maud?' His hand was already brushing the pommel of his blade. Maud was here mob handed but he'd be damned if he went down without a fight.

'Relax, Harlaw, you're in no danger from me. There's no bounty on you... yet. What would be the point in killing you now? Besides, we've known each other years. Not all mercenaries are as treacherous as you think.'

Her words didn't ease the tension. 'So what would you do, if you were me?'

'If I were you, I'd get on that big white stallion and ride north. And I wouldn't stop until the Suderfeld border was ten leagues behind me.'

Harlaw knew it was an opportunity that wouldn't come twice. 'Thanks for the advice,' he said, rising to his feet. He picked up his saddlebags and turned towards the door.

Half a dozen of Maud's men stood in the shadowy recesses of the room. No wonder she had been so relaxed. With his hand still teasing the pommel of his sword, Harlaw made for the door. No one tried to stop him as he left the inn, and outside he was relieved to see the rain had stopped.

The stable boy was quick saddling Mestilus, and Harlaw was quicker securing his bags and climbing atop the horse's back. With a silent thanks to Maud Levar for her mercy, he put heels to flanks and took the long road north.

The walk was hard. He had never known land like this – dry arid scrub, fit for neither man nor beast. No wonder the Cordral Extent was such a lawless place of disparate territories lacking any cohesion. How could one city hold sway in a wasteland like this, let alone a city that had lost its king? Whoever ended up ruling the vast city of Kantor now its king was dead had an unenviable task on their hands.

He had passed a town some miles back. More outpost than vibrant community, with vendors selling their scant wares under the oppressive heat of day. It was there he had been forced to bid goodbye to Mestilus; sold to a trader for a few supplies. It had hurt Harlaw more than he thought, more than losing Selene if truth be told. At least that horse had been faithful to him. And in return he had sold the stallion to some desert nomad who would probably slaughter the beast for meat.

For all his growing disdain of this country, it did not slow Harlaw. He had nowhere else to go now, no allies to turn to. Across the Ebon Sea were savage lands that would consume a man whole. Further north the Ramadi was little better and the Shengen Empire to the east would accept no foreigners into its lands. This was his last chance. One chance.

The road he walked led to Kantor – a city ruled by a regent queen, her son too young to take the crown. Harlaw saw his opportunity. She would need warriors around her. Loyal men she could trust. If Harlaw could persuade her he was such a man, then perhaps he could find some type of redemption here. Perhaps he could be the nobleman he used to be.

The more Harlaw trod the road north the flatter and more arid the landscape became. In this endless barren country he missed the rolling hills of the Suderfeld. Even riven by war the homeland he remembered was a more welcoming place than this. It was with relief that he spied another outpost on the road ahead, and he drank the rest of his dwindling water as he quickened his pace to reach it.

At the edge of the outpost he could hear orders being barked. His heart began to beat that much faster. Perhaps this was a military outpost – a way for him to begin his journey to Kantor could lie amongst the ranks of the Cordral militia.

He made his way past the domed buildings and came out onto a central square. The stench of sewage and rotting meat hit his nostrils, but he put that out of his mind as he saw a group of men at the centre of the main square. They were being watched with some amusement by a gathered crowd, and for a moment Harlaw stood among them and viewed the spectacle. It didn't take him long to realise what had caused their mirth.

'Straight fucking rows,' bellowed a beleaguered militia officer, his accent thick, reminding Harlaw he was a stranger in this foreign land. The men were arrayed before the officer in two rough ranks but they seemed little used to the ministration of a military man. Each wore civilian dress and carried a makeshift weapon like a pitchfork or a farmer's hoe, but there was not a real blade among them.

'Can not one of you stand in a straight line?' shouted the officer. 'If you want to join the Great Eastern Militia, you'll have to use your fucking heads. What kind of bloody recruits are you?'

Harlaw could see they were the shit kind. Old men and naïve boys. Where all the fighting men were, he had no idea. As he continued to watch, his own dismay grew to match that of the recruitment officer, and before he could stop himself he stepped forward.

'You're looking for recruits?' he said, conscious that all eyes were suddenly on him. 'I have experience.'

The officer regarded him with an imperious expression. 'Step back, southlander. I have enough old men already.'

'And yet you have no fighters.'

The officer looked Harlaw up and down, perhaps sensing he was not quite the old man he first thought.

'So you can fight, southlander?'

'Better than anyone here,' Harlaw replied.

'Really?' The officer looked unconvinced. 'Itzhak!' he bellowed.

From the crowd came another militiaman, this one wearing a uniform that was stretched over bulging muscle. His black hair was shorn close to his scalp and Harlaw couldn't quite tell where his neck stopped and his shoulders began.

'Let's see just how good you are,' said the officer.

Itzhak was already drawing a blade that looked more like a short sword in his meaty fist. In response, Harlaw undid his own sword belt, but kept his blade sheathed as he waited for the brute to advance.

As Itzhak swung his first lumbering blow, Harlaw just had time to think how unfair it was he had to fight when the rest of the recruits stood around failing at drill. He stepped to the side, allowing Itzhak's sword to swoop by before slapping his sheathed blade across the back of the man's head. It made a hollow crack, and Itzhak staggered forward. He rubbed the back of his head, confusion turning to annoyance before he lumbered in again. This time Harlaw dodged the blow then slapped the scabbard across Itzhak's rump. It only served to enrage the giant further as the crowd laughed at his misfortune.

The militiaman growled, waving his sword around like it was on fire. Harlaw planted his feet, grasping the scabbard and sliding his sword free. With a downward swipe he disarmed his opponent, bringing the tip of the blade back up to hover in front of the brute's throat. It stopped Itzhak in his tracks and he held up both his meaty hands in surrender.

Harlaw looked over at the officer. 'Good enough?' he asked.

'Good enough for me,' the officer said. 'Welcome to the Great Eastern Militia.'

Harlaw sheathed his blade, forgetting the defeated Itzhak and moving closer to the officer so they might conduct their conversation out of earshot of the crowd.

'That's a fine offer,' he said. 'But I was hoping to reach Kantor and offer my services to its queen.'

The officer barked a laugh. 'Kantor? They will entertain no foreign mercenaries there. The city is in lockdown after the death of the king. Egil Sun holds sway now. Go there and you're as likely to be hung as a foreign spy as given a place in the Desert Blades.'

Harlaw considered the man's words. He could very well believe the city was closed to foreigners. These were trying times in the Cordral as well as the Suderfeld. Add to that the fact that the bag on his shoulder felt light on supplies and he was thirsty as a man lost in the desert.

'The Great Eastern Militia it is then,' he said.

The officer gave him a beaming grin. 'Good man. What's the name?'

Harlaw thought on it for a moment. 'Ermund,' he said finally. He'd never liked his given name, but it seemed apt he use it now.

'All right, Ermund. Feel free to join the rest of the recruits.'

Harlaw looked at the motley group before him. It was hardly the royal guard he had hoped for, but what choice did he have? He had indeed fallen low, but perhaps there might still be some way for him to rise through the ranks and regain some of what he had lost.

Fastening the sword belt around his waist once more, Harlaw stepped forward to stand beside his new countrymen.

17

SUDERFELD dungeon cells were pretty much like any other, apart from a strange stink Ctenka couldn't identify. It was in between damp, rot and fresh straw, and he was hard pressed to work out if he liked it or not. Weird, he knew, but hardly the weirdest thing about this whole situation.

Ermund sat across from him in silence. At some points Ctenka had been tempted to call horseshit on the whole sorry tale, but there had always been something noble and aloof about the man. The fact he was a duke explained everything. His story had to be true. Why else would they have been imprisoned down here in the dark with their hands chained behind them?

'I hope you're happy now,' said Ctenka. He knew it wasn't a helpful thing to say but he was too angry to hold it in.

Ermund regarded him with a look of genuine regret. 'You know I'm not. If I'd thought this was going to happen I would never have brought you into it.'

'Oh, well I suppose that's all right then. That will come as great solace when my head's stuck on a spike on some southern fucking castle.'

'Don't lose hope,' said Ermund. 'We're not dead yet.'

He looked completely relaxed, which only made Ctenka even angrier. It was as though getting locked in foreign dungeons happened to him all the time. Perhaps it was a Suderfeld tradition. Perhaps they spent most of their time locked up in each other's fucking castles.

'Not dead yet?' Ctenka spat. 'You brought us to meet a man who stole your wife and took your lands. What did you think he was going to do? Welcome you back with open arms?'

'We needed his help. Now the war is over I thought—'

'You thought? You fucking thought? We're going to die, Ermund. We should never have come here.'

That much was obvious, made even more plain when the door to their dungeon cell was thrown open. A crowd of men in red, golden lions emblazoned on their chests, burst in. They were shouting obscenities as they grabbed Ctenka by the throat, lifting him to his feet, telling him what a horrible little cunt he was and what horrible things they were going to do to him.

Amid the cacophony of violence, Ctenka forgot where he was and who he was with. All he could hear was shouting. All he could feel were mailed hands pulling at his clothes and hair as he was dragged out of the cell and along a dank corridor. His feet barely touched the ground as he was pulled up a narrow flight of stairs and through an outbuilding. He just had time to look up and see they were being brought out into a courtyard, scaffold in its midst, two nooses up on a gibbet, before he was consumed in a melee once again.

The pair of them were dragged out before the scaffold

and driven to their knees. Ctenka stared up at the gallows, all the fight in him fled. There was sudden silence, no noise but the birds chirruping from the rooftops, an audience for the execution.

From beneath a nearby archway came the woman Ermund had talked about, the one that had seen them arrested back at the inn. Selene, his wife, though Ctenka supposed she was the queen now. Every last inch of her spoke power and authority. It wasn't just the way she looked either. She walked with an air of grace Ctenka had never seen before. For all Ermund's stout nobility, Ctenka couldn't imagine how he, or any other man, would think this woman could be theirs. Not even a king could hope to own this woman as their wife. She was an empress.

'Selene,' Ermund said as she drew nearer. 'This is nothing to do with the boy. Let him go.'

She stopped, gazing down at Ermund like a cat about to pounce.

'So typical of you,' she replied. 'Noble to the end.'

'Does Stellan know I'm here? I must speak with him. There is danger coming, I must speak to the king.'

'He knows you're here, Ermund. He just doesn't care. You were given every chance to escape this place, but still you returned. Surely you knew what would await you?'

'The Suderfeld is in danger, Selene. You must let me speak to the king. Don't let your bitterness lead to the ruin of this land.'

There was a flash of anger in Selene's deep green eyes for a moment, before she wrested back control.

'Bitterness, Ermund?' A smile crept up one side of her perfect lips. 'You think I still care enough about you to be bitter? You're nothing to me. You never were.'

'Then let me speak to him. For the sake of the Suderfeld I must entreat his aid. An army is coming—'

'From beyond the Crooked Jaw,' she said. 'Yes, we know.'

That was enough to silence Ermund for a moment. 'You know? Then you know we must raise an army and ride east before it's too late.'

That made her laugh, the sound tinkling through the open courtyard. It almost made Ctenka forget he was about to be hung by the neck until fucked.

'We need no army, Ermund. There is nothing for us to fear from the Iron Tusk.'

Ermund shook his head. 'How do you know all this?'

'Much has changed in the Suderfeld since you left. The War of Three Crowns is over. We are a country united once more. There is a power here that you cannot begin to comprehend.'

'But what—'

'Would that we had the time, Ermund. But I wasted enough years on you. I don't owe you anything. You should never have come back here.'

With a wave of her hand two men grabbed Ctenka and dragged him towards the stairs. This was it; he'd been saved from death at the hands of lowly bandits and murderous priestesses just to be strung up by royalty. It was little comfort as he struggled in vain against the two knights.

'Wait!' Ctenka shouted. 'Your Majesty, I am just an envoy from the Cordral.' He tried nodding towards Ermund in a last desperate attempt to save himself. 'I don't even know that man.'

As his foot hit the first step of the scaffold he realised how stupid he must have sounded, since his and Ermund's uniforms were identical. It didn't matter anyway, they ignored his pleas and he was unceremoniously bundled up to the gallows, where a rope was affixed around his neck. One of the knights pulled it tight and Ctenka was forced up, as a stool was placed beneath his feet. A firm kick and he'd be left dangling like a marionette.

This was it. This was how he'd die. The story of Ctenka Sunatra, left hanging at the end of a rope in a Suderfeld palace. This was definitely not how he'd wanted to go out.

From the corner of his eye, Ctenka saw someone new enter the courtyard. He tried to shift his head to get a better view but he was so afraid of slipping from the stool he could barely get a sense of who it was. The knights noticed the newcomer too, and paused as though awaiting permission.

'Wait.' The voice was calm, and Ctenka watched as a slim man with a crooked nose came into view. By his side was a little boy, head shaved, watching proceedings with a blank stare.

'What do you mean, wait?' said Selene. 'Do you know who this is?' She gestured to Ermund, still kneeling on the ground.

'Of course I do,' said the man. 'I've been waiting for him to arrive.' He glanced up at Ctenka. 'Don't know you, though.'

Ctenka tried to put on his best smile but it was impossible with the noose so tight around his throat. 'Ctenka Sunatra,' he tried to say, but it came out as more of a strangled croak.

'Someone take him down,' said the man. 'There'll be no need for executions today.'

Selene took a step forward, all her composure gone now. She looked furious. 'These men are—'

'And remove those chains, they won't be necessary.'

The knights ignored Selene, and did as they were ordered. Two of them loosened the rope at Ctenka's neck and gently lowered him from the gallows.

When they were both unchained, the man waved off the knights. 'You can leave now.'

They obeyed him, but Selene remained, her ire only growing. 'This is not—'

'Anything to concern yourself with,' the man interrupted. 'I'm sure there must be other business for you to attend to?'

Selene glared at him, then glanced down at the child that accompanied him. All the fight seemed to leave her, and she stormed from the courtyard. Ermund watched her every step before she was out of sight.

'Gentlemen, my apologies. I wasn't notified of your arrival.'

There was a moment of silence before Ctenka realised it was their turn to speak.

'No apology necessary,' he said, despite having almost been hung like fresh game. 'I am Ctenka Sunatra.' He gestured to Ermund. 'And this is—'

'This is the former Duke Harlaw of Ravensbrooke. But it looks like you've now found gainful employment in the Cordral.' He glanced down at Ermund's weathered uniform.

'I have,' said Ermund. 'I'm glad you recognised me before we were hung for common criminals.'

'Who wouldn't recognise a man of such esteem? Well—'

198

he looked Ermund's dishevelled form up and down, '—former esteem.'

'I don't mean to sound rude,' said Ctenka, fast running out of patience, 'but who are you?'

The man smiled, placing a hand gently on the child's head. 'I am Randal Weirwulf. And I run things around here.'

'You?' said Ermund, the disbelief plain in his voice. 'This is Northold. King Stellan rules here. What do you mean, you run things?'

'Well,' said Randal, turning to take a stroll. 'That's a long story...'

Ermund stepped after him. 'Any chance of you telling it?'

'Every chance,' Randal replied.

Ctenka followed right behind. He would be damned if he'd miss this tale.

RANDAL

I

THE graveyard was empty but for an old dead tree standing mangled and rotten in one corner. A crow cawed somewhere at the grey sky, most likely complaining about the cold, wet air. Randal stood silently as the priest anointed the covered grave, invoking the names of the gods – Aethel, Urien, Juthwara and the rest. They were names Randal had forgotten, but then he had long since stopped believing in the old gods. He knew better than anyone that there were new gods abroad. Vengeful malevolent gods that had been newly awoken from their slumber. His journey north had taught him that, if nothing else.

It had been a lesson hard in the teaching, though. One that had almost killed him, and when he returned he found his mother was already dead. How she must have called for him from her sick bed in those final days. Her only son, gone, and she had no idea whether he was dead or alive. How it must have tortured her until her final breath.

And all because of Livia Harrow.

That girl had led Randal on a merry dance north. And

of course he had followed. Once he had the bit between his teeth there was never any stopping him. It had almost killed him, and even now he couldn't quite believe how he had survived the journey home across hundreds of miles of desert. But Randal had made it. And what had been his reward? Gothelm had admonished him for his failure, humiliating Randal in front of his court. After everything he had done for that bastard. Every trial suffered and he had been treated like an errant child.

The priest had finished now, and they both stood in silence over an old woman's grave. What would she have thought of him if she knew the deeds he had performed in the name of Duke Gothelm? He had slit Ben Harrow's throat in that duty. Randal could only imagine what his mother would have called him for that. Monster, perhaps?

Randal was sure there were worse words. And now his mother was dead she'd never know what lengths he had gone to to keep this realm safe. But what could he do to protect it now the gods had returned? He had seen Innellan rise in the north. Had felt how much power she wielded over the hearts and minds of those beneath her gaze. No mortal could hope to rival that. This realm was powerless, its folk little more than livestock awaiting slaughter. There was no way Randal could have ever made Gothelm understand that, and so he had not even tried.

'I am sorry for your loss,' said the priest, as a none-too-subtle hint that his work was done. Randal deposited a piece of silver in the priest's hand and turned to where his horse was tied up outside the graveyard. There he saw a rider was waiting for him, one Randal didn't recognise.

'Waiting for me?' he said as he drew nearer.

'I am,' said the rider, tipping the front of his brimmed hat. 'Gothelm sends his condolences.'

'That's kind of him,' said Randal. 'What does he really want?'

The rider smirked. Gothelm couldn't have cared two shits for Randal's loss.

'He wants to see you. Now.'

'Of course he does,' said Randal, climbing atop his horse. 'Then I suppose you'd best lead the way.'

The pair rode east along the well-trodden path. The Canbrian countryside looked bleak in autumn, but compared to where Randal had recently been it was like some kind of paradise. Randal almost relished the damp that seeped through his cloak. The oppressive desert heat had nearly killed him, and he found himself looking forward to the wet southern winter.

'Any idea what this is about?' asked Randal as they rode.

The messenger shrugged beneath his riding cloak. 'Your guess is as good as mine. But Gothelm was keen you were to visit with him immediately. You know what he's like – all bluster and no patience.'

Randal could attest to that. Gothelm could be like a spoiled child, albeit a particularly cruel and sadistic one, when it took his fancy. But he was duke of the province. And Randal his tallyman, bound to carry out his bidding, whatever that might be. Better to be servant to a cruel master than his enemy.

The rain was coming down in a fine spray as they reached Gothelm's castle. It was a much-feared stronghold. The depravity that was rumoured to go on within its walls had given the place a grim reputation. As Randal rode into the bailey all he could think was how much it looked like any other castle in Canbria – brick walls, merlons, portcullis. There was nothing demonic about this place or the man who owned it. Randal had experienced the demonic, and in comparison Gothelm's proclivity for cruelty was child's play.

Once inside, Randal was led to the main hall. Gothelm had a throne built at one end, all stone and iron, to rival that of King Stellan himself. Randal could only think how pathetic the fat sot looked, sitting there like a pig on a bench.

To Gothelm's left stood another tallyman, one Randal recognised. Bertrand was younger than Randal, but much more ambitious. Their paths had seldom crossed, but the younger tallyman had already built quite the reputation, in a very different way to Randal. He used his position to curry favour with men of influence all across the duchy and he approached his duties with a much lighter tread than many of his more zealous peers.

'Randal, you're late,' said Gothelm, as the tallyman entered.

'Apologies, my lord. I had other business to attend to.'

Gothelm didn't ask what, so he'd either forgotten or didn't care about Randal's mother. It came as no surprise.

Randal stopped some feet before the throne. He didn't know whether to kneel or simply bow. He decided on neither. Again, Gothelm didn't seem to notice.

'I have a job for you,' said the duke. 'Let's consider it a chance for you to redeem yourself.' Randal bristled at the suggestion he had done any wrong in Gothelm's service but he stayed silent. 'Bertrand here has discovered something to the east of the province. Strange goings on in Murhair County. Children dabbling in witchcraft or some such. I want you to find out what's going on.'

Randal looked at the face of the tallyman standing beside the duke. One of those faces it would have been satisfying to smash with a bat.

'And why can't Bertrand investigate this by himself?' Randal asked.

'I thought this a task perfectly suited to your individual talents, Randal,' Gothelm said.

Again, Randal resented the suggestion. Orphaned children and witchcraft. It was clear Bertrand didn't have the stomach for the execution of children. But Randal...

'Very well, my lord,' he said. 'I will investigate immediately.'

'Good,' Gothelm replied. 'And try to make it clean this time.'

Randal bowed. The thought of old dead Ben Harrow flashed into his mind and it stung him sharper than it ought to have.

'I will, my lord. Cleaner than a priest's conscience.'

The route east to Murhair was more an unused goat path than a road. Randal had taken up the lead with Bertrand close behind. Behind that were more tallymen, four in all, each one a man Randal knew and trusted. Clearly Bertrand thought it was excessive.

'Six of us for an orphanage full of children?' he said as they made their way down a crumbling slope.

Randal shook his head. 'If I've learned one thing, it's never to underestimate your quarry.'

'For children?' Bertrand still didn't seem to get it.

'You were the one who reported the rumours to Gothelm,' Randal said. 'Now you're squeamish about what we might face?'

'No,' Bertrand replied in a tone that suggested every part of him was squeamish about this whole thing. 'I just thought...'

'You thought this would be an easy way to embed yourself in Gothelm's good graces. You thought if there was any dirty work to be done, I would be the one to do it. You thought involving me would keep your hands clean. But here you are. No one keeps their hands clean in this business. Not even you.'

Bertrand stayed silent until he quietly mumbled, 'I was sorry to hear about your loss.'

Randal masked a smile. Clearly he had rattled Bertrand. 'So everyone keeps saying,' was his only reply.

They didn't speak again all the way to Murhair.

The orphanage wasn't what Randal had expected. The building itself was an old temple, a crumbling turret to each of the twelve gods poking up from the dull grey stone like tines on a battered crown. The place was silent, as though its days of reverent worship had never ended.

Randal climbed down from his horse, Bertrand beside him, and together they entered through the front door. Inside were rows of children, each seated on the floor, reciting their letters as a woman at the front pointed to a chalkboard. Nothing sinister about the place, just an ordinary, rural classroom.

On seeing them enter, the woman fell silent, recognising the tallymen who had come to her door.

'Welcome,' she said. Every child turned to look at Randal.

'Please forgive the intrusion. I am Randal Weirwulf. Servant of Duke Gothelm.'

'And I am Lagather Goodwife. Priestess of Maerwynn. What business does Duke Gothelm have at my orphanage?'

'Nothing to alarm yourself with, Mistress Goodwife,' Randal replied. 'Duke Gothelm is merely ensuring those living under his wing are well cared for. Especially those he deems most in need.'

Randal cast his eye over the gathered children, every one of them still staring at him. But no... not every one of them. In the corner were three children sitting in a circle. Each one had a shaved head and they were locked in intense conversation.

'And for that we are grateful,' said the priestess. 'But, as you can see, we are quite content here.'

'I can,' said Randal. 'But I wonder if we might talk in private, Mistress Goodwife?'

She glanced at Bertrand, then at the children under her care, before agreeing to Randal's request.

He and the priestess walked outside. A chill nip of air

hit Randal and he realised how warm and welcoming it had been inside.

'Tell me,' he said, as they both strolled down towards a narrow river that ran past the temple. 'Have you noticed anything strange about any of your children? Anything out of the ordinary?'

'Every one of them is unique in their own way,' the priestess replied.

'I think you know what I mean, Mistress Goodwife,' Randal replied. 'I think you know I'm asking if any of your children have displayed any kind of... gift.'

Lagather thought on his words for a moment. Randal had seen it countless times before. She was weighing up the value of lying to him. In the end everyone told the truth, and fortunately Lagather decided that was her best option.

'Of late... yes,' she said.

'Fear not, Mistress Goodwife. Your children are safe as long as you tell me the truth of what has happened.'

The priestess paused for a moment, her hand grasping tightly to the pendant of Maerwynn she had around her neck. Randal could tell she didn't quite believe him. The reputation of the tallymen was such that no one trusted them, but fear always made people talk.

'Recently, when the children have been at prayer, some of them have shown... signs of communion.'

'Communion?' Randal stopped by the river, the sound of it soothing. 'What do you mean?'

Lagather glanced back towards the temple. 'Some of them are able to perform miracles. As though when they pray to the gods, their prayers are answered.'

'I see,' said Randal. 'And does anyone else know about this? Other than Bertrand, have you told anyone what has happened here?'

'No,' said Lagather. 'No one.' She reached out, taking hold of Randal's sleeve. 'You must understand, these children are under my care. I am duty bound to protect them. No harm can come to them. Please…'

Randal took her hand and removed it from his sleeve. 'Oh, Mistress Goodwife, your children are quite safe.'

He turned back to the temple. His tallymen were already moving down to the riverside. As he passed them he heard the priestess begin to protest, but Randal had long ago learned how to deafen himself to cries for clemency. Mistress Goodwife's struggle was a brief one before the tallymen dragged her into the shallow river and submerged her head beneath its waters.

Bertrand was outside the temple, his eyes wide as the scene unfolded in front of him.

'What now, Weirwulf?' He sounded disgusted, the disdain dripping from his lips. 'We burn this place down with every child still inside?'

Randal was sickened by his cowardice. Bertrand didn't object to what was happening… he was simply too weak to do his own dirty work.

A knife was in Randal's hand and at Bertrand's neck before the little shit could speak further.

'I'll tell you *what now*,' said Randal, close in Bertrand's ear. 'Now we return to Gothelm and tell him there was nothing to report. We tell him these stories of witchcraft were nothing but empty rumour. Do you understand?' Bertrand nodded. 'I hope so. Because if I find out Gothelm has learned anything about this, someone is going to visit your brother in Ankhem. I've heard Meryl is a beautiful girl. It would be a shame if anything happened to your niece's pretty face. Do we understand one another?'

Bertrand nodded.

Randal put away the knife and entered the temple once more. The place was eerily silent. Not something Randal would have expected. Children left unsupervised were rarely quiet for long.

He walked to the front of the classroom, and all eyes were on him once more.

'Children,' he said, a smile on his face. 'Why don't we talk about the gods…?'

II

RANDAL had never thought of himself as paternal. Finding a wife and starting a family had always been something that appealed to other men. It came as a surprise that he then found himself spending longer at the orphanage than he would have previously thought healthy.

The children were receptive, obedient and, after he had evaded their questions about Mistress Goodwife's fate, completely beholden to his every word. It was a strange power he held over these youngsters. A distant change from the power he usually held over people, which was derived via threats of violence and torture.

Of course it had taken no time to discover his favourites – five of them in all, each gifted in their own unique way. Bertrand's rumours and Mistress Goodwife's confirmation of their unique gifts had merely scratched the surface of what these children were capable of, and Randal wasted no time in nurturing their potential.

Hestan was the eldest. His hair was shorn to the scalp – the result of a bout of lice he'd had when younger, but now he kept it that way through preference. He was a quiet boy, as they all were, but there was something unnerving about him. Randal hadn't been able to put his finger on just what, until the boy had wanted something from one of the other children and been refused it. With a word and a gesture Hestan had compelled the child to give him the small wooden horse he coveted. The incident fascinated Randal so much he had ordered one of his tallymen to bring him every book he could find on the Crown Sorcerers. It was clear Randal had some studying to do.

Lena and Castiel were twins. They spoke to no one but each other, though it was clear they could understand anything asked of them. They walked around, often holding hands, their heads inclined towards one another. Lena was always cold, shivering in her brother's arms, whereas Castiel could be seen perspiring even when the weather was inclement. The smell from them both was most like rotten turnips, but Randal was willing to put up with that. He hadn't quite worked out the nature of their gifts but he was more than happy to wait. He was sure patience would be its own reward where these children were concerned.

Little Mabel Fogg's gifts were the easiest to spot. She often delighted the other children with her ability to arrange stones and toys without touching them. The other children had no idea what horrors they were witnessing — how just being privy to such witchcraft put them in mortal danger. But Randal had taken on responsibility for his wards. As long as they stayed within the temple he would see that no harm came to any of them. They were his now, and he took his duties as their guardian very seriously.

Youngest of those gifted children was Olivar. Little more than an infant, Olivar spoke in religious tenets, relaying his scripture better than any nursery rhyme. As a result he too had been gifted, but it was a blessing he was far too young to control. His childish tantrums manifested in displays of inhuman strength. Accompanied with an infant's rage it was a truly terrifying display. As a consequence, Randal had ordered the boy locked away. When he understood more, he would be sure to pay special attention to Olivar's development.

These children were all special in their own way, but for now Randal only needed Hestan. The boy was clever, cunning and, above all, loyal. It was as though he instinctively understood what Randal was trying to achieve, which was a miracle in itself, since Randal wasn't sure exactly what that was. For now, ridding himself of unnecessary baggage was his first priority.

'This is madness,' Bertrand said.

Randal looked over at him, standing there shitting his trews like an infant.

'Show some fucking steel for once, will you?' Randal replied. He looked at Hestan beside him, but if the boy understood the curse word he didn't respond. 'Everything will be fine.'

'Will it?' Bertrand asked. 'Because I think it's highly likely they'll cut us to bits.'

They were in the relic of an old church, far away from

prying eyes. Randal had persuaded Bertrand to summon Duke Gothelm and he needed to conduct the meeting somewhere remote. This wasn't going to be pretty.

'If you've done as I said there is nothing to worry about.'

'Of course I've fucking done as you said,' Bertrand snapped.

Of that there was little doubt. If Bertrand was intimidated by Randal and what he could do, then he was downright terrified of the children and their gifts. Bertrand was a coward, but then that had worked out for Randal well enough. Cowards could be trusted as long as they were scared more of you than of anyone else. And Bertrand was more scared of these gifted children than he was of the gods themselves.

The sound of horses' hooves stomping up the muddy path heralded the truth of Bertrand's words. Randal felt his heart beat a little faster at the prospect of what was to come.

There were six of them, each wearing a thick riding cloak, but Randal could still spot Gothelm's bulky frame. When they reached the church the duke threw back his hood, revealing that permanent scowl. His men jumped down from their horses, one of them helping Gothelm heave his ample girth from the saddle.

'Bertrand?' he shouted. 'I've made my away across hill and dale in this infernal shit storm, this had better be worth my while.'

Randal walked out into the open air, Hestan close at his side. Gothelm squinted through the drizzle.

'Weirwulf? What in Osred's name are you doing here? Where's Bertrand?'

Randal could hear Bertrand shuffling in the church behind him, but it was obvious he had no intention of showing himself.

'My lord,' Randal said. 'I apologise for the inconvenience, but it was important we meet... in private.'

'What are you bloody talking about, Randal? What is going on?'

Randal looked down at Hestan, who glanced up with that look of bewildered innocence he always bore.

'Remember what we talked about,' Randal said, placing a gentle hand on the stubble of Hestan's head.

The boy nodded, taking a step forward as Gothelm advanced.

'I'm warning you, Weirwulf. If this is some kind of lark I'll—'

One of Gothelm's guards pulled a knife and shoved it into the duke's ribs. Gothelm staggered, unsure of what had just happened, as the armoured knight twisted the blade, grinding the flesh to mincemeat.

Gothelm staggered and fell. One of his other guards shouted in alarm, drawing steel. The one with the knife ran at his fellow and was met with a crashing blow to the skull that floored him.

On the ground, Gothelm was yelling blue murder, hand desperately trying to staunch the gaping wound in his side. As one, every guard had a sword drawn and they went at each other with abandon. One of them screamed, 'What the fuck are you doing?' as he was gutted by someone who had moments ago been a friend and ally. Two others fought viciously, rolling around in the mud, beating one another with mailed fists until their faces were bloody pulp.

Randal watched as they went about it. Men killing one another was nothing new to him but he'd never seen anything so brutal. Not even in the Ramadi fortress of Kessel had the warriors attacked one another with such deadly zeal.

In moments it was over. Four men lay dead. One guard was clawing his way across the ground towards Gothelm, his mouth open in a toothy grin, eyes glazed and focused on the duke.

Randal had seen enough.

He drew his blade and walked through the mud and bodies, planting his sword in the guard's back and skewering him to the ground. Then he turned to Gothelm.

'This is you,' said Gothelm, blood spewing from his mouth, body and hands slick with red as he vainly tried to staunch his wound.

'Not all me,' Randal replied. He knelt down beside Gothelm, taking a strange pleasure in watching him die. 'Just mostly.'

If Gothelm had wanted to spout some last curse he wasn't able, as his eyes rolled back and he slumped in the mud.

Randal took a step back, glancing to Hestan, who returned the look with no emotion. A spatter of blood had flown in the melee and hit the boy in the face but he hadn't seemed to notice.

'Fuck,' whispered Bertrand, choosing now to finally show himself. 'Fuck this. Fuck this.' He stared at the carnage with wide eyes.

'Keep your wits about you, man. Don't tell me you've never seen a dead body before.'

Bertrand looked up at Randal and shook his head.

'That's it. I'm out of this. I can't—'

'You can and you will,' Randal replied, holding his gaze, unblinking, unwavering. 'I need you now more than ever. Gothelm is out of the way. The duchy is left without a duke. Who better than…?' He smiled at Bertrand as though he'd just offered a casket of gold.

'But I can't—'

'If you say those words to me one more time Hestan will force you to pluck out one of your own eyes and eat it.'

Bertrand looked down at the child as though he were a viper about to strike. He seemed to physically diminish, conceding defeat.

'So what now?' he asked.

'Now we proceed as planned,' Randal replied. 'And move on to bigger fish.'

'You can't be serious about this.'

Randal let out a sigh as he realised Bertrand still wasn't able to appreciate the level of ambition at play here.

'Hestan.' He looked down at the boy, all innocence. 'Show Bertrand how serious we are.'

The weather had brightened. Northold was almost a pleasant place to be when the sun was shining.

Randal and Hestan sat in a garden on the outskirts of the city, away from the shit smell of the streets. The birds tweeted incessantly, the sound of them rising above the distant noise of street traders. Randal could understand their irritation. He was as impatient for this to be done as they were.

At one end of the garden, Bertrand came running. He had become so much more compliant in recent days, but then the eyepatch he now wore over the socket of his right eye served as a constant reminder that obedience was not a choice.

'She's coming,' he said.

Randal raised a smile at Bertrand's subservient nature. It made a pleasant change from his previous haughty attitude.

Queen Selene's entrance was heralded by a column of stout bodyguards, armour polished and shining in the sun, halberds pointing proudly to the sky. They formed a rank in front of Randal before making an opening for her to step through.

Randal had to admit, Selene was everything he'd heard of and more. A rare beauty in this grim city. It almost made him wish he more enjoyed the company of the opposite sex, but that had never been Randal's preference.

She regarded him closely, weighing him up. Bertrand had done a good job of piquing her curiosity and for that Randal could only be grateful.

'My lady,' he said, standing and bowing just enough to look respectful, not quite enough to seem fawning.

'Duke Bertrand tells me you have important business with the crown,' she replied. 'I must say, I've never seen him quite so animated in his enthusiasm.'

Randal couldn't stifle a smile at that one.

'Because he knows the importance of this meeting, my lady,' he said. Hestan had come to stand at his side now and Randal rested a hand on the boy's head.

'And what is so important that you would have us meet in this quiet place and not in the palace?'

'Well,' said Randal. 'I have a proposition… one that could see an end to the War of Three Crowns.'

Selene raised an eyebrow and Randal felt a twitch of excitement.

'Really?' she replied. 'Then you had best tell me all about it.'

III

R ANDAL had to admit, those children had made him pious. In the past he'd given no more or less credence to the gods than any other man. He knew the gods' names, he knew their stories and their constellations, and occasionally when he passed a church or temple he would offer a prayer, but he would never have described himself as devout.

After several weeks of looking after the children in his care and observing their daily rituals, he found himself making the sign of the Maiden before he slept, or saying a quick prayer of thanks to the wolf god Vadir at repast.

It was obvious now where the children had gained their powers from, and though Randal knew he would never receive the same benefaction, he observed the gods just as devoutly as they did. He came to see himself as their high priest, ensuring that they followed every rite and ritual, and said every new prayer as keenly as the last.

Randal had hunted down every tome, codex and scroll written on the Crown Sorcerers of old, and pored over every last word. Those texts said little of the connection between a sorcerer's powers and the act of prayer, but Randal could easily read it between the lines.

Some of those ancient mages were deeply spiritual, while others seemed to actively shirk the worship of the gods, even hold it in disdain. But the one thing they all held in common was the fact that they were revered. Though the Crown Sorcerers worked in service to one monarch or another, it was they who were held in awe, not the ancient kings. It was they who were feared and exalted in equal measure. That adoration was channelled to a higher power, and in return they were granted gifts beyond those any mortal should have been bestowed with.

The more Randal read, the more he understood. What he had witnessed in the Ramadi – the god Innellan, her inhuman power – it all had to be linked. The gods had returned, and in exchange for worship they would grant divine powers. Randal realised if he could harness that power before anyone else he would be more influential than any Crown Sorcerer who had ruled the Suderfeld from the shadows of a king's throne.

And so harness it he would.

Randal watched Selene from a dark alcove within the palace of Northold. He had to admire her charm as she spoke to Clydus. The man had arrived with an entire cohort of warriors. Perhaps overcautious of him, but the old rat hadn't lived so long by being reckless. Nevertheless, no number of armoured men could protect him now.

Clydus laughed at something she said; whether it was a joke or a proposition of alliance, Randal couldn't quite hear. Either way it didn't matter. Any offers of a truce made by the queen of Canbria were merely a ruse. Honeyed words to put Clydus at ease before Randal made the final coup de grace.

As they walked through the vast and ancient hall of Northold, surrounded by Clydus' guard, Randal had just about seen enough. Placing his hand on Hestan's head he stepped into the light shed through one of the many stained glass windows that lined the huge room. The guards surrounding Clydus spotted him immediately, hands moving to weapons. To his credit, Clydus seemed unperturbed, but who would not be, surrounded as he was by such a formidable guard?

'Ah, Randal,' Selene said, sensing the sudden tension. 'Clydus, please allow me to introduce—'

'That's enough, I think,' Randal interrupted. 'You may leave us now.'

Selene glared at him. He had undermined her authority on numerous occasions but never in front of such a prominent guest. Randal could tell the wound to her pride would never heal, but what could she do against him? He had already shown her that resistance was pointless.

Her fear won over her pride, and Selene turned and slowly walked away, leaving Clydus looking confused.

'It appears I am missing something?' asked King Ozric's consul. Randal admired his shrewdness. Hopefully this was a man who could be bargained with.

'Not for long,' Randal replied with a grin. 'You see, I'm relying on the fact that we both know about crowns and

221

kings, Clydus. We both know there is always a figurehead, a monarch of the people. And then there are those who play the instruments of politics. Those who make that monarch dance to a dainty tune. I know who makes Ozric dance.' Randal looked directly into the consul's eyes. The side of Clydus' mouth turned up into a smile. The man knew he was found out, but he didn't care. No matter. 'Stellan also loves his music. I play the tunes in this palace.'

'And there was me thinking the songstress was Queen Selene,' Clydus said.

'Modesty prevents me,' Randal replied.

'I'm sure it does. So why am I suddenly so honoured? I would have thought a man in your position would covet his anonymity.'

'Some things must be done in person. And proposing an alliance is a tricky subject I would never presume to leave to an underling.'

'Queen Selene, an underling? My, you are a bold one. So what would be the nature of this alliance?'

'The War of Three Crowns has gone on for long enough. Stellan is the clear candidate to wear the crown of Suderfeld. You will persuade Ozric of the sense in this.'

Clydus cackled a dry and grim laugh that echoed in the open hall. He was the only one who found it funny.

'You're a fool if you think I'm about to give up so easily. I control Eldreth. Ozric dances to my tune and when he wins the War of Three Crowns so will the Suderfeld. You were a fool to reveal yourself, Randal. And fools rarely last long in times of war.'

The consul clicked his fingers. A dozen swords were drawn.

Randal calmly placed his hand on Hestan's head, drumming his fingers across that shaven pate. Immediately every one of Clydus' warriors sheathed his sword, turned around and walked away to the edge of the room as though they had been scolded by their mother.

Clydus glared at them, then at the boy.

It was Randal's turn to smile. 'Alone at last.'

'What is this?' Clydus was trying to appear calm but his voice was taut.

'This is the birth of a new era,' Randal replied. 'The birth of a new power. One I hold in the palm of my hand.' He ruffled the stubble atop Hestan's head.

'So what do you want?' asked Clydus. 'To kill me? To wrest control of the crown for yourself?'

'Nothing so crude. I merely want peace. What form that takes is up to you. King Banedon has already been brought into the fold and made to understand the way of things. Your task is now to persuade King Ozric of the same.'

'Surrender? You think I can make Ozric kneel before Stellan's throne? What am I to do? Tell him I have seen some parlour trick and he should fear a child with… magic? You have overestimated my influence.'

'Come now. We both know that's not true. You have more influence in Eldreth than any man alive. And fear a child? You think this is my only weapon? Clydus, don't force me to give a further demonstration of the power I wield.'

'I– It's just…' Clydus was defeated. Randal could see him trying to work out a way to get out of this. He was wondering if it really was a parlour trick. Trying to come up with some rational explanation for his loyal guard to leave him so exposed. Eventually he accepted there was none.

'Banedon is already making preparations to offer his daughter's hand to Stellan's eldest son,' said Randal. 'But a decision has not been made yet. There is still a chance that Ozric's heir could sit on the throne of a united Suderfeld. He must be persuaded.'

'I will try, but there is no guarantee Ozric will listen. He is determined to be the victor in this war.'

'Then I suggest you try very hard, Clydus.'

The two men stood in silence for an uncomfortable moment, but Randal had said all he needed to say.

Clydus nodded politely and turned to leave. Randal took a certain satisfaction from that nod. It was a small gesture but it shouted his victory as loud as any battle cry.

One by one, Clydus' guards seemed to come to, looking around in a daze before they followed the consul from the great hall.

When they had left, Selene walked back into the light. Of course she had lurked in the shadows, listening in like some trespasser. Randal could hardly blame her for that. In her position he would have done the same.

'This is too much of a risk,' she said.

There it was. Her nerve was giving out, and Randal could understand her fears – she had gone from possessing all the cards to holding nothing but a worthless hand.

'Fear not, milady. Clydus will do his part. And if not...'

Randal didn't have to elucidate on what he and his wards

were capable of. He had already given ample demonstration.

'I just—'

'You just need to do as you're told. Keep the king occupied. That is your job. I hear he's become quite the drunken sot in recent weeks, so it shouldn't be all that difficult for you. Just keep that cup of his filled.'

Anger flashed in Selene's eyes. 'You see that as my job, do you? To be serving wench to that idiot? I'm worth more than that. Why don't you just bewitch him? Have your little demons—'

'Careful,' said Randal, placing a protective arm around Hestan. 'You wouldn't want to upset them.'

She glanced down at the boy as though he were a serpent in Randal's arms, before all defiance leaked away. 'I will do my part,' she said, leaving the chamber as fast as she could.

When Randal fell asleep that night the air had been still, the sky becalmed. As he woke from a troubled slumber, he could hear a storm had whipped up beyond the walls of the temple. It took some moments, as he overcame the fug of sleep, to realise it was not just inclement weather that was raging outside his chamber.

A bang at his door and he was roused fully. Randal stood, pulling on his tunic and opening the door to see Forgrim standing there. His face was troubled; Randal had never seen the stoic tallyman look so worried.

'Milord,' he said, an affectation his men used that Randal hadn't seen fit to dissuade them from. 'You must come quickly.'

Forgrim led the way through the temple. As he made his way down the corridor Randal could hear the sound of raging and banging as though an army were trying to batter its way into the building, screaming and shouting as they came. It took some moments for him to realise it was no adult voice, but a child's.

'Is that Olivar? What has happened? Why is he so distressed?'

Forgrim shook his head. 'I don't know, milord, but it's not Olivar that's the problem.'

Randal found that hard to believe, the way the boy was smashing against his cage like a wild beast, but he followed Forgrim as he led the way to where the rest of the children slept.

His tallyman motioned to the door, the fear plain in his eyes. Forgrim would go no further.

Randal opened the door to the dormitory. Candles flickered in the room, casting peculiar shapes on the walls. The four children knelt in the centre of the room facing each other, hands gripped together so they formed a tight ring. Their heads were cast back to the ceiling, eyes blank white, lips moving in a silent incantation.

Despite his fear, Randal stepped into the room. His presence suddenly broke the spell, and the children ceased their silent prayer, bowing their heads.

'Hestan?' Randal whispered. 'Lena? Castiel? What is it?'

It was Mabel Fogg who was the first of them to look up. Randal was relieved to see her eyes had returned to their usual blue. There was a look of fear on that doleful face.

Randal knelt beside the girl, trying to reassure her with

226

a comforting hand. 'What is it, child?' he asked.

She regarded him with eyes that seemed to have experienced a lifetime of worry. 'They are coming, master,' she said.

'Who?' asked Randal, though he dreaded the answer.

'Our gods,' she replied, as though it were obvious. 'Our gods are coming.'

18

'WHAT a pile of stinking horseshit!' Ctenka said.

Or at least that was what he wanted to say. It was on the tip of his tongue, the words threatening to spill out like puke after a heavy night on the grog, but he managed to keep his mouth shut. It would have been stupid to question Randal, despite how ridiculous he sounded. And not just because he was an unnerving character. More because that boy, Hestan, was the weirdest child Ctenka had ever come across. If there was any chance he possessed the powers Randal claimed, then Ctenka was in no mood to get on his wrong side.

Even now the boy was staring curiously in Ctenka's direction, like he was looking through his soul. He would never admit it, but Ctenka was more scared of that boy than anyone he'd ever met.

Randal might have spared their lives but he was a difficult man to trust. And not just from the story he'd told. There was something about him, a single-minded ruthlessness to his bearing. That much of his tale must have been true.

Randal waited for them to respond, but it was clear neither was too keen to start. If Ermund doubted anything

Randal had said he was in no mood to pick the man up on it. He simply stood there like a guard on parade, refusing to call Randal out on his tall tale. Ctenka supposed it would be down to him.

'How do you know those children weren't just having a nightmare?' he asked. 'They said the gods are coming. That could mean anything.'

Randal placed a hand on Hestan's head. The boy didn't react to the man's touch, continuing to stare right at Ctenka.

'These children have proven themselves to me time and again. I would be foolish to ignore their warnings. More of their ilk are revealing themselves throughout the Suderfeld. Those I can find I take into my care. I would expect there are more throughout the lands of the Cordral and Ramadi. Signs are everywhere that things are changing. If what I witnessed in the Ramadi Wastes wasn't enough to convince me that the gods have returned, I have seen enough since to make me certain.'

'Signs of what?' asked Ctenka. 'Some kind of apocalypse? We only came to warn of a warlord rising in the east. Not the end of life as we know it.'

Randal smiled. It was wry and humourless and looked out of place on his face. 'This is just the beginning,' he replied. 'There is a war brewing beyond this realm. One that is set to spill over into the lands of men and reduce its nations to ruin. It has to be stopped.'

'So you'll help us?' asked Ctenka.

Before Randal could answer, Ermund stepped forward. 'Where is King Stellan?' he demanded.

If Ermund was trying to intimidate, Randal looked unimpressed. If his story was true, he had faced more imposing men than Ermund.

'He is in his palace, no doubt,' Randal replied. 'You shouldn't concern yourself with the king.'

'I must see him.' If Ermund had heard and believed that Hestan could make a man eat his own eyeballs with a thought, he clearly wasn't rattled by it.

'You will find your old friend is much changed, Harlaw. Are you sure you want to walk this road?'

'Take me to Stellan,' Ermund demanded. He didn't look like he was about to ask again.

When Randal said, 'Of course,' Ctenka heaved an audible sigh of relief. As Randal and the boy led the way through the palace grounds, Ctenka leaned in to Ermund.

'Try and keep your head,' he whispered. 'We've just been spared the gallows. Try not to get us killed. This man communes with the gods, for fuck's sake. Why don't you just be nice?'

'You believe his stories of gods and magic, Ctenka?' Ermund replied. 'Then you're a bigger fool than I thought.'

'Firstly, that hurts. Secondly, whether that boy can make a man mad just by looking at him is irrelevant. It's obvious Randal holds the power in this place now. Let's try not to upset him.'

Ermund did not answer. His fists were bunched, his jaw clenched. Ctenka could only hope his friend could keep that temper in check.

As they made their way through the palace Ctenka could

see signs of opulence hidden behind the decay. Intricate tapestries hung limply from the walls and ancient gilded weapons were set in skewed sconces, but rats still lurked in the shadows, leaving their tracks in the dust. If Randal truly controlled the throne of Suderfeld it was clear he paid no mind to the upkeep of its palace.

When they drew close to the throne room, Ctenka could hear the sound of a dull and lifeless tune being played on a lute. Like the rest of this place it could have been rousing, but instead sounded like someone was playing a funeral dirge at their own burial.

Randal and the boy led the way, twisting through the corridors of the palace until they reached the throne room. Ctenka glanced around, expecting at least a cursory bodyguard, but there were no towering warriors in their lion livery, just a drunk man on a throne and an even drunker musician at the foot of it.

Ctenka had never met a king before, and if Stellan was anything to go by he wasn't missing much. The man's beard was a matted mess, clothes dishevelled, eyes heavy. He wasn't even wearing a crown.

'May I present Stellan of Canbria, King of the Suderfeld,' said Randal with a sweep of his arm.

The lute player stopped his tune, glancing around groggily. As though sensing he was somewhat out of place he stood on unsteady feet and stumbled away into the recesses of the throne room, bowing all the while.

Ermund took a step towards the throne. 'Stellan?' he said.

The king frowned back at him with little recognition.

'Who seeks... audience with the king?' he replied, the words coming out in a slurred mess.

'Stellan, it's me. Harlaw.'

'Harlaw?' answered the king. 'What would you ask of the King of Suderfeld?'

'Stellan.' Ermund made to move forward but stopped himself. 'It's Ermund Harlaw. Don't you recognise me?'

The king shook his head lazily as though they'd never met. Ctenka moved forward, about to tell his friend he was wasting his breath, when Ermund turned on Randal.

'What have you done to him?' He spat the words, clearly caring little for the stories Randal had told about his sorcerous children. 'What have you done to my king?'

Randal merely shrugged. 'I can assure you, this is none of my doing.'

'None of your doing? Look at him.' He pointed at Stellan, barely containing his fury. 'The king is bewitched.'

Randal pursed his lips as though considering the notion. 'You're right,' he said finally. 'But not by me.'

'What are you talking about?' asked Ermund.

'Did Selene not cast her spell on you?' Randal said.

Ermund looked up at the king, slouched in his throne. 'Selene? She did this? But how...'

'Stellan was always a fighting man,' said Randal. 'The many battles have taken their toll on his body. The queen has seen fit to treat his many ailments with a steady diet of wine liberally laced with essence of the poppy.'

Ermund turned on Randal. 'And you have allowed—'

'Yes, I have allowed it.' There was a hint of irritation

in Randal's tone, as though he had been humouring them both till now and his patience was running thin. 'Would you rather he were bedridden? Racked by pain? This land has finally been united under one king after years of war. I will not allow it to fall into chaos now.'

Ermund turned back to his king, a man who had betrayed him. Who had stolen his lands and wife and forced him into exile. Ctenka could see he was torn between loyalty and anger as he took a step towards Stellan, but then stopped.

'Then it looks like you've got your wish,' Ermund said.

It seemed that was all that needed to be said. All the fight drained from Ermund. Whatever he had wanted from his former king was gone now, he had seen enough.

'Now, to business,' said Randal, gesturing for them to follow him from the throne room.

Again they dutifully followed, but then what alternative did Ctenka and Ermund have? Randal appeared peaceable enough, and he had spared their lives, but it was clear he held a position of power here. If it was due to the reasons he had suggested then they'd be fools to do anything but obey him.

They made their way down through the palace and out into a wide courtyard. The smell of a stable hit Ctenka as they made their way outside, but despite the smell of manure and animal, this place seemed to be in a better-kept state than much of the palace interior.

A groom was brushing down a horse. Three saddled mounts waited for them along with two children, who stood holding hands, a boy and a girl, heads inclined towards one another. Ctenka remembered Randal's story. Remembered two children with strange gifts, and a sense of foreboding began to grow in his gut as he watched them standing there with little conception of what was going on.

'Meet Lena and Castiel,' said Randal as they crossed the courtyard. 'They are my parting gift to you.' He looked down at them with a slight expression of disappointment. 'I cannot speak for their usefulness, but who knows, you might find them indispensable.'

'Cannot speak for their usefulness?' said Ctenka. 'They're children, how much use could they be?'

Randal shook his head. 'Have you not heard a word I've said? These children are gifted. I believe.'

'You believe?' Ctenka stared at the two children, who stared back blankly.

'They haven't manifested any... powers, as yet. But I know there is potential there.'

'We came here to entreat aid,' said Ctenka. 'We need fighting men. Not... whatever these are.'

'I need all the men I have. The Suderfeld is still in transition. We have peace, but it is an uneasy one. Besides, you'll find these children more useful than an entire cohort... probably.'

Ctenka looked at the two children, no more than fifteen summers between them. The boy, Castiel, chewed the inside of his cheek and the girl pulled at the fringe of her dress. Ctenka was doubtful either of them could even speak. What use they'd be against an invading army was beyond him.

'We'll take them,' said Ermund. 'Let's just get out of here.'

'I have provided fresh mounts,' said Randal. 'And supplies for the—'

'Appreciated,' said Ermund, grasping the reins of the nearest horse and checking the tackle was fastened right.

It seemed that was that.

Ctenka lifted the two children into the saddle of the last mount. The girl Lena was cold to the touch, and the boy Castiel was warm and clammy. They both had a strange, ripe smell to them but they looked washed and well tended to, which only added to their oddness. Once they were saddled up, Randal bid the children farewell, then turned to Ctenka.

'Remember, I am passing these children into your care,' he said. 'They're your responsibility now. When they have served their purpose I want them returned home in one piece.'

Ctenka suddenly felt uncomfortable under Randal's gaze. 'You want them returned home?'

'In one piece. Promise it.'

Ctenka glanced at Ermund for help, but he was too busy checking his saddle was set right to care. 'You want me to promise—'

'Make the vow.'

'All right,' said Ctenka, 'I promise. Home in one piece.'

'Mean it,' said Randal. 'These children are precious to me.'

Ctenka shook his head. 'If they're so precious, then why not grant us a cohort of knights instead?'

'With the foe you face these children will be more value than a hundred men-at-arms. Now...'

'All right.' Ctenka was done with arguing. 'I give you my word. I'll protect these children as though they were my own.'

That was enough for Randal, and he took a step back and watched as Ctenka mounted his horse.

As they made their way from the grounds of Northold's palace, Randal raised a hand in farewell. Ctenka made to lift his own in reply, but all of a sudden it felt a foolish thing to do.

Ermund didn't even look back as they left. Ctenka watched as he rode through the gates of Northold and back onto the road. He wanted to say something comforting, but what did he know about comforting people. How did you comfort a man who had lost everything? What words could make up for a life of loyalty wasted?

19

*I*T was an impossible landscape, changing from darkened forest to marshy bog to lush field in the space of mere moments. The time too seemed to change of its own accord, from morning to evening then to bright midday heat, with little regard for the natural order of things.

She followed the woman Hera as best she could, stumbling over rocks and through craggy mountain passes, where the woman seemed to bound, sure-footed and confident. She felt like a newborn foal trying to follow a mountain lion.

It was impossible to tell how long their journey lasted with the environment constantly shifting, but still she trailed Hera until they came to the foot of a mountain range. As soon as they reached the rocky rise the temperature dropped. Looking up, she saw a thick white cloud crest the mountain peaks, blotting out the previously clear blue skies and instantly depositing a thick fall of snow, as though to welcome their arrival at the mountain. The wind whipped up, lashing the snow into a painful flurry.

'We're almost there,' Hera shouted through the downpour, before forging on up the mountainside. All the hag could do was follow, hoping that Hera was right and they would find shelter soon.

The climb was hard, the mountain surface sheer and slick. More than once she found herself slipping, not daring to look down in case she panic at how high they had climbed. Each time she faltered, though, Hera was there, pulling her up. Just as she began to fear her energy might be all but sapped, she spied a cave entrance hewn into the side of the mountain.

Still stumbling, she followed Hera inside. At first they were plunged into darkness, the quiet of the tunnel striking an unnatural contrast to the howling wind outside. They didn't have to travel far through the shadows before she heard Hera knocking against a wooden barrier. A firm shove and a grunt of effort and the barrier moved aside revealing... the warmly lit interior of a homely dwelling.

Sunlight shone in through little round windows, the glass panes framed in dark wood. A fire burned in the hearth and bookshelves lined every wall. Something bubbled on the stove, filling the room with a warm, meaty aroma that made her stomach spring to life with gurgling anticipation. This place was impossible. Not moments before they had been climbing the side of a mountain. Now they were in some idyllic cottage in the countryside. But, despite appearances, there was an unnerving sense about the place that none of this was real.

Hera walked in, unstrapping her sword and casting it aside. 'Come in,' she said. 'Make yourself at home.'

As she entered, a man walked in from an adjoining room at the back of the cottage.

'Ah, you're here,' he said.

He was small, just under five feet, his hair tousled and thick, cheeks full and teeth whiter than any she'd ever seen. His clothes were simple but well-tailored and his shoes shone, winking in the firelight.

'How is he?' Hera asked the man.

'Go and see for yourself.' He gestured to the room he had entered from, and Hera walked past, leaving the two of them alone.

'Please, sit down,' said the man, waving to a chair by the fire.

As uncomfortable as she was, she did as he asked, still too cold to argue. He took the seat opposite, beaming at her all the while.

'You must have many questions,' he said as she rubbed some life into her wrinkled fingers.

'Who are you?' was all she could think of.

'Ah, of course. How rude of me. You can call me the Hermit. That's one of my names, it'll do for now. But I think the better question is: who are you?'

She stopped rubbing her fingers, stunned at the prospect. 'Do you know?'

'Of course. You're Livia Harrow.'

The name brought a rush of thoughts and memories to her.

An old man in the fields. His face agape, throat opened, lifeblood gushing down his chest. Her captors, so many of them. Brutal, hateful... kind. A journey north. A child speaking like a priest. A battle.

She shook her head, the memories coming fast, solidifying, forming a life she had led. One that had ended atop a ziggurat. One that had ended with her murdering a child.

'What is this?' She stood, sending the chair she had been sitting on toppling back to the floor with a loud clatter.

As the curtain was ripped away and her memory returned, the hag's shell covering her body sloughed away. Her skin began to smooth, brittle hair growing thicker. Meat began to fill out the bony frame of her hips and shoulders. Lifting a hand to her face she felt the flesh of her face become youthful again.

'Be calm,' said the Hermit. 'The rush will pass.'

He was right. Already her mind was steadying. Already she knew with dread certainty that she was Livia Harrow. Born on a

239

farm in Canbria. Taken from her home and forced miles to the north. It was all a mass of confusion but she knew one thing – she was no longer in the Ramadi Wastes.

'What is this place?' she asked, picking up the chair and sitting back down beside the fire.

'Safe,' the Hermit replied. 'I am sorry I didn't find you sooner, but—'

'This land?' said Livia, raising her voice. 'Am I dead? Am I in Hell?'

The Hermit smiled, his teeth almost gleaming. 'This place has many names to many people. Hell is as good as any, but this is not the afterlife, Livia. You're not dead.'

'So where am I?'

'Lost between two worlds. The mortal realm, as you know it, and here. A plane ruled by the gods, as you might call them.'

'The Archons,' said Livia.

'Very good,' said the Hermit. 'It seems your connection with Innellan is still strong. You hold much of her knowledge, as she holds much of yours.'

With every one of her questions, more sprang up. 'Who is Innellan?'

'She is one of the Twelve… or the Thirteen if you're picky. But perhaps I should start at the beginning. The Archons were born when your world was young—'

'Wait,' said Livia. 'Is this going to be a history lesson?'

'If that makes it easier for you,' said the Hermit. 'May I carry on?' When she nodded, he continued. 'The gods were born in your world, summoned by the first priests. They grew in power as the centuries passed, gleaning their strength from the worship of mortals

240

and in return bestowing the power you know as magic upon those they deemed worthy. But the gods are a jealous breed, and they coveted their worship like misers, each one seeking more and more mortals to raise their voices in praise. War was inevitable – a conflict that almost destroyed your world. Some of the gods saw where they were heading, predicting the conflict would ultimately end in their mutual destruction. And so they came to an accord. The Archons would banish themselves to an alternate plane, an alternate realm of existence they could neither control nor destroy. This realm.'

Livia shook her head. 'But how am I here? How did I—'

The Hermit raised a finger and smiled. 'In good time. Despite their self-imposed exile the gods still yearned to be worshipped, and so they needed a conduit between the worlds. One that would allow them to glean power from mortals and in turn reward them for their benefaction. For that they created the Heartstone – an artefact of supreme power that would act as a channel between worlds. All seemed well for a time, and the realm of mortals was safe, but for one thing... the Heartstone could also allow the gods to travel between worlds. To inhabit the body of a mortal avatar and become more powerful still.'

'Then, that is what...'

'Yes. A hundred years ago, by the reckoning of your world, the Archon Siff split the Heartstone asunder so that the gods could no longer meddle in the affairs of mortals. All twelve Archons agreed that it should remain broken, placing it atop the Blue Tower and pledging a cohort of their own followers to guard it. But Innellan tricked the Archon Durius into repairing the artefact, once more opening a pathway between worlds.'

'The Blue Tower.' Livia thought back to the dreams she had of a terrible battle. Thousands slain on an open field, their lives wasted. 'I have seen it.'

'Thinking that Durius had repaired the Heartstone and would use it for his own ends, Siff, Innellan and Armadon slaughtered the armies guarding the Blue Tower and raced to stop him. When they reached the summit...'

'Siff realised she had been betrayed.' Livia remembered now as though she had witnessed it with her own eyes.

A noise from the back of the cottage made Livia start. Hera appeared from the adjoining room. With her was a man, hugely muscled, his face handsome but marred by a troubled frown.

'Ah,' said the Hermit, standing. 'You've met Hera. And this is Mandrake.' The man stared back at the Hermit as though he didn't recognise his own name.

Realisation dawned on Livia. 'They're... like me,' she said. 'Lost in this world.'

'Indeed,' the Hermit replied. 'Souls from the mortal realm.'

'But why is he...'

'Ah yes. That is an unfortunate side effect of Armadon's possession. The Archon of War ripped his host's soul from his body. Forcing himself upon unfortunate Mandrake here. The result is... tragic. As you can see.'

'But why did Innellan not do the same to me?' Livia asked.

The Hermit walked towards Hera and Mandrake, laying a comforting hand on the huge warrior's arm.

'Hera and Mandrake were offered as sacrifices. The rites performed and worship offered by the Set of Katamaru's Faithful meant they were like fresh shells to be prised open. Armadon chose to rip Mandrake's soul free and cast it aside, whereas Siff lived within her host for many weeks. When eventually Siff took control, Hera's soul was already halfway across the realms and she managed to hold onto her sanity.'

'And me?'

The Hermit looked at Livia, a strange sadness in his eyes. 'Innellan chose you as her avatar because of the raw power your mortal form possesses. But after inhabiting her host even she was not powerful enough to simply tear your soul free. So she waited until the time was right. Until you—'

'Until I killed the boy.' Livia remembered tearing out the Blood Regent's throat with her teeth and she felt suddenly light-headed.

'Yes,' said the Hermit. 'I'm afraid once a host has tasted the blood of a mortal, has taken a life with their own hands, then there is nothing they can do to halt the possession.'

Livia was surprised at how much of this made sense. It should have been confusing, but she understood every word the Hermit had told her. Only one question remained.

'How do we get back home?'

Livia stared at the Hermit but he looked away, eyes gleaming in the firelight, before he shook his head.

'There is no way back,' said Hera. 'Is there?' She looked at the Hermit, who remained silent.

Livia could not accept that. 'Well? Is there?' she said.

'It has never been done before,' he said.

'That doesn't mean it can't be done,' she said.

The Hermit considered her, and then showed that gleaming white smile. 'I see now why she chose you. But it would be impossible.'

'Impossible?' Livia said. 'This whole place is impossible. Since I've arrived I've been chased through portals, some lizard men tried to eat my soul and I've been threatened by a warrior king with a burning crown for a head.'

'Ah, Ekemon. He always did have a penchant for theatrics.'

'I don't give a shit who he was. What I want is to go to the Blue Tower. If the Archons can make their way through it to the mortal realm then maybe that's how we get home.'

The Hermit thought on her suggestion. 'Perhaps it could be done, but—'

'No buts,' said Livia. 'We have to try, and you have to help. Otherwise why save me in the first place?'

'Well I—'

'No, really? Why did you save me?'

Hera stepped forward. 'He saved all of us. He is the Hermit. That's what he does.'

Livia shrugged. 'Well thanks, that explains absolutely nothing. Either way… we're going. All of us.'

The Hermit shook his head in exasperation. 'I suppose I had nothing else planned.'

Livia felt herself for the first time in a long time.

'Just what I wanted to hear.'

20

The Cordral Extent, 106 years after the Fall

EYMAN sat opposite Laigon at the small table, mulling over his next move on the board. Their game of *khetzak* had gone on for two days now and Laigon had to admit he was growing bored. Before he came to Dunrun he had never played, but there were other games of strategy he was familiar with. *Khetzak* was much the same, only more rudimentary. It hadn't taken Laigon long to master the tactics and his early losses to Eyman soon became fake losses. It was best if he let the young militiaman think he had the more cunning mind. At least for now.

Eyman placed his hand on a thick piece carved in black onyx – the Shieldman, used to block sections of the board – but he let go without moving it.

'You're getting better at this,' he said, running fingers across his wispy excuse for a beard.

Laigon wanted to tell Eyman he could have ended the game six moves ago, but he held his tongue. Beating the militiaman at *khetzak* would be a hollow victory. Better he win the man's trust. Laigon was confident he was almost there.

'So tell me of the women in Shengen,' Eyman said, placing the Shieldman down in a predictable position.

Laigon suppressed a smile at the question. He could understand Eyman's frustration, stuck in a compound miles from any civilised company, with no one but other men for company.

'Strong,' he replied. There was no use coating it in honey. 'Disciplined. Honourable.'

It clearly wasn't the answer Eyman had been hoping for. 'Beautiful?' he asked.

'In their way,' said Laigon, suddenly thinking of Verrana and how much he missed her smile. It was a thought he put out of his head as soon as it arrived.

'The women of the Cordral are the most beautiful in all the world. Well, most of them anyway. My sister is the exception, but then her brother got all the looks.'

Eyman smiled as though he were only half joking.

'I'm sure,' Laigon replied, feeling guilty that he was here, playing games and chatting idly, while the rest of his men were locked away in chains. But it was necessary. If he could gain the trust of the Cordral militia he might ensure those chains did not stay on for much longer.

He turned his attention back to the board, considering his next move, when the door to the chamber opened. Marshal Ziyadin entered, looking more hot and flustered than usual. Slick rivulets of sweat ran from his dark greasy hair and he licked his lips nervously.

'Centurion Valdyr,' he said. 'I require your attendance.'

Laigon rose dutifully, and followed the marshal out into the warm morning air. Ziyadin walked brusquely. Laigon had never known the man move so fast and he could only imagine what had spurred him into such exertions.

They made their way through the gates of Dunrun. As he had done the first time he walked through each of them, Laigon noted how strong they were. How in the past, any army would have struggled to overcome such defences. As they neared the final gate, Laigon began to realise what had caused the marshal such concern.

Militiamen ran around in a panic. Someone shouted for a bow and was told in no uncertain terms where to go. As Laigon neared the foot of the final gate he saw a young boy weeping.

'They are here,' he said to Ziyadin.

The marshal glanced at the boy, then back to the wall ahead, walking with as much determination as he could muster. Laigon wasn't fooled. He could sense the marshal's fear. He could spot a coward from a mile away. It wasn't for nothing that Ziyadin had been given this commission in the back end of nowhere. Clearly his shortcomings as an officer had caught up with him.

Laigon took the stairs with vigour. As he made it to the top of the gate he was greeted by a familiar sight. Ranks of armoured legionaries lined the Skull Road for as far as he could see. They stood to attention, shields raised. It was a pose struck to intimidate – a wall of steel that had seen the enemies of the Shengen surrender at the very sight of it. Laigon knew it well, but had never faced it from this side before. Now he understood.

Ziyadin finally came to stand beside him at the parapet, breathing heavily from the exertion. Laigon could see the marshal was terrified but what could he expect; it was rare that any man in the west had seen the might of the Shengen army arrayed before him.

'What do we do?' Ziyadin asked.

Laigon looked down at the rows of shields. He knew the only sane option was to surrender. No matter how high these walls, they would not hold back the might of the Standings. Surrender was no option though. They had to fight.

Before he could answer, a gap appeared in the wall of shields and a single warrior strode out, carrying his helm in the crook of his arm. By his armour, Laigon could see he was a praetorian, but from this distance he couldn't tell which one.

'They're coming,' said Ziyadin, white-knuckled hands gripping the parapet. 'Should we let them in? Should I have my archers fire on him?'

'Wait,' Laigon replied. 'It would be foolish to kill the messenger before hearing what he has to say.'

The warrior came to stand within the shadow of the gate, looking up at the militiamen.

'Citizens of the Cordral,' he exclaimed, his voice echoing in the silent valley. 'I am Praetorian Kyon of the Shengen Imperial Guard. The Iron Tusk sends his greetings and requests that you allow us to pass peacefully.'

Kyon. It wasn't a name Laigon recognised, but if he was anything like Manse then he would be as ruthless and uncompromising as any of the Iron Tusk's followers.

Ziyadin looked to Laigon for any notion of what to do. He was desperate, that much was clear.

'If you open the gate we're all dead,' Laigon said to him. 'They are not here to parlay. They are here to destroy and conquer.'

Ziyadin nodded, and Laigon was surprised when the man took a breath, puffing himself up into some semblance of the military man he professed to be.

'I am Ziyadin of the Great Eastern Militia. Marshal of the fortress of Dunrun. Loyal to Queen Suraan of Kantor and protector of the Cordral Extent. We are...' He faltered, running out of bluster once the honorifics were done with.

'Marshal Ziyadin,' said Kyon. 'As you can see, the Shengen army has come to your door. I suggest you open the gate and allow us to pass.'

Ziyadin looked out onto the ranks of men, on the pennants of the five Standings flying proudly among the glinting armour, at the impenetrable wall of shields. Then he looked at Laigon. He was a man dragged beneath the waves by the weight of his responsibilities, but without the ability to swim. Laigon had seen enough.

'Praetorian Kyon,' Laigon announced, standing as tall as he could so that all the armies of his homeland could see him. 'The answer is no. The gateway to the Cordral is closed to you. Take your army and return home.'

Kyon raised a hand to shield his eyes from the sun. 'Is that Laigon Valdyr?' he said.

'I am Centurion Laigon Valdyr of the Fourth Standing.'

Kyon shook his head. 'You are Laigon Valdyr, nothing more than a deserter. Marshal Ziyadin, I suggest you throw this traitor from your walls and open the gate. It would be a shame if we had to knock them down.'

Laigon said nothing as Ziyadin stared down at the praetorian. He could only hope the marshal wasn't quite the coward he appeared.

'On behalf of Queen Suraan, I respectfully decline your request,' said Ziyadin.

Kyon shook his head. 'I will grant you time to reconsider, Marshal. But do it quickly. The Iron Tusk is not a patient man.'

With that he turned and strolled back towards the implacable shield wall.

'You've made the right decision,' said Laigon.

'Have I?' Ziyadin replied. 'I have barely fifty men manning this garrison. They have an army of thousands. If reinforcements don't arrive soon we're all dead.'

'I can give you reinforcements, Marshal. All you need do is release them.'

'You have forty-one men. What can I do with forty-one men?'

Laigon leaned in close. 'It's not what you can do, Marshal. It's what I can do.'

Ziyadin shook his head. 'I don't know if I can even trust you.'

'If I'd wanted to open the way for the armies of the Shengen Empire I would have already persuaded you, Marshal. You must bar the way. And I will pledge my life, and the lives of my men, to ensure that happens.'

'Doesn't look like I have much choice then, does it?'

Marshal Ziyadin made his way down from the top of the gate and Laigon followed him, at any moment expecting him to fall and break something. Once Ziyadin had struggled to the bottom he started barking orders. Perhaps he had misjudged the man after all.

The last order was for Laigon's legionaries to be freed.

'You have my thanks,' said Laigon, quietly.

Ziyadin offered a cursory nod. His only choice was to

trust Laigon. Open the gate to the Shengen and they would most likely be slaughtered. Defend it alone and the odds weren't much better. At least with trained men at his side, Ziyadin could make a show of defending the Cordral from the entire Shengen Empire.

As Laigon waited for his men to be freed, he noticed a half-painted wall within the confines of the first courtyard. A thought came to him as he regarded the forgotten scaffold and the discarded buckets of red limewash. Picking up two of the buckets he went to meet his legionaries.

Vallion was the first to appear, squinting in the light as the militiamen held open the doors to his makeshift cell.

'Centurion,' he said with a nod of greeting.

'Have the men form rank,' Laigon replied, placing the buckets down.

Vallion obeyed, and in no time Laigon's forty-one legionaries had ordered themselves into four rows.

'You have all endured much,' Laigon began. 'You have followed me along the Skull Road, turning your backs on your homeland. Your brothers. Your families. Well, I would ask more of you, if you are willing to give it. Every Standing in the Shengen now waits beyond the gates of this fortress. They wish to rape this land at the behest of a tyrant. I would ask any of you still loyal to Emperor Demetrii to stand beside me. To stop them. Any man who wishes to leave may do so without reproach.'

He waited. Not a single man moved or made a sound.

'We are legionaries of the Shengen no longer,' Laigon continued. 'Our homeland is lost. We are the red hand of

251

Demetrii's vengeance.' He picked up a brush from the bucket of red limewash. 'And we will show our colours to prove who we are. Who is with me? Who will join me in the Red Standing?'

Forty-one voices yelled as one, shouting, 'The Red Standing!' as every man raised his fist in unison.

21

The Suderfeld, 106 years after the Fall

CTENKA no longer appreciated the lush Suderfeld countryside as they made their way back north. He couldn't bring himself to enjoy it, knowing they had failed in their mission. There had been a promise of troops from Kantor, but the All-Mother knew how many. It may well have been half a dozen old men, as far he knew. As for Northold, that had been more than a waste. It had been a disaster. No troops, but instead they had two children to take care of. So much for he and Ermund bringing back an army to defend Dunrun.

Lena and Castiel rode their steed in silence ahead of Ctenka. Neither had spoken or as much as glanced his way as they plodded along the road, but still he felt unnerved by them. Randal's tale of gods-given powers had been enough to chill Ctenka to the bone, and he could only imagine what the two children were capable of. Part of him knew he was probably spooked over nothing. They were just children after all, what danger could they possibly pose? The fact remained it would likely fall to Ctenka to take care of them when they reached Dunrun. He could hear Marshal Ziyadin's voice barking at him already.

'Sunatra, you brought these little fuckers here, you can take care of them. And make sure they're fed out of your own rations.'

Curse him for ever volunteering for this mission, not that he'd had much say in the matter. It had been folly from the start.

The journey wore on with no sign of ending, as the sun made an uncharacteristically bright appearance for a Suderfeld day. At least it wasn't raining, in that Ctenka could take some solace, but it did nothing to assuage his boredom.

'We should think about making camp,' Ctenka said to Ermund as the evening was drawing in.

Ermund glanced up at the darkening sky as though thinking on it. 'We'll ride on,' he said eventually.

'What are you talking about?' said Ctenka. 'We can't ride on through the night. Who knows what's lurking out there, waiting for us in the dark.'

'I want to be away from this place as quick as I can. I don't care if we have to ride through hell.'

'I know this place holds a lot of bad memories for you, but riding through the night is madness.'

Ermund turned to him as though to argue, but before the veteran could speak Ctenka spied something up ahead. Through the trees there was a campfire, light glowing through the evening haze.

'Look, they've got the right idea.' And before Ermund could argue, Ctenka kicked his horse forward.

'Wait, you idiot,' Ermund snarled after him, but Ctenka had suffered enough nonsense from his southern friend. Besides, Ermund had nearly got them both killed back at Northold, so he was done taking orders.

Ctenka could hear voices as he came closer to the fire. Sliding from his saddle he tied his mount to a tree and made his way through the brush towards the clearing. As soon as he came out into the open, the voices stopped and half a dozen heads turned his way. And they weren't the friendly kind of heads he'd been hoping for.

One of the men stood up brandishing a nasty-looking blade in his hand. It looked like a filleting knife but Ctenka couldn't see any fish.

'What the fuck do you want?' said the man. His eyes were keen, peering at Ctenka from over a thick grey beard.

All of a sudden Ctenka didn't really know. So far every southerner he'd met had wanted to kill him, and this bunch didn't look like they were about to offer a hug of welcome.

'I… We… There's…'

'Cat got your fucking tongue?' The man gripped that filleting knife all the tighter. The rest of the men were standing now, and they all looked as unfriendly as the filleter.

'I thought—'

'You thought you'd commit suicide?'

Ctenka started to realise what a mistake he'd made. He thought about backing away, but that would just make him look like a coward. Then again, being a live coward was much preferable to being brave and dead. He was filled with relief when Ermund arrived through the undergrowth.

'Bayliss Gunby, you dog,' Ermund said. Ctenka couldn't tell if he was pleased to see this rough-looking bastard or not.

'Duke Harlaw, as I live and breathe. How in the hell are

255

you still alive?' said the bearded man, slipping the filleting knife in his belt.

'I'll live longer than you will, Gunby,' said Ermund. Ctenka could hear a certain levity in his voice that made a refreshing change.

'It's *Sheriff* Gunby now, my lord.'

'It's *my lord* no longer,' Ermund replied.

'So I heard,' said Gunby. 'And I'm sorry about that.'

'Don't be, I'm not.'

Ctenka had heard enough.

'As much as I'm touched by this joyful reunion,' he said, 'is there any chance we can continue this beside the fire where it's warm and I'm not standing in two feet of wet grass?'

Ermund and Gunby both turned to look at Ctenka. Then Gunby laughed.

'Of course,' he said. 'There's plenty of room and plenty of food. Any friend of the great Duke Harlaw is welcome by my fire.'

Simple as that, Ctenka went from being threatened with death to having a new bunch of friends in less time than you could fillet a foreigner.

When they'd tied up the horses and taken their place by the fire, Ctenka found Gunby's ruffians a lot friendlier than they looked. They were generous with their rabbit and other supplies, and Ctenka took it upon himself to make sure the two children were fed. Lena and Castiel accepted the food on offer, but still neither spoke a word.

From the conversation the two men were having, Ctenka got the impression Gunby had been one of Ermund's best

256

men during the war in the Suderfeld. They spoke brashly but fondly to one another, like brothers in arms. It was strange to see Ermund with his guard down, but Ctenka liked this new side to his friend. It made him seem less distant.

'None of us could believe what happened to you,' said Gunby, as evening turned to night. 'Where have you been all this time?'

'The Cordral,' Ermund replied. 'Had to make a living somehow.'

Gunby found this amusing. 'Surprised you're not ruling the place by now,' he said through a mouthful of rabbit.

'Not quite. And there might not be much to rule if I don't find capable men soon.'

'Trouble?'

'You might say that. The whole Shengen army is on its way west. Only thing standing between it and the Cordral is a dusty fort, and fifty raw recruits and old men. Don't fancy coming back with me, do you? I could use a good sword.'

'I'd love to help you,' said Gunby. 'But I've got my hands full here as it is.'

Ermund looked around the camp, unsure what Gunby meant. 'You don't look too busy.'

'Looks can be deceiving. I've been chasing bandits and robbers halfway across the Canbrian countryside. It takes it out of a man, especially one with as many years as I've got under my belt.'

'Bandits and robbers? I take it you haven't found any then?'

'Well, my old friend, that's where you're wrong.'

Gunby stood, and with a wry smile he beckoned Ermund

after him. As they made their way to the edge of the clearing, Ctenka couldn't resist following them. Neither man seemed to be bothered about Ctenka's nosiness, as he blundered after them through the brush.

When he'd made his way a short distance through the trees, a nasty smell hit him. He saw them, illuminated in the half-light given off by the campfire and the dull moon above. There were maybe half a dozen; a bedraggled bunch of men, each one manacled, a chain running through their arms and fastened between two stout oaks.

'See, I found plenty,' said Gunby, sounding particularly pleased with himself. 'We're taking them to Canville to stand trial.'

'What have they done?' asked Ctenka, looking at the sorry row of prisoners.

'What haven't they done?' Gunby replied. 'We got rapers, bandits, murderers. A right sorry selection of bastards. There'll be a big crowd for the hangings in Canville when we get there.'

Ermund stared at the prisoners. Ctenka could see something formulating in his mind.

'What do you think?' Ermund said finally.

It took a second before Ctenka realised that Ermund was talking to him.

'What do I think about what?'

Ermund turned to Gunby. 'I could use these men,' he said. 'How would you feel about handing them over to my care?'

'What?' Gunby said almost at the same time as Ctenka.

'I need men,' Ermund continued. 'And for what I have in store it's best if they don't care about dying.'

'What are you talking about?' Gunby asked.

'I came here to recruit soldiers. So far I've not done a very good job. Seems a waste if you're just going to kill this lot. They could still be useful to me.'

'Are you mad? They'll cut you to pieces first chance they get. You'd be safer without them.'

'For what it's worth,' said Ctenka, 'I'm with Gunby on this.'

Clearly it wasn't worth shit. Ermund ignored them both, moving closer to the band of condemned men.

'You're all on your way to trial,' he announced, as though they wouldn't already know. 'Most of you will end up hanging on the end of a rope. I'm offering you a chance. If you come with me you'll be fed. I'll even put a sword in your hand, but chances are you'll end up dead anyway. Survive what's coming and you'll have your freedom. Who wants to take their chances with me?'

The prisoners were mulling over the proposition. Some of them looked up warily, not sure whether this was some kind of trick. Then one of them said, 'I'll take that bloody chance.'

One by one, the rest started to nod, realising this was no joke, and pledged themselves to Ermund rather than face the hangman's noose.

Ermund turned to Gunby. 'See? Easy as that.'

Gunby shook his head. 'You always were a mad one, my lord. I'll try not to feel too responsible when one of these fuckers sticks a knife in you.'

That seemed to amuse Ermund, and a rare grin crept up one side of his mouth. He turned back to the men in irons. 'Remember,' he said, 'I know what you are. So don't think for a minute I'll hesitate to kill you if you disobey me. Try to run and you're dead. Try to thieve, or rape, or do any of the shit that saw you in irons in the first place, and I'll send you straight to hell.'

Ctenka could see that sinking in. It was clear they believed every word.

Ermund turned, clapping a hand on Gunby's shoulder as they both walked back towards the fire and the sound of men laughing and eating. Ctenka glanced back one more time at the criminals he'd be sharing the road with for the next few days, before following them.

'I hope you're okay with this,' said Ermund to Gunby. 'I'm not your duke anymore, I don't mean to overstep the mark.'

Gunby shook his head. 'Don't think nothing of it,' he said. 'I owe you, don't forget that.'

'Then consider us even,' Ermund replied as they joined the rest of the men.

The laughing and drinking went on well into the night, but all Ctenka could do was watch. He was an outsider and he didn't fit in with these southerners. For his part Ermund looked the happiest Ctenka had ever seen him. It seemed he'd already forgotten about what had happened in Northold.

Well, good for him; at least one of them wasn't troubled by the prospect of hardened criminals joining them as travelling companions.

As Ctenka rolled himself in his blanket and tried to get some sleep, all he could think was that this could be the last night he'd be able to sleep with both eyes closed.

22

THEY passed the waystone marking the border between the Suderfeld and the Cordral. Ctenka should have felt elated leaving the foreign land behind but he still gripped his reins tightly, anxiety eating away at him. How could he feel any relief when he was travelling with murderers and rapers?

There were seven of them, each dishevelled, all still manacled at the hands. Ermund had seen fit to leave behind the chain that bound them all together and so far the threat of what would happen if they ran seemed to be working. Still, they made Ctenka nervous. Truth be told, he wouldn't have minded a bit if any of them made a break for it and fled into the desert. He would have been glad to see the back of them. As it was, Ermund seemed determined to take them all the way back to Dunrun, and there was nothing Ctenka could say to change his mind.

Two of the men were the roughest individuals Ctenka had ever laid eyes on. They both had shaved heads, thick stubble sprouting from thicker chins. Their dark, squinting eyes roved everywhere, always searching for their next chance to escape. Or maybe to kill.

Behind them walked a thin weaselly article with no

teeth. He twitched with every step, grumbling to himself like a crazed lunatic. Ctenka only caught the odd word of profanity, and did his best not to listen.

Then there was a young lad with a sorry expression. He was about Ctenka's age and it was difficult to see what a boy so innocent looking could have done to end up in this company. Ctenka reckoned you could never tell about some people.

At the back of the row walked a man whose face was hidden behind a great brush of hair and beard. He kept his eyes to the ground, and from the thick set of his shoulders Ctenka guessed he was a fighting man, or at least used to be. Something about him spoke danger and Ctenka knew instinctively to keep an eye on this one even more than the others.

For his part Ermund didn't seem to care. They were all his prisoners now, each one a prize to be taken back to Dunrun.

'It's a fine day, my friend.'

Ctenka looked down to see one of the prisoners strolling beside him as though he were out taking a breath of air on a sunny day. But for the manacles binding his hands he could have been an ordinary traveller.

'A fine day indeed,' Ctenka replied, unable to stop himself answering the friendly greeting out of politeness.

'I've never been this far north before,' the prisoner continued. 'Your homeland is a place of rare beauty.'

Ctenka found it hard to drag his gaze away from the man's dazzling white teeth, a rarity in the Suderfeld from what he'd seen. When finally he glanced about him at the barrenness of their surroundings Ctenka wondered if the man was having a lark.

'Rare beauty?' he answered. 'That is clearly a matter of opinion.'

'Aye,' said the man. 'You should see my wife. She's a rare beauty too.' He gave a wink at which Ctenka almost guffawed.

'That bad?'

'Trust me, my friend. You wouldn't even ride her into battle.'

That time Ctenka did laugh.

'I am Daffyd,' the man continued. 'I would offer to shake your hand, but obviously...' He vainly tried to raise his manacled wrists.

'Ctenka Sunatra. And those will have to stay on.'

Daffyd shrugged. 'Of course they will. It's clear that you're no fool.'

'And it's clear that you're a good judge. So tell me, how does a man with such impeccable powers of discernment end up in chains?'

'Ah, that is a question. And one I would love to answer. But would you believe me if I told you? After all, I am a criminal. I could tell you my tale of bad luck. Or perhaps of a miscarriage of justice. Or shall we just dispense with the ruse and say I am in my current predicament because I got caught.'

Ctenka was starting to like this man. His company on the road made a sharp difference to that of Ermund. Perhaps he had at last found someone who would make the journey less dull.

Before they could continue the conversation, Ermund pulled up his horse.

'We'll rest here,' he announced. 'Take some water, see to

your feet. It's a long road ahead, so if any of you are thinking of having a whinge, save it for later when you're really feeling the strain.'

As the prisoners passed around a water skin, Ermund nudged his horse beside Ctenka's.

'Made yourself a new friend?' he said.

Ctenka could hardly deny it. 'We were just talking. No harm in that.'

'These men were on their way to trial. Gunby had them in chains for a reason. Be careful who you take a shine to.'

'What harm can they do? They're still in chains.'

'Just watch yourself.' With that, Ermund nudged his horse back up the road.

When they were done with resting, the group continued their journey east. As they made their way along the road, Ermund's words of warning echoed in Ctenka's head and he made a point of avoiding further conversation with anyone. Instead he kept a diligent eye on the prisoners, determined to do his duty and not let Ermund down.

They'd covered a lot of ground by the time night drew in. Ctenka was surprised that none of the prisoners had collapsed under the heat. But then he guessed they were a hardy bunch, and a march in the sun was far from the worst they'd experienced.

Ermund had Ctenka build a fire while he stood vigilantly watching the prisoners. Gunby had given them a little dried fruit and meat for their journey, almost enough to see them to Dunrun, but they'd have to find somewhere to resupply before long.

Ctenka sat Castiel and Lena at the opposite side of the fire to the prisoners, but he needn't have worried. With Ermund's imposing eye watching them, not one of the manacled men seemed to pay the children any mind.

When they'd eaten, Ctenka walked off a little into the night to take a piss. As he got back to the fireside he felt his throat tighten at the sight of a prisoner sitting next to Castiel, but when he saw it was Daffyd who had decided to entertain the youngsters he let out a breath of relief.

'What's this?' said the prisoner, pulling a coin from behind Castiel's ear. Where he had been hiding it, Ctenka didn't dare to wonder. Castiel merely stared at the coin blankly as Daffyd made it dance across his knuckles before it disappeared into his palm.

'You're a skilled charlatan,' said Ctenka. 'I think I've worked out why you're in chains.'

'Just a trick I used to keep my own children amused with,' he said. There was a distant look to his eyes.

Ctenka felt a sudden ache of pity. 'There's every chance you'll see them again.'

Daffyd stared into the fire, not giving an answer.

Ctenka didn't want to intrude on the man's sorrow, and felt it best to hold his peace. The night wore on in silence until finally Ermund came to him and said, 'You're the first watch.'

Ctenka wasn't about to argue. The long ride meant they would soon be at Dunrun where an army of Shengens might be waiting, which was enough to make sleep difficult.

He sat there in the dark, watching the fire dwindle, thinking about what was to come. When they arrived back at Dunrun there would be a fight the likes of which he had only dreamed of, if there hadn't been one already. Part of Ctenka wanted to be in time for the fight so he could gain glory with the rest of the militia. As he stared into that fire, he realised there was also a part of him that hoped it was already over. That the fort would be in ruins and the Iron Tusk's army already gone.

The shame of that hit Ctenka like a bolt. He pulled his blanket around him, closing his eyes against the night, the chill and the shame.

When he opened his eyes again he realised he must have been more tired than he thought.

He was lying on his side. The fire had guttered to almost nothing. There was a noise, a throaty retch, as though something were choking to death off in the dark. It took him a moment to realise it was a man's voice, and he scrambled to his feet, tearing his sword from its sheath.

Ermund was fighting in the shadows. Struggling with one of the prisoners. Ctenka could see the man was on top of him, trying to throttle the veteran with his manacled hands. The prisoner was a mass of beard and hair and there was blind fury in his face.

As Ctenka rushed forward two more prisoners leapt to their feet. Ctenka tried to block their escape but was sent sprawling into the dirt. He scrambled to his feet, looking for his sword in the darkness. By the time he found it both men had made a dash for the shadows. He shouted at the prisoners to stop, but they didn't take his demands seriously, as they disappeared into the night.

Ermund continued to roll on the ground, struggling with the desperate prisoner. He grappled the man into the embers of the fire, but his attacker ignored the cinders that burned his ragged tunic and continued to fight.

Ctenka ran towards them, his sword held high, but he daren't strike in case he hit his friend.

'Kill him!' Ermund shouted, desperately holding off the wild prisoner.

The thought of killing the innkeeper suddenly rushed back to Ctenka. That man's body, dead and broken, was all he could see, haunting him with its grim memory.

He dropped his sword and grabbed the prisoner's hair, dragging him off Ermund. The man twisted in his grip, lashing out and striking Ctenka in the nose with his elbow. Ctenka staggered back but managed to stay on his feet. It was a shit contribution to the fight but it gave Ermund enough of a chance to smash the prisoner in the face with his fist. The man staggered back, and luckily Ermund had the presence of mind to pick up Ctenka's fallen sword.

The prisoner halted his attack in the face of the naked blade, but there was still hate in his eyes. He was breathing hard, teeth grinding, fists balled.

'Go on then,' the wild man said. 'You tried to kill me once, why don't you finish the job?'

Ermund paused, staying his hand. He stared at the man and Ctenka could see recognition dawning on his friend's face.

'No,' said Ermund. 'It can't be you. Not you.'

'What's going on?' asked Ctenka, willing Ermund to strike.

Neither man seemed to want to answer. The silence went on. Ctenka could see the other prisoners watching from the dark. The two children were standing now, holding each other in a tight embrace.

'Well? Are you going to tell him who I am?' said the prisoner.

'This is…' Ermund couldn't find the words.

The prisoner had stopped seething now. His mouth twisted into a grin. 'Aren't you going to introduce your old friend?'

'This is Josten Cade,' Ermund said.

Ctenka was none the wiser, and neither man seemed to want to provide an explanation.

'So are you going to kill me?' Josten asked. 'Or shall we just stand here, holding our dicks all night?'

Ermund lowered the sword. 'Guess we should take a seat,' he said to Josten. 'And you can tell me what in the hell has happened to you.'

That was enough for both of them, and they sat by what remained of the fire like two old comrades.

Ctenka couldn't quite believe what he was seeing. 'What the fuck is going on? This man just tried to kill you.'

Ermund looked up at him, seeming amused by the notion. 'He was only returning the favour.' He turned his attention back to Josten. 'Now, what the hell are you doing here?'

JOSTEN

HONEST work they called it. Fair work for a fair wage, some others mentioned.

Back-breaking fucking toil, was what Josten Cade thought. He'd fought in more battles than he could count. Traded blows with tyrants and kings. Walked miles through endless desert, and back again. Been a pirate on the Ebon Sea. But none of that had prepared him for the misery of ploughing a field.

It wasn't just his back that ached – it was his shoulders, his hips, his bloody knees. The hard calluses on his palms had torn, his skin not even having the decency to blister before it started bleeding. And yet no one else working the fields gave a word of complaint, so Josten was damned sure he wasn't going to. Not that their silence surprised him. They were ordinary folk, just glad to have survived the war.

He certainly didn't share their enthusiasm for that.

Peace had broken out overnight. Stellan, Ozric and Banedon had reached an accord. Marriages had been arranged and now Stellan was High King of all Suderfeld. No wonder every labourer in the land was rejoicing. No longer did they have to risk being recruited under the banners. No longer did they have to leave their families behind and risk death on the battlefield. They could go back to their farms and start ploughing again. Good for them.

Shit for Josten Cade.

What was a fighting man supposed to do in times of peace? The answer to that one was staring him right in the face as he slammed the hoe into the ground. Lift and strike, lift and strike, all bloody day. Josten thought he was a lean article after days walking the desert and a few weeks at sea, but now he was like a racing snake, all sinew and muscle.

If there was something noble to this life he had no idea what it was, but what choice did he have? Sit on the streets and beg? Go back to life as a criminal?

No. He'd had his fill of that. Best make do with what he had.

He'd come here to start again and had given his name as 'Larren' in case anyone he didn't like came looking for Josten Cade. Not that there'd be much starting again. Josten had seen what was coming from the north. Had seen the witch who ruled there. War might be over in the Suderfeld but he was sure it wouldn't last long before the death cults came down from the Ramadi looking for blood.

When the day was done he slept in a barn with the rest of the labourers who ploughed Duke Coffick's lands. There were a couple of snorers, but on the whole it was quiet and safe and he had a roof over his head. Two meals a day stopped him starving to death and he had to admit, he'd had it worse. In the morning he woke to a sunny sky and the knowledge that he wouldn't have to kill anyone. What more could a man ask?

270

He was washing the sleep from his face in a cold bucket, when Farnal came to talk.

'Larren. Fancy a day away from the field?' asked the foreman.

Josten couldn't quite believe his ears, but he nodded back at the grey old man. 'I reckon I could stand it.'

'Good. I need supplies,' said Farnal. 'Wagon'll be leaving soon. Be on it.'

Josten dressed as fast as he could. Farnal was already waiting for him on the wagon when he emerged from the barn. As soon as he sat beside the foreman the horses set off and they left the long open fields behind them.

'Why me?' Josten asked as they trundled along the road. 'Why not any of the other lads?'

Farnal whipped the reins to urge the horses on. 'Guess you seem to be a man that can think. That can reason. Not like the others.'

Josten supposed he was right enough about that. The other labourers could barely string two sentences together.

'So what? You're taking me to a library?'

Farnal smirked at that. 'No. But I'm getting old and there's lots needs doing on the land. Now the war's over we can go back to the way things were. I need someone to take some of the slack.'

'You want me to act foreman?'

'Aye, I suppose that's exactly what I'm saying. I'm guessing you've led men before?'

Josten wasn't sure how to answer that one. He'd not wanted to give too much of himself away and risk yet more enquiries.

'Maybe,' he said, realising that was as good as saying *yes*.

'Well, you ain't no farmboy that's for sure, but I'd reckon a fighting man. It's all right. You don't have to say and I don't care. Whatever reason you've got to be here is your own. But I need a capable man. If you're up for it, I'd like it to be you.'

Josten wanted to tell the old man the truth but he was all out of trust. He'd been betrayed enough times to know when to keep his mouth shut. That said, Farnal wasn't the double-crossing kind. He seemed genuine in his offer, and right now options were slim.

'All right. I'll do it,' he replied.

'Glad we've got that settled then.'

The rest of the journey went by in silence. Farnal wasn't one for conversation and that was exactly how Josten liked it. Less they said to one another, less chance he had of revealing something that would land him in the shit.

They pulled up at a little hamlet. Part of it had been burned down in the war, blackened wood not yet cleared away. As for the rest, it was carrying on as though war had never happened. A blacksmith hammered, someone was selling river fish to a less than enthusiastic crowd and an inn stood alone at one end of the main thoroughfare.

'Get yourself an ale, if you fancy one.' Farnal must have seen his gaze lingering on the inn.

'I'm all right,' Josten replied.

'Have it on me.' The foreman flipped him a coin, which Josten caught deftly. 'We should celebrate your promotion. I just have some business to do and I'll join you in a bit.'

Josten couldn't refuse that offer.

They climbed down and Josten took a seat on the porch that surrounded the inn. A serving girl took his order for two ales and he sat there taking in the air. It seemed an odd turn of events. This had been the first time he'd had to sit down and think where his life had taken him in recent days, and here he was; foreman on a farm. Josten Cade, man of the land.

Three riders appeared as the girl placed his beers down. They looked like they'd been on the road for days – two of them wore rough, bushy beards, the third was older, greyer, and much shorter. He had a shifty look to him Josten had seen a thousand times. Trouble.

They tied up their horses and moved onto the wooden porch, one of them shouting at the girl for ales. The grey one took a long look at Josten before moving closer.

'Afternoon,' he said.

This was all he needed.

'Good day,' Josten replied.

The man took a seat at Josten's table, his companions taking up two more tables not far away. Josten suddenly felt naked without a weapon. He didn't even have a knife.

'Name's Bayliss,' said the man, friendly enough, but Josten could see his hand next to a sword at his side.

'Larren,' Josten replied.

'What brings you out here, Larren?'

He was tempted to tell Bayliss it was none of his fucking business, but the odds were stacked against him so it was probably best to keep things civil.

'Just on a supply run,' Josten replied. 'I'm foreman over on Duke Coffick's land.'

273

'Farmer. That's good. With the war over, this country needs men with good strong backs now there's no longer a need for good strong blades.'

'You're right there,' Josten said, picking up his ale jug and taking a drink. He could see the other two men were looking nonchalant but it was a ruse. They were all ready for a fight.

'How long you been a farmer, Larren?' This Bayliss was one nosy bastard.

'Pretty much all my life,' Josten replied.

Bayliss looked him up and down in an appraising manner. 'Tough life.'

'Has its ups and downs,' Josten replied. He took another draught from his ale and was almost halfway to finishing it.

'How's the pay?'

'Stops me starving to death.'

'I only ask,' said Bayliss, 'because you look strong and capable. We're looking for men just like you to join us. Men who can swing a sword, think on their feet.'

Josten shook his head. 'Not me. I can swing a scythe, but that's about it.'

'Shame,' Bayliss replied. 'It pays a fortune.'

Josten took another drink, finishing the jug. 'It is a shame. Anyway, I must be off.'

'But you haven't finished your other ale,' Bayliss said, as Josten stood up.

'That's okay. Why don't you—' He stopped as the serving girl brought Bayliss his own drink.

'Not going to make me drink alone are you?' Bayliss said.

Josten could see the man's companions waiting patiently

at the other tables, but clearly Bayliss didn't value their company. Slowly Josten sat back down.

'You see, I'm a tracker,' Bayliss continued. 'Used to be a bounty hunter, mercenary, sword-for-hire. But now the war's over Duke Lensmar decided it best to make me sheriff.'

'Good for you,' Josten said, picking up the second ale and taking a sip with less enthusiasm than he had the first.

'It is good for me. But bad for the local bandits, eh?' Bayliss laughed. Josten gave him a smile in return, then drank as much of the second ale as he could stomach. It had been a while since he'd had a drink and it was hard to keep down.

'So what do you say?' Bayliss asked.

'What do I say to what?'

'Fancy joining me? Leaving the life of a farmhand behind you? See a bit of the country?'

Josten took another drink, feeling it stick in his throat before he shook his head. 'No, I've got fields to turn. Crops to harvest. But thanks for the offer.'

He stood up once more, not caring he'd left half the ale in the jug.

'Sit down, Josten,' Bayliss said.

His two cohorts had stood up now, hands on their swords. The game was up and Josten knew it. Whichever of his past misdemeanours they'd pegged him for he had no idea, but it was bound to be something bad. His choices weren't plentiful or particularly appealing. Surrender and hang or fight and be cut down. Though there was a third option.

He flipped the table and made a run for it. One of those big beardy bastards was quicker than he looked, drawing his sword and blocking the way down from the porch. Josten vaulted the wooden balcony, landing on the soft earth, but no sooner had he got his footing than one of Bayliss' henchmen landed right on top of him.

They struggled in the dirt, Josten managing to land an elbow to that bearded face, but the other one was on him before he could do any more damage. They had him by the arms, rolling in the mud, until Bayliss appeared, sword in hand. It was doubtful he'd be afraid to use it.

Josten let the men take him by the arms, hearing the clink of manacles before they secured his wrists behind him.

'I knew you wouldn't make it easy,' Bayliss said. 'When we took the brand to those pirates back in Ferraby your name came up, clear as a bell. It's taken me weeks of looking but no sign of Josten Cade anywhere. I'd all but given up hope, but it looks like the gods are against you.'

And not for the first time.

As Bayliss and his men dragged Josten off he caught sight of old Farnal coming out of a hut, arms laden with supplies. The man stared in disbelief as Josten was manhandled away and lashed to the waiting horses.

Josten didn't have the heart to say anything. How would he explain this anyway? How could he tell anyone how bad luck followed him around like a shit stink wherever he went?

So much for new beginnings.

23

The Cordral Extent, 106 years after the Fall

'So what now?' Josten asked when he'd finished his story.

Ermund looked at him after taking in all he had learned. 'Nothing has changed,' he said. 'We still need to get to Dunrun. You're still in my charge. You'll fight for us, or you'll die.'

'Same old Harlaw,' Josten said. 'Single-minded to the last. You haven't changed at all.'

Ermund seemed unmoved by the comment. 'And you have?'

Josten didn't have an answer for that.

'Maybe we should get some rest,' Ctenka said, trying and failing to interrupt the dark mood that had fallen across the camp.

'Maybe you're right,' Ermund said. 'I'll keep watch for the rest of the night. That way at least nobody will be sleeping on the job.'

Ctenka opened his mouth to make his excuses but thought better of it. He'd almost got them both killed, best just do as he was told.

After he'd made sure the children were safe, he curled up in a blanket of his own. This time though, sleep refused to come and he lay there for the rest of the night, staring into the dark.

The next day they rose in silence. No washing, no food, just back on those horses and on the road east. They only had five prisoners left now. Ctenka had been hoping he would rise and find the rest of them had run off into the desert too, but no such luck.

Ermund set a good pace, and Ctenka wondered if the prisoners would be able to keep up. There was no doubting that this was a hardy bunch, but Ermund seemed determined to march them into the dirt.

Eventually, Ctenka found himself riding beside Josten. The man walked with a steady stride, his eyes fixed on the road ahead. Ctenka wanted to talk to him, to find out who he was and more importantly who Ermund really was. Yes, Ctenka knew his friend used to be a duke, but that meant little now. Since they had begun their journey together Ctenka had learned a lot about the southerner, but there was still so much mystery. How he would have loved to find out from someone who knew the man in his prime. Looking down at Josten though, Ctenka doubted there'd be any conversation. Say one thing for the men of the Suderfeld – they were a surly bunch.

As evening drew in, Ctenka noticed an edifice protruding from the sand. It was a few hundred yards from the road, easily visible, and he pointed, drawing Ermund's attention to it. Ermund glanced across the sand, not seeming to pay much mind.

'We must have passed it on the way from Dunrun,' said Ctenka. 'How come we didn't see it then?'

Ermund gave him a long look of disinterest. 'How do I know? Maybe it was buried in the sand. Maybe there was a storm in the past week that uncovered it.'

Ctenka thought that was possible but unlikely, his curiosity getting the better of him. 'Night will be drawing in soon,' he said. 'Maybe it would be a good place to shelter.'

'As good a place as any,' said Ermund. 'We might not lose as many men tonight if they're all inside.'

Ctenka ignored the barb as they led the prisoners across the sand to the stone edifice. On closer inspection he could see it was some kind of ancient temple swallowed by the sands. It might have been centuries since anyone had last explored its depths and this made Ctenka nervous. Anything could have made its home inside and there might be jackals or worse lurking within. Perhaps this hadn't been such a good idea after all.

'Well? What you waiting for?'

Ctenka looked down to see it was Josten who had spoken. It was clear he and Ermund shared the same impatience, as well as the same gruffness. All eyes were on him now. Ermund, the prisoners, even the children were looking at him expectantly. With some reluctance he climbed down from his horse.

The entrance to the ancient temple was a weathered hole in the stone. Ctenka pulled a torch from his saddlebag and deftly lit it with flint and tinder. Holding it ahead of him, he had no choice but to plunge into the dark. The entrance dipped down. There might once have been stairs, but now there was just a steep ramp of sand beneath his feet,

279

leading down into gods knew what. He picked his way down carefully, until eventually he came out into a massive cave.

Ctenka could see there were carvings on the walls, depictions of ancient figures. On closer examination he saw they were of the Cordral pantheon – Vane the Hunter, Anural the Cupbearer, Karnak the Reaver, all carved into the stone. This was a holy place, or at least it had been. Now it was as dead as the desert.

He had never put much store in the gods before. Maybe if he had worshipped in a place as magnificent as this when he was younger he might have paid them more than mere lip service.

A noise made him turn, his heart beating like a drum. He let out a long breath as the light from his torch showed him it was just the others entering the confines of the cave.

'We got bored of waiting,' said Ermund. 'What have you found?'

'I think this must have been some kind of temple,' Ctenka replied, looking back at the walls. 'A place of worship.'

'And sacrifice.'

Ctenka turned at Josten's voice, seeing him lounging atop an altar of some kind. In the light shed by his torch, he could see that gutters had been carved into the stone to let blood run from the altar and puddle in troughs set in the floor.

Thinking about it, perhaps he wouldn't have liked it so much as a child.

'Whatever went on here hasn't happened for a hundred years,' said Ermund. 'This is as safe a place as any to make camp. Best get some rest. We're still at least a day away from Dunrun.'

This time, before they settled for the night, Ermund tied a rope through the manacles of the prisoners. He was taking no chances that any of them would escape, so feeling a little safer, Ctenka settled down to sleep in the dead temple.

He woke to Ermund shaking him like a madman. Ctenka sat up. He could hear a noise like the distraught keening of some trapped animal.

'What the fuck is that?' he said.

Ermund shone his torch towards the corner of the cave. Ctenka could see Lena standing, gripping herself tight. The little girl was making a hell of a noise, eyes wide as though she had seen some unspeakable horror.

'The boy's gone,' said Ermund. 'And so is that prisoner you were having such a romantic talk with the other day.'

Ctenka rose to his feet. The prisoners were all still manacled together apart from one. Daffyd had managed to slip his chains in the night and flee, and it looked like he had taken Castiel with him.

'How long have they been gone?' asked Ctenka.

Ermund shook his head. 'I have no idea. They must have slipped past me in the dark.'

'Then how the fuck are we going to find them? They could be anywhere.'

Ermund looked like he was about to argue, when Josten stood up, manacles jangling. 'I can find them,' he said. 'Just let me loose.'

'You must be fucking joking,' said Ermund. 'You think I'm just going to set you free?'

'You know I can track anything that walks. If you want them back you need me.'

Ermund looked defiant, but Ctenka had heard enough. 'All right. I'll go with you.'

'Not a chance,' said Ermund. 'You don't know how dangerous this man is.'

'And I don't give a damn,' said Ctenka. 'I'm not leaving Castiel out there alone with a complete stranger.'

Ermund wasn't about to argue with that, and he stayed silent as Ctenka unlocked Josten's manacles.

'Cross me and I'll kill you,' Ctenka said, trying to sound as convincing as he could.

'I believe you,' Josten replied.

That was just the reply Ctenka had wanted, but it did little to bolster his confidence. If it came down to it he wasn't sure he could kill another man. Not after the innkeeper.

Before they left, Ctenka turned to Ermund. 'If we're not back by tomorrow you may as well leave without us.'

Ermund said nothing, and Ctenka realised that was the best he was going to get.

Outside, the sun was just rising, casting a red pall across the desert. Josten checked the ground, laying his hand on the sand. All Ctenka could see was a mass of footprints from the night before. Clearly Josten had a better eye... or at least Ctenka hoped.

'This way,' said Josten finally, rising to his feet and pointing back down the road to the west.

'Wait,' said Ctenka.

He untethered two horses before offering the reins of

one to Josten, who looked at him quizzically. 'You sure about this? I could just ride off.'

'I guess I'll have to trust you then,' said Ctenka. 'Try not to let me down.'

Josten mounted the horse without a word, and as Ctenka sat in his own saddle he half expected the man to gallop off into the distance. Instead Josten set a steady pace back along the road.

They travelled for almost the whole morning, occasionally stopping to check for signs on the road. Eventually, Josten veered his mount off the path, following a barely visible set of footprints over the harsh scrub.

'Tracks are fresh,' said Josten. 'I reckon they're just over that—'

A scream cut the air. It chilled Ctenka to the bone. Josten had no such qualms, kicking his horse and guiding it over the ridge. Ctenka took a deep breath and shook his head, then followed.

When he crested the rise, he saw Josten had dismounted. He was kneeling next to Castiel, who stood silently, staring into space like he always did. Beyond them was a derelict building, not big enough to be a temple, but perhaps some kind of abandoned outpost.

Ctenka kicked his horse forward. 'Is he all right?' he asked.

'Seems to be,' Josten said. 'Not a mark on him, from what I can see.'

'What about Daffyd?'

Josten looked up to the building, then walked towards it with purpose.

'Wait,' Ctenka said, about to offer his sword until he realised what a stupid move that would have been.

Josten ignored him anyway, moving to the building. Ctenka dismounted, kneeling beside Castiel.

'Are you okay?' Ctenka asked. 'Did he hurt you?'

Castiel's eyes were fixed on the horizon, as if he'd spotted something that fascinated him. It was then Ctenka caught the smell, like someone had set fire to horseshit.

Josten reappeared, his expression telling a tale all its own. He clearly hadn't liked whatever he'd seen inside.

'What is it?' Ctenka said.

Josten shook his head. 'You don't want to know.'

'Is that bastard in there?' Ctenka rose to his feet, feeling his anger rising. 'I'll kill the fucker.'

He walked towards the building. 'Don't say I didn't warn you,' Josten said, but Ctenka was too angry to stop himself. As soon as he stepped inside he instantly regretted following his fury.

Daffyd sat in the corner of the room. His leggings were slipped down to his knees, flaccid cock wan and useless. Half his torso and face were burned off, flesh cracked and still smouldering.

Ctenka's stomach flipped, bile rising in his throat. He made it into the open air before vomiting onto the ground.

'I tried to tell you,' said Josten.

Ctenka looked up to see the prisoner had already mounted his horse. Castiel was sitting in front of him, face still blank.

'Can we go now?' said Josten. 'Or do you want to see anything else?'

Ctenka mounted his horse and let Josten lead the way back. On the way east all he could see was that immolated corpse.

Glancing at Castiel he wondered what else the boy was capable of. It seemed Randal truly had given them a gift after all.

24

H E knelt in the tower of the Chapel Gate surrounded by foreign idols. This was a holy place, albeit neglected in recent years, and despite the fact he did not recognise the statues that surrounded him, Laigon was at peace here. He had always been a pious man, had always worshipped his gods as much as his emperor, but now Demetrii was gone and the gods were all he had left.

Laigon felt the pewter figurine, cold in his palm. It was reassuring to have it so close – something familiar in this strange place. Portius the Trickster was not a god soldiers would pray to in times of war, but Laigon had long since chosen him above all others. Better Portius' cunning than the strength of the war god Galles. Especially now they were so sorely outnumbered.

Laigon gripped the tiny figure and invoked his ancestors, invoked the gods, invoked the memory of the emperor, anything he thought might help. He and his men faced impossible odds and they needed all the help they could get. If there was the slightest chance any of the gods were listening he had to try.

All the while he tried not to think about his family back

in the White City. He could only hope that Verrana and Petrachus had been spared. That the Iron Tusk had not seen fit to make an example. He prayed for that hardest of all. Laigon didn't care if he fell in battle as long as his family was safe.

'Centurion, my apologies.'

Laigon recognised the voice of Primaris Vallion. He stood, slipping the figurine into the pocket at his belt.

'No need to apologise, Primaris. I was just taking a moment.'

'I understand, Centurion. But you are needed at the gate.'

'Today is the day?' Laigon asked.

Vallion nodded.

They both made their way down from the chapel and out onto the courtyard. As they walked through the fort of Dunrun they could see preparations for battle still frantically being made by the Cordral militia. Some men lugged fallen blocks of stone to erect makeshift barricades while others sharpened weapons or practised their swordplay.

At the Sandstone Gate, Marshal Ziyadin gave Laigon a nod of respect. It might not have meant much, but still Laigon answered in kind.

'You know your orders, Marshal,' Laigon said.

'Yes, Centurion,' Ziyadin replied.

Laigon was pleased that any doubt as to who was in charge had now been expunged.

Ziyadin and his militia were to wait at the Sandstone Gate. The Red Standing would have the honour of being the vanguard.

As Laigon walked through the Sandstone Gate, his

legionaries were waiting for him in the courtyard beyond. Every man was bedecked in red, shields and spears at the ready. High atop the Eagle Gate was a single legionary watching the Skull Road.

Vallion took his place with the men, and Laigon observed them for a moment, all those faces he knew so well. He had led them to this, and they had followed. A more loyal group of soldiers he had never known and it made him proud to be standing beside them.

'The enemy is coming,' Laigon announced. 'And we are all that stands between them and this foreign land. We are all that stands between them and the slaughter of innocents. Every man here knows what the Iron Tusk will do if he is allowed to pass through these gates. We have seen it. We have lived it. And so we must stand as the last barrier. We must hold this place. We must prove to him that not everyone will kneel before his tyranny. The Shengen we knew is lost. All that remains of it is here, the ground upon which we stand, for we are the last true warriors of the empire. This is our homeland now. Who will help me defend it?'

As one, the Red Standing began to beat their shields against the ground. Laigon wanted to say more, wanted to tell these men of his faith in them, that their sacrifice would not go unnoticed by the gods, that they were the pride of the Shengen and the Emperor Demetrii. But none of that seemed to matter now. All that mattered was they were fighting for the right side. Not one of them doubted that.

The legionary at the top of the gate began waving his hand frantically. Their enemy was coming.

'Form rank,' Laigon ordered.

As one, his men turned to face the gate. They locked shields, spears thrust forward. There were forty-two men standing between an empire and a country they didn't know. Forty-two men willing to fight their brothers to face down a tyrant. Laigon knew they would most likely die here. He had no doubt it would be glorious.

Arrows began slamming into the gate with an unmistakable thud. Each one was followed by the splash of oil as the bags that were attached to each arrow burst. More arrows followed, flaming tips igniting the oil that had soaked the dried timbers of the gate. Before long the first lick of fire appeared as the gate took. Still the Red Standing stood and waited as the flames turned from a flicker to a roaring inferno. The heat was intense but still they waited, shields locked.

It seemed to take an age for the gate to burn, but eventually it began to split and crack, crumbling in burning embers. Laigon could see past the fire now, see an army on the other side of that burning gate. He knew his men could see it too, and only hoped their resolve was as sturdy as their honour.

A warrior burst through the gate, body in flames, set alight by the firestorm still burning around him. He ran forward screaming, throwing himself at the shield wall. With a single spear thrust, the screaming was silenced and the body fell, but it was quickly followed by a cacophony.

Savages, half naked and armed to the teeth, threw themselves through the burning gate, heedless of the danger. Laigon recognised the tribal scarring of the Hintervale. These were warriors from a province beyond the north-eastern border of Shengen. Tribes that had never been subdued by Emperor Demetrii. Clearly the Iron Tusk had used other methods to bring them to heel. Now they fought for him with a fanatical zeal Laigon had never witnessed before. The warlord was throwing his expendable minions into the vanguard. Of course the Iron Tusk would not sacrifice his elite. Not yet anyway.

Like a wave of fury they hit the shield wall, snarling, screaming. Bone weapons clanked against shields like a relentless storm, but still the Red Standing held. Spears thrust out, the naked flesh of the Hintervale's tribesmen easy meat for sharpened steel. Before long a pile of bodies lay dead and dying in front of the wall of armour, and Laigon felt himself swell with pride once more. Forty-one were all he had, but he could have been commanding an army for all the courage and discipline they displayed.

Before he could shower himself with further platitudes, a tribesman burst through the wall, laying low one of the legionaries. Laigon's blade was already drawn, his legs already pumping as he sprinted to defend the rear of the shield wall. Just as the shields locked together once more, blocking the way, Laigon hacked down at the interloper, splitting him from shoulder to abdomen. It took a foot planted on the body to release his blade.

'Step back,' he bellowed.

As one, his shield wall retreated a step away from the burgeoning pile of corpses. If the men of the Hintervale were affected by the sight of their fellow tribesmen being butchered they didn't show it. More of them poured through the Eagle Gate until the courtyard was a clogged mass of screaming barbarians.

Another tribesman leapt over the wall, his feat of strength exemplary. Laigon rewarded him with a sword to the chest, impaling him before he could think about attacking.

'Step back,' he ordered again.

Once more the Red Standing retreated closer to the Sandstone Gate, closer to Ziyadin's waiting militia.

Laigon allowed himself a brief glance back, seeing the men of the Cordral watching in fear and awe. It would be their turn soon enough. Best they saw what they were letting themselves in for.

Laigon ordered his men back another pace, and again they obeyed him with uniform precision. To his right, he saw one of his legionaries go down under a torrent of violence. Instantly the men to either side of him locked shields to plug the gap, and Laigon ran forward. The young soldier clutched his side. To his shame, Laigon had forgotten his name. He had always prided himself in knowing the name of every last man, but in the heat of battle this one escaped him.

He dragged the boy back from the wall, but before he could begin to assess the extent of his injury, two militiamen had rushed forward to help. Laigon was pleased to see that one of them was Eyman.

'We'll take him, Centurion,' Eyman said, and together the men dragged the legionary away.

The shield wall was wavering now. Sheer weight of numbers was becoming too much for forty men to bear.

'On my mark, retreat,' shouted Laigon.

At that order his men began to fight all the harder, spears thrusting forward maniacally, slaughtering the tribesmen like they were livestock, easy for the kill.

'Mark,' Laigon bellowed.

With that, the shield wall broke. The Red Standing retreated back the ten yards to the Sandstone Gate and Laigon ran with them, keeping a watchful eye for any man who might falter. To his relief they managed to retreat beneath the gate tower without another casualty. There the shield wall reformed and was instantly battered by the pursuing Hintervale tribesmen.

'Marshal Ziyadin,' Laigon shouted above the cacophony. 'Now would be a good time for your men to begin.'

Ziyadin nodded, shouting orders to his dumbfounded men. Some of them obeyed immediately, others having to be nudged into action by their fellow militiamen.

The Sandstone Gate housed a portcullis, but try as they might the militia had been unable to release the ancient iron barricade from its housing. Laigon had decided the archway itself would act as a barrier, and for the past days the militia had worked frantically at undermining the gate's foundations. Now the Sandstone Gate stood on a few fragile stone blocks.

As Laigon's men held the narrow gap through the gate, the militia went at the blocks with their hammers. Laigon only hoped that his rudimentary understanding of siege engineering would be enough that the gate did not come crashing down on all of them.

'Hold,' he shouted to his men, as the tribesmen battered themselves against the shield wall in a last-ditch attempt to break through. As far as the tribesmen were concerned, their enemy had retreated in front of them and the savages of the Hintervale could now taste victory.

The Sandstone Gate suddenly shifted as one of the blocks was smashed to dust. Laigon looked up, for the first time doubting his plan. Another block cracked, giving way under the weight of the gate, and Laigon could delay no longer.

'Full retreat,' he cried, and just in time.

As his men moved back from their defensive position, the gate gave way. The huge portcullis came crashing down, flattening the tribesmen beneath it. Immediately after, the gateway itself gave out, blocks toppling down, smashing to the ground, crushing their enemy and blocking the way through.

Laigon and the rest of the defenders rushed back to the safety of the Tinker's Gate, closing the wood and iron doors behind and barring the way.

As his men regained their breath and inspected their wounds, Laigon could only watch in relief.

'You think that will hold them?' Ziyadin asked, panting all the while.

Laigon shook his head. 'They will move the rubble aside before the night is out. Then we will have another gate to defend. For now, Marshal, you should prepare your men. Before long they will see real battle.'

The solid oak barrier that was the Tinker's Gate would certainly hold better than the other two had, but Laigon knew it would not keep the Standings of the Shengen out for long.

He could only hope help was on its way.

25

I F nothing else, these men of the Cordral knew how to celebrate. Even though it had been a small victory, they were keen to congratulate themselves, and Laigon sat and watched as they shared their meagre reserves of wine, patting one another on the back, telling stories of their contribution to the battle, no matter how paltry. He could have been angry at them. Could easily have found himself chastising these men for their hubris. But what did it matter? Let them have their moment. They would find out soon enough what it was like to fight in a real battle. They would learn that after the killing, if they were still alive, there would be little time for celebration. There would be wounded. There would be mourning. There would be nights haunted by the dead.

A militiaman burst into the chamber. His face was flushed, eyes wide.

'They're back,' he blurted, staring around the room, desperate for someone to take charge.

Laigon stood, and his men of the Red Standing stood with him. Together they marched out into the morning sun and across the courtyard to the Tinker's Gate. More militiamen were standing there, unsure of what to do, an air of fear and doubt hovering around them like a bad stink. At least they hadn't fled.

He mounted the stair to the turret above the gate, fully expecting to see the Shengen army arrayed before him when he reached the summit. As he peered over the parapet there was but a single man waiting below.

Praetorian Kyon stood in the midst of the courtyard. Behind him the rubble of the Sandstone Gate had already been cleared aside. Beyond that, Laigon could see the shields and armour of a thousand legionaries shining in the sun. For his part, Kyon had chosen to face his enemy alone. Laigon couldn't help but have a grudging respect for his bravery. Then again, he was a servant of the Iron Tusk. It wasn't bravery; just a fanatic's zeal that made him face Laigon single-handed.

'Ah, Centurion Valdyr,' said Kyon. 'I see you are well.'

It seemed Kyon had changed his tune. Where before he had called Laigon 'traitor', now he used his title of centurion.

'And so are you,' said Laigon. 'But then you haven't sullied your armour in the fight yet. Will you be sending more tribesmen to sacrifice themselves in your stead?'

Kyon seemed to find that amusing. 'Your bravery and ingenuity is without question. You have proven yourself yet again. The Iron Tusk admires your skill as a general, Laigon, but he still demands your surrender.'

'Then perhaps he should ask for it himself,' Laigon replied.

'The Iron Tusk will be here soon enough. For now, I speak with his voice. You know you cannot win. This place will fall, your men will be slaughtered. If you surrender we can avoid any further bloodshed.'

'Do you think me a fool? I have seen the Iron Tusk's mercy with my own eyes.'

Kyon shook his head. 'You underestimate him, Laigon. He is not without compassion.'

Laigon had heard enough. 'There will be no surrender, Praetorian. We will fight to the last. The only way the Iron Tusk will pass through this fortress is over our rotting corpses.'

'That is regrettable,' said Kyon. 'If I cannot persuade you, then perhaps a gift from the Iron Tusk himself will make you see sense.'

Kyon turned and signalled to his men in the distance and there was movement among the ranks of armoured troops. Laigon had a sudden feeling of dread. He knew this would be no gift he would want to receive.

'What is this, Kyon?' he shouted. 'Have you brought innocent captives to be slaughtered before my eyes? You think that will soften my resolve?'

The praetorian shook his head. 'The Iron Tusk is no monster, despite what you think. Do you think he would punish innocents for the sins of an errant general?'

Laigon could see now that prisoners were being brought forward, marched in ranks through the fortress, through the rubble, through the fallen gates and past the corpses. As they drew closer he saw they were his own men – legionaries of the Fourth Standing, hands tied and stripped to the waist. They were marched all the way to the gate and Laigon could only watch helplessly, seeing the faces of men he knew, men he had fought with, bled with.

'These are all that remain of the Fourth Standing,' said

Kyon. 'When you fled like a coward, the Iron Tusk was furious at his loss. His retribution was swift and violent, but these forty men have been spared. For now. You can save them, Laigon. All you need do is surrender yourself to me and they will be spared.'

Laigon stared down at the men. They looked beaten, a shadow of what they had been. Once-proud warriors reduced to slaves. But he could save them. Just give himself over and they would be spared. Remain behind this wall and they would be slaughtered before his eyes.

As Laigon watched, Kyon laid his hand on the shoulder of the nearest prisoner. Laigon could see he was young, smaller than the rest, and as he squinted in the noonday sun he realised who he was seeing. It made his throat tighten in fear.

'Your son Petrachus also decided to join us,' Kyon announced. 'He was most eager to prove himself to the Iron Tusk.'

Laigon slammed his fist against the parapet. He was being left with no choice. His son stood defiantly, suffering his humiliation in silence, and Laigon wanted nothing more than to call out to him. To tell him how proud he was of his son's bravery.

Instead he steeled himself. He had to face this with dignity.

'And I should trust you to keep your word?' he said.

'What choice do you have?' said Kyon.

'What of the rest of my men? What of the defenders of this fortress?'

Kyon shrugged. 'They will make their own fate. For now, the Iron Tusk just wants you.'

Laigon stepped away from the parapet. As he made his way down he saw Vallion waiting for him at the bottom.

'Open the gate,' said Laigon.

Vallion shook his head. 'You're not serious?' he replied. 'You cannot trust the word of the praetorian. He is the Iron Tusk's puppet. He will never honour the bargain.'

Laigon had never seen Vallion so disconcerted. Not even in the heat of battle did he show such emotion.

'That is my son out there,' said Laigon.

'These men are your sons too. You led them here. You can't just abandon them.'

Laigon shook his head. 'I'm not abandoning them, Vallion. They have you. I know you will lead them just as well as I have.'

'You cannot just hand yourself over to the Iron Tusk. He will kill you. Slowly.'

'They have my son!' he growled. Laigon saw in his friend's face that Vallion knew he could not win this battle. Laying a hand on his second's shoulder, he said, 'Fight to the last, my friend. And may the gods watch over you.'

'Don't do this,' said Vallion.

'Open the gate,' Laigon shouted.

With reluctance, the militiamen began unbarring the gate. Vallion stared at Laigon as the gate was swung open, his sadness and frustration clear.

'You are the centurion now,' said Laigon. 'Farewell, my friend.'

Laigon turned, and walked out through the gate to face Kyon. He had been expecting the praetorian to bear an imperious grin, relishing Laigon's defeat, but to his surprise Kyon looked almost respectful.

As the gate slammed shut behind him, Laigon suddenly felt exposed. He had opened himself up to treachery, bared his throat to the enemy. Now he would find out just how foolish that had been.

The only thing Laigon had for protection was hidden in his belt, and he reached inside, feeling the small pewter figure of Portius in his grip. If the trickster god held him in any regard, now might be the time to show it.

'I am here,' Laigon said. 'Now release them.'

Praetorian Kyon glanced back at the prisoners. Behind each of them was a legionary loyal to the Iron Tusk, sword drawn ready to execute Kyon's order.

'Not so simple, I'm afraid,' said Kyon. 'These men are still traitors. They have yet to prove their devotion to the Iron Tusk.'

'I knew I could not trust you,' said Laigon.

'On the contrary. You are here and these men have been spared. Now they just need to demonstrate their worth and earn the Iron Tusk's mercy.'

Praetorian Kyon turned, walking back between the two rows of men.

'Men of the Fourth Standing,' he announced. 'You have a chance at redemption. The Iron Tusk, in his mercy, is willing to give you a chance. All you need do is show your loyalty.'

The legionaries had made the prisoners stand now, each

one with the rope that bound his wrists cut. They formed two rows, with Praetorian Kyon standing at the far end of the corridor they made. Laigon already knew what was about to happen. It was a punishment common in the Standings, reserved only for the worst transgressions. He would be made to walk the mill.

'You will have one strike each,' said the praetorian. 'If Centurion Valdyr manages to reach me before you have killed him, the Iron Tusk will show you no mercy.' A smile crossed Kyon's face and he laid a hand on Petrachus' shoulder. 'Valdyr. If you don't manage to walk the mill we'll hang your son's body from the same gibbet as yours.'

The legionary standing behind each of the prisoners drew his sword. Laigon could see their doubt, their apprehension. After all, he had walked out of a fortress to save their lives. Laigon had been leader of the Fourth Standing. He had recruited these men, trained them, prepared them for war. Now they were being asked to kill him. He should have let them, but if he did not make it to the end of the mill then his son would be slaughtered like a pig. Laigon had no choice.

He walked to the first pair of men. They stared at him, Dragus and Gaiovar. Laigon had recruited both of them as boys. Had practically raised them. Dragus looked mournfully at him, reluctant to strike, unwilling to be the first to betray their former centurion.

'Do it, boy,' said Laigon.

It was Gaiovar who struck first, a punch hard enough to make Laigon stumble. Then Dragus hit him, a blow harder than the first. It sent sparks flaring at the periphery of Laigon's vision, but he managed to stay on his feet. Only another thirty-eight men to go.

When the next five men hit him he felt every blow. The five after that he stopped feeling the pain. Laigon concentrated purely on staying on his feet. *Just keep walking,* he told himself, *get to the end.*

Halfway through the mill and Laigon stopped caring. His body was numb, his legs ready to betray him with every step. There was no pain in his face, just emptiness. He could already feel his eyes swelling, teeth loosened, blood flowing freely from his nose.

He took a blow to the jaw, spinning him, and he blacked out for the briefest moment. When he opened his eyes he found himself on all fours. He had lost the figurine of Portius and he scrabbled in the dirt for it, probing the sand until eventually his hand closed around the cold metal.

Two men reached to help him up, but with a shout from Kyon they left him to rise of his own volition. Laigon managed to struggle to his feet, his knees weak, the men surrounding him spinning in his damaged vision. Gripping the figurine tighter, Laigon carried on.

When he was four men from the end of the mill he stumbled, a blow driving him to one knee. The punches were becoming more desperate now as the prisoners saw he was nearing the end of the row. It was them or him.

Laigon looked up, seeing Kyon waiting, hand on the shoulder of Petrachus. There was no pleasure in the praetorian's expression, no pity either.

As the last legionary hit him, Laigon stumbled forward

on hands and knees. He didn't know if he could stand. Didn't know if he wanted to. Looking up he saw Petrachus standing there. He wanted to speak, wanted to tell his son how much he loved him, but no words would come from his swollen jaw.

Kyon knelt beside him. 'Never known a man survive a mill of forty before. That's quite a feat.' Laigon could barely hear him through the ringing in his ears. 'But then you're a man used to achieving the impossible.'

Laigon tried to stand, but his legs had given in now. Instead he sat back on his knees, head throbbing, body sapped of all its vigour. All he could feel was that figurine in his hand.

Two legionaries grabbed him under the arms, dragging him away from the gate. Behind him he could hear Kyon giving orders. Through the ringing he could not hear what was said, but he knew the last survivors of the Fourth Standing were about to meet their end.

Again he tried crying out to his son. Was Petrachus about to meet the same fate as the Fourth? Laigon didn't find out before a merciful darkness consumed him.

26

*J*UST when she thought she was getting used to this place it changed again. One moment they were travelling across a loose shale cliffside, the next they were on an open plain of grass. When grass turned to sand and they were suddenly surrounded by open desert, Livia was in awe at the sight, transported back to her time in the Ramadi Wastes. But no sooner had she acclimatised to that than they were trekking along the edge of a rocky cliff, wind whipping the sea beneath an ominous grey sky.

The Hermit took the lead. He wore a battered hat at a jaunty angle and a moth-eaten jacket that apparently shielded him from the conditions, despite its many holes. No matter the state of the elements he set a heady pace, whistling some tune she didn't recognise, swinging his walking stick like he was out for a summer stroll. Behind her, Hera helped Mandrake along as best she could. He seemed even more befuddled now they had left the safety of the cottage, as though the environment were robbing him of his few remaining faculties. Hera did her best to gently coax him along but at times it was difficult. Despite the trouble she had, Hera stoutly refused any help from Livia, determined to struggle along on her own.

'So what's the deal with this place?' Livia asked the Hermit, finally sick of his whistling. 'Why does everything shift and change of its own accord?'

The Hermit turned and gave her a wry smile, before splaying his arms and looking upwards. 'Why does the sun shine? Why does the wind blow? Why do the—'

'You're about as much use as shit in a pair of new shoes, you know that?'

The Hermit seemed genuinely hurt. 'I was only trying to answer your question.'

'You mean you don't know?'

He looked a little sheepish. 'Yes, that's probably what I was getting at in a roundabout way.'

'It's madness,' Livia said.

'Only because it's not what you're used to. This place simply doesn't obey the same rules as your world. Its geography is not beholden to any law, and neither is time.'

'Neither is time? What does that mean?'

'It means a day here could be a year there, could be a century somewhere else.'

Livia felt that hit her like a dart. 'You mean I could get back home and find everyone I've ever known has been dead for a thousand years?'

The Hermit gave her a piteous glance. 'Firstly, the chances of you getting back home are infinitesimally small. Secondly... yes, I suppose you're right.'

She shook her head. 'You know, you really are a tiny bundle of joy. Has anyone ever told you that?'

The Hermit smiled, missing her sarcasm. 'Why yes. Several times, actually.'

Livia went back to plodding behind the strange little man, wondering if this had been such a good idea after all. Maybe she should have accepted the safety of that cottage in the mountains. Maybe this had been folly all along.

But of course it wasn't. A tiny chance was better than no chance.

As they rounded the jutting headland, the Hermit stopped. Following his gaze Livia saw a monument standing in the middle of some flat grassland. It was a portal, fully ten feet tall, its stone frame carved with strange sigils and sprouting outlandish sculptures. In its centre was a pulsating mass, like some kind of gelatinous pool that occasionally bulged and beat with life.

'Short cut,' said the Hermit.

'We're going through that?' Livia asked, remembering the last time she had passed through a similar portal and the feeling of utter emptiness it had given her.

'Unless you'd rather walk for another hundred years?' said the Hermit.

'Let's go,' Livia replied, taking the lead and striding down the hill towards where the huge gateway stood.

When she was within twenty yards of it, the sporadic pulsing of the portal's surface changed to a violent throb. With a hollow popping sound, like when she had to pull her leg from the muddy earth, three figures emerged from the other side.

They stood tall, unaffected by their journey through the portal. Each was bare-chested, head bedecked in a grey wolf pelt, animal hide covering pitch-black skin. They held spears adorned with feathers and bird bones. Livia had never seen a group of more muscular men, their waists impossibly thin, their shoulders bulging impossibly broad.

'Ah,' said the Hermit, stepping in front of Livia. 'We have company.'

His voice bore none of its previous humour, and it scared her.

One of the wolfmen came to stand before the Hermit, looking down on the tiny man as though he were about to pounce.

'This portal leads to the sovereign territory of Lord Luphir,' he said, voice deeper than a well. 'You will pay tribute.'

'I see,' said the Hermit nervously. 'That's a new one. Last time I passed this way Kastion was in charge.'

'Luphir ousted that bitch from her perch a year ago. Now, are you going to pay tribute or am I going to take your head?'

The Hermit glanced back at his travelling companions. 'I... don't really have much to offer,' he said.

The wolfman looked up, seeing Livia standing there. The look on his face made her feel like she was part of a forthcoming banquet.

'What's wrong with her?' said the leader.

The Hermit shook his head. 'Luphir won't want her, trust me. She'd be very stringy. Probably repeat on him later.'

'We'll let Luphir be the judge,' said the wolfman, shoving the Hermit out of the way and taking a step towards her.

Livia backed away, fear rising within her as the huge beast of a man loomed down.

Suddenly the warrior braced himself, brandishing his spear defensively, as Hera rushed past Livia, sword raised. She went at the wolfman with abandon, and he was at pains to parry her blows. The other warriors rushed forward to meet Hera, their spears held at the ready. Livia turned, seeing Mandrake on the ground, hands over his ears as he rocked back and forth like a scolded child. Livia wanted to shout at the bulging idiot, to scream

306

for him to help, but he was clearly no good for anything.

The Hermit stood to one side, watching proceedings with a curious look on his face. Hera was going to die and he was just standing there. The woman was surrounded now, her attack turned to defence as the wolfmen jabbed at her with their spears. For every lunge she responded with a parry, but she couldn't hold them off forever.

Livia's rage grew inside her like a wellspring. Something was boiling up within, churning like the strange sea she had looked out on moments before. Roiling like the surface of that portal. This place fuelled a fire within her she couldn't quench... not even if she'd wanted to.

She rushed forward, not knowing what she was going to do – just that she had to do something. The first of the wolfmen turned to regard her. He brought his spear about, ready to impale her where she stood.

Feeling that rage inside, that primal hate, all Livia could do was bellow at the warrior.

Her voice was a cacophony, all her fury and pent-up aggression funnelled through her mouth. The wolfman was thrust into the air and thrown into the sky until he disappeared into the distant grey cloud.

Everybody stopped.

'What the fuck?' Livia said.

She barely had time to dodge to one side as another spear was thrust at her. Hera jumped in, sword flashing, but one of the wolfmen batted her aside with his muscular arm, a crunching blow that sent her sprawling.

Two warriors bore down on Livia now. She tried to summon that power once more, tried to channel whatever magic she had conjured, but she was spent. There was nothing left inside her to call upon.

One of the wolfmen kicked her in the chest and she fell in the dirt, teeth clattering together. From the ground she stared up helplessly at the tip of a spear, waiting for it to slice through her flesh.

Before the wolfman could impale her, he exploded. Blood spattered Livia's face and her front was covered in guts. She barely had a chance to lock eyes with the last wolfman, who looked as surprised as she was, before he too exploded into red ribbons of flesh and ichor.

Livia wiped the gore from her eyes and found the Hermit standing there. He was pointing his walking stick as though ready to shoot an arrow from it. Instead he smiled, spinning it in his hand, then leaning on it jauntily.

'Right, that's it,' Livia said, rising to her feet. More guts slipped from her frock and spattered onto the ground. 'No more lies. No more vague, ephemeral riddles. Who the bloody hell are you?'

The Hermit nodded, as though she had found him out. As though he'd been hiding some big secret but Livia had gotten to the bottom of it and now he had to confess.

'My name is Durius,' said the Hermit. 'Though in Canbria you would know me best as the god Urien the Trickster. Hera would call me Duchor, although the legends they ascribe to me in the Ramadi are invariably false. It's all very bloodthirsty up there and they do have a tendency to exaggerate.'

'You're a bloody Archon?' Livia said.

'I'm afraid so,' said Durius. 'But the more pressing question is – who are you?'

Livia shook her head. 'What's that supposed to mean?'

'What you just did. We all saw it. Unbridled power booming from your tonsils. Only the most devout sorcerer should be capable of that, and yet you come from a land that has been cut off from magic for a hundred years.'

308

'Well, you're the expert,' she said. 'You tell me.'

Durius placed a finger to his lips, pondering the problem. 'Could be that you spent so long with Innellan inside your head you took a part of her with you. That's rare but not unheard of.'

Livia shook her head. 'No, that bitch is gone. Completely. I had power in the other place, the mortal land, and that was her acting through my body. But here, it's just… me.'

'Well then, I have no idea,' said Durius with a shrug.

'Great,' Livia replied. 'All-seeing, all-knowing Archon, and you don't know where my power comes from.'

'I'm a god, my dear. But no one's perfect.' With that he flipped his stick into the cruck of his arm and headed towards the portal.

Hera had managed to get Mandrake to his feet now, and they followed Durius to the edge of the pulsating door.

'Any surprises on the other side we should be ready for?' asked Livia.

Durius turned. 'Isn't that the point of surprises? You don't get to find out in advance.'

With a wink he jumped through the portal and disappeared.

Hera stumbled past her, looking up with a defeated expression. 'Count yourself lucky,' she said. 'I had weeks of this before you turned up.' With that, she and Mandrake stumbled through the magical gateway.

Livia gave one last look around at the mournful sky above and the remains of the bodies on the floor.

Well, she wasn't going to get any answers waiting around here. Stepping forward, she let the portal take her.

27

The Cordral Extent, 106 years after the Fall

THE closer they got to the Crooked Jaw the more ominous the mountains seemed. Ctenka had set off on his noble quest to find an army to defend Dunrun. Now he was returning with half a dozen criminals and two mute children. That might well have been classed as a failure in some people's eyes.

If the armies of the Shengen Empire weren't already at the gates of Dunrun they soon would be, and Ctenka Sunatra, along with a bunch of poorly trained militiamen, would be all that stood in their way.

The closer he came to those mountains, the more it dawned on him that he was going to die.

The fortress of Dunrun appeared at the foot of the mountains all too quickly. Ctenka found himself checking the road behind, wondering if it was too late for him to make a run for it. But there was no escape now, or at least that was what he told himself. The old Ctenka might have wanted to take the coward's way out, but he was done with all that.

When they finally reached the fortress, the gates lay open. Ermund pulled up his horse at the front, and sat there watching the open gateway.

'Where is everyone?' asked Ctenka. Perhaps the Shengen army had already ransacked the place. Perhaps they were even still waiting inside.

'Only one way to find out,' said Ermund, nudging his horse forward.

Ctenka followed him through the open gate. The courtyard was empty, but there were no signs of a fight. It was like the place had just been abandoned. Maybe it had. Maybe the Great Eastern Militia had turned tail and fled in the face of the Shengen forces.

Ermund dismounted as the prisoners stumbled into the courtyard, collapsing on the floor. It had been a hard trek, and the men were on their last legs. Of all of them, Josten seemed in the best shape, but after all he had been through it was clear he was fashioned from harder stuff than most men.

'Do you think we're too late?' said Ctenka.

'How would I know?' said Ermund, moving towards the well that sat in the middle of the courtyard.

When Ctenka didn't answer Ermund turned and looked at him expectantly. 'So? Go and find out where everyone is.'

As Ermund pulled up a bucket of water for the prisoners, Ctenka did as he was told. He gripped his sword in a sweaty palm as he moved towards the main barrack building, thinking that any minute half the Shengen army might burst out of it and cut him into so much offal. As he approached, he thought he could hear talking.

Ctenka paused at the door, craning his neck to listen. He could hear muffled voices raised in anger, but no one he recognised. Surely this couldn't be the Shengen army? Surely their soldiers would be all over this place like maggots on a rotting dog if they had already broken through?

Taking a breath, he opened the door. Ctenka was hit in the face by the raucous noise, but he was relieved to see people he knew.

What looked like the entirety of Dunrun's militia sat around the long dining table in the mess. Marshal Ziyadin was at its centre, with a harried expression. Since Ctenka had been away it looked like the man had aged ten years. Several of the militia seemed to be calling for him to order a retreat and every man looked desperate and scared. Ziyadin had little to say, but one of the Shengen deserters seemed opposed to the idea of fleeing. He sat in his armour, which was now painted a familiar shade of red, stoically taking every shouted barb from the militiamen.

'We have to get out of here,' one of them cried.

'This is insane, we're all going to die,' said another.

'All we're doing is delaying the inevitable,' said one more, who Ctenka recognised as Fat Diyazim. There was no wonder he would be among those ready to mutiny.

The Shengen warrior continued to sit calmly amid the tumult but could be silent no more. 'The centurion gave up his life to try and save forty men,' he said. 'And you would not sacrifice yours to save thousands? I had heard the men of the Cordral were better than this. I did not think you cowards.'

That shamed them into silence for a moment.

Ctenka realised that Laigon was not present, and his second in command spoke with authority on behalf of the Shengen. Already they had lost the most capable commander

312

among them. Now probably wasn't the best time for Ctenka to enter and announce he and Ermund had failed in their mission. But then Ctenka's timing had never been the best.

'Sunatra,' said a voice. One of the militia had spotted him.

'All-Mother be praised,' said Marshal Ziyadin, rising to his feet. 'You're back. Tell me you've brought reinforcements. Tell me we are to be relieved.'

'Well…' Ctenka didn't really have the heart. He glanced around the room, every eye on him, expecting, or even demanding, he give them good news.

Ermund walked into the room behind him, and it was like a huge weight had been lifted.

'I am sorry, Marshal,' said the southerner. 'But we have failed.'

'Failed?' said Ziyadin. 'But you must have brought someone?' He stood, pushing past the militia in the crowded room and making his way outside.

Ctenka followed Ziyadin as he stumbled into the courtyard, seeing half a dozen bedraggled men in chains drinking heartily from a bucket, and two children, still atop a horse, staring around them like they were in a stupor.

'Is this it?' Ziyadin said. 'How many days have you been away? And this is all you could find?'

The rest of the militia had spilled out into the courtyard now, seeing the shabby gang of prisoners on their knees. One of them laughed, another wailed, pulling at his hair.

'We're dead,' one of them said. 'We're all going to die.'

That sparked a wave of despair. Ctenka got the dread feeling that a mutiny was about to kick off, when one of the militia pointed through the open gates to the west.

'Look,' he said. 'Along the road.'

Everyone moved towards the gate. Ctenka followed, peering past the other militiamen. A cloud of dust had risen in the distance, heralding the arrival of someone. By the shape of the cloud it looked like a sizeable group.

They waited in silence, every man peering intently to the west. Eventually, when they could see a group of marching men, some of the militia cheered.

'It's a force from Kantor,' one of them said.

'The Desert Blades,' said another.

Suddenly there was a wave of excitement. If Queen Suraan had sent her elite fighting force then surely they were saved. But as the marching column came nearer, their hopes were dashed. The flag they flew was not the rising sun symbol of the Desert Blades but the crossed scimitars of the Kantor Militia.

Nevertheless, the men of Dunrun moved aside to allow the marching column to enter. They were led by a man on horseback, beard oiled, uniform immaculate, in contrast to the dishevelled appearance of his men. Ctenka counted roughly two hundred warriors, but from the look of them they weren't seasoned campaigners. He could see the pale faces of raw recruits among their number and not a few old men. It seemed this new contingent was the same standard of waif and stray as already manned Dunrun.

'This is it?' bellowed Ziyadin. 'This is what Queen Suraan sends me to defend her nation?'

The man on horseback glared down at Ziyadin with an imperious look.

'I am Marshal Aykan Cem of Her Radiant Majesty's Third Royal Militia. I assume you are Ziyadin?'

'Marshal Ziyadin,' he replied. 'And where are the rest of you?'

'This is what could be spared, Marshal. Count yourself lucky you have this many. I am to assess the situation then—'

'Assess the fucking situation?' Ziyadin's red face looked ready to burst like a melon. 'We've already lost two gates. The next attack is imminent. We need the Desert Blades. We need an army, not this…' He motioned pathetically to the two hundred who stood around in the courtyard.

Aykan Cem's imperious look wavered. Clearly he had not expected the rumours of an attacking army to be true.

'Fear not, Marshal,' he said, climbing down from his horse. 'I am ready to take charge.'

'You're what?' Ziyadin's brow furrowed. 'I am in charge here. This is my posting.'

Aykan glanced around the dilapidated fort. 'And what a posting it is. Look at this place.'

'I don't need you to tell me—'

'Enough!' The Shengen deserter stepped forward. 'We don't have long until the next attack. We must consolidate our forces and prepare—'

'What is this?' said Aykan. 'A Shengen warrior walks free? Why is this man not in chains?'

'He…' Ziyadin didn't have an answer.

'I am Shengen no longer. My name is Centurion Vallion of the Red Standing. And my men are ready to defend this place to the last.'

Aykan shook his head. Ziyadin seemed unable to explain himself and now Ermund stepped forward, hands raised, ready to be the great conciliator. Clearly there was nothing Ctenka Sunatra could add now that Duke Harlaw of Canbria was about to get involved.

As the men argued, he walked to where Lena and Castiel still sat patiently, and helped them down from the horse.

'Come,' he said, as voices rose behind him. 'Shall we go and find something to eat?'

Neither of them seemed too concerned, but Ctenka decided he'd best act like the only responsible adult in this whole damned fortress.

Taking each of them by the hand he led them through the Hangman's Gate and out into the courtyard. As soon as they caught sight of the Chapel Gate, both the children let go of his hands and ran straight towards it.

'Wait,' he cried, setting off after them. 'Where are you going?'

The children reached the stairs ahead of him. Ctenka saw that more of the Shengen warriors were standing guard. Their armour was also coloured red, and he realised it was with the pitch they used to paint the walls. Whatever had gone on here in his absence was strange indeed. Stranger still was the children heading straight into the chapel, leaving the door wide open behind them.

By the time Ctenka reached them he was out of breath. They were both kneeling now amongst the idols of the Cordral gods. Sol looked down from a makeshift altar. Flanking him were Anural and Lilith. Set all about were clay figures of many sizes depicting Vane and Essena and the Fallen King. All twelve were depicted in one way or another.

As Ctenka came closer he could hear Lena and Castiel mumbling, their eyes shut tight, hands clasped as though their lives depended on prayer.

He knelt down beside them, listening for some time until he could listen no more.

'These are not your gods, little ones,' he whispered, as much to himself as to them. 'These are the Cordral gods, and they cannot hear your prayers.'

Both of them stopped at the same time, and Ctenka was taken aback. He'd never got so much as an acknowledgement from them and now he had their full attention.

Lena looked at him, right in his eyes, before saying, 'All the gods are the same, Ctenka. No matter the land you pray in. Names make no difference. They can hear us wherever we are.'

They were the first words he had heard her say.

'How do you know this?' Ctenka asked eventually.

'Because they answer us,' replied Castiel. 'Pray with us and you might hear them too.'

Ctenka shook his head. 'No one listens to my prayers. Otherwise I wouldn't be in this shithole waiting to be slaughtered.'

'Pray with us, Ctenka Sunatra, and you will see.'

For once, it didn't seem like such a stupid idea.

For the first time in as long as he could remember, Ctenka knelt in a chapel, closed his eyes and prayed.

28

IT was the hottest day Ctenka could remember. Sweat was dripping down from within his helmet, soaking his cheeks, stinging his eyes.

Just a few hundred of them were gathered in the courtyard, and a single gate was all that stood between them and a vast army. They were a thin shield wall holding back an insurmountable tide. Centurion Vallion had told them they could defend that gate with half their number. Ctenka was buoyed by his confidence but now, waiting for the attack, he wasn't so sure. He'd preferred the other man, Laigon. He'd borne an air of confidence and certainty that any man would follow, but he had apparently surrendered himself to the enemy. Given himself up to save his son and had the shit beaten out of him for his courage. Ctenka couldn't imagine being that brave. He was standing here amidst stone cold warriors and he was still scared stiff.

Vallion had taken the vanguard. His warriors were at the front, shields locked, a red barrier of discipline. Apparently he hadn't had to argue very hard to take the honour of being front and centre. For all his imperiousness, Aykan Cem had given up easily, instead forming his two hundred into four ranks behind them.

The rest, the fifty men of the Dunrun militia, were waiting at the back. Looking around, Ctenka noted that they didn't look quite so disciplined. Their uniforms were threadbare, weapons rusty and ill-assorted. Not that it mattered. If the enemy made it past the men of the Red Standing a full rout would probably be on the cards. What was he talking about 'probably'? There was no doubt these men would flee at the first sign of real battle, and Ctenka would be running right alongside them.

To his left was Ermund. Now there was a man he could believe would stand tall in the face of any threat. And on his right stood the prisoner, Josten. He too looked like he'd fight anything that walked. Ctenka should have felt like a hero of legend standing between these two titans. As it was he felt like he was going to piss. Someone had already done that in the rank in front and was now standing in wet sand. Ctenka would have laughed if they weren't all just waiting here to die. Nothing seemed funny anymore.

Something hit the gate, rattling the bars that held it in place. Ctenka jumped, but so did half the men around him. A second blow and the timbers cracked. This time men began to shuffle backwards.

'Hold,' growled Ermund. It was enough to steady their nerves. For now.

Another smash of the ram, another crack of the timbers. Ctenka looked up at the summit of the gate, suddenly wishing they had archers, but Vallion had assured them archers were useless against the shields of the Shengen troops. Better the men were down in the courtyard ready to stand against the tide that would come smashing through those gates.

And smash through they did.

With an almighty crack the gate buckled. Ancient hinges were wrenched from their housing in the solid stone archway and the Tinker's Gate fell. Vallion shouted something to his men that Ctenka couldn't hear. Aykan Cem also raised his voice, calling for his men to fight for the honour of the queen.

'Here they come,' yelled Ziyadin.

No fucking shit, thought Ctenka, as a wall of shields burst through the opening. He could just see over the heads of the men in front as the enemy clashed with the thin line of the Red Standing. A cacophony resounded throughout the courtyard, the cries of the attacking army bouncing off the mountain walls that soared up to either side.

'Bring back memories?' Josten said suddenly.

Ctenka looked to his right and saw a deathly grin on the man's face. Memories? Ctenka had no memories of ever being in such a hopeless situation.

'None I'd care to remember,' Ermund replied.

Ah, Josten wasn't talking to him.

'What about when we fought at Baldun Rock?' Josten said, as though recalling happier times.

'Ah yes,' Ermund laughed. 'We were lucky to survive that one. Two hundred mounted knights charging at us and all we had was a rundown stockade to hide behind.'

'We got bloody that day,' said Josten.

'Not as bloody as those knights.'

'When you've both finished reminiscing...' Ctenka said over the din.

A sudden volley of arrows fluttered past their position, shot by a unit of Shengen archers. It was like listening to a flock of birds flying low overhead, a whispered breath that brought death with it. Ctenka could hear the screams as men were hit. It sent panic through their ranks, but standing between Josten and Ermund, Ctenka knew he was going nowhere.

The enemy piled through the open gate. Ctenka could hear shouts from the front. The clash of weapons.

'Advance,' shouted Marshal Cem.

'No... What's he doing?' said Ermund.

'He's going to pen in the shield wall, the fucking idiot,' Josten replied.

Ctenka craned his neck, but all he could see was the odd spear being thrust or a sword raised.

'Pull back,' someone cried. 'Pull back to the Chapel Gate.'

There was a mass of confusion. Some shouted that they should retreat, that Marshal Ziyadin had given the order.

Ermund desperately shouted for the troops around him to hold their position, but it was useless. The men of the Great Eastern Militia were already flocking back through the gate behind them.

'What do we do?' asked Ctenka desperately, but he already knew what the answer would be.

As the militia fled, Josten and Ermund pushed forward through the mess of bodies. For a moment Ctenka had a choice. Flee and live, or walk forward with these two mad bastards and die on the end of a Shengen spear. A month ago it would have been an easy choice. Now though, Ctenka Sunatra would have liked to think he was a different man.

Gripping his sword tighter to stop his hand shaking, he pressed through the fleeing mob, hearing the sound of battle grow louder. Josten and Ermund pressed on harder, only too eager to reach the fighting.

When they had moved twenty yards though the mass of bodies, Ctenka could see the Red Standing shield wall was broken. Aykan Cem's men were in disarray, fighting without any cohesion. Where Marshal Ziyadin had disappeared to was anyone's guess. Vallion stood shouting at his men to reform, but against the overwhelming weight of the enemy shield wall his calls were in vain.

This was a disaster. The gate would fall, the defenders had been beaten in a single attack. None of that seemed to deter Ermund.

He howled as he charged forward, slashing out with his sword, batting an enemy shield aside and leaving the Shengen warrior exposed. Another slash and Ermund had bent the warrior's helm, blood spurting from his mouth as he fell.

Josten also ran in like a man possessed, shield battering against the enemy, knocking them back with his bulk.

Ctenka's sword remained limp and useless in his hand. All the fury he'd used to cut down that innkeeper had seeped away like bilge. Now he faced trained killers, who were more likely to hit back, and the prospect of battle didn't seem so desirable.

'Withdraw,' screamed Vallion above the din. 'Rally to me!'

Out of nowhere the Red Standing seemed to coalesce from the fighting, building a wall of shields around their centurion. Josten and Ermund likewise joined the group, forming a tight defensive unit in the midst of the battlefield.

Ctenka ran to them, slotting his shield into the defensive wall as they withdrew towards the Chapel Gate. The Shengen attackers smelled blood, advancing on them with all their might. Ctenka raised his shield in time to bat off the rain of spears that descended on him. The shield rattled on his arm, the wood cracking, split by the keen spearheads.

'We're not going to make it,' Josten cried above the battle, batting a spear to one side with his shield.

Ermund glanced back. 'Not if they shut that gate on us we won't.'

Ctenka looked back. To his horror he could see the militia were already closing the Chapel Gate behind them, more than willing to leave the remnants of their men to be slaughtered.

'Retreat,' yelled Vallion, also noticing the danger. 'Back to the gate.'

With that, all thought of defending themselves was gone. The Red Standing and what remained of Aykan Cem's militia turned tail and fled. Ctenka ran with them, any moment expecting to feel a spear between his shoulder blades.

His breath came in hot gasps, sweat pouring from him now, but miraculously there was no fatal blow to slay him.

They were almost there. The first of the Red Standing legionaries reached the gate, pushing it back open. Ctenka was going to survive the day.

His foot caught on something and he went down, sword and shield rolling from his grip. He looked down, noticing what he had tripped over. Marshal Ziyadin's fat sweaty face glared up at the sky, the shaft of an arrow protruding from the side of his head.

Ctenka scrabbled away, turning to see the entire Shengen army bearing down on him. He was never going to make it now. Never going to do anything again.

'Get up, you fucking idiot.'

It was Josten, grabbing his arm and pulling him to his feet. Ermund was also by his side, and together the three of them stood, facing the oncoming enemy.

'You ready?' asked Ermund.

'Of course I am,' Josten replied. 'It was always going to end like this. Just a matter of where and when.'

No. Ctenka hadn't thought it would always end like this. He'd always wanted to die in bed at the age of a hundred and six, with a nubile young thing riding him like a prize stallion.

One of the Shengen legionaries raised a spear, aimed right at his heart. This was it. This was the story of Ctenka Sunatra.

The advance of the Shengen troops suddenly stalled. They slowed their charge until it halted completely, and they came to stand stock still in front of the trio. Ctenka could see their armour begin to mist over, then whiten with frost. As he watched with amazement, the whole front row seemed to freeze in place, faces turning blue beneath their armour.

With a deafening blast of hot air, the Shengen warriors suddenly burst into flames. Ctenka could hear some of them howling, but he was too busy shielding his face from the conflagration to see what was happening.

When the noise died down, he finally looked up. The front row of the army had crumbled, some of them blackened and still burning. He turned, jaw dropping when he saw Lena and Castiel standing before the Chapel Gate. Their little faces were a mask of innocence, but no one else could have caused this.

'What in the hell was that?' said Ermund.

'Did I not mention?' Josten said, pulling both men to their feet. 'The gods may have returned.'

'The what?' Ermund replied.

'I'll tell you about it later.'

Lena mumbled words beneath her breath, as though she were speaking some forbidden language. At her command, more of the Shengen attackers froze where they stood. As soon as she had cast her magic, Castiel blew into his hands, closed his eyes tight, then flung his arms forward as though throwing a stone into a lake. More Shengen legionaries went up in flames, screaming as they burned.

It was too much for the invaders. Their cries of fear as they fled made Ctenka whoop for joy.

'We're fucking saved,' he said, as the last of the surviving Shengen ran back through the Tinker's Gate. He clapped Ermund on the arm. 'This is a gift. I knew it. I knew it.'

He wanted to grab both children and hug them, but he paused when he saw they were both now staring ahead at the Tinker's Gate fearfully, as though they had seen something terrifying.

Ctenka knelt beside them. 'What is it?' he asked. 'Lena, what's wrong?'

She carried on staring at the gate. 'He is coming,' she said, taking a step back.

As the little girl clasped hands with her brother, an inhuman roar echoed from down the Skull Road.

'What the fuck was that?' asked Josten.

'What does it matter?' said Ctenka. 'We've got these two.' He turned to point at Lena and Castiel, but they had already fled back through the gate.

Ermund backed away. 'Whatever it is, I for one would like to greet it from behind this wall.'

There would be no arguments from Ctenka.

Together the three men retreated beyond the safety of the gate.

It wasn't until it was closed and barred that Ctenka realised how much he was shaking.

29

THERE was weeping. But then there was always weeping afterwards. Josten remembered when he'd first seen battle. When he sat there in the long aftermath, thinking about what he'd witnessed. About what he'd done. He didn't remember crying though.

As he'd expected, this ramshackle mob hadn't put up much of a fight. He could tell they were runners as soon as he laid eyes on them. Old men put out to pasture and young boys just finished sucking on their mother's tit. They weren't going to do anything but flee in the face of a trained and disciplined army. The Shengen Empire wasn't renowned the world over for nothing.

Over a score of militia had already fled this place. Josten had half a mind to join them, but he'd had enough of stumbling through the desert. At least here he'd get to go down with a sword in his hand, not dying of thirst under the relentless sun.

So rather than flee he sat in the coolest corner he could find and watched proceedings.

It didn't take long for the reprisals to start. The shouting and the arguments. Whose fault was it they lost and what were they going to do now? Josten could have answered both those questions for them – because they were a useless bunch of fuckwits and they should do themselves a favour and surrender. As it was, no one wanted to say the obvious.

'We need to retreat immediately,' said Aykan Cem. That wasn't surprising though. The man was clearly a weakling. He'd managed to get from the front of the battle to the rear without anyone noticing. In fact he was most likely the one that ordered the gate shut when there were still men out fighting.

'Go then, if you must,' said Vallion. 'But your men stay.'

Josten quite liked the stoic Shengen, not least because he clearly took no shit.

'You are not in command here,' Cem snapped back. 'I hold seniority.'

'You are a coward who flees at the first sign of danger. You should be flogged to death, not left in charge of fighting men.'

'And who will do the flogging? You?'

Both men were on their feet now, nose to nose. The legionaries of the Red Standing and the men of the royal militia were gathered behind their respective leaders as the tension brewed. If they'd all been as keen to fight the Shengens as they were to fight each other then maybe they wouldn't be licking their wounds right now.

'Enough. This is the last thing we need,' said Ermund, stepping forward.

What a surprise, great Duke Harlaw of Ravensbrooke. Everyone relax, Ermund was here to save the day.

To his credit, his appearance did calm the men down, but then Harlaw had always had a talent for conciliation.

Perhaps he should have tried it with his wife once in a while, then maybe she wouldn't have betrayed him and he wouldn't be stuck in this dump.

'We cannot just abandon Dunrun. We must hold it,' he continued.

'We need reinforcements,' said Cem. 'This place is doomed.'

Ermund nodded in agreement. 'It is,' he said. 'So you must inform the queen. When I visited Kantor to tell her of the threat there was no way of knowing what kind of force we would face and I didn't have the authority to demand more troops. Now you've seen first hand, Marshal. You must go to her. Tell her what we are up against. But we will need your men to hold this fortress until you can return with the army we need.'

Vallion made to protest, but Ermund silenced him with nothing more than a hand on his shoulder.

'Very well,' said Cem, feigning reluctance. 'I will ride to Kantor immediately and take word of your plight.'

Josten couldn't help but admire Harlaw. He'd got rid of the incompetent Aykan Cem but managed to keep his men. Quite the diplomat.

He had seen enough now. Josten was hungry and thirsty and needed some sleep before the next wave of Shengens came knocking. He stood, leaving Aykan Cem to stammer his false regrets to his men before fleeing like someone had set his arse on fire. Harlaw and Vallion were more than capable of concocting the next battle plan. Not that they had many options beyond standing and fighting until everyone here was dead.

As Josten made his way to the main courtyard he could see two men arguing over a piece of dried beef. It was obvious there wasn't enough food to go around for the militia, let alone a prisoner brought all the way from the Suderfeld to die. His stomach was rumbling and he started to wonder whether it was worth joining in the fight for scraps when he spotted the boy Ctenka sitting with those two children.

Ctenka was genuinely caring for the pair of waifs and had managed to find them food from somewhere. He certainly made a better nursemaid than a fighter, that was for sure.

The rest of the men gave those children a wide berth, but that was only to be expected. They had conjured enough magic to decimate an entire unit of legionaries. Two little children. The fact they were dangerous was plain for all to see, but Josten didn't share their apprehension. He had seen magic manifested as pure evil. He had faced the witch Innellan and lived, so he was hardly going to be frightened of two little children.

He walked to where Ctenka was trying to get the girl to eat some rancid-looking jerky, and sat down with them.

'Keeping our secret weapons well fed?' he said.

Ctenka looked up at him, not seeing the funny side. 'They're not weapons. They're children. Or can't you see that?'

'I saw them slaughter about fifty men with a gesture. They looked like weapons to me.' Ctenka ignored him. 'You know when this is over you won't be able to keep them.' Josten remembered how Livia had been relentlessly pursued across three nations. He knew full well these children would be coveted for their power much the same.

'They're not mine to keep,' Ctenka replied. 'But someone will have to take care of them.'

'So you're just going to take them back to where you found them?'

'I—' Ctenka clearly hadn't thought it through.

'Best thing you can do when this is all over, is take them far away from here. Far from anyone who knows what they can do. It's the only chance they've got for a life.'

'You seem to know a lot about it,' said Ctenka.

'Let's say I've seen this kind of thing before. And it won't end well for anyone if people know what they're capable of. If you want to keep them safe, keep them hidden.'

'Why do you care?' Ctenka asked.

Josten remembered a conversation he'd had not too long ago with a lad called Lonik the Fidget. He'd tried his best to help that boy. To keep him alive. He remembered how that had turned out.

'I don't.'

Ctenka shook his head. 'Even I can see through that lie. You care more than you're willing to say. You saved me out there. Stood by me, ready to die. That's not a man who doesn't care.'

'Maybe I'm just not choosy about where I die… or who with,' was all Josten could think to say.

He stood, the conversation leaving a sour taste in his mouth.

Aykan Cem was mounting his horse, spewing platitudes to the men he was leaving behind. Assuring them that he would return swiftly at the head of an army. Josten couldn't help but grin at the prig as he rode off. He doubted he would ever see Aykan Cem again.

As he watched the man ride away, his horse galloped past a figure approaching down the Skull Road. Perhaps a deserter who had changed their mind about running away, returning to die by the sword rather than be taken by the desert. Perhaps a lone traveller lost on the road. Well, they'd be in for a surprise if they thought they'd gain any succour here.

Before long he could discern it was a woman. A few moments more and he realised it was a woman he recognised. But it couldn't be. She had been killed at Kessel. Slaughtered in a battle between fanatics, or so Josten had assumed.

Silver walked into the fortress of Dunrun and the courtyard went silent.

'Fuck me, what's this?' said one of the militia.

'What's a woman doing here?' said another.

Josten walked forward, standing in front of her. She glanced back at him, as though not recognising the man she had travelled through the desert with not more than a year ago.

'Silver?' he said.

She frowned at him, as though searching her memory for any sign of familiarity.

'I know you,' she said. 'Yes, I remember you.'

'It's Josten,' he said. 'Josten Cade. We travelled through the Ramadi together. We fought together at—'

'Yes,' she said. Then walked past him.

'What are you doing here?' he asked as she walked away.

Before she could answer, the two children Ctenka had been looking after appeared at Silver's side. She looked down at them as they stared up adoringly.

'We knew you would come,' said the little girl.

Silver knelt down beside them. 'Sweet child,' she said, running a weathered hand across the girl's head. 'You shouldn't be here.'

'None of us should,' said Ctenka, rushing over. 'Come away, children.'

They both ignored him, continuing to stare at Silver. 'Will you stop him?' the girl asked.

Silver nodded. 'That is why I have come,' she replied.

'Stop who?' asked Josten. 'What are you doing here?'

Again she ignored him, rising to her feet and making her way through the fort. He followed her beneath the Hangman's Gate, the two children running after her like she was leading them by an invisible rope.

As they made their way through to the next courtyard every eye turned towards them. Josten had to admit they struck an odd group, a woman fresh from the desert followed by two children. This was a fortress besieged. It was no place for any of them. But then, Josten had seen what Silver could do. Had seen what these children were capable of. They had more right to be here than anyone.

When she reached the Chapel Gate, Vallion and Ermund were discussing tactics. They had put the remaining militia to task shoring up the wood–and–iron gate. It already looked sturdier than the last one. Only time would tell how long it kept the enemy out.

Silver stopped before the gate, as though waiting for someone to knock.

Vallion and Ermund stopped their conversation, noticing Silver standing there, the two children waiting behind, watching her every move.

Ermund looked at Josten with a quizzical expression. 'Who is this?'

'This is Silver,' Josten said. 'She's…'

'I am here to kill your enemy and send him back to where he crawled from,' Silver said, still staring at that gate.

Vallion walked forward, sizing Silver up. 'You are here to kill the Iron Tusk?' he asked.

She turned to look at him, and Josten was surprised to see this implacable warrior unable to hold her gaze.

'Whatever you choose to call him,' she said gently, 'I am here to stop him, before he can do any more damage to this place.'

There was silence, until Josten could stand it no more.

'Well I for one am glad of the help,' he said to her. 'You're very welcome to stay and die with the rest of us.'

No one seemed to want to argue with that. Least of all Silver.

SIFF

*S*HE *opened her eyes to watch the world burn. Fire consumed a sea of corpses. A funeral pyre of thousands, flames licking the heavens. A dead world slaughtered in sacrifice to the gods.*

Temples towered above the dead, erected in tribute to her rule. Factories churned with activity, cogs perpetually spinning, bellows pumping, chimneys coughing out poison. The sky was black with the ashes of the dead. There was no more life in this place. No relief. She had seen it laid low and now, in her victory, she had a carrion realm to rule over.

This was what Siff's triumph had cost, but it was the only price that could be paid. She had defeated every enemy. The Archons were dead and there were no lands left to conquer, in this plane or the next.

She looked down from her tower and wept.

Her tears splashed to the ground, running in rivulets, coalescing into streams that poured in rivers to quell the fires that consumed the world. But it was too late. Too late for this place or any other.

Too late.

She screamed, body convulsing, tortured, wracked with pain.

It was a familiar agony. A body burned. Useless.

Only this time she was not alone in the desert. This time she was surrounded by life.

No, not by life. By life-givers.

Siff opened her eyes to the night. A sea of stars spread across the sky. She could make out every one pinpointed in the blackness, swirling in concentric patterns, forming sigils and glyphs, verses and stanzas… symphonies in the night.

Surrounding her, mortals kneeling in the dark. They mumbled ancient tenets and credos. Prayers she had not heard for a century, but they were familiar to her ears. They filled her with a strange sensation, as though a restorative light were glowing in the pit of her stomach. Healing her. Bringing her back from the brink.

Even when she stood from the makeshift altar they continued to pray. Her legs were weak, unsteady, but as she stumbled she could feel the muscle and sinew knitting back together. Her flesh blossoming with life, sloughing off the burned flakes of dead skin.

Slowly, one of the worshippers stood. A woman, face time-worn and back stooped by the weight of her years. She looked up with rheumy eyes shining with tears.

Siff looked down at the woman, opened her mouth to speak, but before she could the light from the stars suddenly went out…

★ ★ ★

336

The next time she woke she was inside, surrounded by a hide shelter that swayed gently in the desert breeze. Siff raised a hand; every inch of her was wrapped in linen bandages. It stirred a memory...

A mortal. A beautiful mortal and his two beautiful sons. They had bandaged her body, healing her, but not with their worship. They had done it with kindness. With patience. With love.

She had been different then. Forged from the desert and born anew as Silver. But that woman had been no one. Not the mortal whose body she had taken. Not the goddess, Siff, who she eventually became. She had been both of those and neither, and now she was gone. Killed in the desert when Siff had taken her vengeance. Now all that remained was the Archon.

The hide was pulled back, letting in the bright sun, and she turned away from its glare. Someone entered, shuffling to her bedside, and when Siff looked up she saw the old woman from the night before. She was smiling kindly.

Before Siff could try to speak, the woman lowered herself to her knees, bowing her head.

'We are truly blessed,' she said. 'Truly blessed that you have returned.'

Her reverence sparked memories. Old memories of a different age. A different time, when she had been worshipped by mortals. When entire nations had fallen to their knees and given themselves to her willingly in supplication. It sparked a forbidden desire within her she had fought to repress for a thousand years, a desire that nagged at her, pulling at her with its temptation. She tried to rise, to stop the woman before she could continue, but her body would not respond.

'Do not kneel,' she managed to say through cracked lips.

Slowly the woman stood, smiling down. 'I am the *umma* of this caravan,' she said. 'We have waited so long for you.'

'How long have I been...'

'With us once more? Weeks? Months? We have not counted the number of moons. We have simply prayed for you to be restored.'

'Who do you think I am?' asked Siff.

The woman seemed fazed by the question. 'Why, you are Anural. Cup Bearer to Sol the Father. The Life Giver.'

It became clearer now. In the Cordral they had called her Anural, and Brachius was known as Sol. She cringed at the thought; she had never been cup-bearer to anyone, least of all that sot Brachius.

She tried to sit up, but the *umma* put a gentle hand on her shoulder.

'You must rest,' said the old woman. 'Your journey from the heavens was a hard one. We will take care of everything. Soon you will be restored.'

Siff shook her head. 'No. I will recover without your help.'

'But we have already prepared for you. We pray day and night. We go without food or water.'

This was exactly what Siff had feared. 'No,' she said as firmly as she could. 'You are not to suffer in my name. You are not to offer me worship. It is too...'

But Siff could already feel it filling her with power. That exquisite sensation she had spurned for what seemed an age. But then, it had been an age.

338

'Fear not, goddess,' said the woman, pushing Siff back to the bed. 'We will take care of everything. Soon you will be healed. Then you may lead us.'

Siff wanted to argue but she couldn't. The combination of fatigue and the fact that she could feel the life returning to her body made her lie back and close her eyes.

To accept such veneration was forbidden. She had been the one to forbid it. But now all she could think was how exquisite it felt…

Her dreams had changed. No longer did they plague her with visions of what could be. Now they seemed to show her a picture of what was.

She floated over the sands, further and further north, the miles flashing past impossibly fast as she soared, the hot air rushing in her face.

The Ramadi Wastes burned. Slaves toiled deep beneath the earth, reconstructing palaces that had been empty for a hundred years, reclaiming ancient temples from the sand. The death cults were uniting, their ancient wars now all but forgotten. Wherever there was resistance to this new order it was crushed, dissenters sacrificed to the gods… no, not the gods. To one god.

Innellan towered over them all, consolidating her power, destroying all who did not kneel before her. And all the while she did it in the body of an innocent child. The White Widow ruled her empire from a tower that teased the sky, and all worshipped her for her beauty. All lusted after her. All would have flung themselves on their swords for a word of approval from her perfect lips.

She had very nearly united an entire nation in less than a year. Only a small cell of resistance remained and it would not last long. Then she would clutch the allegiance of every death cult in her wicked grip. Every warlord and chieftain would kneel before her. Where before there had been chaos, now there would be unity. And once she held ultimate power in the Ramadi, Innellan would turn her eye south...

Before she could see more, Siff was moving again, flying east over blasted desert until she reached the mountains. Over the peaks, over valleys and jutting crags, until she reached the land of the Shengen. There she saw an emperor die. Legions falling to their knees in worship of an inhuman warlord mounted on an armoured beast. Where before there had been order, now there was only violence. Only pain and suffering. Again, dissent was quelled in the cruellest fashion. A nation that had once prospered was falling to ruin, but still Armadon pressed on. All he yearned for was conquest and he had already begun his march west.

He was already well on his way through the mountains and there was no one to stop him.

When Siff woke, it was night. She could still hear them praying outside, but where before she had accepted their praise, now it only served to raise her hackles.

Gingerly she rose from the bed, limping from the tent and out into the night. Torches burned at the edge of the camp and she could hear the high-pitched keening of some animal off in the distance.

Siff had been expecting a score of worshippers on their knees in prayer, but there was no one waiting for her outside the tent.

She stumbled on through the dark, following the distant sound of the animal. As she moved on broken feet she could soon hear worshippers at prayer, feeling their benefaction eking into every fibre of her being. When she had walked far enough she saw them, more torches burning in the night as the whole tribe seemed to be kneeling in prayer. They had erected an altar upon which the *umma* stood. Her arms were raised as she led their rite and Siff could see in one hand she held a curved dagger.

That keening noise rose up into the desert night once more and Siff realised it was made by no animal. On the altar in front of the *umma* was laid out a child, struggling against its bonds.

'Stop,' Siff cried.

The *umma* looked up from her mumbled prayers. More than one of the congregation shrank from Siff as she appeared, but the rest carried on with their devotion.

'This is for you,' said the old woman. 'It will restore you, that you might lead us to salvation. Our sacrifice shall be your—'

'I said no!' Siff yelled over her worshippers' droning noise.

Even as she forbade it, Siff yearned for the sacrifice. The blood of that child would grant her great power. Would make her invincible, for a time. It was everything she desired and it took all her will to quell the need.

'This is our way,' said the *umma*, raising that dagger high. 'This has always been our way.'

Siff wrenched one of the torches from the ground. She could barely comprehend what she was doing as she flung the pole at the woman. The flames made a hissing noise in the wind before the torch impaled the woman atop the altar and flung her back into darkness.

One of the congregation screamed, fearing the wrath of a god. Two more leapt to their feet and fled into the night. Then, like a dam breaking, the rest of them ran.

Siff walked to the altar, climbing atop it, seeing the infant there, still struggling, still wailing into the night.

This was what the world had become since the Archons had left. This was why she had demanded the Heartstone be broken. This was why she had to stop Innellan.

But there was a more pressing danger. A conqueror was already on his way to subjugate these lands.

First she had to defeat Armadon.

30

CTENKA watched the Shengen legions mustering as he stood at the top of the Tinker's Gate. They were bringing death with them now. There was no chance of clemency. No surrender. They would have to fight or die.

When he looked over at Josten and Ermund he knew they had embraced the prospect of death. They showed no fear, they'd survived more battles than they could count and here they were again, ready to throw themselves at the enemy, despite the odds.

Ctenka wasn't that confident yet. He'd only killed one man, and that had been in a forest in a different country. After the way that had made him feel he didn't value the prospect of killing anyone else, not that there was any chance of him slaying the enemy. The Shengens were a wall of armoured might. How would this band of rag-tag defenders ever defeat them?

When Ctenka saw the woman, Silver, approaching, he felt a little spark of hope.

There was something about her that unnerved him more than the Shengens, but then she seemed to unnerve everyone. All apart from Josten. He knew the woman of old, had travelled with her and fought with her. Beyond that

Ctenka had no idea what was between them and he didn't have the guts to pry.

She surveyed the killing yard below. Bodies still rotted in the sun, neither side having the courage to claim their dead. Ctenka watched her from the corner of his eye, wondering what could be going on in that head of hers. An unseasonably cool breeze blew down the valley from the east, and she closed her eyes as it ruffled the dry, blonde hair on her head.

'He is coming,' she said.

Ctenka looked out from the gate to the far end of the courtyard but could see nothing at first. He squinted across at the distant legions, silent and still as statues, until finally he saw movement. Ranks of men were turning aside in regimented order, making a corridor for someone to pass through. Eventually he spied a towering shape advancing, a rider on a mount, moving relentlessly past row upon row of legionaries.

With wide eyes, Ctenka stared as the Iron Tusk approached the Tinker's Gate. He rode on the back of a vast armoured bear, the beast appearing docile as it walked, but Ctenka could see the enormous power in its limbs as its claws churned up the sand, slaver dripping from jaws that could tear a man in half. But this beast was nothing in comparison to the warrior who rode upon its back. The Iron Tusk was a formidable being, head encased in a helm, single horn curling upwards. He was huge about the shoulders, the sinew of his arms standing out starkly in the sun. In his right hand he held a double-headed axe, in the left a sword wider than any blade Ctenka had ever laid eyes on.

The Iron Tusk stopped in front of the gate, raising his

344

arms wide, those impossibly heavy weapons seeming like wooden toys in his grip.

'Defenders of the Cordral,' he proclaimed, voice resonating from within his helm. 'You have my admiration. You have fought valiantly, and for that I grant you mercy. Open your gates. Pledge yourselves to me and you will be spared. Continue to defy me and you will all die.'

Ctenka could feel something radiating from the warlord as he spoke. All he wanted to do was rush down and push open the gates. To fall at this monster's feet and beg for mercy. To pledge his loyalty and give over his very soul. He looked down and saw his hands were gripping the parapet tightly, knuckles white, fingernails almost breaking as he fought to resist.

No one was brave enough to answer and Ctenka could see doubt falling across everyone else's brow, as though a dark shadow of uncertainty had crossed them all, leeching their resolve in the face of this titan.

Only one of them dared to defy him.

'I see you, Armadon,' Silver shouted down.

The Iron Tusk slowly lowered his arms. A dry chuckle emanated from behind a helm that seemed to be bolted to his face.

'So you have come to stop me? Even here,' he said. 'I thought I could feel you, slinking in the dark, stalking me like the spider you are.'

'Will you face me? We can end this here,' Silver said. Ctenka couldn't believe what he was hearing. Of all the heroes that might defend the Cordral Extent, it appeared the only champion willing to step forward was this wild-looking woman from the desert.

'How can I refuse?' the Iron Tusk called.

Silver turned and made her way down to the gate below. Josten and Ermund followed her, and despite his better judgement, Ctenka went with them. At the bottom, Vallion ordered his men to unbar the gate.

As it opened, revealing the Iron Tusk awaiting her, Silver took a spear from one of the legionaries.

'Don't interfere,' she said as she walked forward through the gate.

Ctenka wanted to assure her there was no danger of that, but he kept his mouth shut.

She walked out to stand before the Iron Tusk atop his mighty bear. Ctenka couldn't help but notice how tiny she was in front of this behemoth. How was she ever going to defeat him? They'd been mad to allow her to go. But then, who was going to stop her?

'We could rule this land side by side,' said the Iron Tusk. 'We could defeat that bitch Innellan and take this world for ourselves.'

In answer, Silver hefted the spear, effortlessly bringing it to her shoulder and drawing it back. In one smooth motion she flung it directly at her target. The spearhead pierced the bear's right eye, sinking in halfway up the shaft. The creature made no sound as it collapsed.

The Iron Tusk rolled aside as the beast fell dead, and rose deftly to his feet. Silver was already running at him, her sword ringing free of its scabbard. The warlord managed to parry her first blow with his sword, swinging his axe to counter. She ducked, spinning aside, slashing in again and catching the Iron Tusk a glancing blow at the hip.

Ctenka could hear him grunt in pain, the sound hollow from within that vast helm. Josten and Ermund had walked in front of the gate now, eager to watch, not wanting to miss a thing, and Ctenka went with them, barely comprehending that he was putting himself in harm's way.

The way they went at each other was a sight to behold. Ctenka had seen skilled combatants fighting before – had even been in the thick of it himself – but he'd never seen anything like this. The Iron Tusk was fast, too fast for his size. He should have been a lumbering brute, but he seemed to move with a wicked grace, swinging those mighty weapons like they weighed nothing. For her part, Silver dodged and sidestepped every blow, ducking low, dancing out of range, and for every miss from her opponent she struck in with a counter, jabbing and slicing at the huge warlord.

Blood was flowing freely from him now, running in rivulets down his great barrel chest, soaking the armour on his legs. He howled in frustration, a terrifying bellow that rang throughout the fortress and made Ctenka want to flee. But he didn't flee; he stood and watched as they went at one another.

Silver leapt impossibly high over a devastating sweep of the Iron Tusk's sword. Her blade flashed, cutting a rent in the warlord's shoulder. He grunted again, dropping his axe to the ground and staggering back. He was mortally wounded, a cut that would have laid low the strongest warrior, but still he stood his ground, broadsword flashing in the sun. Silver ducked the blow, rolling along the ground, coming up to run him through the midriff.

This time he faltered, falling to one knee, barely able to parry another flurry of strikes from Silver.

Ctenka heard a shout from across the courtyard. The Shengens were rushing forward, seeing their warlord on his knees, determined that he would not be vanquished by this woman.

Armoured warriors ran to aid their faltering leader. Shengen archers launched a volley of arrows that struck the ground around the combatants. Silver raised her blade for a final strike but an arrow impaled her shoulder. She stumbled back and Ctenka was already running. Josten and Ermund were by his side, Vallion also sprinting, shield at the ready.

The Shengen warriors had reached the Iron Tusk now, half a dozen of them trying to drag him to safety, but he would not go, easily brushing two of them aside, determined to finish the fight. His men were dogged in their determination, and yet more of them piled forward, grabbing the Iron Tusk, fighting against his enormous strength and dragging him bodily back to safety.

Another volley of arrows flew across the courtyard, but Vallion was already there, planting his tower shield in front of Silver. Ctenka heard the arrows strike the steel, but he was already helping Silver to her feet. She barely seemed to notice the wound in her shoulder as the legionaries dragged the Iron Tusk back across the courtyard.

More archers ran forward. Ctenka had to duck as he and the others retreated back towards the gate. Arrows peppered the ground all around him as they moved back behind their defensive wall. With a cry from Vallion the gate was slammed shut behind them. They could still hear the bellowing of the Iron Tusk echoing up through the mountains.

Everyone was breathing heavily apart from Silver, who stood glaring at the gate, the arrow still impaled in her shoulder.

'We need to get that out,' Ctenka said, trying not to be sick.

She looked down at the arrow as though she hadn't noticed it. Then she snapped off the flight, reached behind and pulled the head from the back of her shoulder.

'No, bastard!'

Ctenka turned at the voice. It was Josten, crouched on the ground where Ermund lay in the dust, Vallion leaning over him. Ctenka could see the arrowhead protruding from Ermund's chest and he ran forward, kneeling by his friend's side. 'Help him,' he shouted. 'Somebody help him.'

Nobody came. It seemed obvious to everyone but Ctenka that Ermund could not be helped.

'You have to save him.' Ctenka looked up at Silver. There was something about her, anyone could see that. If anyone could save Ermund it was her. Instead, she just turned and walked away.

Josten knelt beside them, looking down at Ermund and grasping his hand.

'You can't die. Not like this,' he said through gritted teeth, biting back tears. It was the first real emotion Ctenka had seen from the man besides rage.

'This…' Ermund said, fighting the pain, '…is as good a way as any.'

'Fuck that,' Josten snarled. 'You and me aren't fucking done yet. Not by a damn sight.'

Ermund smiled at that, a line of blood running from his mouth and down his cheek. 'I forgive you, Josten Cade. I forgive you for all of it.' He grabbed Josten's tunic and pulled him close. 'Now you just have to forgive yourself.'

'No,' said Josten, as though he could heal Ermund with his anger. 'I said we're not fucking done.'

Ermund ignored him and turned to Ctenka. 'Do one thing for me, lad,' he whispered.

'Anything,' Ctenka replied. 'Just name it.'

'Don't die here.'

Ctenka was about to say he had no bloody intention of dying here, and he had no intention of letting Ermund die here either.

But his friend had already gone.

Josten stood and left Ctenka holding Ermund's hand.

It was a stupid fucking death. But then, weren't they all?

31

H<small>E</small> was alive. No matter how much Laigon might have wanted death, he was still here. One of his eyes had swollen shut and he could barely see out of the other. His breath came in laboured wheezes, his nostrils filled with clotted blood. His jaw was most likely broken, his nose definitely.

Though Laigon's vision was impaired, he could still make out details of the command tent he was in. This was the Iron Tusk's lair, he had visited it enough times to know. It was decorated simply, but then the Iron Tusk was a simple man. Cruel, ruthless, deadly, but still simple. Candles burned in their stands but by their light Laigon couldn't see a bed. It was like the warlord never slept, always on the hunt, always eager to conquer.

Laigon strained against his bonds, his hands tied behind him to the main prop post in the centre of the tent. It was useless, there would be no escape. No hope of redemption. No hope at all. All that was left for him was execution. If he was lucky it would be quick, but then luck had abandoned him of late.

It seemed that for Laigon all that was left now was his faith. Before the coming of the new warlord, when he had been a true servant of the emperor, Laigon had worshipped the gods. Even after the Iron Tusk had conquered the Shengen Empire, Laigon had still secretly prayed. But what good had it done? The Shengen were defeated, now led by a usurper. Its faithful servants turned into little more than slaves. And here was Laigon, defiant, faithful to the old gods and the old ways, tied to a post waiting to die.

Had the gods abandoned him? Was he to be left to die at the whim of a tyrant? Or perhaps... perhaps this was a test. Perhaps now more than ever Laigon would need his faith.

He still had the metal figurine of Portius in his hand and he squeezed it, not wanting to let it go, comforted by the feel of it against his palm. It was all he had left. The only thing connecting him with the past. To those days of glorious righteousness. Laigon closed his one good eye, summoning up as much conviction as he could. He had never seen any evidence of the gods, never been offered a sign, never heard of a miracle performed. But still, if he prayed for salvation could it be granted?

He never got the chance to even try. The side of the tent opened and Laigon looked up to find the hulking figure of the Iron Tusk enter. The warlord glared down, the one eye visible within that twisted helm burning into Laigon like a hot brand. He was wounded, blood covering his bare chest, arms and legs. Cuts marring almost every inch of his flesh.

The Iron Tusk drew in breath after furious breath, that eye staring at Laigon all the while. At any moment Laigon expected him to reach forward with those huge hands and crush his skull. Instead the Iron Tusk stood there and bled.

'You have defied me,' he said at last. 'You have all defied me and it will not stand. It cannot stand.'

Laigon didn't know if he could speak, even had he wanted to. His jaw ached, teeth feeling loose in his head.

The Iron Tusk's breathing became more regular and slowly he knelt beside Laigon, blood still running down his bare flesh. There was a stab wound in the warlord's side that would have laid even the mightiest warrior low, but if Laigon had learned anything by now it was that the Iron Tusk was like no mortal man.

'You must pledge yourself to me, Laigon Valdyr. You must worship me. You must become mine. Follow me, Laigon, and I will give you this world.'

'Why don't you just kill me?' Laigon managed to say through broken lips. 'Isn't that why you brought me here?'

The Iron Tusk murmured a laugh beneath his helmet, his shoulders shaking. 'You were my greatest warrior. My greatest leader. My greatest failure. Do you think I would just abandon you? I need you, Laigon. If you follow me then they will all follow me. I need you to prove that I am to be revered. To dispel any doubt that I am the absolute ruler of the Shengen Empire. That my conquest is a righteous one.'

Now it was Laigon's turn to laugh, but doing so sent pain coursing through his jaw, into his head. 'You are the tyrant of Shengen. You can slaughter us by our thousands but that doesn't make you our ruler. Murder and enslavement will not give you men's hearts.'

'You cannot hope to fight me, Laigon. But you can fight *for* me. Lead my armies to victory.'

Laigon met the Tusk's eye, green and piercing. 'You are losing. Finally you see that you're not invincible. Well, I will not help you. You will have to kill me.'

'No,' said the Iron Tusk. 'I will not have to kill you, because you will serve me. You will follow me and you will do it of your own free will.'

The Iron Tusk stood, taking a step back from where Laigon was tied to the post. Someone else entered the tent. At first Laigon couldn't see who it was. Then he felt panic tighten in his gut as he recognised his son.

Petrachus stood silently, hand on the sword by his side. It looked far too big for the boy – a ridiculous ornament given to a child. Petrachus stared at Laigon, but it was as if his own son did not recognise him. But then Laigon's face was swollen and bloodied. He imagined his own mother would have struggled to recognise him.

'Your son has chosen to join me,' said the Iron Tusk. 'He has chosen to share in my glory. It's only a matter of time before you do the same.'

'He has chosen nothing,' Laigon snapped. 'You have bewitched him. Just like you have bewitched the rest of them.'

'Bewitched? I have merely chosen to lead a weak nation to glory. I have bewitched no one.'

'You are a usurper, and you will fall.'

The Iron Tusk shook his vast helmed head. 'No. I will rise and I will conquer. And you will be by my side. Petrachus, explain to your father.'

The boy seemed to recognise Laigon for the first time.

Where previously he had shown only contempt and treated him like a traitor, now he looked on him like a father.

'It is true,' the boy said. 'All of it is true. I have been shown the way. Do not turn your back on us, father. We need you. We all need you.'

Laigon stifled his tears. For an instant he thought he saw the Petrachus he knew, but his words spoke a different story.

'Petrachus, this is not you,' said Laigon. 'You are no man's slave. Think, son. Remember me. Remember your mother. The gods. This tyrant is not the one you should follow.'

'He is with me,' said the Iron Tusk, moving around the prop post. 'Loyal. As you once were.' Laigon could feel a pull at the bonds tying his wrists together. With the deft slice of a blade the Iron Tusk cut him free. 'You should follow his example. The father taught by the son.' The Iron Tusk stood in front of Laigon now, a blade in his hand; a cruel jagged knife designed for inflicting pain. He jammed that knife into the ground between Laigon's legs, then he knelt, his hands behind his back. 'But if you will not follow your son, if you will not join the men and women of your nation, then save them. End my life. Strike me down, Laigon Valdyr.'

Laigon sensed treachery. This had to be some kind of trick. He knew the Iron Tusk was fast, despite his size, but maybe Laigon was faster. Maybe, despite what they had done to him, despite his injuries, he would be able to take that knife and end this madness.

Even as he lunged forward he expected the Iron Tusk to lash out with one of his huge fists. As his hand closed around the knife handle he knew he was slow, he would never be quick enough. The knife came out of the ground with ease, and still Laigon never believed he could finish the warlord.

His aim was true. Yet before he could finish his strike a sword sliced down, knocking the knife from his hand with a clash of steel. That sword came up again, resting beneath Laigon's chin. He looked to his right and Petrachus was holding the blade, too big in his little boy's hands, but still he held it. He stood there stock still, his stance perfect, eyes fixed on Laigon. There was no emotion in them, and Laigon knew that one command from the Iron Tusk and Petrachus would have cut his throat.

'You see,' said the Iron Tusk. 'What once was yours is now mine. But I can give it back to you. All you need do is pledge yourself to me. Let yourself believe, Laigon Valdyr, and you will have everything you ever wished for.'

Laigon stared at his son. Petrachus still stood, that blade held tight in his hands, not wavering, not faltering. Laigon could never have hoped to train a recruit so young to demonstrate such impeccable form. A power was at work here beyond his understanding.

He fell back, defeated, leaning against the prop post, fighting his tears once more.

Petrachus sheathed his sword as the Iron Tusk rose to his feet.

'If I cannot persuade you, if the loyalty of your son does not inspire you, then perhaps another can sway you onto the right path.'

A woman entered behind Petrachus. Laigon knew who it was before he even looked at her face. Verrana rested her hands on Petrachus' shoulders and Laigon heard himself whisper 'no' involuntarily. Not his wife. Not his love.

'You see,' said the Iron Tusk. 'It is foolish to resist the inevitable. If you still insist on this stubbornness, this hubris, then let me show you the true power of devotion.'

Laigon looked up fearfully, wondering what the Iron Tusk would do. Whether the warlord would wring his wife's neck. Whether he would order Petrachus to run her through. He did neither.

The Iron Tusk merely stood there as Laigon's wife and son knelt down before him. They bowed their heads, clasping their hands together and raising their voices in prayer. With every well-practised word they pledged their devotion, they wished for his victory, they begged for him to be restored to health. And as Laigon sat there and watched, he saw the warlord's wounds close up. The deep rents in his side and shoulder knitted together before Laigon's eyes, the myriad cuts and bruises on his flesh healing over.

When they had finished their prayers, the Iron Tusk fixed Laigon with his steely eye once more. 'What say you now? What will you do now your family is mine?'

Laigon still held the pewter figurine in his fist. He squeezed the tiny statue of Portius until his hand bled, gritting his teeth against temptation until his head throbbed.

'I will kill you,' he said.

'Traitor,' spat Verrana. 'You are the one who will die.'

Laigon knew then he had lost her. He had lost his son. There was nothing else to say.

'It is clear you have much to think on,' said the Iron

Tusk. 'I will leave you to reflect. But do not take forever, Laigon Valdyr. Time is not on your side.'

The Iron Tusk left him alone. Petrachus and Verrana left too, neither deigning to look at him.

The Iron Tusk's guards entered, and Laigon was bound once more to the prop post. As he was finally alone in the dark and the candles burned down to nothing, all Laigon was left with were his own prayers.

32

Ermund's body lay wrapped in linens in the middle of the chapel. Ctenka kept watch as the children knelt beside him. Lena and Castiel had been praying all night. Ctenka wondered where they got their energy.

For his part, Ctenka was done with praying. What bloody good was it doing them anyway?

It hadn't done Ermund any good.

His friend lay there, still and lifeless. Ctenka was finished with crying as well as praying. There were no more tears left. Who the hell was going to cry for him when he was run through by a Shengen spear? There'd be no prayers said for poor, dead Ctenka Sunatra. Just a shallow grave, if he was lucky.

The door to the chapel opened and Josten stood there. Sweat had gathered on his brow and his shirt was drenched from the noonday heat.

'It's ready,' he said.

Ctenka nodded, moving to help with the body, but Josten raised his hand. The southerner lifted Ermund's corpse, hefting it over his shoulder and making his way from the chapel.

Ctenka followed him out, past the legionaries of the Red Standing preparing for battle. Past the scared and tired militia. Past the wounded and the not-so-wounded as they cowered in the shadows of Dunrun's walls.

They walked out into the desert and Ctenka could see the makeshift markers designating a forgotten graveyard. There was one freshly dug hole.

As Josten gently laid Ermund in the grave, Ctenka knew it was time to stop feeling sorry for himself. Ermund had given his life to defend this place. Would Ctenka do the same when the time came? When Josten picked up the shovel and started covering up the body, Ctenka told him to wait.

'Shouldn't we say something?' he asked.

Josten stabbed his shovel into the ground and looked up, squinting in the sun. 'You a priest all of a sudden?'

'No, but I… I just thought…'

Josten sighed. 'All right then,' he said. 'Here lies Ermund Harlaw. One time Duke of Ravensbrooke. Always a bastard.' He paused, seeming suddenly regretful. 'And he was my friend once.'

The genuine sorrow in Josten's voice surprised Ctenka. He doubted Josten Cade had many friends, it was clear he was a difficult man to like, yet here he was burying one of the few that had. For the first time, Ctenka felt sorry for the man.

'Now,' said Josten, turning from the grave. 'Feel free to finish burying the fucker.'

As Josten walked away, Ctenka did as he was bid. He'd expected to be more emotional as he put Ermund in the earth, but all he felt was numb.

Just as he finished he heard a bell ringing from inside the fort.

Before he realised what he was doing, Ctenka was running. Once inside the fort he was relieved to see other men were running with him. The Red Standing had already positioned themselves in front of the gate. Silver stood with them, sword drawn. If her shoulder was still hurting from the arrow wound she didn't show it. Beside her were Lena and Castiel, determined to be by her side when the Shengen army burst through.

Ctenka pushed his way to the front, where the two children were standing. He had seen what they could do, knew they were more than just children, but still he felt the need to protect them. Despite how devastating they were, despite the way they might have turned the tide of the battle, Ctenka couldn't let them stay to face the enemy spears. He was responsible for them. When he'd given that oath to Randal, pledged his word to keep them safe, he hadn't meant it. To his shame all he'd been concerned with was himself. Things were different now. Lena and Castiel had been gifted to him like slaves, but Ctenka would be damned if he'd see them treated like that.

'Come away,' he said, grasping Lena's freezing cold hand.

She pulled away from him, not moving from Silver's side.

The woman looked down. 'Do as you are bid, little ones,' she said.

When they hesitated, Silver knelt down, motioning them closer. The two children moved in, listening as she whispered something in their ears. They both smiled at her words, then obediently turned and took Ctenka's hands. He walked back with them through the mess of bodies and fearful men who looked ready to weep. All that stood between the might of an army and his country.

Once they were through the Hangman's Gate and back in the main courtyard of Dunrun, Ctenka knelt beside them.

'You have to wait here,' he said. 'And if they break through, you have to run and hide.'

Both of them looked at him as though he'd been speaking a foreign language.

'Do you hear me? Stay here.'

'And do what?' Lena said.

Ctenka couldn't think of much. 'Pray,' he said finally.

To his surprise, the children immediately knelt in the courtyard and began to quietly mumble their prayers. For all the good it would do them. For all the good it would do any of them.

Ctenka left them and went back to the gate. On his way he heard the sonorous beat of a ram smashing against the gate and, for a moment, wished he was back there praying with the children. It echoed ominously, the gate below the high chapel rumbling and cracking with every slam.

At Vallion's word, what remained of the Red Standing braced their shields. Silver stood impassively, like a dust-covered statue. Ctenka stood beside her. Josten's gaze was fixed on the gate as though willing the enemy to break it down so he could wreak his vengeance. To his surprise, Ctenka felt ready to do some avenging of his own.

Timbers smashed. The head of the ram crashed through. Shengen axes went to work, taking down the loose timbers. Ctenka braced himself, expecting the attacking army to come bursting through, but it wasn't a unit of armoured men that came charging.

It was the Iron Tusk himself.

His flesh was unblemished, the devastating wounds Silver had inflicted on him the day before miraculously healed. Again he carried axe and sword, swinging them as though they weighed nothing. With one mighty blow he swept aside the shield wall of the Red Standing, sending half a dozen legionaries sprawling.

Silver ran forward to plug the gap, her sword striking at the Iron Tusk, but Ctenka could already see she was slower than before, and her thrust was easily batted aside by the warlord. Where before she had dodged and sidestepped every blow, dancing around him as though he were a tethered animal, now it was the Iron Tusk's turn to dominate.

He roared as he hacked at her, Silver barely able to parry axe and sword. Their weapons rang off one another, the sound rising above the noise of the battle. Ctenka watched in awe and fear as Silver ducked a sweep of the axe, then stepped out of range of the sword as it swung down and thudded into the ground.

Silver lunged in again, blade striking true at the warlord's heart, but the Iron Tusk merely turned it aside with his sword, axe countering. It caught Silver at the hip and she yelled, staggering back. The Iron Tusk's blood was up, sensing victory, howling as he rushed forward for the kill.

Ctenka was already running. He sprinted straight at the Iron Tusk and when the monster raised his axe for the killing blow, Ctenka brought his sword up. He had no thought other than to defend Silver, no matter what it would cost him.

The Iron Tusk's blow would have felled a tree, but when it clashed against Ctenka's steel it halted. Ctenka could see the Iron Tusk glaring with that one eye and disbelief seemed to cloud it for a moment. Everything stopped about them. Ctenka's weapon was locked with this inhuman beast. The sinew of his muscle felt as though it would burst through his flesh, but still Ctenka held his weapon there.

Reality hit him like a hammer. Suddenly the stench of the warlord, sweat and raw meat, almost knocked him over in a nauseating wave. His arm began to falter under the incredible weight of the Iron Tusk's strength. The stunned silence rang out louder than a thunderclap as he realised both armies had stopped to witness what was happening.

Ctenka was about to die, that's what was fucking happening.

The Iron Tusk pulled back, hefting his weapon for another killing blow, and this time Ctenka knew he didn't have the strength to stop it. All he could do was watch as the axe came crashing down.

A weight hit him from the side, knocking him out of the way as the axe slammed into the ground, sending up a cloud of dust. Ctenka looked up to see Silver sprawled on top of him.

She leapt to her feet, one hand grasping the wound at her side, sword in the other, ready to take on the Iron Tusk once more.

Before she could attack, the Red Standing rallied.

Vallion led them in a mass of red armour. Where before they had been well-ordered troops, their shields locked in a disciplined wall, now they were a furious horde, bent on murdering the warlord.

Silver staggered towards the melee but stumbled, the wound in her side deep, blood spilling from between her fingers. Josten was suddenly by her side.

'We have to go,' he growled, fresh blood on his sword and a wound across his cheek.

Ctenka rose to his feet, still shaking from his encounter with the Iron Tusk, still feeling what little power he had ebb from his tired muscles.

Silver tried to move back towards the fray but Josten stopped her.

'This gate is lost. We have to retreat.'

Ctenka could see her glaring at the fight, yearning to join in, but they knew this was a battle they could not win. The Iron Tusk could not be defeated.

Limping from the encounter, they moved back as the rest of the militia withdrew to the Hangman's Gate. Ctenka heard Vallion cry 'To the death!' as he retreated to the relative safety of Dunrun's final courtyard. Before they closed the gate, he saw the last men of the Red Standing swarming all over the Iron Tusk like wolves taking down a bear. Only this bear would not be beaten.

When the gates were closed the sound of battle dulled.

'We left them,' Ctenka said, still listening to the Red Standing fighting to the last.

'There was nothing we could do,' said Josten.

Ctenka knew that wasn't true. They could have fought alongside them till the end. They could have died heroes instead of cowering behind the last gate of Dunrun. He had taken on the Iron Tusk and survived, at least they could have tried.

No. They would have fought and died, just like Vallion and his men.

Ctenka staggered back through the courtyard as Josten tended to Silver's wound. Lena and Castiel were still kneeling, still praying by the dried-up well. All around them the militia were recovering from the skirmish, some bleeding, some weeping. The place looked doomed.

As Ctenka approached them, the children finished their prayers and stood, turning to him expectantly.

'Whatever you asked for, it didn't work,' Ctenka said. He'd had enough of trying to lie about it. There was no help from the gods here.

'Yes it did,' said Lena, as though Ctenka were an idiot.

'Well, Silver survived I guess. So that was something.'

Lena shook her head. 'No, Ctenka Sunatra. We did not pray for her.' She looked up at him with those innocent eyes. 'We prayed for you.'

Ctenka could only watch as the children turned, joined hands and skipped away to the edge of the courtyard.

Of course the gods were watching over him. How else could he have faced the Iron Tusk and survived?

Whatever gods those children were praying to, he could only hope they were listening when the Shengen army finally broke through the Hangman's Gate. After that, the gods would be all that could stop them.

33

'*H*ow *much further?' Livia asked.*

They pressed on through driving rain so dense she could hardly see ten yards in front of her.

'*Not much,' Durius answered. His collar was turned up and he'd pulled his hat down almost to his nose. Somewhere he'd abandoned his walking stick, proving it had only been for show in the first place.*

'*There must be an easier way there than this,' she replied, feeling the cold and wet creeping into her bones.*

'*What would you have me do?' Durius shouted above the torrent. 'Summon a convocation of giant eagles to carry us there?'*

Livia had no idea what a convocation was, but riding on giant eagles seemed greatly preferable to slogging through this downpour.

Glancing back she could see Hera helping Mandrake through the harsh conditions. She refused any help, though his head was becoming more fuddled with every passing step.

Just as Livia began to think this had been a fool's errand, they walked out of the rain and into bright sunshine, as though passing through a curtain. She looked behind her, seeing no sign of the downpour they had just endured, only endless open fields.

Durius took off his hat, beating off the rain against his thigh.

'*See,' he said, motioning across a grassy glen. 'We're here in no time.'*

Livia looked across the lush green grass, speckled with yellow and blue flowers. It rolled along for miles to the foot of a bright blue tower that spiralled up to the heavens. Of all the strange and wonderful sights she had seen since arriving in this place, this one struck her with the most awe.

There was a sudden cry of pain behind her, and Livia turned. Mandrake was on his knees, clutching his side as though he'd been stabbed. Hera held onto him tightly, powerless to do anything but cradle her lover.

'What's wrong with him?' Livia asked.

Durius looked on gravely. 'Armadon must be in battle in the mortal realm. The Archon of War can endure any amount of pain, but it appears Mandrake cannot.'

'We have to get to the tower,' Livia said. 'We have to help him.'

Durius shook his head. 'There is nothing to be done, Livia Harrow. You cannot stop this, no matter how hard you try.'

'I don't accept that. There must be something that can be done. You don't know what might happen once we reach the Heartstone. You said so yourself.'

Durius placed his hat back on his head with a sigh. 'Very well.'

He turned and walked on towards the Blue Tower.

This time Hera accepted Livia's help and they both carried Mandrake, following the path Durius led across the verdant glen. The closer they came, the more Livia sensed something emanating from the tower; a power lurking at its summit.

Detritus was scattered on the ground. At first a rusted sword discarded in a tangle of grass, then a magnificent winged helmet dulled by age. Soon the ground was littered with the scraps of an ancient army. Bones protruded from the soil alongside the desiccated corpses of huge mounts, all wallowing amidst the ragged and dulled pennants of some forgotten kingdom.

'This place is a graveyard,' Livia breathed. 'Was there a war here long ago?'

Durius inclined his head. 'Yes and no,' he replied.

'Which is it?' Livia snapped, losing patience with his cryptic twaddle.

'In this place the war was an ancient one. Elsewhere it may only have happened a day or two ago. Let's just say what's done is done and let that be an end to it.'

Livia was happy to do just that, sick of asking for a straight answer to anything Durius said. Besides, she'd need all her energy if she was going to reach that tower's summit. From a distance it had seemed huge, but now they were almost at its base the thing looked higher than any structure she could imagine.

When finally they reached the foot of it, Livia looked up. The top of the Blue Tower was impossible to see, but Durius for one was undeterred. Without a word he walked inside, and they followed him beneath a huge archway crested by winged seraphs. They appeared to shift in aspect as she passed beneath, closer to demons than angels.

'If this place is so important, why is no one guarding it?' Livia asked as they made their way up the winding stairs.

'There were once guardians here, servants who followed each of the Archons, loyal slaves specially picked to ensure no one entered here. What's left of them is rotting out on that field. For now, no one guards the Heartstone.'

'So what's to stop someone passing through into the mortal realm?'

'All-out war,' Durius replied. 'Three Archons have already gone through. As yet the consequences of that are unknown. The rest are merely waiting, plotting, deciding what their next move should be. Should Siff fail to bring Armadon and Innellan back to the fold I fully expect this place will become very busy.'

'So why doesn't one of you go and help her?'

Durius winked. 'Waiting. Plotting. Deciding. Don't you listen to what anyone tells you?'

'When they talk bloody sense I do,' she replied.

Durius found that one amusing, and he skipped along up the stairs with renewed vigour.

Livia saved her breath for the climb. She helped Hera carry Mandrake, who had managed to calm himself, the pain he previously felt now miraculously gone.

'At least he's no longer suffering,' Livia said, as they struggled with the weight of him.

'The Iron Tusk must have healed himself of his wounds in the mortal realm,' Hera said, her face still marred with concern.

'That's good… isn't it?'

'For now,' Hera replied.

On they went, feeling the weight of their burden with every laboured step. Just as Livia thought she could go no further, that her legs would not allow her another step, they finally reached the top.

Despite her fatigue, Livia looked out, open-mouthed. She could see for miles, rolling country, soaring mountains, blasted desert. A myriad of vistas in one. But the sight paled in comparison to what lay at the pinnacle of the tower.

The Heartstone was like a giant diamond, easily as big as a man. Every facet shone a different colour, winking in the sunlight,

370

shifting and changing as Livia moved around the dais on which it rested. It pulled her towards it with an irresistible attraction like a long-lost lover. It wanted her and she felt the same. Desiring it. Needing it. Beyond the veneer of that stone lay her homeland, and she could almost hear it calling to her.

Livia reached out to the Heartstone, her fingers tingling as though the stone were trying to take her hand and lead her home.

'What if I just... What if I just went through?' she asked.

'Through to what?' Durius replied. 'You have no physical form there anymore. Innellan now possesses your earthly body. You could wind up drifting as a lost spirit for the rest of time.'

'You know that for sure?'

'I don't know anything for sure, but it's as likely an outcome as any.'

Livia felt the Heartstone pulse with life at her presence, trying to communicate with her, trying to tell her something.

'What's it doing?' she said.

'The Heartstone has a story to tell,' Durius replied. 'You just have to listen.'

Livia closed her eyes, silently waiting for the answer to a question she hadn't asked. Willing the Heartstone to tell her.

She sat on a dark throne, white hair cascading down her shoulders, crimson gown flowing to the floor. Kneeling before her were the fallen masters of the Ramadi death cults. Blood regents, warlords, eidolons all. Former rulers of the desert now subjugated to her will.

Innellan rose like a snake from its lair, and climbed the

stairs down from that onyx throne. She passed the servile leaders of her army of fanatics, across a darkened hallway and out through a high arch to the balcony that overlooked her realm. The desert air was scorching, but she did not feel it. All she felt was victory.

This place was hers. A land ripe for the picking, and pick it she had. Every mortal in the realm now worshipped her as a god. Every prayer was in her name, and she could feel them filling her with power.

But it wasn't enough.

It could never be enough.

Innellan turned her eye to the south. For centuries the Ramadi cults had fought one another. It was the only thing that had kept their neighbours safe. But they were safe no longer. She would mobilise, unite, conquer.

And there would be nothing to stand in her way.

'She is preparing for war,' Livia said, reeling from the vision, feeling the Heartstone releasing her from its pull. 'We have to do something. The Archons have to do something.'

Durius raised a hand to placate her. 'Someone will,' he said. 'Siff will not stop until Innellan is defeated. Or until she dies trying to stop her. But first she must defeat Armadon.'

Livia looked over to Hera and Mandrake, both kneeling on the marble floor. Hera cradled her lover as his lips moved in a soundless rant.

'I need to see,' Livia said, turning back to the Heartstone.

This time it pulsed brighter; Livia felt somehow she had gained the artefact's trust. As though she were part of it now, and it a part

of her. They were connected, and with that joining the Heartstone
showed her what she asked for...

The brute raged against the gate. It was all that stood between him and conquest of the western nations. He roared from within a horned helm, the sound echoing through the mountains. At his back was an army built to conquer. United behind their immortal master and devoted to executing his will. All that stood in their way was the last fragile gate of a fortress.

Beyond it a tired militia. Ordinary men, some too scared to stand.

Before them was a woman: stout, resolute, but... she was wounded. Weakened.

Where the warlord commanded an army's worship, she stood alone. All that might stop this monster. All that could save the west from devastation.

Livia fell back from the Heartstone. 'They're all going to die,' she
whispered, staring at the stone.

'Well, it certainly looks that way,' Durius said. 'When
Armadon finally breaks through the mountain pass, he and Innellan
will start a war that will ravage the entire continent.'

'There must be something you can do to stop them.'

Durius shrugged. 'What would you suggest? Shall I fling myself into
the mortal realm and join in the fray?' His expression turned incredulous
when she didn't argue with that idea. 'Do I look like some god of war?'

'Is that it?' Livia was on her feet now, shouting at this little

man. This god. 'That's all you're going to say? There must be something you can do.'

Durius approached the Heartstone, staring into its depths. It reacted to his gaze, the facets dulling, becoming more transparent. Inside Livia could see a core of roiling smoke, becoming ever more agitated at Durius' presence.

'It's been so long,' he said, staring intently into the stone.

'Since what?' Livia asked.

He dragged his gaze away. 'Since I listened,' he said. 'Since I felt the exquisite pleasure.'

'For fuck's sake, of what?'

'Of worship. Of you mortals falling to your knees in adoration. Not that I'd feel it now. Not that there's anyone praying to little, insignificant Durius. And without it I'm powerless to do anything. I can't help you.'

'Try,' she demanded. 'Please just try. Listen, just for a moment. Maybe there's someone. Anyone.'

Durius shook his head. 'It is forbidden.'

'Balls to forbidden,' Livia cried. 'You said yourself, the rest of the Archons are just sitting on their hands, weighing up their next move. Aren't you supposed to be the trickster god? Aren't you supposed to be one move ahead of them all?'

Durius stared at her, his despondent look gradually becoming a gleeful smile.

'You might just be right, Livia Harrow,' he said, turning back to the Heartstone.

He reached out a hand towards it, closing his eyes. Livia could see the mist inside become increasingly violent, until it swirled in a furious vortex.

'I… I have been all but forgotten,' Durius said. 'Looked over in favour of warrior gods and temptresses. But…' the smile on his face widened. 'But there is one.'

'One worshipper?' It didn't sound like much to Livia.

'Yes, one,' Durius replied. 'But it could be all I need.'

34

LAIGON sat, still tethered in the tent, as the Standings of the Shengen army mustered for a final push. He heard prayers, as a thousand men dropped to their knees in front of the Iron Tusk. A warlord revered like a god.

He had been a fool to think that he could defy such a man. To think that he could lead a few legionaries in defence of the Cordral Extent. That coming to this place would make one iota of difference. He had led them to their deaths, and what did he have to show for it?

In his hand he could still feel that pewter figurine, cold against his palm. No matter how hard he squeezed, it was still cold to the touch. What good would such an empty trinket do him? But then, what good had any of this done him?

Feeling as foolish as the first time he had tried, Laigon closed his eyes and prayed.

'You're not fucking listening, are you?' he said. Laigon had never been prone to cursing, but this seemed like just the occasion cursing was created for. 'But if you are, if you're up there, I need you to show it. Show me this wasn't all for nothing. Prove that there's someone there, that this was all worth it. Gods! Tell me to shut up if it makes you feel any better, but please tell me something.'

Nothing.

He knew he was wasting his breath. No one could hear him. All Laigon could hope for now was that the Iron Tusk would have him executed before he was forced to witness the fall of every kingdom in the west. Deep down, he knew that would never happen. The Iron Tusk needed him. It was only a matter of time before Laigon would succumb to his will.

'Damn you then,' he whispered to no one. 'Damn you, Portius, and damn all the—'

The figurine, cold for all this time, suddenly burned white hot in his fist. Laigon cried out, dropping the tiny statue to the ground, feeling the pain still stinging his palm.

He lifted his hand to examine it and was suddenly shocked by two things – first that there was no mark on his flesh, second that his bonds had miraculously come loose.

Laigon stared at his hands. Then slowly he climbed to his feet, using the prop post for support. Looking down he saw the rope that had bound his hands sitting in a neat little pile next to the figurine of Portius.

This couldn't be. The gods had never listened to any of his prayers. They had abandoned the world long ago, no more than legend.

He bent down, picked up the figurine and stared at it. It stared back, that portly face still looking full of mischief. Of all the gods that had chosen to favour him it was the jester. What luck. Laigon Valdyr, Centurion of the Fourth, favoured by the trickster god. He would have laughed, but there was little to raise his mirth.

What now? Escape? Surely he could not fight. There was an army in front of him. An immortal warlord. Even if he had the favour of the gods, of just one god, he could never hope to vanquish the Iron Tusk in battle. No, he had to flee. Head back along the Skull Road and claim his freedom beyond the Shengen Empire.

But Laigon could not leave. Not when his wife and son were still slaves to a tyrant.

Gripping the figure of Portius tight in his hand, Laigon stumbled from the tent. He was still unsteady on his feet, head filled with a fug. Through his one swollen eye he could barely see, but out in the bright sunlight there was little to see anyway. The entire Shengen army had advanced on the fort; in the distance he could hear their noise resounding along the causeway. The sound of the Iron Tusk bellowing his anger against those that chose to defy his will echoed in the distance.

The camp was ordered, tents erected in regimented lines as he would expect from such disciplined troops. If Petrachus and Verrana were here they would be towards the rear, close to the supply tents.

He stumbled along the pass, kicking over a discarded pot as he went. It clattered along the ground, the sound bouncing off the valley walls. Laigon paused, waiting for someone to come racing to see what the commotion was about, but no one seemed to care. A camp follower was cleaning plates beneath an awning and looked up at him as he staggered by. Laigon stopped, staring at the woman, expecting her to cry out in alarm at any moment, but instead she looked on blankly. Somehow she had not succumbed to the temptation of the tyrant of Shengen. Perhaps this was the sign he had been hoping for. If one of his fellow Shengen had resisted the allure of the Iron Tusk then maybe there were others.

As though knowing what he might be searching for, she pointed along the causeway. There was a single tent at the end of the camp, and he shuffled on towards it. When he reached the tent he could hear the mumbled sounds of prayer emanating from within. Though their voices were muffled, Laigon recognised Petrachus and Verrana instantly.

When last they had seen him they had proclaimed him a traitor. Nothing had changed since then, but Laigon was not about to give up. He was determined not to abandon them to the whims of a warlord, no matter the cost.

When he opened the flap to the tent neither his wife nor his son looked up at him. Laigon waited for several moments before their prayers petered out. He had to listen to them begging for victory, lauding the Iron Tusk, pledging their undying devotion to that brute. It was all Laigon could do to listen to their litanies, but still he stood and watched them, fighting back the tears.

Eventually, Petrachus ceased his prayers and looked up, sensing someone watching him. Upon seeing his father his expression turned from serenity to hate, lips creasing into a snarl, eyes burning with hatred.

'You,' he snapped. 'What are you doing here, traitor?'

Verrana opened her eyes and on seeing her husband she cringed in fear, crawling away to the far end of the tent, terrified of what Laigon might do.

He stepped inside, kneeling down before them. 'It's me,' he said, almost pleading with them. 'Your husband. Your father.'

'You are no one,' said Petrachus, rising to his feet.

'I am your—'

Petrachus lashed out in anger. The blow was a swift one, but Laigon snatched Petrachus' wrist before his son could strike him.

'I am your father,' Laigon growled, pulling Petrachus close, holding the boy to him, squeezing him in a loving embrace.

'Don't hurt him,' Verrana cried. Laigon could see she was terrified.

'I would never...' Petrachus squirmed in his grip but still Laigon refused to let go. He could not release his son. He knew that if he did he might never win him back.

'Then why are you here, traitor?' Verrana screamed.

Laigon released his son. Petrachus scrambled back to the corner of the tent, clutching his mother close.

'Because you are mine,' said Laigon. 'Because I am yours. We are a family, Verrana, we belong together. All three of us.'

'No,' she spat. 'You are a monster. A betrayer.'

'You have been poisoned,' said Laigon.

'You are the poison. Get away from us.'

Laigon stood. He watched as his wife cradled his son in fear. In that moment he felt his heart break. They had been taken from him. Stolen by the Iron Tusk, and there was nothing he could think to do that would win them back.

He turned and left them. For a moment he looked east along miles of valley to Shengen and his home. Along the Skull Road. It would have been so easy to take it. To leave all this behind and start anew. But there would be no new beginnings for Laigon Valdyr. Only endings.

He turned back towards the fortress of Dunrun.

Squeezing the figure of Portius tight in his fist, Laigon set off west. The warmth of the small idol filled his palm, radiated up his arm, filling his chest, his limbs; even his head began to clear. His stooped gait straightened, becoming a powerful stride. Laigon could see everything sharply now. If he was to free his family from bondage he had to claim one last victory. One impossible victory.

He approached the first gate of Dunrun, the timbers lying blackened and burned. Corpses had been moved to the side of the pass and left to rot in the sun. When he crossed beneath the arch he saw the Shengen army ahead, the ranks of the Fifth Standing waiting at the rear. Laigon gave no warning, no greeting as he walked past them, and for their part they ignored him at first. Soon though, heads began to turn, whispers spread of his appearance, travelling through the ranks like a forest fire.

On he walked, hearing the legionaries' growing disquiet. Men turned up ahead as they heard of his coming. Legionaries, centurions and praetorians alike turned to witness him, faces twisted in disgust. Someone said 'traitor', another 'betrayer', but no one made a move to stop him.

As he reached the next broken gate he could see the collapsed stones had been moved aside to create a passage through. More legionaries watched his approach now, but Laigon kept his faith, gripping the figure of Portius, its warmth invigorating him.

A legionary spat in his face as he carried on walking, but Laigon ignored the insult. The massed ranks up ahead knew he was coming, but instead of barring his way they made room, a guard of dishonour for him to pass through.

Did they think he had changed his mind and decided to pledge himself to the Iron Tusk? Were they keen to see him fall to his knees in supplication, or did they merely wish to witness him executed at their warlord's hand? Laigon had no idea, but he walked on regardless through what remained of the Tinker's Gate, through the Chapel Gate until he came to the final courtyard.

Word had already reached them of his approach. The yard was lined with warriors standing behind their shields, presenting him a channel right up to the gate.

In front of it stood the Iron Tusk himself.

'You see,' proclaimed the warlord, as Laigon approached. 'Our brother has returned to us. Turned to the right path. We were wise not to abandon our faith in him.'

Laigon stopped in front of the brute. The immortal warrior whose wounds had healed before his very eyes. He looked up, drinking in the stink of him, the size of him.

'Kneel before me, Laigon Valdyr.' The Iron Tusk's voice cut through the silence, filling the void like the words of a high priest. 'Pledge yourself to me and we will become conquerors.'

'It is over,' Laigon said. 'Your reign is at an end.' As he said the words, he believed them. Despite what he faced, Laigon's faith did not waver.

'You disappoint me again,' said the Iron Tusk. 'And for the last time. If you will not kneel in fealty, then kneel for

382

your execution. I promise I will make it a swift one.'

'If you want to take my head, you savage bastard, then go ahead. But it won't be easy.'

The Iron Tusk laughed, discarding his huge sword and letting it fall to the ground with a thud. He hefted his axe in both hands, raising it for the final swing.

Laigon felt the figurine of Portius burn hot in his hand once more. This time he gripped it tighter, letting the pain course through his flesh. As the Iron Tusk swung the axe it was as though the warlord were moving through tar. His attack was laboured, like an old man was swinging that weapon and not an immortal overlord.

The axe swept past Laigon's head, inches from his face. The Iron Tusk grunted as he missed his target, and Laigon picked his moment to strike. He lunged forward, gripping the figurine of Portius like a dagger, plunging it into that one baleful eye. It struck true, and Laigon grasped the horn protruding from the Iron Tusk's head with his free hand, shoving the figurine in deeper, hearing the warlord's laboured scream of agony as he did so.

With a bellow of fury, the Iron Tusk shoved Laigon back, sending him sprawling in the sand. Laigon looked up to see the warlord gripping his eye, trying to pull the figure of Portius free. But it was stuck fast.

Then, with a sudden flare of light, it burst into flames.

The Iron Tusk's screams filled the courtyard as he fell to his knees. His head within that helm was burning like a funeral pyre, the eyeholes flaring bright, the metal glowing white hot.

Laigon leapt to his feet, pulling a sword from the scabbard of a stunned legionary. Then he rushed in, his form perfect as always, striking at the Iron Tusk's neck. It should have struck the head from the beast, but instead it merely hacked a divot in the flesh. The Iron Tusk bellowed louder, swinging his huge blade blindly at his attacker. Laigon leapt aside, the axe whistling past his head. He rolled, coming up on his feet as the Iron Tusk thrashed about him, hacking that axe into the ground but finding no target.

With a final burst of energy, Laigon leapt again, raising the sword high. He screamed, a feral roar, and the Iron Tusk turned his head, axe sweeping back to hack Laigon in two. But he was not fast enough.

With a final hack of the blade, with all his strength and hate, Laigon struck the head from the Iron Tusk. He landed, hearing the warlord's huge body collapsing to the dirt.

The courtyard fell silent. Laigon was panting heavily as he stood over that hulking corpse, the charred helm lying next to it. All around him were the legionaries of the Shengen. Men of every Standing looking on in awe.

Then, one by one, they fell to their knees and bowed their heads before him.

35

THE scream was more an animal howl than anything that might come from man or woman. Livia turned away from Durius, whose face had been contorting into myriad different expressions, to see Hera kneeling next to Mandrake. The warrior woman gripped her lover tightly. His face was serene, eyes staring vacantly. As Livia watched in growing horror, his flesh began to decay, body crumbling like ash from a burning log and floating away on the breeze.

Hera desperately tried to hold onto him, tried to keep the crumbling body in one piece, but it simply fell through her fingers. There was nothing she could do to stop Mandrake from vanishing before her eyes.

Livia ran towards her, but she was already too late. Mandrake had drifted away on the wind, leaving nothing but wisps of ash in his wake. All she could hear was Hera screaming, raging like an animal. For so long she had tried desperately to save her lover, but now he had simply disappeared before her eyes.

Hera looked up at Durius. 'You did this,' she spat. 'You killed him.'

The little man shook his head sorrowfully. 'Armadon had to be stopped. You have to understand—'

'Understand what?' Hera was on her feet now. Livia could see

385

her gripping the handle of her sword as though it took every fibre of her body to stop her from drawing it. 'That you're all the same? Gods, Archons, whatever you want to call yourselves. You don't care about us. We are pawns in a game. What happens when my turn comes? Will you just stand there and shrug your shoulders then?'

'What have you done?' asked Livia. 'What's going on?'

Durius shook his head. 'With Armadon's defeat, and his earthly body vanquished, Mandrake no longer has a link to this plane or the mortal one. He has simply ceased to exist. His pain is finally over.'

'Did you know this would happen?' said Livia.

Durius made to answer, but he stopped as a high-pitched keening sound emanated from the Heartstone. Livia watched in horror as something squirmed within. Something vile was roiling within the mist, like a giant leech in the centre of the jewel.

As they watched, it grew, limbs sprouting from the amorphous blob, head forming, mouth open in a woeful scream. Livia could see with increasing revulsion that the thing was taking shape, a horned head, cloven-hoofed hindquarters, spindly arms. It was like some foul by-blow of man and goat.

With a ghastly sucking sound, the Heartstone spewed out the creature as though retching up a maggot. Stinking ichor and birthing fluid were thrown out with it, as the beast flopped onto the marble floor of the tower. It lay helpless, mewling like a newborn lamb, eyes blind, limbs flailing in the muck.

'What.... the hell... is that?' Livia asked, not sure if she wanted to know the answer.

'His mortal body destroyed, Armadon has been banished back to this realm.' Durius said. 'As you can see, it's quite a disgusting process.'

Hera stepped forward, drawing her sword and glaring down at the bantling beast. 'This. This is what took Mandrake from me?'

'Wait,' said Durius. 'You cannot kill it.'

'Watch me,' Hera replied.

Livia stood helpless as Hera raised her sword, but the killing blow never came.

In an instant, the blue sky that surrounded them turned iron grey, plunging the platform into darkness. Hera stayed her hand as the sudden chill enveloped them all. An ominous wind blew through the tower. It heralded the most majestic beast Livia had ever laid eyes on.

With a beat of leather wings, another gust blew through the tower. Livia turned in time to see a huge winged reptile approaching. Clawed feet gripped the edge of the platform as it dipped its long and ancient head beneath the lintel. Cruel, reptilian eyes surveyed them – Durius, Hera, Livia, Armadon – before the serpent transformed. Its wings folded and shrank, vast head becoming humanlike, clawed feet turning to slender human legs. In an instant a woman stood there, the most regal figure Livia had ever seen; gown of green and purple swaying about her perfect form, hair arranged in intricate braids about her shoulders.

'Durius.' Her voice was silk and honey. 'You were warned.'

'My dear Mortana,' said Durius, bowing low. 'I can explain everything.'

She gazed down on the foundering form of Armadon. 'Yes, I'm sure you can.'

There was a noise from down the winding stairwell. A click followed by a shuffle. Another figure appeared, this one as old and wizened as the mountains. He laboured up the stairs, aided by a long and ancient staff. His back was hunched, and to all intents he resembled an ancient tortoise as he shuffled along, head like beaten leather poking forward to survey the room with glassy eyes.

'Don't start without me, Durius. I'd like to hear this too,' he said, voice rumbling and phlegmy.

'Of course, Hastor, my old friend.'

Durius bowed again, and Livia began to get the feeling she ought to as well. Not that these newcomers had even acknowledged her presence.

A flash of lightning momentarily blinded her, and the rumble of thunder that followed made her heart pound. When she opened her eyes again, standing in the centre of the tower was a sight that had previously struck her dumb with fear. The burning king stood tall and proud, a flaming crown atop his head, his armour cracked and molten and constantly shifting. The pungent reek of brimstone filled the air around him as his vast head moved to scan the summit of the tower.

'Ekemon, my brother,' Durius laughed nervously. Ekemon chose not to reply, if indeed he could speak at all with no mouth.

No sooner had the burning king appeared than yet another majestic winged form drifted onto the tower's platform. This time it was on white-feathered wings, porcelain flesh perfect in every way, a seraph of the utmost beauty, but for the blood-red eyes housed within that exquisite face. He was naked, curling his wings around him as he landed softly. The tousled, white hair atop his head was perfectly styled, as though this being were more sculpture than man.

'I hope you weren't planning on leaving me out?' said the seraph, glancing around the room. His gaze paused on Livia for a moment and in that instant she almost fell to her knees to worship in front of

388

this paragon. The creature was undeniably beautiful, but at the same time he had an aura of wickedness she found impossible to resist.

'Kastion,' said Durius. 'Always a pleasure.'

Durius seemed to be growing more and more agitated with each new arrival. It was clear he hadn't expected so many Archons to make a personal appearance.

There was a deafening caw, as a huge corvid figure swooped down to perch on the edge of the platform. This huge beast had a human torso, armoured in intricate carved iron, but its head and wings were those of a giant raven.

It cawed once more and Durius nodded in greeting. 'Badb, so good of you to join us. And yes, of course I will make this as quick and painless as I can.'

'Do we think there will be any more?' asked Mortana. She moved languidly, in a way that reminded Livia of a giant lizard in the sun, but she was the most beautiful woman Livia had ever seen.

'Who cares,' said the seraph Kastion. 'Let's get on with this.'

'Of course,' said Durius. 'Now we're all gathered it might be a good time—'

'What are you up to, Durius?' asked Hastor. The ancient old man's rheumy eyes narrowed in suspicion.

'I… Well, I'm ensuring our covenant is upheld. Look.' He motioned to the squirming form of Armadon. 'Duly returned to the fold.'

Mortana walked forward and stooped to pick up the mewling creature, seemingly oblivious to the fact its slimy body was ruining her magnificent gown. She cradled the newly birthed Archon as she might her own infant. 'And these?' she said, glancing at Hera and Livia.

'Mortals,' Durius replied. 'In my care.'

'In your care?' said Kastion. 'Since when did we care for mortals?'

'Some of us have always cared,' Durius answered.

The ancient Hastor stepped forward, staff clicking on the marble floor. He regarded Livia with suspicion. 'This one is powerful,' he said.

Livia felt a swell of fear under the Archon's attention but she dared not move.

'That is of no matter,' Mortana said, as Armadon reached up with a child's hand and grabbed one of her ringlets. 'We must decide what we are to do.'

'Siff has vanquished Armadon and returned him to us,' said Durius, failing to mention his own part in Armadon's defeat. 'She will do the same with Innellan. We have to allow her the time to accomplish what she set out to do. Then order will be restored.'

'The Heartstone is here, restored to its original form,' said Kastion. 'We can use it. We can travel through and take back the mortal realm. Or we could remain here and force them to worship us as the gods we are. We can be returned to power. Why don't we just—'

The great crow head of Badb interrupted the seraph with a mighty caw. Livia couldn't tell if it was in agreement or not.

'I agree with Durius,' Mortana said. 'Siff must be given time and allowed to destroy Innellan.'

Hastor nodded in agreement. 'Mortana is right. Once Innellan is brought low, Siff will return and we can once again render the Heartstone useless. It was agreed. We have had centuries of peace because of it.'

There were rumblings from the other Archons but no one disagreed. No one but Livia.

If Innellan was vanquished wouldn't Livia suffer the same fate as Mandrake? She would cease to exist, her form in this place floating away like petals on the wind.

'No,' she shouted.

As every Archon turned at her outburst she instantly regretted it. These were gods, and now she had brought their attention down upon her.

'No?' said Mortana. 'You think to bray at us like an animal?'

'I– It's just—'

'Durius, let me eat this sow,' said Kastion, his wickedness clearly matched only by his appetite.

Durius stepped in the way. 'My apologies. She doesn't understand.'

But as the Archons continued to bicker, Livia realised she did understand. This was a game to them. One they had been playing for millennia. She was merely a passing diversion, just like every mortal they had ever influenced.

She felt the Heartstone pulse once more. It called to her as it had done once before, only this time it didn't merely want to show her the way home… it wanted to take her there.

Right now, floating like a spectre in the mortal realm seemed far preferable to being made a plaything for the gods.

Livia took a step closer to the huge gem. It pulsed at her presence, and for the briefest of moments she saw something beyond the glittering veneer. There was a way through and… a mortal body awaited her. Unsuspecting, innocent, perfect to host her in its mortal flesh.

She understood now; she could not return to reclaim her body from Innellan, but she could still inhabit someone else. The notion repulsed and excited her all at once.

Another step closer and she heard the caw of the raven Badb. The Archons had noticed her now. They had seen what she was doing. Knew what she was thinking and spotted the danger.

There was no choice. It was now or never.

'Livia, no!' Durius shouted. 'You cannot. It is forbidden.'

But she was already gone.

Livia Harrow stepped forward, and let the Heartstone take her.

36

SHE could hear them screaming. Calling out in alarm, their raised voices muffled but still unmistakable. The Archons had gathered about the Heartstone, their call passing through it, travelling the infinite distance between the ethereal plane and the mortal realm.

As Siff heard them she knew she was running out of time.

The Archons would not wait forever. Their covenant was held together by a gossamer thread. If just one more of them were to submit to temptation and pass through to this realm it would spark a new war. To avoid that, Siff had to defeat Innellan as swiftly as possible.

But how? Innellan had already carved out an empire in the desert but that would never be enough for her. Armadon had been stopped, but Innellan was much more cunning. She would not simply attack head on. She would already be preparing her conquest and if Siff didn't act soon, all would be lost.

As she made her way through the fort of Dunrun, the militia were still shifting bodies, carrying them out to a mass grave just beyond the fortress walls. Makeshift gates were being built for each of the vast archways. The sound of saws and hammers echoed through the fortress courtyards. Someone was even painting pitch on the scorched walls of the Eagle Gate as she approached it. This was the most industrious the place had been since she arrived.

Out through the gate and along the Skull Road to the east, Siff could smell embers still burning in the morning air. The Shengen had cremated their warlord in the night and the flames had burned almost to the peaks of the mountain pass, filling the valley with fire. It had been beautiful, and now all that remained was a blackened pyre. As Siff approached it she saw the battered and bruised figure of the new Shengen emperor standing and watching the fire dwindle to nothing.

She stood beside Laigon for some time. His face was a mass of pulped meat, yellow and black flesh fighting for dominance, but still he managed to look every inch the noble leader. He stared at that pyre, at the body of the warlord he had vanquished, but Siff could tell his victory had been a hollow one.

'I know what you are,' Laigon said eventually, without turning to look at her.

Siff had no doubt. Laigon had communed with the Archons, or at least one of them. He knew their power now. In all likelihood he could sense her true nature.

'And I know what you are,' she replied.

'What's that?' he asked.

'You are the new warlord. A conqueror. Slayer of tyrants.'

Laigon barked a laugh.

'You saved them all,' she said.

'And yet I don't feel victorious,' he replied, his eyes not leaving the ashes. 'So many of my people dead. So many of my brothers.'

'Those who remain worship you now. You are a god to them. Would you still have them in thrall to the Iron Tusk?'

'I am no god,' said Laigon. 'I never asked for this.'

'Some men crave power. Most have no idea what to do with it when they finally hold it in their hands. Now it is yours. Whether you like it or not, Laigon Valdyr, you must use it.'

'I am a soldier. Not an emperor.'

'You are a leader of men,' she said. 'You have an army that would follow you anywhere. There is no choice but to accept that.'

'All I wanted was to free my family,' he said, turning to look at her. 'Now that is done. I have once again searched the eyes of my wife and child and found only love there.'

Siff could see the relief in his bloodshot eyes. 'You did that. You were the one who freed them, and an empire along with them.'

'And what am I supposed to do now?' he asked.

'You are a soldier, Laigon. You must fight your next battle.'

Laigon shook his head. 'There are no more battles left to fight. And I am tired. So tired of it all.'

'There is one battle left. You have vanquished one tyrant. Now I would ask you to join me in defeating another.'

Laigon shook his head. 'I've done enough. I have seen brother kill brother. All that remains is to go home and rebuild my homeland.'

'And for how long do you think you'll be safe? An empress is risen in the Ramadi. She looks to conquer the western nations and once she is done, she will not stop there. Go home now and you will only be building on a foundation of sand. Come with me, Laigon. Bring your army north and we can defeat her before she is too powerful to be stopped.'

Laigon looked down, as though the right answer might be written in the dirt. 'I never asked for this,' he whispered.

'Few of us do,' Siff replied, knowing full well how he felt. She had asked for none of this, and yet here she was.

Laigon turned to her. All doubt was gone from him now. 'You will have your army,' he said.

With that he left her by the dying pyre and walked back towards the waiting Shengen legions.

Siff watched him go. Despite his pledge, all she could feel was sadness. She would take his army north. She would face down Innellan in the thin hope that she could save these people, but it would not be she who would suffer and die should they fail.

But then it was never the gods who suffered. Only those who worshipped them.

With the mountains and the fortress behind him, all Josten could see was open scrubland in every direction. He'd endured enough sand and heat to last him a lifetime, but here he was again. Not that going home would have been much better. At least no one was trying to hang him from a gibbet here. Not yet anyway.

They were still digging the huge grave. As soon as they'd excavated a big enough hole it would be full of bodies. Those militia lads couldn't dig fast enough. Josten considered lending a hand, but he'd dug one grave already and that had been enough for him.

He looked down at where he'd laid Ermund Harlaw's body in the ground, and had no idea why he was standing here. It wasn't like he was going to say any prayers. Still, here he was with all his bloody regret and guilt and there was Harlaw. Dead as a fucking doornail.

'You could have given me a chance,' he said to that grave. 'If not to kill you myself, then at least to…'

He couldn't say it. Couldn't bring himself to tell Harlaw how sorry he was, even now the man was dead.

Josten had betrayed him. Harlaw had given him everything and still Josten had fucked the man's wife. Maybe Josten had believed he was in love. Looking back he knew it was just an infatuation. A story that had been written a million times before, but still that hadn't stopped Josten Cade.

He suddenly got that prickly feeling he was being watched. Looking behind him he saw Ctenka standing there, looking all sorrowful. For a moment he felt angry. Who did this little prick think he was? He hadn't known Harlaw – not the real Harlaw. Not the ruthless bastard Harlaw who would have fired his mother from a trebuchet if he thought it would win him the battle.

'What are you after?' Josten asked.

'Just…' Ctenka shook his head. 'Answers, I guess.'

'Well you won't find them in a graveyard, son. No point

asking dead men questions; most of them don't have much to say.'

'I just don't know what to do. Where to go. Who am I supposed to be?'

'How the fuck should I know?' said Josten, not entirely sure what Ctenka was on about.

'Is this how it feels to be victorious? Is this what it is to be a hero?'

Josten turned to look at Ctenka full in the face. 'I don't know much, but I do know that you're no bloody hero.'

Josten hadn't meant to be so harsh, but then he never did. Just the way it came out of his mouth, he supposed.

'But… I matched the Iron Tusk's blow,' said Ctenka. 'Did you not see? I parried that sword. It should have cut me in two but…'

'I've seen a lot of strange shit I can't explain,' said Josten. 'And most of it's been men riding their luck. Trust me, eventually it runs out. Take my advice, pack up, go home, farm or trade, do whatever. But don't be a soldier. It's not for you.'

'So what are you going to do?' Ctenka asked. 'Carry on fighting until someone kills you?'

Josten glanced over Ctenka's shoulder. He could see Silver approaching from the fort and knew exactly where she was headed.

'I reckon I'm going to find that out soon enough,' he replied.

Silver came and placed her hand on Ctenka's shoulder. The young lad glanced at her, his wrinkled brow suddenly untroubled at a mere touch from the woman.

'Go in peace, Ctenka Sunatra,' she said.

Ctenka shook his head. 'I can't. I don't know—'

'You will,' she said. 'You will.'

That seemed enough for the lad, and he nodded his thanks to her before walking back towards the fort.

Then there were two.

'What did you hope to find here, Josten Cade?' Silver asked.

He glanced down at that grave. Whatever he wanted, he knew Ermund Harlaw wasn't going to give it.

'Maybe some peace and quiet?'

'The redemption you seek is not here,' said Silver. 'Punishing yourself will not bring you what you want.'

'Punishing myself? Trust me, there's plenty of people all too willing to do that without me joining them.'

'You will not find the peace you desire until you forgive yourself, Josten.'

'What the fuck are you talking about?' he asked. Her dumb statements were making him uncomfortable. Or maybe they were a little too close to the truth he'd known all along.

'I cannot promise to give you what you want,' she said. 'But if you come with me I can try.'

'Why? Where are you going?'

'North,' she replied. 'Innellan is raising an army to conquer the world. I need—'

'I'm in,' Josten said.

'So eager? Most likely we will all be slaughtered.'

'Why didn't you say that in the first place? When do we go?'

A smile crept up one side of Silver's face.

Without another word, she left him by the grave as she went to prepare their journey.

Josten looked back down at it for the last time.

He had no idea whether dying for a cause would bring him any kind of redemption, but even if it didn't he knew one thing...

...eventually he'd get exactly what he deserved.

EPILOGUE

The Cordral Extent, 106 years after the Fall

C TENKA squinted up at the sun. The last time he'd ridden the trade road west it had been hot, but this was just ridiculous. Every crevice was moist, his clothes were sticking to him like tar and his own stink made him want to gag. And he'd not even got started on the disgusting excuse for a horse he was riding yet.

Turning in the saddle, he saw that the children were enduring the journey much better than he was. Castiel was at the front, clutching the reins. Lena was behind him, her arms around his waist. Ctenka had to admire the boy's horsemanship. When they had first left Dunrun the steed had appeared keen, ready to bolt at the first opportunity. Now under the boy's ministrations it plodded along, docile as any cow.

When they had been riding for two days, Ctenka saw a cloud of dust in the distance. He gripped his reins the tighter as he stared westward, his nerves getting the better of him.

What was it Josten said? 'You're no bloody hero,' or some such. And he'd been right. Ctenka Sunatra was many things, but hero wasn't one of them.

And if nothing else, a man had to be honest with himself.

So here he was, riding along with two silent children, away from the Great Eastern Militia. Riding away from his ambitions. He couldn't bring himself to regret it.

The closer they got to the dust cloud, the more tightly Ctenka gripped his reins. He knew Lena and Castiel could more than look after themselves, but the less they explored what they were capable of, the better for everyone around them. Most of all, Ctenka.

Eventually he could make out details of the approaching riders. They flew the crossed scimitar flag of the Kantor Militia, and he could even pick out the preened figure of Aykan Cem at their head. Suddenly his fears disappeared like dust on the breeze. Even Ctenka had nothing to fear from the likes of that cowardly bastard.

He guided his horse to the side of the road and signalled for the children to do the same. Castiel pulled his reins to the right and his mount duly obeyed, plodding slavishly onto the side of the road. There they sat, waiting for the army to pass by.

When Aykan Cem reached them he reined in his horse, motioning for the column to carry on.

'What's this?' he said. 'A deserter running from the fight? If I wasn't in such a hurry I'd have you clapped in irons.'

Ctenka gazed at him, wondering if he should deign to answer. It was probably polite. 'The fight is over, Marshal,' he replied. 'And you're late.'

Aykan Cem's expression immediately altered. If Ctenka didn't know better he'd have thought the man was relieved.

'I see,' he said, running a hand thoughtfully through his well-oiled beard. 'I take it we won?'

'If we hadn't I doubt I'd be here to tell you the truth of it, Marshal.'

Aykan nodded. 'Very well. And where do you think you're going?'

Ctenka motioned towards the children. 'I have orders to take these two to safety.'

Aykan looked towards Castiel and Lena. Now his relieved expression turned to one of fear. His horse seemed to sense his unease, and it grew restless beneath him.

'Well, carry on then.'

With that, he put spurs to his steed and joined the column eastward.

Ctenka sat there, watching the men of the Kantor Militia pass by, before he guided his horse back onto the road and led the way west once more.

He'd made a promise, more of a bargain really, that he would take Lena and Castiel home when they had served their purpose. In recent days Ctenka Sunatra was becoming more and more a man of his word. He had to admit, it felt good.

The sun was falling by the time they reached the little farm on the edge of Ankrav Territory. Darkness had almost crossed the entire field of crops but still Markhan was out there, hoe in hand, carving a furrow into the harsh landscape.

The farmer was too busy with his labours to notice them, and Ctenka led his horse to the little white house at the edge of the fields. He climbed down, his damp clothes now starting to chill him in the cool evening air. When he turned to help Lena and Castiel down from their horse he saw they had already dismounted and were waiting patiently.

Felaina opened the door before he could even knock, and Ctenka was greeted by her big gap-toothed smile just as before.

'Ctenka, come in,' she said, hugging him to her ample bosom. 'And who are these two?'

Ctenka introduced the children, and Felaina knelt beside them, giving them an equally huge hug. Neither of the children seemed to mind, and if Felaina noticed that one was burning hot to the touch and the other freezing, she didn't mention it.

The woman didn't even ask what he was doing back here, just eagerly invited them in, sat them at her meagre table and offered a share of their even more meagre meal.

Ctenka was struck by how much he had missed this. Honest hospitality. It made him feel a sudden sting of guilt at the arrogant way he had treated the pair when he last stayed.

As it grew dark outside, Markhan returned to the house. He greeted Ctenka like a long-lost brother, ruffling the hair of both children before taking his seat at the table. To Ctenka's surprise, he saw both Lena and Castiel were smiling as they tucked into a bowl of lukewarm broth. It was the happiest he'd seen them.

That's how he knew this was the right thing to do.

'You'll be staying the night,' said Felaina. It wasn't a question, and Ctenka gladly accepted her offer.

As the few candles in the little house began to flicker down to nubs, Felaina and Markhan bid Ctenka and the children good night. They'd been given ample blankets, and the floor wasn't the worst place they'd slept in the past few weeks, so Ctenka had that to be grateful for.

He waited in the dark until he heard Markhan's gentle snoring before he got up.

Lena and Castiel got up with him, following him across the room as he went. Ctenka signalled for them to stop before kneeling down beside them.

'You can't come with me,' he said.

'Why? Where are you going?' whispered Lena.

It was a pretty good question. One Ctenka didn't have the answer to.

'Look, these are good people. They will take care of you. But you both have to promise me one thing. Can you do that?'

Both children nodded in unison and he took them both by the hand, one red hot, one freezing cold. 'You mustn't use your gifts on anyone. Neither of you, unless it's to protect yourselves or someone you love. Do you promise?'

Both children nodded again.

'Say it,' Ctenka said.

They both said, 'I promise,' in unison.

'Good. Then go back to sleep, and when you wake up you need to do whatever Markhan and Felaina tell you to. They'll do their best by you. Try and be grateful.'

With that, Ctenka stood. He took the little note he'd written the day before from his pocket, and left it on the kitchen table before creeping out of the house. It wished Markhan and Felaina well, and apologised for leaving the children. He doubted they would mind.

Out in the chill night, Ctenka felt a mix of emotions. He was at once guilty for leaving those children behind and relieved to be free of them. Which emotion would rise to destroy the other remained to be seen.

After untying his horse he quietly mounted up and rode it away from the farm. He let the steed lead him on through the dark until the sun started to rise. Looking around in the newborn light, Ctenka found himself at a crossroads and wondered which way he should go.

If the tales were true, an army was coming from the north. A horde of warriors determined to conquer the whole world. Riding south as far and as fast as he could go seemed the only sensible option.

Ctenka had already risked his life for the Cordral and for Queen Suraan, and what did he have to show for it? What was there to gain by going to Kantor other than more suffering? More danger? More... glory?

'Don't be an idiot,' he said to himself.

It was a stupid idea. One that would only see him dead. Ctenka Sunatra had not been raised a fool, he had more sense than to put himself in mortal peril once more.

Didn't he?

'You've got no bloody sense at all.'

With a pull of the reins, Ctenka set off west.

With luck he'd be in Kantor before sundown.

ABOUT THE AUTHOR

Richard Ford originally hails from Leeds in the heartland of Yorkshire but now resides in the wild fens of Cambridgeshire. His previous works include the raucous steampunk adventure, *Kultus*, and the grimdark fantasy trilogy, Steelhaven.

You can find out more about what he's up to, and download free stuff, here: www.richardsfordauthor.com/.

And follow him on Twitter here: @rich4ord

A DEMON IN SILVER
R.S. Ford

In a world where magic has disappeared, rival nations vie for power in a continent devastated by war.

When a young farm girl, Livia, demonstrates magical powers for the first time in a century there are many across the land that will kill to obtain her power. The Duke of Gothelm's tallymen, the blood-soaked Qeltine Brotherhood, and cynical mercenary Josten Cade: all are searching for Livia and the power she wields.

But Livia finds that guardians can come from the most unlikely places… and that the old gods are returning to a world they abandoned.

"Mixes the epic and the earthly, delivering gory battles and well-crafted banter." *SFX*

"*A Demon In Silver* is a brilliant book, and happily the first in a trilogy so there is more excitement to come."
The Book Bag

THE PAGAN NIGHT
Tim Akers

The Celestial Church has all but eliminated the old
pagan ways, ruling the people with an iron hand.
Demonic gheists terrorize the land, hunted by the
warriors of the Inquisition, yet it's the battling factions
within the Church and age-old hatreds between north
and south that tear the land apart.

Malcolm Blakley, hero of the Reaver War, seeks to end
the conflict between men, yet it will fall to his son, Ian,
and the huntress Gwen Adair to stop the killing before
it tears the land apart. *The Pagan Night* is an epic of mad
gods, inquisitor priests, holy knights bound to hunt
and kill, and noble houses fighting battles of politics,
prejudice, and power.

"Generations clash… in this emotionally involving
epic fantasy, in which elders embrace a new faith and
their youngsters rediscover old beliefs… as gods long
imprisoned seek freedom and vengeance."
Publishers Weekly

DUSKFALL
Christopher Husberg

Pulled from a frozen sea, pierced by arrows and close
to death, Knot has no memory of who he was. But his
dreams are dark, filled with violence and unknown
faces. Winter, a tiellan woman whose people have
long been oppressed by humans, is married to and
abandoned by Knot on the same day. In her search for
him, she will discover her control of magic, but risk
losing herself utterly. And Cinzia, priestess and true
believer, returns home to discover her family at the
heart of a heretical rebellion. A rebellion that only the
Inquisition can crush… Their fates and those of others
will intertwine, in a land where magic and daemons are
believed dead, but dark forces still vie for power.

"A great new fantasy epic."
Library Journal

For more fantastic fiction, author events, competitions,
limited editions and more

VISIT OUR WEBSITE
titanbooks.com

LIKE US ON FACEBOOK
facebook.com/titanbooks

FOLLOW US ON TWITTER
@TitanBooks

EMAIL US
readerfeedback@titanemail.com